MS. ETTA'S FAST HOUSE

Also by Victor McGlothin

BORROW TROUBLE

DOWN ON MY KNEES

SINFUL

Published by Dafina Books

MS. ETTA'S
FAST HOUSE

VICTOR
McGLOTHIN

DAFINA BOOKS

DAFINA BOOKS are published by

Kensington Publishing Corp.
850 Third Avenue
New York, NY 10022

ISBN-13: 978-0-7394-8881-2

Printed in the United States of America

*This novel is dedicated to the elite
African-American physicians and nurses
who trained and served at
Homer G. Phillips Hospital.
Long ago, you
lit a torch in St. Louis
that burns even brighter now
in the hearts of those who followed
in your magnificent steps.*

ACKNOWLEDGMENTS

Special Thanks: My wife, Terre McGlothin, M.D., and her brother Kenneth Powe for introducing me to the historic hospital during my first tour of St. Louis. Dennis and John Quinn, former St. Louis Police Department's finest. Katherine Quinn Park and Jenny Robinson, former nurses, for their insight into the once-famous institution affectionately known as "Homer Gee," where most Black folk in St. Louis went to be born, be healed, or die. Dr. Renee Obey, M.D., "The Obstetrician" with all the answers. Agnes Quinn, for her love and hospitality. Dwayne Nelson, my li'l cousin and the best plumber in "the Lou." Last but certainly not least, I'd like to thank my editor on this project, Karen Thomas, who upon hearing about this story said, "Drop everything and get started on it immediately!"

1

PENNY WORTH O' BLUES

Three months deep into 1947, a disturbing calm rolled over St. Louis, Missouri. It was unimaginable to foresee the hope and heartache that one enigmatic season saw fit to unleash, mere inches from winter's edge. One unforgettable story changed the city for ever. This is that story.

Watkins Emporium was the only black-owned dry goods store for seven square blocks and the pride of "The Ville," the city's famous black neighborhood. Talbot Watkins had opened it when the local Woolworth's fired him five years earlier. He allowed black customers to try on hats before purchasing them, which was in direct opposition to store policy. The department store manager had warned him several times before that apparel wasn't fit for sale after having been worn by Negroes. Subsequently, Mr. Watkins used his life savings to start a successful business of his own with his daughter, Chozelle, a hot-natured twenty-year-old who had a propensity for older fast-talking men with even faster hands. Chozelle's scandalous ways became undeniably apparent to her father the third time he'd caught a man running from the backdoor of his storeroom, half-dressed and hell-bent on eluding his wrath. Mr. Watkins clapped an iron pad lock on the rear door after realizing he'd have to protect his daughter's virtue, whether she liked it or not. It was a hard pill to swallow, admitting to himself that canned meat wasn't the only thing getting dusted and polished in that backroom. However, his relationship with Chozelle was just about perfect, compared to that of his meanest customer.

"Penny! Git your bony tail away from that there dress!" Halstead King grunted from the checkout counter. "I done told you once, you're too damned simple for something that fine." When Halstead's lanky daughter snatched her hand away from the red satin cocktail gown displayed in the front window as if a rabid dog had snapped at it, he went right on back to running his mouth and running his eyes up and down Chozelle's full hips and ample everything else. Halstead stuffed the hem of his shirttail into his tattered work pants and then shoved his stubby thumbs beneath the tight suspenders holding them up. After licking his lips and twisting the ends of his thick gray handlebar mustache, he slid a five dollar bill across the wooden countertop, eyeing Chozelle suggestively. "Now, like I was saying, How 'bout I come by later on when your daddy's away and help you arrange thangs in the storeroom?" His plump belly spread between the worn leather suspender straps like one of the heavy grain sacks he'd loaded on the back of his pickup truck just minutes before.

Chozelle had a live one on the hook, but old man Halstead didn't stand a chance of getting at what had his zipper about to burst. Although his appearance reminded her of a rusty old walrus, she strung him along. Chozelle was certain that five dollars was all she'd get from the tight-fisted miser, unless of course she agreed to give him something worth a lot more. After deciding to leave the lustful old man's offer on the counter top, she turned her back toward him and then pretended to adjust a line of canned peaches behind the counter. "Like what you see, Mr. Halstead?" Chozelle flirted. She didn't have to guess whether his mouth watered, because it always did when he imagined pressing his body against up hers. "It'll cost you a heap more than five dollars to catch a peek at the rest of it," she informed him.

"A peek at what, Chozelle?" hissed Mr. Watkins suspiciously, as he stepped out of the side office.

Chozelle stammered while Halstead choked down a pound of culpability. "Oh, nothing, Papa. Mr. Halstead's just thinking about buying something nice for Penny over yonder." Her father tossed a quick glance at the nervous seventeen-year-old obediently standing an arm's length away from the dress she'd been dreaming about for weeks. "I was telling him how we'd be getting in another shipment of ladies garments next Thursday," Chozelle added, hoping that the lie sounded more plausible then. When Halstead's eyes fell to the floor, there was no doubting what he'd had in mind. It was common knowledge that Halstead King, the local moonshiner, treated his only daughter like an unwanted pet and that he never shelled out one thin dime toward her happiness.

"All right then," said Mr. Watkins, in a cool calculated manner. "We'll put that there five on a new dress for Penny. Next weekend she can come back and get that red one in the window she's been fancying." Halstead started to argue as the store owner lifted the money from the counter and folded it into his shirt pocket but it was gone for good, just like Penny's hopes of getting anything close to that red dress if her father had anything to say about it. "She's getting to be a grown woman and it'd make a right nice coming-out gift. Good day, Halstead," Mr. Watkins offered, sealing the agreement.

"Papa, you know I've had my heart set on that satin number since it came in," Chozelle whined, as if the whole world revolved around her.

Directly outside of the store, Halstead slapped Penny down onto the dirty sidewalk in front of the display window. "You done cost me more money than you're worth," he spat. "I have half a mind to take it out of your hide."

"Not unless you want worse coming to you," a velvety smooth voice threatened from the driver's seat of a new Ford convertible with Maryland plates.

Halstead glared at the stranger then at the man's shiny beige Roadster. Penny was staring up at her handsome hero, with the buttery complexion, for another reason all together. She turned her head briefly, holding her sore eye then glanced back at the dress in the window. She managed a smile when the man in the convertible was the only thing she'd ever seen prettier than that red dress. Suddenly, her swollen face didn't sting nearly as much.

"You ain't got no business here, mistah!" Halstead exclaimed harshly. "People known to get hurt messin' where they don't belong."

"Uh-uh, see, you went and made it my business by putting your hands on that girl. If she was half the man you pretend to be, she'd put a hole in your head as sure as you're standing there." The handsome stranger unfastened the buttons on his expensive tweed sports coat to reveal a long black revolver cradled in a shoulder holster. When Halstead took that as a premonition of things to come, he backed down, like most bullies do when confronted by someone who didn't bluff so easily. "Uh-huh, that's what I thought," he said, stepping out of his automobile idled at the curb. "Miss, you all right?" he asked Penny, helping her off the hard cement. He noticed that one of the buckles was broken on her run over shoes. "If not, I could fix that for you. Then, we can go get your shoe looked after." Penny swooned as if she'd seen her first sunrise. Her eyes were opened almost as wide as Chozelle's, who was gawking from the other side of the large framed window. "They call me Baltimore, Baltimore Floyd. It's nice to make your acquaintance, miss. Sorry it had to be under such unfavorable circumstances."

Penny thought she was going to faint right there on the very sidewalk she'd climbed up from. No man had taken the time to notice her, much less talk to her in such a flattering manner. If it were up to Penny, she was willing to get knocked down all over again for the sake of reliving that moment in time.

"Naw, suh, Halstead's right," Penny sighed after giving it some thought. "This here be family business." She dusted herself off, primped her pigtails, a hairstyle more appropriate for much younger girls, then she batted her eyes like she'd done it all of her life. "Thank you kindly, though," Penny mumbled, noting the contempt mounting in her father's expression. Halstead wished he'd brought along his gun and his daughter was wishing the same thing, so that Baltimore could make him eat it. She understood all too well that as soon as they returned to their shanty farmhouse on the outskirts of town, there would be hell to pay.

"Come on, Penny," she heard Halstead gurgle softer than she'd imagined he could. "We ought to be getting on," he added as if asking permission to leave.

"I'll be seeing you again, Penny," Baltimore offered. "And next time, there bet' not be one scratch on your face," he said, looking directly at Halstead. "It's hard enough on women folk as it is. They shouldn't have to go about wearing reminders of a man's shortcomings."

Halstead hurried to the other side of the secondhand pickup truck and cranked it. "Penny," he summoned, when her feet hadn't moved an inch. Perhaps she was waiting on permission to leave too. Baltimore tossed Penny a wink as he helped her up onto the tattered bench seat.

"Go on now. It'll be all right or else I'll fix it," he assured her, nodding his head in a kind fashion and smiling brightly.

As the old pickup truck jerked forward, Penny stole a glance at the tall silky stranger then held the hand Baltimore had clasped inside his up to her nose. The fragrance of his store-bought cologne resonated through her nostrils for miles until the smell of farm animals whipped her back into a stale reality, her own.

It wasn't long before Halstead mustered up enough courage to revert back to the mean tyrant he'd always been. His unforgiving black heart and vivid memories of the woman who ran off with a traveling salesman fueled Halstead's hatred for Penny, the girl his wife left behind. Halstead was determined to destroy Penny's spirit since he couldn't do the same to her mother.

"Git those mason jar crates off'n the truck while I fire up the still!" he hollered. "And you might as well forgit that man in town and ever meeting him again. His meddling can't help you way out here. He's probably on his way back east already." When Penny moved too casually for Halstead's taste, he jumped up and popped her across the mouth. Blood squirted from her bottom lip. "Don't make me tell you again," he cursed. "Ms. Etta's havin' her spring jig this weekend and I promised two more cases before sundown. Now git!"

Penny's injured lip quivered. "Yeah, suh," she whispered, her head bowed.

As Halstead waddled to the rear of their orange brick and oak, weather-beaten house, cussing and complaining about wayward women, traveling salesmen and slick strangers, he shouted additional chores. "Stack them crates up straight this time so's they don't tip over. Fetch a heap of water in that barrel, bring it around yonder and put my store receipts on top of the bureau in my room. Don't touch nothin' while you in there neither, useless heifer," he grumbled.

"Yeah, suh, I will. I mean, I won't," she whimpered. Penny allowed a long strand of blood to dangle from her angular chin before she took the hem of her faded dress and wiped it away. Feeling inadequate, Penny became confused as to in which order her chores were to have been performed. She reached inside the cab of the truck, collected the store receipts and crossed the pebble covered yard. She sighed deeply over how unfair it felt, having to do chores on such a beautiful spring day, and then she pushed open the front door and wandered into Halstead's room. She overlooked the assortment of loose coins scattered on the night stand next to his disheveled queen sized bed with filthy sheets she'd be expected to scrub clean before the day was through.

On the corner of the bed frame hung a silver-plated Colt revolver. Sunlight poured through the half-drawn window shade, glinting off the pistol. While mesmerized by the opportunity to take matters into her own hands, Penny palmed the forty-five carefully. She contemplated how easily she could have ended it all with one bullet to the head, hers. Something deep inside wouldn't allow Penny to hurt another human, something good and decent, something she didn't inherit from Halstead.

"Penny!" he yelled, from outside. "You got three seconds to git outta that house and back to work!" Startled, Penny dropped the gun onto the uneven floor and froze, praying it wouldn't go off. Halstead pressed his round face against the dusty window to look inside. "Goddammit! Gal, you've got to be the slowest somebody. Git back to work before I have to beat some speed into you."

The puddle of warm urine Penny stood in confirmed that she was still live. It could have just as easily been a pool of warm blood instead. Thoughts of ending her misery after her life had been spared fleeted quickly. She unbuttoned her thin cotton dress, used it to mop the floor then tossed it on the dirty clothes heap in her bedroom. Within minutes, she'd changed into an undershirt and denim overalls. Her pace was noticeably revitalized as she wrestled the crates off the truck as instructed. "Stack them crates," Penny mumbled to herself. "Stack 'em straight so's they don't tip over. Then fetch the water." The week before, she'd stacked the crates too high and a strong gust of wind toppled them over. Halstead was furious. He dragged Penny into the barn, tied her to a tractor wheel and left her there for three days without food or water. She was determined not to spend another three days warding off field mice and garden snakes.

Once the shipment had been situated on the front porch, Penny rolled the ten-gallon water barrel over to the well pump beside the cobblestone walkway. Halstead was busy behind the house, boiling sour mash and corn syrup in a copper pot with measures of grain. He'd made a small fortune distilling alcohol and peddling it to bars, juke joints and roadhouses. "Hurr'up, with that water!" he shouted. "This still's plenty hot. Coils try'n'a bunch."

Penny clutched the well handle with both hands and went to work. She had seen an illegal still explode when it reached the boiling point too quickly, causing the copper coils to clog when they didn't hold up to the rapidly increasing temperatures. Ironically, just as it came to Penny that someone had tampered with the neighbors still on the morning it blew up, a thunderous blast shook her where she stood. Penny cringed. Her eyes grew wide when Halstead staggered from the backyard screaming and cussing, with every inch of his body covered in vibrant yellow flames. Stumbling to his knees, he cried out for Penny to help him.

"Water! Throw the damned . . . water!" he demanded.

She watched in amazement as Halstead writhed on the ground in unbridled torment, his skin melting, separating from bone and cartilage. In a desperate attempt, Halstead reached out to her, expecting to be doused with water just beyond his reach, as it gushed from the well spout like blood had poured from Penny's busted lip.

Penny raced past a water pail on her way toward the front porch. When she couldn't reach the top crate fast enough, she shoved the entire stack of them onto the ground. After getting what she went there for, she covered her nose with a rag as she inched closer to Halstead's charred body. While life evaporated from his smoldering remains, Penny held a mason jar beneath the spout until water spilled over onto her hand. She kicked the ten gallon barrel on its side then sat down on it. She was surprised at how fast all the hate she'd known in the world was suddenly gone and how nice it was to finally enjoy a cool, uninterrupted, glass of water.

At her leisure, Penny sipped until she'd had her fill. "Ain't no man supposed to treat his own blood like you treated me," she heckled, rocking back and forth slowly on the rise of that barrel. "Maybe that's cause you wasn't no man at all. You' just mean old Halstead. Mean old Halstead." Penny looked up the road when something in the wind called out to her. A car was headed her way. By the looks of it, she had less than two minutes to map out her future, so she dashed into the house, collected what she could and threw it all into a croaker sack. Somehow, it didn't seem fitting to keep the back door to her shameful past opened, so she snatched the full pail off the ground, filled it from the last batch of moonshine Halstead had brewed. If her mother had ever planned on returning, Penny reasoned that she'd taken too long as she tossed the pail full of white lightning into the house. As she lit a full box of stick matches, her hands shook erratically until the time had come to walk away from her bitter yesterdays and give up on living out the childhood that wasn't intended for her. "No reason to come back here, Momma," she whispered, for the gentle breeze to hear and carry away. "I got to make it on my own now."

Penny stood by the roadside and stared at the rising inferno, ablaze from pillar to post. Halstead's fried corpse smoldered on the lawn when the approaching vehicle ambled to a stop in the middle of the road. A young man, long, lean, and not much older than Penny took his sweet time stepping out of the late model Plymouth sedan. He sauntered over to the hump of roasted flesh and studied it. "Hey, Penny," the familiar passerby said routinely.

"Afternoon, Jinxy," she replied, her gaze still locked on the thick black clouds of smoke billowing toward the sky.

Sam "Jinx" Dearborn, Jr., was the youngest son of a neighbor, whose moonshine still went up in flames two months earlier. Jinx surveyed the yard, the smashed mason jars and the overturned water barrel.

"That there Halstead?" Jinx alleged knowingly.

Penny nodded that it was, without a hint of reservation. "What's left of 'im," she answered casually.

"I guess you'll be moving on then," Jinx concluded stoically.

"Yeah, I reckon I will at that," she concluded as well, using the same even pitch he had. "Haven't seen much of you since yo' daddy passed. How you been?"

Jinx hoisted Penny's large cloth sack into the back seat of his car. "Waitin' mostly," he said, hunching his shoulders, "to get even."

"Yeah, I figured as much when I saw it was you in the road." Penny was one of two people who were all but certain that Halstead had killed Jinx's father by rigging his still to malfunction so he could eliminate the competition. The night before it happened, Halstead had quarreled with him over money. By the next afternoon, Jinx was making burial arrangements for his daddy.

"Halstead got what he had coming to him," Jinx reasoned as he walked Penny to the passenger door.

"Now, I'll get what's coming to me," Penny declared somberly, with a pocket full of folding money. "I'd be thankful, Jinxy, if you'd run me into town. I need to see a man about a dress."

2

OH, DOCTOR!

Delbert Gales stretched his legs when the train pulled into Union Station. The train had teetered through seven hundred miles of track along the Missouri Line, all the way from Texas. Delbert had sworn to himself, every hour on the hour, that the next time he boarded a train he'd have enough money to secure a bed on the Pullman car. The crook in his back proved that a man's body wasn't made to sleep propped up against a bench seat. And, after sitting down for nearly two days straight, he was eager to land his best pair of shoes on the cemented streets of St. Louis. With fifteen dollars to his name and a medical degree to his credit, Delbert had his sights set on a lot more. The letter he received two months ago informed him he had been accepted into the residency program at Homer G. Phillips Hospital, one of the few places a colored man could train to become a full-fledged surgeon. Despite Delbert's thin frame and boyish appearance, he was twenty-two, educated and anxious to match wits with some of the brightest medical minds in the country.

Feeling that he owed it to himself to take in the sights while strolling through the busy train station, Delbert spotted several tight skirts, attached to some of the nicest legs he'd ever seen.

Red Cap baggage handlers darted here and there as he watched hordes of travelers scatting about, nearly all of them seeming to be in one big hurry. Delbert tried to ignore one shapely woman's assets, who'd strutted out in front of him with a large suitcase in tow, but there was no denying her big city curves harnessed beneath a pink chiffon dress fitting so tightly it could have used some letting out in the back. After Delbert traced her steps all the way out of the depot, he realized he'd erred in judgment. The pink chiffon dress fit that woman's behind just fine.

"Hey, kid!" someone shouted at him from an opened taxi window. "You gon' stand there all day wishing you was that pink dress or you gonna get to going where you need to be?" The taxi driver turned his palms up when Delbert's puzzled expression fell flat. "Suit yourself then." As the checkered cab pulled away from the curb, Delbert flagged him down.

"Yeah, yeah. I need you to carry me to the Ambrose Arms, over on Lexington Avenue."

"Now you talking," the driver cheered. "If that's the onliest bag you got, jump on in. I'll have you there in no time."

Delbert would have been all right with anchoring himself to that sidewalk for the rest of the afternoon, wishing he was that pink dress and countless others that clung just as tightly to other female travelers, but he figured he had better not get caught up doing anything that didn't benefit his surgical training, big city girl-watching included. Delbert's father, an automobile salesman, wouldn't have stood for anything to get his only son off track after making numerous sacrifices to send him to Prairie View A&M University, outside of Houston, and subsequently to Meharry Medical College in Nashville. To show his appreciation, Delbert had taken life seriously, and made his father the proudest man in Ft. Worth, Texas. He had no designs on disappointing dear ole dad now. Delbert knew that being smart merely qualified him for success but didn't guarantee it. He'd be forced to overcome the three things stacked against him. He appeared too young to be as accomplished as he was, he wasn't tall, or well-built, like some of his contemporaries and his skin was two shades darker than most colored people considered acceptable for a surgeon at the time. Discrimination among Negroes was at its height, and many patients shared a common belief that doctors with lighter complexions were the smartest because they had more of the white man's blood coursing through their veins. Delbert had proven that theory wrong hundreds of times and he was prepared to do so again, and as often as necessary.

On that warm spring afternoon he wandered through the lobby of the apartment building, realizing for the first time how nervous he had become. Nervousness about surgical training, becoming the man everyone back home expected and making it on his own without the benefit of his father's bank account, caused his chest to tighten.

"I need to check in," Delbert said to the male desk clerk. "There should be a room reserved for Gales, Delbert Gales," he said, after the man glared his way and quickly blew him off to complete his current task. The clerk, who looked to be nearing age fifty, finally began perusing a list of names from a tablet of some sort on the back credenza.

"Uh, we have a room for Mr. Delbert Gales," the older clerk replied, without lending much thought to the young man standing before him. "Uh-huh, a-uh Dr. Gales from Texas. He's not in yet but you can wait for him over there if you like."

Tired and hungry, Delbert wasted no time as he set out to clear up the man's misconceptions. He extended his hand across the reception counter to offer his credentials. "I am Dr. Delbert Gales. Here is my identification. As you can see, I am from Texas and I'd like to have the key to my room. Now, unless you want me to call the hospital superintendent and have you explain why I'm standing here trying to convince you to hand them over then—"

"I guess I'd better check you in . . . doctor," the clerk backpedaled. He asked Delbert to sign the log, then handed him the key in a flash. "I hope you don't hold it against me none but you

appear kinda young to be a doctor. I got socks older than you."
He didn't have to say another word. Delbert had seen and heard
it all before.

"Then I suggest you get yourself some new socks," he advised, while turning to walk away.

"Oh, Dr. Gales," the clerk called out, "you forgot your identification. It sure will be nice having y'all stay here. Mr. M.K.
Phipps and Mr. William Browning just arrived a little bit ago."
Those were the names of two other promising young doctors.
Sure, Delbert had heard of them and he couldn't wait to size
them up for himself. He snapped out of a hazy daydream when
the clerk informed him for the second time that a lounging suite
had been prepared for the other arrivals throughout the afternoon. "So feel free to go right on up and knock off some of that
traveling dust before you get settled in. That's room number
four-oh-seven, on the top floor. Take a right at the end of the
hallway, you can't miss it."

"Thank you kindly." Delbert said, after returning the I.D. to
his billfold resting atop the granite counter. "And who would I
speak to about having a few extra towels sent to the room?"

The clerk tossed a comfortable smile at him. "I'll see to it personally, Dr. Gales. Wow, we sure are proud to have y'all here."
There was something peculiar in the way the older man's per-
ception of Delbert had transformed into overwhelming respect,
just shy of adoration. The desk clerk's expression begged to be
addressed.

"Is there something else?" Delbert asked evenly.

"Well, now that you mentioned it, I get a little pain in my side
after I eat my Maybelline's chili." The clerk poked at his side to
point out exactly where his wife's cooking had tormented him
the most.

"I have a surefire remedy for that. Don't eat any more of her
chili," Delbert answered matter-of-factly. "Apologize to her but
turn it down from now on. Obviously, it doesn't agree with you.
Trust me, she'll understand." He left the clerk standing near the

bottom of the staircase, grinning and rubbing his side as if he'd been miraculously healed.

When Delbert wandered down the hall toward the hospitality suite, laughter and merriment poured through the thin walls. As he lowered his bag to the floor outside room number four hundred and seven, the door whipped open from the other side. He poked his head in the doorway and almost had it knocked off in the process, as a wooden ice bucket, hurled in his direction, slammed against the door.

"Don't forget the ice this time, M.K.," a man's deep voice shouted with exuberance from inside the oversized room. The ice bucket bounced off the solid oak door and ricocheted into the capable clutches of M.K. Phipps, who had once been an All-American tailback at Howard University.

"Bill, you just make sure to save me a seat at the table. I've been telling everybody back in Washington how I couldn't wait to get you tangled up in a card game. I'm just the man to take some starch out of that pumped up ego you got going on and lighten your pockets while I'm at it."

M.K. Phipps was still as fit as ever, after serving two years in the Army, and wore the same wide-toothed grin Delbert remembered seeing in newspaper photos. William Browning was taller with a slighter build, a paper-sack brown complexion and a full head of curly hair. He'd had the good fortune of assisting in a successful kidney operation, one of the first performed by a colored surgeon. William's name was included in a national journal article discussing the ground-breaking procedure. William Browning, M.D. became an overnight star in the medical community.

"M.K. Phipps, well, I'll be. I'm Delbert Gales." When Delbert shook hands with the man who was built like a monument of steel, he understood why most would-be football foes feared going head to head with this one time hero of the gridiron. Delbert's hand disappeared in the man's colossal grasp.

"Delbert, nice to meet cha'," M.K. beamed. "The boys are inside. Hop in and make yourself at home but keep an eye on Bill.

He's a much better card cheat than he is at suturing, so watch out for his slow finger drag on the shuffle. Don't get distracted with his high-toned signifying or you'll miss it when he's dealing off the bottom."

"Heyyy! I resemble that remark," trailed M.K.'s off-beat comment, as William stepped to the doorway to get a look at who was holding up the card game.

"Bill, take care of Gales here," M.K. said, as he started down the long hallway. "Delbert, I'd keep one hand on my wallet, if I were you."

"Don't take stock in anything that comes out of that kickball-sized head of his. M.K.'s been losing money to me for years and I'm not so sure he don't like it that way. Ain't nobody that bad at cards without trying to be." William picked up the bag and carried it into the room.

"Thanks, uh . . . William," Delbert replied awkwardly, having been thoroughly impressed with papers William published regarding early studies on Sickle Cell Anemia.

"Call me Bill. Come on in and meet the boys." He sat the leather luggage down and whistled loudly, cowboy-on-the-open-range style, above the noise spurred by numerous conversations all going on at once. Delbert didn't know what to make of this conglomerate of gifted young talent, exercising an opportunity to yuck it up with other noted contemporaries. Eventually, the noise subsided enough for Bill to make a swooping introduction. "Fellas, this here is Delbert Gales, the boy-genius from Texas we've been hearing so much about. Make him feel at home and save some of his money for me." Hearty chuckling rang throughout the room. As soon as it occurred to Delbert that his accomplishments had been discussed, a strange but warm feeling of fraternity swept over him. In that instance, he felt like one of the fellows, even though he'd still have to find his place among them. Along with the men in that room, he would be tried, tested and twisted beyond anything he could have imagined. Seven out of one hundred and twenty-two medical students were selected for surgical internships at the famous hospital, which prided itself on training the best Negro surgeons in the country.

"Delbert," Bill continued, "the slick dresser over there is Charley Morrow. The big fella across from him is Claude "Frenchy" Babineaux. Now, Claude, he's no bona fide Frenchman, mind you, but I'm sure somebody responsible for hatching him was." The fair-skinned man waved hello then went back to studying his cards as if they'd changed for the better since the last time he stared them down. "That one sitting next to him is Harry Johnson. Course, you might have heard of him 'cause of some national colored citation with his name on it." Every black medical student, and most white ones, had heard of Harry Johnson's name after he achieved the highest scores possible on every standardized medical examination. "Ollie Washington's the joker of the bunch," Bill added, "and the long one stretched out on the divan with the forty-five caliber charmer is Baltimore Floyd. He's a friend of M.K.'s and a good man to know."

"Glad to meet y'all," Delbert said, after the introductions ended. Baltimore's revolver, resting in his shoulder holster, suggested to Delbert that he wasn't interested in saving lives, taking a few every now and then, perhaps.

Bill observed Delbert, somewhat awed by the assortment of men who had traveled from the outstretched corners of the United States to become skilled in surgery. "Now, look, Tex, I know this might appear to be a premiere collection of medical Einsteins but your talents have earned you a place here as much as the rest of these high-minded low-brows."

"Yeah, and if he sits his talents down at this poker table," M.K. quipped, "his spending change will belong to me." Delbert now laughed as loud as the others. "Delbert, we sent out for sandwiches, if you're hungry. We should've smuggled a few of 'em out of the cafeteria in wax paper when we had the chance."

Bill shook his head, protesting the idea. "And have Hiram Knight looking at me cross eyed? Hell, naw. I might be crazy but I've never been mistaken for stupid." Hiram Knight, the legendary Director of Surgery, was responsible for seeing to the moral conduct of his interns as well as to their technical mentorship.

"From what I hear, the Little General keeps count of every cotton ball and bandage at HGP," Ollie said, looking up from his cards.

Delbert scratched his head, took out a small piece of paper then read over it. "Did I miss something? I thought orientation was Monday morning."

"Some of the fellas got in early and went over to scout around," Bill informed him. "Said they had a nice time grazing over the weekend stock."

"I heard there're over two hundred nurses on staff," Delbert said with a mischievous leer, eager to have his way with every last one of them. "I guess that's why they call Homer G. Phillips Hospital, HGP, the Halls of Good and Plenty."

M.K. poured himself a stiff shot of whiskey and sampled it. "Round these parts, it's also known as the House of Good Pussy." Everyone in the room laughed and applauded that particular acronym.

After the laughter died down, Ollie tapped his shirt pocket insinuating there was something vitally important inside it. "Matter of fact, I had the notion to test out that theory and I convinced one of the madams of the house to meet me for dinner. Hope she don't mind springing for it 'cause I'm busted."

"Just keep ole M.K. Phipps on deck in case she does mind," M.K. offered. Whether Ollie's date was interested in either of them was of no concern, they were in St. Louis and itching to blow off some steam in the way of female companionship. Soon enough, they'd get their fair shot at releasing a lot more than just steam.

Delbert had been waiting over two months for an opportunity to prove himself in the operating room and now he realized he had to do the same with the ladies in order to keep step. There he was in the midst of other talented black men, who had also taken it upon themselves to endure the rigors of long hours and intense scrutiny for little to no money. Improving the quality of life for their patients, along with the perks associated with being single physicians was their reward. Delbert was feeling better about his chances to make a big splash in a deep pond and although he felt more at ease than he'd anticipated, he quickly came to discover that keeping his head above water wasn't quite so easy.

3

OLD DOGS, NEW FLEAS

The following morning rolled in nice and easy. As the community came alive, Penny was there to witness it. Watkins Emporium had closed by the time she made it back to town the evening before, so she sat on the curb outside of the dry goods store all night, with her knees tucked against her chest, waiting and watching. She watched a large woman in the gray house across the street open the front door and kiss a fellow good night. Then, Penny's eyes were glued to the milkman as he parked in the driveway, stepped inside, and made a fifteen minute in-home delivery before returning to the dairy truck while zipping up his pants. She also witnessed another man arrive in a work uniform, with a meal pail in one hand and the *St. Louis Comet News* in the other. Penny scratched her nappy hair wondering how the poor woman in that gray house managed to get any sleep between the second and third shifts. By the end of the week, Penny would come to learn that the woman wasn't all that interested in sleeping.

While the revolving door across the street kept on spinning, an attractive woman, satin-brown skinned and jazzy, strolled along humming a pleasant tune. She sashayed in her tangerine colored cotton dress and matching pumps as she surveyed the young girl curiously. "Penny King, that you?" she asked, surprised to find her there.

Penny glanced up, smiled cordially then went back to spying at the gray house where all the activity had taken place. "Yeah, it's me. Morning, Ms. Etta." Jo Etta Adams was the closest thing there was to a society woman without actually being one. She owned the most popular nightclub in "The Ville," St. Louis's upper-crust colored neighborhood. Negroes from all over the country visited Ms. Etta's Fast House, the rhythm and blues haven of the Midwest, where national celebrities made frequent appearances to shake up the local scene. Dizzy Gillespie played a nearby theater to a packed white-only audience the month before. After the theater owner paid him, Dizzy loaded up the tour bus and drove it thirteen blocks to the front door of Ms. Etta's so his band could cut up with the colored folk all night long. The famous musician wouldn't accept money from Etta but he didn't pass up on the free beer and all the home cooking his band members could eat.

"What are you doing, sitting there on the sidewalk this early in the day?" Etta inquired with her brow furrowed, as if this was one of the strangest things she'd ever seen.

"I was waiting for Watkins to open up while watching how these city folk start off their day," Penny answered nonchalantly. "Now I'm just waiting."

"I don't understand. You waiting for Halstead?"

"Nah, he' dead," Penny told her, as if he'd merely skinned his knee. "I'm waiting to see what happens now since that man showed up after working all night and finds the milkman's hat in his bedroom. See, he had it on going in but not when he come out."

Etta was even more confused than before. "What's this about some dead milkman?"

"Uh-uh, Halstead is the one who died." Before Penny continued her ragged explanation, they heard a loud commotion coming from across the street. There was shouting, screaming and things getting smashed inside that gray house. Penny's eyes sparkled when the man in the work uniform came barreling through the screen door with the milkman's hat clutched in his hand. "Ooh, she sure is strong," Penny marveled, thrilled that a woman had the strength to body slam a grown man.

"I'll say," Etta agreed.

"And stay out!" the woman's voice shrieked from the front porch, as she lumbered back inside. "I don't take to getting roughed up by no man, for no reason!"

"Looks like he found the hat," Penny assessed. "But he's gonna have to find another place to lay his head now." As the man crawled to his car, Penny cheered the woman's decision to fight back, even if she had been in the wrong for shuttling men in and out under his nose. "Wow! This is even better than the picture show. You think she'll let him come back, Ms. Etta?"

"She'll have to," Etta answered, keeping an eye peeled on the action. "That's his house. She's just renting a room." After the man of the house cranked up his sedan and sped away, something dawned on Etta. "Did you say Halstead passed on?" Penny quickly explained how Halstead caught on fire, how she'd burned down the house and a few other secrets Etta made her promise never to share again. "Don't tell anyone else you were there when the still blew up and never mention anything about setting fire to the house," Etta warned. "People go to prison for stuff like that. If there's something to be said, let me handle it." Since Penny couldn't imagine trading one prison for another, she shook her head ferociously.

"Yes, ma'am. I mean, no, ma'am," Penny stammered. "I ain't gon' say nothing else about it, to nobody. I'm free and aim'n' to stay that way."

"Good. You look hungry. I was on my way over to Clarisse's Beauty Parlor but we can stop and grab a bite along the way."

"*We*, Ms. Etta? I can come and wait with you at Madame Clarisse's?" Penny had seen women coming and going from the neighborhood hair salon since she could remember, but Halstead only slowed down long enough to ogle at the customers through the storefront window.

"Seems to me all you've been doing is waiting," Etta said, trying to imagine how Penny would look if she had the chance to spread her wings. "It's high time you started living."

Penny's mouth watered when that familiar cream-colored convertible came to a stop in the street behind Etta. It was him again, the stranger who said nice things, threatened Halstead and helped her off the ground. He'd even winked. He winked! With him showing up again unannounced, Penny was really living now and each moment appeared to get topped by the next. " 'Morning, Jo Etta," he hailed, after killing the engine.

"Baltimo' Floyd," Etta announced. She was genuinely happy to see him, not ecstatic but happy enough to hug him around his neck. "When'd you get into town? Billy Eckstine fell in last night and bunched 'em in from wall to wall. He mentioned how you'd relieved him of his new automobile while he was up in Philly."

"Well, some people ought to stick to what they're good at. Billy happens to sing a lot better than he plays poker."

"He might be catching on, 'cause that's pretty close to what he was cackling about last night," Etta informed him. "Now that I get a look at that fine coach, I can see why he was putting up such a fuss."

When Etta noticed Baltimore's eyes drifting past hers, she turned to see what had drawn them away. She sighed when his expression hardened. It appeared that Penny was hiding something from him, by purposely concealing the left side of her face from view. "Penny, I think I need to have that talk with your papa," Baltimore declared solemnly.

"Naw, suh, ain't no need for that now," she assured him, like he had to ease her troubled mind the day before. "He beat on me for the last time. God made sure of that. You might say He fixed it." Suddenly, Penny raised her head, stuck out her chin and nodded to both Etta and Baltimore.

"There's nobody better for setting things straight," Baltimore said, sincerely. "Let's get some grub, then see if there're any loose ends The Man Upstairs might have overlooked." He opened the car door to help Etta into the front seat, while Penny gladly jumped in the back.

"So, how do you know Penny?" Etta asked Baltimore, while admiring his classy automobile.

"We met yesterday on that very spot, right, Penny?" She nodded again, as he placed the sack in the seat next to her. "Yeah, she put me in the mind of the first girl I fell hard for," he reminisced, climbing in behind the wheel. "Uh-huh, I was stuck on her for some time too."

"Whuu—whut happened to her?" Penny asked anxiously.

"We had nine children together before I came to realize we had nothing in common," Baltimore replied, displaying his best poker face.

Penny was astonished. Her eyes were about to pop clean out of her head until Etta howled with laughter. When Penny caught on that it was a friendly joke at her expense, she doubled over in unbridled giggles. "Ooh, Mistah Baltimo'," she squealed with delight like a kid on an amusement park ride. "Ms. Etta, how you keep up with him?"

"Lucky for me, I ain't crazy enough to try," Etta snickered, as the car pulled away.

Madame Clarisse's shop was a few blocks south, over on Papin Avenue. By the time they had eaten breakfast, Etta filled Baltimore in on what needed to be done with Halstead's remains and the possible methods of facilitating it. The threesome was as thick as thieves. Penny had no doubts that Baltimore was the kind of man who made things go down easy and she couldn't wait to see what lay in store next.

Baltimore glanced through the beauty parlor window and then eyed his wristwatch. "Jo Etta, I'm 'a take care of that Halstead matter, but I need to run by Henry Taylor's to let him know I'm back." When she pursed her lips instead of saying what she thought about it, he suspected something was wrong. "Etta? What you holding out on?" His stern expression demanded an answer.

"Go on inside, Penny," Etta directed firmly, so she could discuss grown folks' business, including her own. She held her tongue until the girl was out of earshot. "Not that it's any of my affair, but you won't find Henry in that cramped apartment over by the train yard. He went and talked himself into getting hitched. He," she sighed before the rest came out slowly, ". . . married a country girl, who moved up here from Tennessee. They got a little place on Tenth." It was obvious that Etta still carried a torch for Baltimore's oldest living friend. Most of his other friends had long since perished. Some of them received their send-off by Baltimore's own hands. Etta was very much in love with Henry, but hadn't fooled herself into thinking she was the marrying kind.

Caught by surprise, Baltimore started to comfort Etta but thought better of beating a dead horse. He offered a warm smile in place of empty words as Etta tapped his hand, signifying her thanks for leaving well enough alone. Then, as if she didn't have a care in the world, Etta eagerly strolled inside to direct Madame Clarisse in orchestrating a miracle, converting years of shameful neglect into a vibrant young lady. That transformation would take some time, providing Etta with the opportunity to figure out what to do with Penny after that. When the owner of the ritzy salon took one look at Penny's bruises and matted hair, she winced.

"Etta," Madame Clarisse groaned wearily, "I'll do it 'cause you're my best customer and 'cause I like you." She shook her head at Penny's faded overalls and run over shoes. "But I'ma need me a cigarette first."

"I know, Clarisse, I know," Etta agreed, smirking alongside her girlfriend. "Light up two and hand me one." Both of the women sat there, smoking and staring at Penny's long twisted pigtails while she gawked at the expensive leather chairs, polished furnishings and spotless red and white checkerboard linoleum floor. Madame's shop was a lot classier than Penny had envisioned when passing by in Halstead's old truck all those years. Beginning to feel like she was something special, Penny laughed to herself on the inside because all of the anticipation kind of tickled. If she didn't know better, she would have sworn she was dreaming.

A few miles away, Baltimore set out to find Henry using the information he'd received from Etta. When he'd located the house matching her description, he parked along the street instead of pulling into the driveway, considering the outside chance he'd stumbled on the wrong address. The small red brick house had a cozy feel to it from the outside. The smell of fresh cut grass reminded Baltimore of spring baseball and all the great times he'd experienced barnstorming with colored teams while touring the country's back roads and Negro ballparks from coast to coast.

When he climbed the steps and knocked at the door of the red brick house, Baltimore saw a pair of bright eyes staring up at him from the other side of the small paned window. He assumed he'd chosen the wrong house for sure then and started to walk away until he heard a woman's voice yell out, "Henry, it's that man again!" Baltimore's face lit up like a Christmas tree. He wore a wide smile when the door flew open and his old pal Henry Taylor appeared in navy Dickies' work pants and a white undershirt. Henry was more than six feet, two inches, two hundred thirty pounds of sheer brawn, and waving a bat. Most men would have bolted for safety or at least flinched in close proximity to someone that menacing, tight-faced and huffing mad. But all Baltimore did was call the man's name.

"Henry Taylor!" he grunted. The oversized field hand blinked rapidly. "Thangs so bad you got to come to your front door like this?" Henry's hard scowl faded slightly when Baltimore stood up to him. "Get to swinging that lumber or invite me inside."

"Sure, Baltimo', come on in," Henry offered half-heartedly. "Excuse my manners." He leaned the bat against the door frame and shoved his thick hands into the front pockets of his pants. Suddenly, a woman in her late twenties wandered into the room with a small boy on her heels. "This is my wife Roberta and Denny, her . . . uh, our son," Henry explained. His wife was considered more handsome than pretty, light brown in complexion with full thighs and large breasts. The child's face was the mirror image of his mother's and Baltimore couldn't see his daddy's presence stamped anywhere yet.

"My goodness, Henry, you've got yourself a beautiful family," Baltimore marveled while smiling cordially at Roberta. "Congratulations. Me and Henry go way back and . . ."

"And I'm sure not interested in hearing about it," the dutiful wife snapped rudely. "Yes, I've heard your name, Mr. Floyd, since the day Henry and I met and every day in between. He's not the same kind of man he used to be and I like it just that way."

"Nice meeting you, too," Baltimore said when nothing else seemed appropriate. He was interested to know what kind of man she had turned Henry into. Baltimore later learned that Roberta was a war widow. Her husband didn't make it back and her son longed for a father. She moved to St. Louis and found a teaching job about the same time Henry had picked up some casual money on a painting job, through a friend of his in the school superintendent's office. By the time that schoolhouse had received a second coat, Henry had the bright idea his time had come to settle down. Oddly enough, the thought of saddling an educated woman appealed to him and they were married before the paint dried.

"Honey, let me and Baltimo' talk," Henry proposed. "Go on now, it'll be all right." The minute she left the two of them alone, Henry's eyes fell to the floor.

Baltimore bent over to get a better look at him then he began to pace back and forth. "Man, I gotta get you outta here. She's got you asking if you can have a private conversation with your best friend, not to mention coming to the door ready to hurt somebody." Baltimore frowned as he stopped on a dime. "Well, what you waiting for? Get your coat."

Henry looked up at him, peculiarly, as if he was out of his

mind. "Fool, sit your ass down. I ain't leaving here. This is my home. The first one I ever owned."

"Henry I hope you don't take this the wrong way but playing house don't suit you."

The overgrown man popped to his feet. "This suits me just fine. I got a good woman and don't have to go 'round looking over my shoulder like I used to. Yeah, this suits me down to my shoes and the only reason I carried that lumber to the door was 'cause I figured you was that sneaky outfitter. He got us all this front room furniture and we's paying him back, on time, with interest." Henry grimaced while thinking about the hole he'd dug for himself. "Roberta warned me it was a bad move. Now we's behind, so they sends this man 'round to collect."

Baltimore shook his head slowly. "I don't believe this. You let a outfitter get his hooks in you?"

Avoiding eye contact, Henry reluctantly admitted the real reason behind getting the trendy furniture. "The minister lives next door and Roberta and them always over there having teas, garden parties and such. I guess I was trying to make a good impression."

"And you call me a fool." Disgusted, Baltimore took a seat next to Henry on the rented sofa. "I've been gone nine months and you've managed to get hitched to a dictator, father a four-year-old boy and let some fella soak you in a interest scam. Henry, what's gotten into you?" Baltimore waved broadly at the man's den full of high priced department store trappings, still trying to understand his friend's new lifestyle. After a few moments of silence trampled by, he looked at Henry from the corner of his eye. "And what about Jo Etta?"

Henry raised a finger to his lips. "Man, it ain't smart bringing up that name around here." He craned his thick neck as best he could, with hopes that Roberta wasn't listening in. "What about Jo Etta?" he replied eventually, in a hushed tone.

"Forget it. You're too far gone to understand." Baltimore reached into his pocket and came out with a thick roll of assorted bills. "How much you need to get that collector's boot off your neck?"

"Don't you mind what I owe," Henry objected. "This is something I've got to figure a way out on my own. Mr. Bellows, he'll be in today. Chances of getting that Negro League charter are looking good. That means more than enough money to settle thangs." Scarcely believing his own rhetoric, Henry sat down on the chair and stroked his chin.

"Come on, Henry, you need to wise up," Baltimore advised. "Mr. Randolph Bellows and the other owners are running scared. The white teams are talking about raping the Negro League and it won't be long before Satchel Paige or "Cool Papa" Bell gets invited in to play with Jackie Robinson. The time for colored baseball in St. Louis has all but dried up and blown away. Sure you can go on barnstorming in exhibition games but every year the crowds are getting smaller. Let me help you out with this before that man comes back to get his merchandise and leaves you and that dictator wife of yours sitting on the floor."

"What you saying I ought to do, give up playing baseball?"

"I'm just saying you might oughta consider another line of work?"

Henry leaned away from Baltimore in direct opposition to his suggestion. "Uh-uh, the kinda of work you do always seem to put the police on my trail."

"Naw, man, I'm through with all that. I'm what they call an entrepreneur now."

"A which?" Henry asked, scratching at his thick head.

"A self-made business man."

"Oh, no! I've seen how you do business and the way you operate scares the hell out of me."

"I'm not asking you to throw in with me, Henry. I just thought I'd stop by and see how you were getting along and tell you personally that I'm done with baseball. So don't be looking for me to lace up today against them Metro white boys. I've got something big cooking and it's gonna take all the time I got to see it play out. I'm staying at the Ambrose Arms if you change your mind."

Henry extended his hand to Baltimore as he stepped off the front porch. "You know I can't take your money without a way to pay it back, but thanks just the same."

"Shoot, you should have thought about that before you went and filled your house with that crooked salesman's window dressing."

"You think I feel better with you showing up in a fine car rubbing it in?"

"No, I didn't figure on anything but looking in on you and wishing you well against those boys aiming to put one over on you today." The St. Louis Blacksmiths were a bunch of talented young players who worked the spring and summers providing exhibition games in black communities but started each campaign by opening with a grudge match for bragging rights against the St. Louis Metropolitan Police Department, an all-white team representing an all-white force. The game offered the city a chance to come together collectively to celebrate the birth of spring. This time, however, there'd be more to play for after the game ended and far more to mourn than celebrate by the time spring had come and gone. "You watch yourself out there this afternoon," Baltimore warned, remembering games in the past ending in all-out brawls. "Besides, I hear they got a third baseman who played some college ball. Say he's supposed to be something to see."

"Well then, you'd better hurry over to the gate and get yourself a ticket," Henry retorted playfully. His eyes followed Baltimore as he started off in the direction of his car. "Baltimo'!" Henry called out to him, with a pinch of sadness. "I ain't forgot."

"Me neither, Henry," Baltimore shouted back with the same tenor in his voice. "Me neither." Baltimore had rescued his friend from more scrapes than either of them could remember and over the years, they shared everything from the last can of soup to bunking on the same sofa. But more importantly, they shared a solemn promise to back each other's play until death, although there was always something standing between them. Henry wanted to pretend he wasn't cut out for murder. With Baltimore, there was no need for pretending.

4

GOOD LUCK AIN'T BAD

Madame Clarisse's was packed by noon. Several society women, nurses and working girls observed Penny's extreme makeover. The posh parlor was one of the few places where a black woman didn't have to be concerned about status, because at Madame's, cash money was the only thing that meant anything. Neither pretentiousness nor credit was allowed, under any circumstances, especially not on the third Saturday in March. This Saturday was special. It featured a baseball game between the 'Smiths and Metro Police, the first major event of spring for colored St. Lucians, which meant scrounging up something new to be seen in at the ball park and then chasing the blues away at Ms. Etta's Fast House later that evening. Penny hadn't previously imagined attending either of those majestic events but that was before she'd started living like Etta suggested.

Penny's head was still spinning while Madame's clients hollered suggestions to the team of stylists engaged for the young girl's coming out party. Etta spent most of the first hour shaking her head and grimacing as they wrestled with Penny's thick, coarse, untamed mane, which seemed to grow each time a comb was raked through it. Etta covered her mouth to keep a litany of dirty words from spilling out when the spectacle began, but she laughed hysterically at the sight of Madame Clarisse working so hard that she actually broke a sweat between cigarette breaks. Soon enough, there were rays of hope after Clarisse thoroughly administered a maximum strength hair relaxer treatment, which left a huge black ring inside the rinsing sink. Once Penny's tresses had been washed, pinned and set to go under the dryer, Etta realized that Penny never got a shot at being a young lady. What she lacked were a befitting wardrobe and the right kind of training. Suddenly, Etta had an idea. She informed the shop keeper of an emergency that she needed to attend to then headed out of the salon and up the boulevard.

When Etta returned nearly an hour later, strutting through the door with three store clerks following closely behind her with bags under each arm, Penny awakened beneath the hairdryer. She didn't know what to think. The clerks were paid well for their trouble and then hastily ushered out. As soon as Madame Clarisse locked the door and drew the shades, a hoard of chattering women who hadn't laid eyes on Penny before that morning began fussing over her and the array of new outfits. Subsequently, Penny was pulled, prodded, poked and perused. It felt more like an examination than anything else, but she loved the overwhelming attention. Before she knew what was happening, she had been disrobed and whisked into the backroom.

Penny put up a good fight but proved no match for three determined groomers as they submerged her up to the neck in a gigantic washtub filled with satiny bubbles. Even though it required considerably more scrubbing than previously predicted, Penny was finally squeaky clean, powdered and perfumed. All of the clothes she'd brought from home were thrown away in the alley trashcan. She pleaded with Etta to keep a small embroidered cloth hatbox, the only personal item her estranged mother left behind. Etta agreed, selected a suitable outfit for the occasion, assisted the make-up girls with lip rouge and skin cream, then presented Penny to the impatiently awaiting clientele.

As the tall, anxious seventeen-year-old emerged timidly out of the backroom, a hush fell over the salon. Penny touched her face nervously with wandering fingertips, as if something went terribly wrong. Not sure how to read the women's startled expressions she hurried in front a full length mirror and took a look at her new and improved appearance. The poor girl fainted right on the spot. After being revived, she explained how it appeared that someone had replaced her with the person she'd always dreamed of becoming. The grown-up hairstyle, beautiful clothes and frilly undergarments were beyond anything she could have conceived. Her fantasy was made complete when there was a rap on the salon door. When Madame Clarisee she saw who it was, she smiled and primped her hair.

"Oh, yes, come on in," she said, escorting the man inside her shop as if she wouldn't mind doing the same if he happened to knock on the front door of her home. "Etta's still here," Clarisse sang. Her clients began straightening their clothes and eyeing one another while looking over the visitor in the meantime.

When Clarisse cleared her throat to get Etta's attention, she turned to find a memorable scene she'd viewed before, an entire room full of women shamelessly ogling the outrageously handsome Baltimore Floyd. "Baltimore, did you forget something?" Etta asked curtly, as if her teenaged brother had barged in on an all-girl slumber party.

"No, ma'am," he replied, all cool and smooth. "But I do believe that you may have." He gestured to someone at the window. One of the clerks from the department store strolled in with a collection of women's footwear. "Penny appears to be a nine-and-a-half narrow but I've been wrong before."

Penny nodded appreciatively. "Uh-huh, nine-and-one-half . . . narrow," she said, mostly guessing because she'd worn oversized men's hand-me-down work boots for years. Several of the ladies held their breaths as Baltimore whipped a silk handkerchief with a paisley print from his breast pocket. He snapped it in the air and placed it on the floor and the collection of onlookers was thoroughly impressed. He gestured for the young clerk to remove every lid from the assortment of shoe boxes. When Penny pointed tentatively to the pair she liked most, Baltimore kneeled down on one knee over the handkerchief and fastened the light green sling backs onto Penny's skinny feet. She grinned affectionately while standing from the chair. Baltimore held her hand tightly, as if she were a small child trying her mother's heels on for size for the first time.

Applause rang out in Madame Clarisse's while Penny paraded in circles. She giggled and blushed at Baltimore, then at Ms. Etta, who was quite accustomed to Baltimore sweeping women off their feet with such generous displays. She'd seen him at his best and worst, kindhearted and cold-blooded. There was no getting around it, Baltimore had taken a liking to Penny and he was prone to protect things he'd grown fond of, people included. Unfortunately, it was his association which often put them in harm's way. Etta had witnessed that first hand, too.

When the hoorays were well spent, Etta made an attempt to compensate Clarisse for Penny's new look but the shop owner declined it initially. "Hell, Etta, what would that make me, taking money from you when I enjoyed seeing that child blossom more than anybody?" It wasn't until Baltimore threw her one of those winks of his, that she understood the payment was from him. With a thankful nod, she gladly tucked the money away in her brassiere for safe keeping. "That's my kind of man, up and down," she said, watching Baltimore load Penny's things in the trunk of a taxi.

"Yours and mine both," one of her oldest customers agreed cheerfully, to the delightful roar of everyone listening in. "Huh, I can still get it going every now and then but he'd have to be packing something just as long as nine-and-a-half narrows!"

The parking lot at Medsker's Field was full to the gills. Baltimore circled it but didn't catch a break. He slipped the attendant a few bucks to park his convertible near the player's clubhouse, since the game had progressed farther along than he anticipated. By the time he purchased a ticket and scaled the stairs to the colored section, it was almost over.

Bottom of the ninth, with one out, the 'Smiths were up on the police department by a run. The crowd cheered, each section rooting for the team which represented them. Growing concerned, Baltimore reached inside his pleated pockets and came out with only forty-two dollars. He'd made a bet for two-fifty at two-to-one odds, which meant he stood to win five hundred if the 'Smiths pulled it off. He didn't want to think about the alternatives if they didn't. To ward off troubling thoughts he cheered and whistled like every other Negro in the upper balcony, although pride wasn't fueling his motivation. Facing the police officers he'd bet against without the money to pay them off was.

Henry Taylor was poised in the outfield, waiting for Jinx to throw the batter something wicked to take a slice at. On the next pitch, the batter took the bait and popped a fly ball directly into Henry's glove. He tipped his hat, took a bow and relayed the baseball to Willie B. Bernard, an undertaker's son and one heck of a mean-spirited shortstop. Jinx received the toss on the mound and took a deep breath. One more out and Baltimore's pockets would be bulging again, but another Metro run would tie the game with a runner in scoring position. As Jinx rolled into his wind-up and hoisted his knee into the air, Baltimore wondered if the pitcher had given any thought to helping him bury Halstead behind his own barn earlier that day.

As the batter whiffed at a smoking hot fast ball, there was no reason to wonder any longer. Baltimore took the back stairs down to the field assuming the game was in the bag. Suddenly he heard an all too familiar sound, a bat smashing against an errant pitch. He hustled to the fence as the runner flew down the first base path. At the same time, another one headed for home. Willie B. fumbled the ball in the dirt, a puff of red clay dust rose from the ground. The shortstop gritted his teeth as he gathered the ball into his right hand. The runner galloped. The ball sailed toward home plate. The umpire positioned himself for an impending collision. Then, the runner ducked into his slide just as the ball arrived. The 'Smiths catcher caught the ball in his mitt. He squatted along the base path to block the plate. After the runner slammed into the catcher six inches from home plate, the umpire waded through the cloud of dust to make an educated guess. He looked at the runner's cleats trapped beneath the catcher's knee. "Where's the ball?" the umpire yelled while the entire stadium watched attentively. Time stood still as the catcher raised his glove with the ball stuck firmly inside it. "He's out!" the umpire shouted. "He's out! That's the ball game!"

Baltimore sighed with relief, white fans flopped into their seats, the colored congregation cheered on their feet. The 'Smiths formed a congratulatory pile on top of Willie B. Bernard and the Metro Police team argued with the umpire like angry dogs. It was baseball in all its glory, with winners, losers and fans, who paid their hard earned money to see grown men play a child's game. Eventually, the on-field celebration concluded. Both teams lined up and shook hands like always, but neither of them knew it would be the ending of their rivalry and the hallowed spring classic.

The 'Smiths locker room bubbled over with joyful elation and red cream soda. Baltimore congratulated the boys, patted Henry on the back then hugged Willie B. like a long lost brother.

"It feels mighty good to be on top. Even if it's only once a year, I'll take it," Henry hailed loudly.

"Y'all almost gave it away out there," Baltimore said, wrapping his hands around the neck of a wooden bat.

"Could've used you on first," Henry replied, noting Baltimore's snazzy street clothes. "What you doing here anyway? This is the players' clubhouse. Last I heard you gave up baseball."

"Yep, but I didn't give up winning," Baltimore chuckled.

Within minutes he was sitting in the back seat of his sporty roadster, parked directly outside the opposing team's locker room. The Metros spilled out one by one until the man Baltimore had business with emerged from the shadows. When it appeared as if a certain police sergeant planned on ignoring his participation in a certain gaming arrangement, Baltimore perked up. "Barker, now don't act like we're not old friends," he teased. "I'd hate to tell everybody you crawfished on me and welched on a bet."

The tough officer growled. He was so agitated that his red hair seemed to stand up on end. He dug into the ball bag hanging off his shoulder and spit a hunk of brown tobacco extremely close to Baltimore's car. "You know gambling is illegal in this state," he threatened.

"It didn't appear to be illegal yesterday when you thought you'd come out on the other end of this thing," Baltimore smarted back.

Barker's jaw clenched tightly as he made a violent stride toward the smart-mouthed colored man. He couldn't stand to listen to him any longer. Baltimore observed him as he approached, fuming mad, but he held firm and didn't flinch. Barker's younger brother Clay grabbed him by the arm. The strapping police corporal, who not only mixed it up with Barker on a regular basis, was opposed to nearly everything he stood for. Clay was just as tall as Barker and gave up about thirty pounds or so, but he more than made up for it with sinewy muscle. "You want to start a riot, big brother?" he commented coolly, asking him to be mindful of the sea of colored fans spilling out of the ballpark. "Well then, give the man what you owe him, let's grab a couple of beers and call it a day. Better luck next time. It was one helluva game today. Let it go at that." After Barker wiped venom from his mouth, Clay tipped his hat to Baltimore and tugged on his brother's arm to move him along.

"Yeah, next time," Barker hissed as he shot another stream of brown saliva in Baltimore's direction. Finally, he pitched the bulky envelope into the front seat of Baltimore's car in passing. "You might want to consider making tracks back to Maryland before wearing out your welcome."

Once the standoff ended, Baltimore settled in behind the steering wheel. "Huh, next time," he mused, glaring at the envelope. "You set the time, I'll name the place. Throwing my money around like that." As he thumbed through his winnings, a pretty brunette, riding in the passenger seat of Barker Sinclair's automobile caught his eye. Baltimore didn't think of looking away once their eyes met but then neither did Mrs. Sinclair. Colored men had been hanged from tall trees for less, although that didn't seem to bother Baltimore and his fistful of money. It was then he knew he'd see that brunette again. If he had anything to say about it, he'd see all of her.

The thought of giving it to Barker's wife stayed with Baltimore as he drove to the other end of town to meet with a very powerful mobster. Schmitty Rosenberg, a dangerous man if not handled correctly, had his hands in every illegal industry in St. Louis. Baltimore had asked for a meeting with the aging mobster to pitch a partnership. Rosenberg wasn't likely to refuse, although he was known as a ruthless greedy gangster, who avoided doing business in "The Ville" despite extending his reach into every other black community in the city. It was rumored that shady enterprises within the neighborhood ran smoothly and unmolested as long as the police received their cut on the back end. Shakedowns were common place for protection from outside racketeers. Baltimore was tired of living on crumbs, so he set out to carve up his own piece of the pie.

As soon as he reached the main gate, fashioned with wrought iron and barbed wire, his car was thoroughly searched. When he received the go ahead to pull forward, he was searched from head to toe at the front door, then physically detained by two of Schmitty's thugs until another brutish looking man, wearing an expensive dark blue all-weather wool suit, stepped into the small room off the kitchen.

"The Boss wants to see you now," he mumbled, staring through Baltimore instead of at him.

"About time," Baltimore thought aloud, returning the same disrespectful look he'd received. "He ain't the only one got things to do."

The square-shouldered henchman showed Baltimore into an impressive den decorated with fine antique furniture and brass fixtures. Baltimore stared at a collection of stuffed animals and foreign warrior masks until a short round man entered from the far end of the room. He took a seat behind a mammoth rosewood desk, picked a white handkerchief from inside his pin-striped suit and wiped moisture from his severely pitted skin. Then, he brushed back what was left of his thinning gray hair. "Sit down Mr. Floyd," he commanded. *Not please have a seat or please make yourself comfortable, but sit down.* Baltimore made note of it but put the crude salutation aside for the sake of gaining the man's allegiance.

"So, what makes you think I'm interested in doing business with niggers from 'The Ville'?" the gangster asked, while puffing on a Cuban cigar.

"Mr. Rosenberg, I'm gonna overlook your unflattering remark." Baltimore paused to glance over his shoulder at the wool-wearing brute. His boss hadn't told him to react so he didn't. "But what I will do is explain why you should be in business with me." He acknowledged the police had the community under wraps and explained how he planned to put together a crew to handle things from the inside without them getting wise until it was too late to do anything about it.

Within five minutes, Mr. Rosenberg was intrigued. After another five he'd heard enough. He rose from the desk, circled around it and shook Baltimore's hand. The other details were to be fleshed out when the time came, to guarantee there wouldn't be a threat of a double-cross squeezing Baltimore in the middle. Rosenberg respected that part of the proposition most of all. It revealed a fair amount of cunning and forethought. There was room in his shady enterprises for Baltimore, Rosenberg had decided, for the time being at least. The very least was all the time Baltimore expected to get. Time enough to work his magic in the streets then hit the road with more cash than he could have hustled in twenty years by himself. In parting, Baltimore grinned sheepishly. "Oh, yeah," he said in parting, "I'ma need a big truck."

5

EVENING AT MS. ETTA'S

Baltimore backed his convertible into a parking space between a brand new Chrysler Imperial and a late model Studebaker. He figured that those car owners valued their expensive automobiles as much as he did, and after previously paying to repair a dented door, the thought of shelling out another seventy dollars to have it done all over again didn't appeal to him. "Lock that back door for me," Baltimore instructed Delbert, while M.K. assisted him with fastening the rag top.

A group of women, all dressed to the nines, entered what appeared to be a three-story fire station on the other side of the busy boulevard. "Man, it's going to be a hot time in the ole town tonight," M.K. predicted, with his mind set on having the hottest time possible.

"Yeah, I'm in the mood for some devilment myself," Baltimore admitted. He stroked his curly hair back with his fingertips then checked to see if he'd remembered packing his charmer. The revolver often came in handy when a drunk or jealous boyfriend needed a little persuading to back down. Saturday nights in St. Louis offered plenty of both.

"That's it?" Delbert asked, stepping onto the curb in front of

Ms. Etta's. He squinted at the mushroom-colored brick building. "Looks like a firehouse to me."

"Used to be one, now it's a fast house," Baltimore answered, casting a broad smile over Delbert's obvious disappointment. Always the dresser, Baltimore popped the lapels on his tan plaid blazer, adjusted the white linen pocket kerchief and leather suspenders. "You boys ready?"

After observing Baltimore's primping ritual, Delbert and M.K. did likewise to spruce up their attire. The off-white cotton suit Delbert sported was his favorite of the three he owned and M.K. felt like a movie star when a young lady gawked at him while he buttoned his double-breasted houndstooth jacket and straightened the silk tie he'd won in a friendly dice game.

"Would you look at that? M.K.'s already got 'em going and we haven't even broke in yet," said Baltimore. "If you can't get lucky tonight, man, you ain't trying."

Music poured out of the nightclub when M.K. opened the entrance door. Charles Brown tickled the ivories while his band laid down some California blues. The dance floor was hopping. Couples boogied heartily to exorcise their work week demons as others swayed to the soulful rhythms, everyone celebrating the birth of spring at the hottest joint this side of Chicago.

Delbert put his money away when Baltimore offered to spring for the libations. "Y'alls' with me, so ain't no need for patting your pockets tonight," he told the other two. "I'm a head over and whisper a few hellos while y'all rustle up a table."

Delbert's heart pounded in his narrow chest, thinking it was possible to fall in love with just about every woman he saw. Ten dollar hairstyles, glad rags, drugstore makeup and painted on lips were very appealing, especially to a young man who had committed himself to examining lacerations and injured appendages over the past three years. When Delbert realized what he'd been missing, he was determined to make up for lost time. "M.K., look at all these grown women," he marveled.

"Yeah, man, I see 'em," he answered, licking his chops. "I see 'em."

Delbert's mouth watered as his eyes bounced from skirt to skirt. "I've died and gone to heaven."

"Naw, this ain't heaven but it's the closest I'll ever get. Delbert, see that one wrapped up in all that green, she's easy on the eyes and built for speed. Two things a man needs."

"She's high class all right." Delbert helped himself to a second glance when M.K. searched in the other direction. "Well, I hope she's got a friend."

"Two friends, don't go forgetting about our sponsor. Baltimore can close any deal. You'll see."

M.K. recognized a woman he'd seen the day before. When he noticed she was accompanied by two female associates, he abandoned the woman in green for a friendly face. He took Delbert along and waited until Baltimore returned, completing a cozy six-pack. "Come on, the train is pulling into the station," M.K. said, with his horns showing.

They approached the table near the back staircase, where it was understood that lovers could pay extra to get better acquainted in one of the bedrooms on the second level, previously used as firemen quarters. Although it had been several years since the fire house was utilized in its initial capacity, the upper rooms more than compensated for the decreased activity. On the second floor, a man with some money in his pocket and a smooth line on his lips could get all the activity he wanted. That's what Delbert had in mind when he studied the woman sitting on the right, wearing a cinnamon complexion as well as she did her black and white off-the-shoulder dress. She grinned brightly when the two men stood by. Her hair was done up in a criss-crossed bun with short bangs dangling in her face. M.K. had met her at the hospital when he and Ollie went out on their scouting expedition.

"Dr. M.K. Phipps," the woman greeted loudly, "you said you were gonna call me. My phone hasn't rung once."

"Hey, Ruth Anne, I've been meaning to call you. Ladies, pleased to meet you."

"I'm Belle and I'd be more pleased if you ordered some cock-

tails . . . doctor," the middle one sang sweetly. M.K. was beginning to think the arrangement just might work out. He'd take
Ruth Anne upstairs. Delbert could try his luck with Belle, because her complexion was fairer than most and Delbert seemed
to fancy that. However for Delbert, she was a bit thicker than he
was accustomed to, but seeing as how it was his first night at
Ms. Etta's he wasn't in any position to be all that particular. Delbert had already caught himself imagining how easy Belle's wine-
colored strapless gown would be to unzip and toss in the corner
of a dimly lit room.

"Why, sure, let me get a couple of seats, then we can have a
ball," M.K. answered cautiously when the third member in the
trio didn't make any efforts at introducing herself. Once he'd returned with additional chairs and taken a seat between Delbert
and Ruth Anne, he fired a questioning leer at the attractive mys-
tery woman. Bearing a close resemblance to Dorothy Dandridge
and decked out in a fashionable violet-colored dress with matching high heels and hat shaped like a Christmas bow, she was a
looker, but didn't appear to be all that eager to be admired.

M.K. leaned in closer to Ruth Anne. "What's her story?"

"Oh that's just Dinah, being Dinah. She's high-strung like
that, but she'll loosen up when a reason to happens by." Before
she went on to elaborate, Belle flicked M.K.'s muscular arm with
the back of her hand.

"So, who's the pup you brung with you?" she said, inspecting
Delbert peculiarly. "He sure ain't much for words."

"Oh, this here is *Dr.* Delbert Gales from Texas," M.K. told
her, emphasizing his profession.

"*Doctor?*" Belle laughed, taking in his youthful appearance.
Her voluptuous breasts heaved every time she took a breath to
speak. Delbert couldn't hear anything above his heart beating so
loudly. "Kinda frail from where I sit, but some say big things
come in small packages."

"Yeah, yeah," M.K. agreed for his friend's sake. "They also
say, everything is bigger in Texas."

"That might be true but he's in Missouri now and this is the 'Show Me State',," quipped Ruth Anne.

"I don't know Ruth Anne, he's kinda cute though." Belle thought the doctor part of Delbert was his most appealing attribute. "Delbert, you one of them *cat* doctors?" she purred seductively.

"Uh-uh, I'm a people doctor," he replied, completely unaware of her seedy insinuation.

"Ooh, and he's green too," Belle hollered gleefully. "I got me a real live Texas greenhorn. Just wait 'til I get you alone, so I can teach you a thing or two about cats."

"Yeah, he's a real quick study too," M.K. chimed in, continuing to do Delbert's bidding because he was failing to hold his own.

Ruth Anne sneered at Belle, who seemed more intrigued by the moment. "As long as he ain't . . . too quick," Ruth Anne remarked rudely, just as Baltimore arrived with a platter-toting waitress.

"Hey, everybody. I've been noticing y'all cutting up over here and figured you'd be getting as thirsty as you are lovely." Baltimore smiled at each woman, knowing that they'd already decided on who was going home with whom before the last how-do-you-do was done. "This young lady will get whatever tickles your fancies. Meanwhile, she brought an assortment of drinks to wet your whistles."

Belle was ready to throw Delbert over at the drop of a hat for Baltimore's company but she never got the chance. Suddenly, the quiet one in the bunch snapped out of her calm sedation. "You figured correctly," was her way of welcoming the newcomer into her midst.

"That there, ladies, is Baltimore, Baltimore Floyd," M.K. announced, as if his friend was a well-known celebrity.

"I'm sure it'll be a change of pace getting chummy with you, considering tickled fancies, wetted whistles and whatnots?" Dinah was testing him to see how well he'd fare when her exam had begun. "I typically despise a man like you, Mr. Floyd. I don't truck with no sheiks because your harem is bound to keep getting in the way of a good night's sleep."

Baltimore had taken the time to study Dinah from the bar before he made his way over to meet her. After having run across his share of dolled up headaches like Dinah in the past and always coming out on top, he was more than capable of maneuvering his way through dicey waters. She was well kept, high-yellow and seemed to be adequately flawed in the morality department. The jury was still out on whether she was a lady but there wasn't any doubt that she was all woman.

After Baltimore considered Dinah's opening bid, he upped the ante to get a peek at all of her cards. "Ma'am, you don't know me as well as you think," he challenged, in his velvety lovemaking voice. "I'll come back around when you've changed your mind." While Belle and Ruth Anne swooned over Baltimore's candor, Delbert turned to M.K.

"Hey, you ever see anything like that before?" he asked in utter amazement.

"Man, I ain't ever heard of anything like that before."

"I'll drink to that." said Delbert, sipping from his glass and desperately trying to gather exactly what had just transpired between Baltimore and Dinah.

Baltimore made his way to the main bar, just passing the time so that Dinah could mull things over while spinning her wheels. "Jo Etta, this is the kinda night that belongs in a picture frame. Charles Brown is a real crowd pleaser."

"He's just getting started, but he's bound to leave a mark before he's done."

"I see you got yourself a real nice billiards table," Baltimore mentioned casually.

"Don't try that with me. I know you the one who sent that pool table," Etta spat, her lips curling into a smile. "Had to give up half a sitting section to fit it in the back. Could you just for once ask me before you squander your bank roll on my account?"

Baltimore planted a sisterly kiss on her cheek. "Who said the pool table was for you?"

Before Etta got the notion to argue about it, he was on his way to discuss another gaming possibility. Madame Clarisse exited the business office with a stack of dollar bills fastened by a rubber band. "Here's the change you wanted, Etta. That was the same fella from the shop, huh?"

"Thanks, Clarisse. Yeah, that's him. None other than the sneak bearing gifts," she answered, handing the strap of bills to Gussy, the overbearing bartender. "Gus, put these up, we'll be need'n them in about an hour."

Clarisse couldn't take her eyes off of Baltimore even if she wanted to. His kind of man was made for staring. "Etta, why is it that you two haven't gotten together?" she wanted to know. "Appears he enjoys being pretty close to wherever you are, if you ask me."

"Nah, it ain't that way at all. For one, I'm still sweet on his best friend. And two, Baltimore ain't nothing but lightning in a bottle. One day, somebody's gonna be foolish enough to break that bottle and lots of people are gonna get hurt behind it. I'd hate to be standing too close when that happens." Clarisse was fanning herself, puffing on a cigarette and thinking how she wouldn't mind getting struck by his kind of lightning.

When Baltimore set his drink down on the corner of the pool table, the man who'd been hustling there all evening smacked his lips. His head was shaved clean, his eyebrows arched, and his skin was smooth and darker than a cool winter's night. When he smiled, the solid gold caps on his teeth glistened. "So you're looking to get embarrassed next, is that it?"

Baltimore ignored him initially. He nonchalantly made his way over to the shoeshine stand where the braggart sat like a king on a throne. Cheap cologne resonated from his spiffy clothing, a powder blue and white seersucker suit. Since men from the south favored the soft fabric enough to be caught dead wearing it, Baltimore thought he'd dig right in at the heart of the matter.

"Only one gon' get embarrassed is the fool wearing that flimsy *cocksucker* suit."

The pool player bit into his bottom lip then eased up when he recognized what Baltimore was up to. Had he paid attention, he would have noticed someone spying his game from the upstairs deck. "I don't get riled up so easily but nice try," he said with a light-hearted chuckle.

"How much you want me to take off your hands?" Baltimore asked rudely, to provoke the gambler. "I ain't got all night."

The fellow accepted Baltimore's challenge and slithered his thin frame down off the shoeshine stand. He studied Baltimore, the tall good looking man with a big mouth and even more imposing confidence. "Let's say we shoot twenty bucks a rack—or is that too steep for you?"

"Actually I was thinking more like a hundred per rack?" After chalking one of the pool sticks delivered with the table, Baltimore pursed his lips then blew lightly at the tip of it. A tiny puff of blue chalk dust scattered into the air. Blinky, the teenaged shoeshine boy swallowed hard, because he'd witnessed Seersucker run every other competitor off the table and he wasn't easily impressed by Baltimore's swagger.

6

OLD HABITS DIE HARD

"A hundred it is then," the gambler hissed, slipping off his summer suit coat. "Mind if I break 'em?"

"That'd be all right with me, 'long as I get to do the honors next time around."

"So you's counting on contributing two hundred of yo' greenbacks? If that's the way you want it, that's the way it ought to be." I'll be proud to knock some of that polish off your high-glossed self."

Baltimore had promised himself to resign from pool hustling after having to kill a man, one night in Kansas City, after a fast game took a wrong turn. Baltimore had kept his vow to steer clear of pool tables until this one called out to him like a sultry siren's song. His hands trembled slightly as he unbuttoned his blazer, succumbing to his addiction of pool hustling, yet again.

Seersucker had taken chunks out of several hardworking men's take home pay and he'd heckled them harshly while doing it. The way Baltimore figured it, the time had come to even out a few things, so he pushed his hand into his front trouser pocket and came out with two quarters. "Blinky, you know my car?" The boy nodded his head then excitedly awaited instructions.

"Go on and get what ever you find out of the trunk. Bring it to me and I'll have four bits for your trouble."

Blinky had a speech impediment that caused him to speak in rapid, short, choppy sentences, sort of blinking his words instead of saying them. "Yeah-yeah. I'll-fetch-it. For-you. I'll-fetch-it."

"Run along now and hurry back," Baltimore prompted him. "Me and this man's got business to 'tend to."

While his slick opponent fired the cue ball into the pack, Baltimore sat quietly and observed. Seersucker sank three balls and heckled at Baltimore's stupidity for raising the stakes. After making two more shots, he faltered. "I decided to let you play so you wouldn't feel left out, but don't go getting too comfortable."

"Oh, you gon' *let* me play?" Baltimore studied the remaining setup on the table then quickly dropped four out of five balls in the same corner pocket. When he peered out the window, he saw that Blinky was crossing the street with what he'd been sent away to retrieve. Baltimore went out of his way to pass on an easy shot in order to set the table for his own defeat.

As planned, the slick stranger put the eight ball away to beat him solidly. In no time flat he was back to flapping his gums. "Sonny, it occurs you got in way over yo' head," the man teased. He folded Baltimore's money in half then added it to the substantial wad he'd amassed from his other victims. "Now, I'ma hafta drown you."

Baltimore unfastened his blazer and slipped it off his broad shoulders. He did likewise with his empty gun holster. The missing forty-five was harnessed to his shin. While reaching to hang his belongings on the coat rack, those same chilling memories he wanted to forget were staring him in the face again.

Baltimore couldn't help recalling how sorry he was for murdering a man after he'd fallen in love with his young wife. Baltimore had spent a whole afternoon talking him into a pool match, then goading him until he went and did something he couldn't apologize for. After losing his rent money, he'd taken two slugs in the chest before swinging his rusty ice pick once. The dead man's wife was a widow before his body hit the floor. Despite all the wrong Baltimore had committed in his lifetime, that was his only regret. He was the only man Baltimore had killed who he didn't believe deserved it or at least had it coming to him.

Moments later, Blinky brought in a thin alligator case to the back. "For. Another-two-bits. I-can get-all-this . . . rrred-paint off'n this-here-fffine-case . . . Mistah-Floyd."

The expensive case, including its contents, were willed to Baltimore in a poker game outside of Cleveland, when the previous owner met his untimely demise after going up against a gun with a hair trigger. "That ain't no paint, boy, but never you mind. Go on and see Ms. Etta about a bite to eat," Baltimore said. Blinky and Seersucker realized simultaneously what the large red stain was: blood.

With his jaw quaking, Blinky pocketed the two quarters and scampered out of sight. Seersucker lined up behind Baltimore. Grinning cautiously, he chalked his stick. "Floyd?" he said, with a stiff pause. "That wouldn't be the same Baltimo' Floyd what shot a man over a pretty little thing in Kansas City?"

"That man's pride killed him, I only officiated," Baltimore replied calmly. "He died over a wager he couldn't pay and a lack of common sense."

"Common sense huh? Is that what they calling being full of piss and vinegar?"

"When a man's wife slips up and hollers out another fella's name, he ought to have the common sense to let it go and get himself another woman," Baltimore rationalized evenly. Sweat began beading up on the southerner's forehead. He loosened his collar and then inched toward his coat but Baltimore stopped him. "Something wrong, Seersucker?"

"Naw, just remembering how I thought it was a shame when I heard about the killing is all." He stared out of the window while a single thought ran laps in his head. "What about you, Mistah Floyd? Ever make a wager you couldn't satisfy?"

"You thinking of trying me?" was Baltimore's answer.

"I'd rather leave you alone and broke like you did that dead fella's wife." The southerner stuffed all of his money into the side pocket directly in front of him. "If you can't match it, I'll play you for that prized coach of yours sitting out yonder." He glanced out of the window again. "But you understand this. One of us is gon' leave this place tonight." Without questioning which place the man was referring to, Baltimore pitched in both his car keys and the stack of bills he'd won off Barker Sinclair.

Seersucker studied Baltimore's every move now that twelve hundred dollars and a new car lay in the balance. He watched as Baltimore opened the fancy alligator box, whistled a slow melody, slapped his hands together and then stroked at his wavy black hair. Then Baltimore doused his hands with talcum powder he'd taken from the case. Those pretty-boy antics ruffled Seersucker. "You ready yet or you gonna prance around all night?"

With that said, Baltimore knew which place one of them would be leaving. "Naw, I'm done," he said coarsely, taking two pieces of African ebony wood from the case. He glared at the man while screwing the top of one into the bottom of the other. He was not only prepared to rain harm down on Seersucker, he'd already decided it was justified. "Eight ball, corner pocket," Baltimore called before the break.

"You crazy as a shit house rat for even thinking about trying that shot."

"Well, you're half right," Baltimore corrected him. He steadied his left hand on the table, cocked his right arm at the elbow then snapped his wrist forward. The cue ball crashed into the pack, scattering the other balls across the table. Blinky reappeared from underneath it. Seersucker's condescending smirk faded as the black eight ball rolled toward the corner pocket. Just like that, the eight ball fell, the game was over and the man's seven hundred dollars were gone.

Baltimore huffed. "Now, I'd appreciate it if you got the hell away from my money."

"But, that's an impossible shot. Impossible!" the loser whined. "I don't know how but you cheated me, you rotten bastard!"

Infuriated, Baltimore marched toward him. Seersucker pulled a six-inch blade from his waistband. He jabbed at Baltimore twice before feeling the brunt of ebony wood smacking against his head just over the left eye. "I should end this right now but I'd hate to ruin all these good folks' evenings," Baltimore barked. He told Blinky to keep watch over his cash and then he grabbed a handful of Seersucker by the collar. Tossing him out in the back alley with his skull cracked opened was doing him a favor. "If I see you again, I'ma shoot you on sight. Understand that!" As the man writhed on the ground in pain, Baltimore gathered himself and headed back inside.

After collecting his things, Baltimore dropped sixty dollars on the table where M.K. and Delbert were teetering on public intoxication. Ruth Anne and Belle were not far behind them. M.K. peered up with his eyes glazed over, a perplexed expression hung on his face. "Hey, y'all, it's Baltimo'. Boy, where you been? Keeping Dinah company is a lot of work and the kinda job I don't want."

"Fellas, that ought to be enough wind to sail your ships right on into the dock, but I've gotta make some waves." Baltimore extended his hand to Dinah, who frowned as if he'd held a dead fish in her face. "Dinah, we both know your mind ought to be good and changed by now."

Slovenly Belle slapped her hand down on the table in protest. "And what's wrong with fine upstanding ladies like us?" she solicited, followed by a jolting hiccup.

"No disrespect. I have a great affection for fine, upstanding ladies such as yourselves, but I'm in the market for a woman who can keep up."

"Dinah isn't going anywhere with you," Ruth Anne cackled. "She already said she's opposed to joining up with harems. And another thing—"

"Don't you mind her," Dinah protested in her own stead. "I was starting to think you'd gone and changed your mind about me." She stood up to leave as Baltimore covered her shoulders with her mink stole.

"Meet me by the door, would you? I've got an itch I feel compelled to scratch," he whispered, against the back of Dinah's neck. She cooed agreeably as Baltimore slipped out the back door. He glanced up the alley then down to the other end. When he saw Seersucker crawling around on his hands and knees, he reached for his palm-sized twenty-two caliber pistol from inside the alligator-skin case. Pop! Pop! Seersucker's body fell over against the cruddy pavement.

"I told you how it'd be if I saw you again and I told Lucinda's people I was sorry but they sent you anyway. Well, I'm all out of apologies now." He had too many irons in the fire to be peeping over his shoulder due to some girl's family seeking retribution. That night at Ms. Etta's Fast House, Baltimore was fortunate. Next time around, it would walk right up and grab him by his throat.

7

ALL THAT GLITTERS

Monday morning, while waiting on the streetcar, Delbert shook off the stale memories of his Sunday lunch date with Belle. She'd fallen asleep on him the night he walked her home from Etta's. She ate twice as much as he expected and almost more than he could afford. Delbert was actually looking forward to moving into the residence quarters at the hospital, considering that his pockets were as flat as day old beer.

M.K. read the sports page in the *St. Louis Comet*, the city's black newspaper and the only source that documented the existence of colored people's society events and other noteworthy stories. The white-owned dailies neglected to include events involving blacks unless they were disparaging or riddled with details stemming from crimes.

"Hey, M.K., why surgery?" Delbert asked, as if there was another part of the question he'd purposely left out.

Without taking his eyes off the morning paper, M.K. smiled softly. "You mean why subject myself to three years of blood and guts when I could take up another discipline and start a private practice in one?" He knew what Delbert was driving at because he'd asked himself the same question many times before. "I'm in it for the rush I get, same as you." He glanced at Delbert to note his reaction. When Delbert frowned, M.K. folded the newspaper over his knee. "That is why you've come all this way, to train at Homer Gee, I mean?"

"Sometimes I don't really know," Delbert admitted. "Seemed like the right thing to do. Book learning always came easy to me. I was too small for sports and my daddy had all of this mapped out by the time I was twelve years old." Traces of a smile played around Delbert's lips. "'You gon' be a doctor,' he'd say. 'Not only that, a surgeon. That's the smartest kind of doctor. They got this hospital up there in Saint Louey where they train colored mens on surgery.'"

M.K. slapped Delbert on the back. "Well, looks like you made it, 'cause there's lots of surgery to be done around here. Once you've heard ole Hiram Knight's speech, you'll be glad you listened to your daddy."

"How's that?" Delbert questioned.

"You mean to tell me you haven't heard about the first day grilling Knight gives to every class of interns before he let's 'em see to the patients?" Delbert's expression was blank, not sure what to make of this supposed "talking to" from the chief administrator. "Bill, Ollie, Claude," M.K. beckoned as three of the other residents walked out of the hotel with their luggage in hand. "Delbert here hasn't caught wind of Hiram Knight's fire and *tombstone* first day speech."

"Sure, I've heard surgical grads mention it back home, but you're the only one who's actually faced it head on," Bill replied. What he said was true. M.K. had been accepted in the program three years earlier but his number came up for the draft. He could have fought with the war department over his exempt status as a medical resident and been awarded a deferment, but going to war meant seeing surgical action up close and a lot of it. The eighteen months he spent operating alongside white doctors proved invaluable. M.K. assisted with several procedures that most non-military surgeons only read about in national journals months after the fact.

Ollie sat his bags down on the stoop. "What is this first day business, a stiff-necked orientation?"

M.K. threw the paper aside and hopped up from the bench. He clasped his hands behind his back then struck a pious pose before pacing back and forth on the sidewalk. The two remaining residents arrived just in time to catch the sideshow. "*You all sit down and learn something about the man's legacy you'll be honoring, as well as the inspiration behind his dream,*" M.K. instructed them, in a voice two octaves lower than his own. The fellas were amused by his antics as they listened attentively. "Now, I feel it's my humble responsibility to share a story with you, so that you might come to understand the magnitude of your calling. Young men, this is the first of the best days of your lives. What you will learn here, see here, and hear here . . . take with you and abound vigilantly, blah . . . blah . . . blah . . . so on and so forth. Homer G. Phillips, the man for whom this great institution was erected, was a determined individual and likewise you too shall become . . . as determined. And remember most importantly, that I am king!"

Delbert held back a chuckle out of respect for the famous surgeon M.K. was imitating while the others joined together in a band of unabated hooting. "You'll see," he warned them, "that little man's got a way with words and he don't mind spending some of 'em on shaping us into finely-tuned surgical machines." The streetcar arrived before M.K. enlightened his companions on Knight's passion for the institution in which he'd dedicated his life's work and the events that led up to building the colored hospital nine years before. Perhaps M.K. had forgotten the details surrounding the overwhelming need for an adequate medical facility to serve the Negro populace in a segregated city, where the infant mortality rate for colored babies more than doubled that of white ones. Perhaps he'd forgotten how colored infants were delivered in basements of white hospitals then placed in dresser drawers, shoeboxes, and egg crates as a standard practice while white ones had access to cribs, bassinettes and heated rooms merely two floors above. And perhaps, it had somehow slipped M.K.'s mind that countless men and women died without proper medical care when hospitals stopped accepting black patients once their basements reached full capacity. Whether he had forgotten or merely neglected to grasp its importance, the famed 'first day grilling' he heard later that morning stayed with him for the rest of his life.

Residing on forty acres of prime real estate, Homer G. Phillips Hospital opened with 685 beds, performing 1200 births a year and 1500 surgeries, 700 of which were major. Homer Gee, as it was commonly called, was the pride of "The Ville" but not all of the blacks in St. Louis shared the same adoration. Patients often refused treatment from colored physicians in hopes of receiving attention from one of the white doctors visiting on behalf of the local university hospital, contributing their services a few hours a week. The situation was so incredibly skewed that a colored patient, who had survived a devastating automobile accident nearly went to his grave screaming, "Where all the white doctors at? I ain't gon' let one of these niggas kill me!" Fortunately, he collapsed in the emergency room and was subsequently saved by one of those Negro doctors he was so adamant against receiving treatment from.

As the streetcar slowed to a stop on North Whittier Street, butterflies danced a two-step in the pit of Delbert's stomach. After walking less than a block, he stopped dead in his tracks. No one had informed him that the hospital was a six-story magnificent buff-colored complex flaunting its art deco architecture, sprawled across an impressive emerald green lawn. Built in 1937, the jewel of black St. Louis cost over $1,000,000 and it was worth every penny.

When Ollie noticed Delbert's feet were glued to the pavement and his mouth hung open, he understood fully. "She sure is something, isn't she?" Ollie said as Delbert eyed the massive building with its measure of boldness and majesty rivaling a royal castle.

"My daddy won't believe this," he whispered.

"If you make me late for the meet and greet with Hiram Knight, you gonna need your daddy to help get me off your ass,"

Ollie jested, tugging on Delbert's sleeve. "Come on now, we've got a date with the Li'l General."

Delbert brought up the rear as the group of new interns jaunted through the front entrance, turning the heads of patients, utility staff and nurses alike. The fine indigo marble beneath Delbert's feet shined brilliantly as he glided along the path made by the others, although he'd soon grow to despise the unyielding stone after treading miles over it each day.

"M.K., hold that elevator!" yelled Ollie, as the golden hued doors begun to close.

"Hurry up then," M.K. hollered back. He stuck his bulky arm between them. "We're pushing it as it is." Ollie shoved Delbert inside the elevator car, pressing his face against Bill's chest. "You may as well get used to close quarters, Tex. The resident's dorm isn't much bigger than this."

When the doors opened on the sixth floor the herd stepped off, swinging luggage and anxiety to and fro, except for Delbert, who examined every inch of the white hallway like a New York tourist. Bill didn't have the heart to tell Delbert he'd left his travel bag on the elevator that descended toward the first floor. For the time being, Delbert was in the promised land and couldn't see any further than his bright future.

"Doctors, please store your luggage in this nurses' lounge, then fall in down the hall. Take the last room on the right," a stern, petite, senior nurse with her uniform starched to the utmost perfection instructed. The blue and white striped dress, white hat, white short-sleeved shirt and stiff white collar under a white apron and matching bib were every bit as striking as any military-issue ensemble.

M.K. chuckled aloud. "Fall in, Nurse Robinson? I thought I'd quit the army?"

"Nice to see you again too, Dr. Phipps," the nursing director sneered sarcastically. "You haven't been gone that long to forget how the line is toed around here." Her assessment was correct, as always. Geraldine Robinson was responsible for running the nursing academy and seeing to it that interns respected the nurses' sharpness and professionalism. "The Director will be along shortly so don't get any ideas of wandering off," Nurse Robinson warned. It wasn't any secret that young doctors spent a major part of their training plotting opportunities to wrinkle the nurses' uniforms, with the nurses still in them.

Twenty minutes later, a fair-skinned man with thinning black hair hastened into the room where the interns were twiddling their thumbs. He carried a clipboard in one hand and a rubber ball in the other, which he squeezed continually until he'd worked out what ever had him trapped in a pensive mood. The diminutive white-on-white starched cotton uniform he wore, buttoned up to his Adam's apple, could have doubled for a child's Halloween costume but that fact was lost on the other men who jumped to attention when they recognized him as the great Hiram Knight, in the flesh. "Right on schedule," he stated boldly. "Gentlemen, if you wouldn't mind lining up so I can get a look at the finest class of promising interns on God's green earth." The men quickly assembled shoulder to shoulder. "Dr. Marion Kennesaw Phipps," Dr. Knight read aloud, from his clipboard. Although Ollie wanted to bust a gut over M.K.'s given name, he dared not make a sound. "I'm glad the good Lord saw fit to bring you back to us in one piece."

"I am as well, sir," M.K. answered, while holding in a scowl over his given name having being openly shared.

"Because you've seen more than your fair share of acute war injuries, the previous time you spent here has been reinstated. You'll work an abbreviated rotation for three months and then join the resident's program already in progress."

"Thank you, sir," beamed M.K.

"Don't thank me so fast. Remember, of whom much is given, also much is expected, sayeth the good book, which means I plan on working your ass like a Hebrew slave." Noting the burly intern withheld his gratitude, the director glared up at him. "You're welcome."

"Dr. William Browning?" he called next.

"Here, sir," Bill answered sharply.

"Hell, I can see that. You're standing right in front of me," Dr. Knight commented irritably. He was noticeably annoyed as he went back to his clipboard, bothered that Bill had stated the obvious; the one thing that the seasoned surgeon despised most. He couldn't stand having his valuable time wasted. After he'd called everyone's name but Delbert's, Dr. Knight searched the floors from wall to wall. On cue, Nurse Robinson sauntered through the doorway carrying a brown leather bag. She placed it at the administrator's feet then exited as suddenly as she had appeared. "Ah, yes, Dr. Delbert Gales," Knight sighed as if he was severely displeased.

A lump about the size of Texas formed in Delbert's narrow throat. "Sir?" he managed to say, eventually.

"How do you plan on dazzling us with your talents when you can't remember to hold on to your drawers?"

At a loss for words, Delbert expressed his confusion. "Sir?" was the only thing that came out of his mouth.

Knight looked Delbert up and down in a curiously manner. "You do wear drawers, don't you, Dr. Gales?"

"Well, yes, sir?"

"And we're all the better for it son. I'll chalk this up to your exuberance to get started, although forgetfulness will not be tolerated from any of you. Nor will my patience suffer your incompetence, lack of sleep, stubbornness, thickheadedness, lewdness, drunkenness or whiny half-baked excuses. Technical errors are inevitable but only acceptable in minimal quantities. However, failure to acknowledge those errors is immoral." Dr. Knight had the complete attention of each man standing in that room and the one woman listening closely just outside the door. Nurse Robinson hadn't missed out on one "first day" grilling in over eight years and she wasn't about to miss this one either. "Furthermore, Knight continued, "you have all taken the Hippocratic Oath and you will live up to it. 'First, do no harm,' gentlemen. Do no harm. There are six hundred and eighty-five beds generally filled with six hundred and eighty-five patients under my care. Those are my patients, entrusted to me. I'm only allowing you to administer your knowledge and efforts to heal them." Dr. Knight laid his clipboard on a small brown table behind him then he wiped his brow with a crisp handkerchief. His countenance was more deliberate than before.

"Just in case there may be one of you who doesn't know of the man's legacy that you'll be honoring as well as the inspiration behind his dream, I want to share a story." Ollie almost snickered when Knight used the exact same words M.K. had earlier to get a rise out of his contemporaries, but the solemn manner in which their chief spoke deterred him from making the biggest mistake of his fledging career.

"Years ago, a very determined individual for whom this great institution was erected worked diligently to manifest his dream, a dream that colored people in the city of St. Louis could receive the best medical care possible, despite the Jim Crow laws or segregation. Homer G. Phillips, a civil law attorney, held the mayor's feet to the fire until he agreed on appropriating funds for the very place you are standing now. It saddens me to inform you that the honorable Homer Phillips was assassinated, in broad daylight while awaiting a streetcar. He never lived to see this glorious facility and all the miracles performed here. And, gentlemen, that is a shame before God."

There wasn't a dry eye among the interns. M.K.'s tears ran free and without regard to what the other men might have thought about it. Obviously he had forgotten the magnitude of his calling.

The head nurse stifled her emotions, as best she could. "God bless you, Dr. Knight," she said tenderly. "God bless you."

"Go on and pull yourselves together," Knight instructed them. "There are a few more items I need to cover before I move on to the rest of your rotation appointments. I am going to expect and inspect, that is what I'm here for. I will expect your best, then inspect to assure that's what I get, your very best. Watch, learn and heal, gentlemen, in that order. I'd like to think that I have selected the best and the brightest when choosing each of you from a selection pool of two hundred candidates, so don't prove me wrong. I detest being wrong."

Afterwards, Dr. Knight informed his prized pupils of their assignments. Bill Browning and Charley Morrow drew pediatrics, Harry Johnson and Claude Babineaux were selected to train in radiology, Ollie Washington was close to throwing a fit when Dr. Knight followed his name with a stint in urology, M.K. was sent to the general medicine wing and Delbert drew the inside straight and the envy of the others by landing obstetrics and gynecology. Only Delbert feared one thing the others didn't, the little secret which had him quaking in his shoes. Despite Ollie having been slated to spend the next three months fondling other men's penises, Delbert was convinced he had the worst luck of all. One man's prison is another man's paradise, after all, or vice versa.

8

Bottom of the Ninth

Over the past three years the Blacksmiths baseball team met with their team sponsor, an industrious tycoon named Randolph Bellows, to discuss the upcoming season and schedule. This Monday was supposed to be special because Mr. Bellows had been working diligently to secure a team charter to join the popular Negro Professional Baseball League. Late into the afternoon the players sat around restlessly, not only waiting for the man responsible for financing their future, but also for Henry Taylor, the captain and the soul of the organization.

Baltimore had driven by Henry's house twice but his wife Roberta insisted he wasn't home. Out of places to search, Baltimore cruised by Ms. Etta's, which was typically closed until five P.M. He noticed that several cars belonging to the 'Smiths' players were parked alongside the curb in front of the Fast House.

Feeling slighted, Baltimore huffed as he pushed the door open, quickly discovering a lively room of athletes reminiscing over old times. Etta and Penny stocked drinking glasses while Gussy, the bartender, offered complimentary sodas to the team while they killed time. When they noticed Baltimore strolling in, they assumed incorrectly that Henry wouldn't be far behind. Instead they got an earful of Baltimore's discontentment.

"Somebody want to tell me what this collection of hideaways is up to and how come not one of ya'll gave me the heads up to get in on it?"

Before any of the men could pony up a response, Henry barged in. "'Cause this don't have nothing to do with you," he said. "You done gave up on us, remember?"

"Henry, what's the matter with you?" asked Trace Wiggins. Trace studied Henry's demeanor over the top of his reading glasses. "I thought you and Baltimore was friends?"

"You tell him, Trace," Baltimore seconded. "Friendship goes deeper than baseball, unless your woman done stripped you of those privileges too."

When Etta heard that, she pulled Penny by the arm. "Get your pocketbook, child. We need to leave the menfolk to work a few things out on their own without us getting in the way. Gussy, don't you let nobody else in here until what ever it is wedged between Baltimore and Henry gets knocked loose," Etta warned. "Nobody!"

The bartender agreed vehemently, staying close to the two-by-four peace keeper he kept behind the bar in the event of customers getting out of hand. "You won't need that," Etta told him on her way out, "'Cause these boys just gonna *talk* through their growing pains." The last comment was a bit of advice to the fellows, if they happened to be in the mindset of accepting any. Although that was the first time Henry had set foot inside the Fast House since he got himself hitched seven months earlier, Etta had the same old feelings racing inside her—the deep-seated feelings Henry inspired when he was hers.

Near the bar, Smiley Tennyson threw a grin over the whole situation as he was accustomed to doing when a dim state of affairs needed some pep. "Now, hold on! Baltimo', Henry, I didn't come here to talk about women, especially not mines. Y'all know the only reason I'm with her is 'cause of her momma's cooking and her sister's good looking."

"When is Mr. Bellows supposed to get here?" another player asked wearily.

"He ain't coming back here," answered Henry, putting off his quarrel with Baltimore for more pressing business. "Mr. Bellows ain't going nowhere else for that matter." The men grumbled, confused over Henry's riddling statement. "They sent this here telegram this morning and Roberta brought it to me while I was down at the club house wondering what happened to y'all." When Baltimore heard that woman's name, he turned his head away as if he couldn't stand the sound of it.

Trace shoved his chair back and stood up like a gunfighter in the old west. He stared at the yellow envelope Henry had tossed on the round table in front of him. "Give me that," Trace demanded, not wanting to put off the inevitable. He adjusted his glasses with one hand and picked up the envelope with the other. "Let's see what Bellows has gotten himself into. 'URGENT! Dear Henry Taylor . . . stop,'" he read. "'Please be advised that Randolph Ulysses Bellows was killed on March 19, 1947 in plane crash . . . stop. Deepest regrets and sympathies . . . stop. It's signed, Turner Wilson, Attorney at Law . . . stop." Trace removed his bifocals when he couldn't see the benefit of reading another word. "It goes on, but . . ."

Strange, how much that small yellow telegram changed those men's lives in an instant. Mr. Bellows' death meant no financial backing, no team management or Negro League Charter. What it also meant was a death sentence to the Blacksmiths. Baltimore wasn't the least bit bothered, seeing as how he'd moved on with his life, much like the others would be forced to do now. Needless to say, the 'Smiths found themselves disenfranchised and void of direction. Most of the players couldn't remember a time when they weren't playing some form of organized ball. Spring was invented for baseball, they believed, instead of it being the other way around and it was simple as that. Without warning, a little yellow piece of paper changed everything.

"Gussy!" Baltimore summoned loudly. "Get these boys something to hold 'em, and put it on my tab. It's gonna be a long evening." The bartender exhaled heartily then brought out bottles of hard liquor and drinking glasses. After lining them up on the bar for self-service, Gussy headed out into the back alley to feed his heroin habit.

Shortly after the bartender's departure the atmosphere quickly twisted into a mangled distortion when what used to be a promising baseball franchise began knocking back shots of liquor, one right behind the other, each of the players looking for a way to say goodbye to their dreams. All but Jinx Dearborn, the most talented pitcher in the state, colored or white, drowned their sorrows with libations on Baltimore's ticket. Jinx was a baseball player more than he was a man. He didn't know how to be anything else so his decision came easy. Jinx decided he'd have to scratch out a living until the game found a way to reclaim him. That's all there was to it. For the others, it wouldn't be nearly that simple.

After the cocktails began watering down the bad news, Smiley Tennyson lit up the joint with a sporting tale that turned Baltimore beet-red every time he heard it. "O.K., so we's out to the fairground in Dallas, on this Negro Appreciation Day they had down there, playing a group of boys up from the Austin Tamale League. Ole Baltimo' was putting 'em to shame. I mean he was slapping that pitcher all around the field. Even hit a curve ball so far, he broke a car window in the parking lot." Henry's lips creased, when remembering his friend's finest hour as a player and exhibitionist.

"After Baltimo' made a fool of the first fella let outta the gate, they had some fat-headed mug to relieve him, on account of how Baltimo' was firing his pitches into the deep bleachers. It got to be so much trouble, for the home team you know, because Dapper Dan here went to signing his name for all the pretty women while he was covering first base. Yeah, right while the game was going on, Baltimo', he'd take a bow before and after he'd hit until something what you might call *occurred* to mix things up a pinch."

Baltimore pleaded for Smiley to forego telling the rest of the story, but he wouldn't hear of it. The jokester had the floor and didn't plan on relinquishing it until he was good and spent. "Well, now, after his sixth home run, a man came out of the stands. Heck we didn't know what he wanted until he walked over, all gangly-like, to the pitcher's mound. And I'll be damned if that fat-headed pitcher didn't hand over his ball and glove like he was pulled from World Series Game Seven." Smiley downed another shot of bourbon then commenced tying up the tale. "All of us laughed at the tall skinny fella with big flapping feet. We didn't know no better and plus the man had on street clothes. Who was to know it was Satchel Paige, visiting a sick relative?"

The players shouted raucously. None of them had been fortunate enough to face the best pitcher in Negro League history. "Yeah, Satchel didn't even warm up his arm, just went to work on Baltimo like he'd been taking liberties with the man's kid sister. Satch used the first ball to brush Baltimo' back a ways. You know how he likes to crowd when he gets in a heated rhythm. The next pitch sailed across the plate and it was smoking like a run-away choo-choo. That ball was sitting in the catcher's mitt before the folks in the stands knew it was strike one. Baltimo' settled in the batting box then and dug in for the next flamethrower. He held out his bat and pointed it toward that car out yonder in the lot with a hole in the window. The crowd roared over the duel going down on the baseball diamond. Satchel cocked his knee up damned near to his chin and hurled his 'hesitation pitch'. Ole Baltimo', he was looking for another high heater so he whipped that lumber around with all his might before the ball was halfway to plate. Hell, he almost screwed himself into the batter's box.

"With only two strikes on him, the umpire called Baltimo' out. Satchel had pitched the man's pants down around his ankles and that long tool of his'n done tumbled out of his pants and hit the dirt. While Baltimo' was busy stuffing it back in his jock strap, the old ump took one look at that thang and accused him of playing with two bats. Damned if he didn't disqualify Baltimo' for cheating." All of the men fell over laughing at the story Smiley told, which actually took place in Peoria, Illinois, but did happen just about the way he remembered. After the game, Baltimore was the most popular bachelor in town until the team's bus pushed off toward the next city two days later.

Within hours, news of Randolph Bellows's death had spread throughout the community, and beyond. Clay Sinclair walked into Ms. Etta's wearing his police uniform. Etta, who hadn't too long returned, threw a hawking glance at Gussy. She held it just long enough to demand he keep his cool. Baltimore assumed that Clay had come all the way to "The Ville" to relay a message from his brother Barker, but he delivered more disturbing news at their feet instead. "Ms. Etta. Fellas," Clay spoke cordially, sniffing empty glasses while his partner posted himself by the door. "None of this hooch would happen to be 'shine, would it?"

"Now, Officer Sinclair, you know I'm law abidin'," Etta told him as nicely as she could, although she was unhappy about his presence. The only reason police came within spitting distance of her establishment was to be paid off for the goods they already had on her beforehand. Luckily, Halstead didn't get the chance to deliver the order she'd placed before he died, so she had nothing to serve but store-bought spirits

"Uh-huh, would this meeting have anything to do with a missing pool shark taking murder-for-hire business on the side?" That accusation drew Baltimore's attention because he was unaware that Gussy cleaned up the mess he'd made in the alley. Seersucker's body had floated half way down the Mississippi River by the time Clay learned of his disappearance.

"Naw, suh, we'ont know nothing 'bout no shark killers," Gussy joked. "The Mississippi's too muddy for anything except for catfish."

Clay grinned at Baltimore, who was leaning back in the wooden chair without a care in the world and a good deal of Barker's money still in his possession. "Well, I guess this might be as good a time as any to say how sorry I am to hear about Mr. Bellows's death. I thought he was a fine man," Clay said with the utmost sincerity. He paused, helped himself to a sip of whiskey and then smacked his lips. "Oh, yeah, not that any of you care, but the climate in this town is changing." He tossed the evening edition of the *St. Louis Dispatch* on the table where Henry sat. "The city council voted today on accepting colored applicants interested on joining the Metro Police Department. Vote passed six to three." Clay gestured to his partner that it was time to leave. "If you do happen to see that missing shark killer, who doesn't know he's missing, let me know." He smiled at Gussy, who didn't offer one in return on general principle. "Evening, Ms. Etta, fellas," the officer hailed, while making his exit. Baltimore was one hundred percent certain that Clay suspected him in Seersucker's disappearance. He was just as certain that the real reason the cop stopped by was written all over the front page of that newspaper.

As soon as Clay Sinclair's patrol car drove away, Trace snatched the paper from off the table and read it aloud like he had with the telegram. "Says here that amidst long term efforts to integrate the city's police force, the day has finally come to provide opportunities for colored males between the ages of twenty-one and thirty-four to become an intricate part of law enforcement in St. Louis." Trace chuckled under his breath. "Let them tell it, we sure have been an intricate part of the *crime* in St. Louis. Oh, it also says that the day to take this giant step toward integration is tomorrow. The civil service exam begins at nine o'clock sharp."

"They giving us that much time to get our giant steps ready, huh?" Henry joked.

Smiley stroked his chin while adding a little seasoning to the conversation. "They cutting it kinda close, almost like they didn't want us to find out they was up to their so-called push for integration until it was too late."

"I suspect that's the general idea," Willie B. added. He'd been a mortician's son since he was born. The thought of being something else for a change was alluring. A chance to venture from beneath his father's shadow was downright beautiful.

"I'm thinking the same thing, Willie B." That was Henry, fingering the edges of the newspaper.

Silent up to then, Baltimore finally reacted. "What else you thinking, Henry? I trust you're thinking about us as friends, 'cause if you pass that test, things gonna change between you and me."

"This is where I get off," Willie B. decided, "if I want to kick my daddy in the ass by joining the Metro. Baltimo', thanks for the drinks. Ms. Etta, Gussy." He tipped his hat to Penny, acknowledging her as an adult before leaving for home to sleep off the party that ended on a staccato beat.

Henry reached into his pocket, resisting Baltimore's hospitality, to settle his own account. Just about broke, he couldn't see his way clear to telling Roberta that her husband was a bust with no lines on putting in for the overdue bills, so his assessment of the situation was clear.

As Henry turned toward the door, Etta heard someone's voice yelling his name before she realized it was hers. "Henry, wait! Does having a steady job mean so much to your wife that you'd quit on Baltimo'? Good friends mean more than that."

Without thinking, Henry answered out of desperation. "I'm starting to believe friendship is overrated," he answered coldly. "Besides, I ain't got nothing better to do than work on feeding my family. 'Night, Jo Etta. Y'all."

One by one, the men filed out of the Fast House to contemplate their own giant steps toward progress. Feeling as if he'd witnessed a tragic funeral procession, Baltimore played a collection of depressing songs on the piano and indulged himself way past seeing straight. Penny nuzzled up next to him on the bench seat, wanting to share in his pain. He kissed her on the forehead and sighed before gently suggesting that she send for Etta so he could discuss the likelihood of Henry jumping the fence to the other side of the law after all they'd been through together. There was also something else to mull over, the likelihood that either or both Baltimore and Henry would get killed as a result of it. But, before traveling down that bumpy road, Etta looked on from a distance as Baltimore poured out a measure of his soul into sorrowful rhythmic measures.

Penny stood beside Etta, while choking back on her tears. "Ms. Etta, what's that ailing him so?" the girl asked sadly. "I ain't known him to drink like that."

Etta exhaled and placed her arm around Penny's shoulder to comfort her. "I've never seen him pick up a drink in all the years I've known him. But then again, I've never seen him get his heart broken either." Etta couldn't believe she'd witnessed it first hand and wished she hadn't. The storm brewing between Henry and Baltimore had her trapped in the middle of it.

In the meanwhile, Etta avoided the imminent conversation with Baltimore regarding Henry as long as humanly possible. She took the path of least resistance when joining him at the piano. With an eager smile, she asked him why he'd taken such a liking to Penny. He let his fingers dance over the keys in a light effortless manner while running her question through his troubled mind. "Penny's pure at heart," he answered. "She's likely the purest thing I've had close to me since I left home years ago. My younger sis, she's probably grown with her own children now, used to look at me with those big doe eyes like Penny . . . like I could do no wrong, you know. I miss her but my old papa, he'd die before allowing me to check in on her. Don't much blame him though, after all I did."

Baltimore's father was a minister, strict as any, although Baltimore was fully aware of the good pastor's reputation with the ladies and his numerous illegitimate children peppered throughout the congregation. He caught wind of Baltimore's gambling, hustling and running women for profit before the age of eighteen. Without hesitation, the minister was prepared to hand him over to the police to save face. Baltimore was so distraught over his father's resolution to turn him in that he pulled a gun, cocked it then labored over committing murder. Since that day, Baltimore had been on the run. From what, he didn't understand, although he was confident of one thing, that he sure was tired of running. And as for his best friend Henry, he was the closest thing there was to family left in the world. It hurt deep down in his heart to think of losing him too.

9

NOTHING IS AS IT SEEMS

After lying awake for most of the night, Henry cursed silently when the sun peeked through his window. He tossed an envious leer at Roberta as she jerked the covers over her head to drown out his rustling. Henry hadn't done anything but think since leaving the Fast House with both Etta and Baltimore stunned and salty. He'd thought about picking up the phone to call in his apology but that just didn't seem right. He'd even deliberated over scrapping the whole idea of joining the police force. Henry's mind was going in several directions all at once. It was all of that thinking that cheated him out of a good night's sleep. The only thing he didn't bother to waste any mental energy on was telling his wife what he'd planned on doing for the good of his family. He feared that she'd suggest how ill-prepared he was to take the civil exam and how he'd have a better chance using his back as opposed to his brains down at the shipyard. More than that, he feared that she might have been right.

With a hearty sigh, Henry flung his long, muscular legs over the side of bed. He washed his face and cleaned up in record time because he'd begun to lose his nerve. If he gave his chances of passing any real consideration, he'd crawl back into bed and catch up on the rest he didn't get. However, the line he'd crossed in his mind wouldn't allow for self-pity, self-doubt or selfishness. He wasn't willing to face Roberta, and continue dodging the outfitter without a prayer of satisfying his account, nor was he ready to admit that he'd passed up an opportunity to make her proud of him. That's what fueled his ambition as he spit shined his church shoes and later wrestled on the secondhand suit he'd bought off a mortician to get married in. Several months had passed since he laid down five dollars and hightailed it to the wedding chapel after Roberta promised him she would start looking for another man to spend the best days of her life with if he didn't. Getting the jacket to fit decently took some doing. It was quite a bit snugger than Henry remembered but that didn't stand in his way. He sucked in his stomach and held his breath until the jacket fastened.

As soon as Henry stepped out onto the porch, he saw two things that he wouldn't have deemed possible. Baltimore was sitting on the front fender of his convertible, wearing the same clothes from the night before, obviously hung over and disgusted at the sight of him. The second vision was several times more unexpected. A line of cars stretching three blocks idled in the street, each one full of anxious colored men waiting for Henry to come out and lead the convoy to the courthouse, where the exam was to be administered within the hour.

Baltimore scowled as he held firm to the steering wheel, blocking Henry's rusty old Buick in the driveway. "If you want to take that police test, you gonna have to walk," Baltimore huffed at him. "That car there done went and popped a clutch." A closer look revealed Henry's clutch was wrapped in newspaper on Baltimore's front passenger seat. "You want to do likewise and blow a fuse, go head on," he threatened, feeling sicker by the minute. "I'll . . . match you blow for blow," he added before hanging his head over the side of his car to vomit.

"Henry, we's gonna be late," Smiley hollered insistently from the first car, his usual jovial countenance nowhere to be seen. "Stop fooling around with Baltimo' and come on."

"You heard the man," Roberta seconded from inside the screen door, wearing a floral printed housecoat and wooden pin curlers in her hair. She stood vigilantly, watching with a spiteful expression as Baltimore heaved and sputtered helplessly. "Don't let him drag you down any further than he has already. Stand up for yourself and for your family. Don't matter the outcome. It's the right thing to do."

Although Henry didn't know how his wife had learned of his decision, he knew that she was right. That still didn't make it any easier walking past Baltimore in his time of need. "I'll be back later on, 'Berta," Henry declared without facing her. "Don't mind him. He'll be gone before you know it." Henry was focused on a brighter tomorrow and a steady paycheck when he eased into the car along with three other ex-teammates. "Hi ya, boys. Let's get down there and see what gives. It can't be no harder than what I've had to put myself through already this morning."

Trace put the car into gear and lurched forward. "Maybe not, but it appears Baltimore caught the worst of it." Fighting the urge to sneak a look back and see how his old friend was making out, Henry unbuttoned his jacket and contemplated his own fate instead.

Two hours later, it seemed that all of St. Louis was out and about. The buzz around town pushed everybody in the same direction. Countless herds of interested colored and white folk gathered near the courthouse to witness the city relax its hiring policies, grow up and usher in a multitude of growing pains at the same time. Not too far away, Roberta strolled along the sidewalk hand-in-hand with her little boy. It didn't matter that she was only window shopping, the two white women who approached from the other direction stared her down until she acquiesced and stood aside to let them pass. Roberta thought her heart would rupture for sure when she found her child's eyes peering up at hers. He was too young to comprehend what had transpired on that sidewalk and how the social climate dictated what was seen as appropriate, but he sensed that it left his mother wounded. With a tug on her dress, he signaled that he was ready for a change of pace. Roberta squeezed his tiny fingers, thinking how she was way past being ready for the same thing.

On the other side of town, Penny blushed and waved gleefully as a car horn honked when passing her outside of the hat shop. Etta exited the upscale store just in time to observe how a man's crude interest moved her young protégée. "My, my," Etta teased. "If you ain't the cat's meow, I'll eat this hat I just dropped a knot on."

"Oh, that wasn't nobody but Joe Simpkins. He's been coming over to the fast house, joking around mostly," answered Penny. "He don't mean no harm."

"There're a couple of things you need to know about men, chile. For one, just cause they hoot and holler don't mean you have to encourage it by flashing your pearly whites every time they do. You should also take into account that not too many men mean you harm when they set out chasing. The harm generally comes later, after they done caught you a few times." Etta tossed a sly wink at Penny to inquire whether she'd been caught yet.

"Oh-oh, naw, Ms. Etta," she stammered. "I've been walking around all my life with a bag over my head until Halstead met his maker. I wouldn't know the first thing to do with a boy."

Upon entering Watkins Emporium, Etta leaned in closer to Penny, so as not to be overheard by other shoppers. "It ain't what you don't know to do that worries me," she whispered. "It's those grown up boys and what they'd like to teach you." Penny's mouth flew wide open but she'd learned to restrain her laughter in calmer settings. Etta tutored her every chance she got and Penny was happy to pick up each tidbit of etiquette thrown her way. On the other hand, being a woman sometimes required straying from the blueprint mapped out for her. It began when Chozelle Watkins sneered at Penny in her new red dress that caused things to stumble off course.

"Morning, Ms. Etta," Chozelle mumbled, while flirting openly with a male customer. "Cool your heels, honey," she said to the man standing only a few naughty inches away from her, which was extremely inappropriate for the circumstances. "I'll be back before you forget what we's getting at." Chozelle left him with a sensual smirk to hold his attention in the meanwhile. She followed Penny around the store with her eyes until she felt the undeniable urge to draw nearer. "That sure is a nice dress, Penny," she said finally. "It'll look a might better still, when you fill it out some."

Etta saw that Chozelle was simply baiting Penny into a war of words because the younger woman's stock was soaring. Penny had also won Baltimore's affection and happened to be wearing the hell out of that red dress, which Chozelle wanted but couldn't maneuver over her curvy hips. Against her better judgment, Etta determined that it was time for Penny to spar as best she could before jumping in to save her from the embarrassment of being out done by the likes of a much craftier adversary.

"Oh, thank you, Chozelle," Penny replied, choosing her words carefully. "I declare menfolk will do just about anything to get a peek at what's shaping this fabric from underneath. When the larger sizes roll off the truck, why don't you have at one of 'em and see what I mean?" Etta's eyes widened when she heard Penny stand her ground like a budding lightweight.

Chozelle jutted her chin forward and cocked a bow in her back. "You might want to be more respectful where you go to flapping those big feet of yours before somebody's pulling them out of your mouth."

"Uh-huh, right after I pull 'em out your fat be-hind," Penny spat back, her tight clenched fist posed close to Chozelle's face. Etta thought it as good a place as any to step in, and save Chozelle.

"All right, girls, the bell done sounded for a break," Etta joked. "Both fighters need to head on back to their corners and settle down."

"Naw, I ain't hardly finished yet," Chozelle hissed, her voice rising heatedly. "This little bony-kneed scrap off the moonshine truck isn't going to floss her new look in my store like she owns it. She probably don't have more than a few nickels to rub together anyhow. Halstead might've given her a couple of dimes but that don't amount to a dollar."

"Halstead ain't got nothing to do with this," argued Penny, foolishly buying into what information the catty vixen wanted to gather in the first place.

"Just wait 'til I see him. I'll get to the bottom of why he's letting you run around on a long leash."

"Then you'll be waiting 'til hell freeze over!" shouted Penny, much to her mentor's dismay. She quickly bunched herself between both the young ladies and cast a hard glaring expression to illustrate she really meant business.

Subsequently, as soon as Chozelle stomped off to the backroom in a royal tizzy, Etta doted on Penny like a county-fair-blue-ribbon heifer. The measure of approval painted across her face was nothing short of prideful adoration. "Hold your tongue, Penny," Etta suggested calmly. "You sure told her where to get off, but you almost said too much." What Penny nearly confessed to while exposing Halstead's lack of involvement during her shining hour could have easily closed the lid on her. Although it came too close for comfort, the skirmish gave Etta an idea and a remedy against future potentially incriminating outbursts. The time had come to save Penny from herself.

Etta didn't ask the girl what she thought about having a proper burial for Halstead. He'd been covered over in an unmarked grave for a few days so a couple of more wouldn't make that much difference at far as Etta was concerned. Penny was liable to get flustered again and go to shooting her mouth off like she'd just done with Chozelle. Etta was not going to let that happen. If a "preacher-fied" funeral is what it took to remove the temptation from Penny's lips, Etta was prepared to stage a decent send-off as an ends to a means. In Penny's vexed comprehension, Halstead was dead but he wasn't gone, yet.

10

LITTLE SECRETS

In the obstetrics and gynecology wing of the hospital, Delbert had spent the better part of the morning seeing to one pregnant patient after another. So far, Delbert's secret was secure, despite the unnerving feeling that the third-year nurse assigned to him would catch wise when his training was upstaged by his lack of carnal experience. With only one remaining scheduled patient on the roll before his lunch hour, Delbert breathed a sigh of relief as he read over her chart. "Mrs. Samuella Collier, she's been complaining of pain on her lower right side, mostly," he read aloud, outside of Examination Room Number Two. He glanced up from the chart and turned toward the nurse, who he hadn't noticed was as pretty as she was intelligent because of his bouts of anxiety. "Her lower right quadrant, *mostly*?" he asked peculiarly.

"Yes, doctor," answered the petite and perturbed duty nurse. Her name was Sue Jacobs, a pleasant twenty-four year old with a penchant for blowing off doctors who exhibited a healthy appetite for casual affairs with nurses. Since Delbert hadn't looked at her twice, she felt quite comfortable in his company until now.

His strange behavior was puzzling so she flashed her soft brown eyes innocently, riddled by his question.

"That sounds like a typical appendicitis. It's odd that she isn't being seen in the appropriate unit," he reasoned.

"One of the staff has had a look at her, decided the pain wasn't caused by her appendix and they sent her over for you to give your opinion," the nurse said, as if to ask why any of that mattered.

Delbert was oblivious to the nurse looking upside his head like it had a hole in it. "So, she's not expecting?" he asked, in the same confused manner as before.

"I'm sure by now she's *expecting* for a qualified physician to walk into that room and examine her, doctor," smarted the nurse, after momentarily forgetting herself.

Delbert read over the chart a second time, praying he'd missed something. He stalled long enough to raise the nurse's suspicions. "Is she prepped for examination?" he asked, while moving toward the door to open it.

"Yes, doctor, at least she was before we started this conversation," Sue answered, her voice trailing off at the end of it.

"Mrs. Collier, I'm Dr. Gales," Delbert announced as he entered the small room with white walls, a standard examination table and a short desk which doubled for a place to situate instruments and write evaluations.

"'Bout time Doctor!" the frumpy older woman grumbled with both eyes cut sharply at him. "I been shuffled around this place like a damn dairy cow and I want you to know I don't care for it."

Delbert took one look at the large brooding woman and smiled. "Yes, Mrs. Collier, I don't blame you for being upset. It's been a long day and I aim to move things along for you if I can. How'd that be?"

"That'll be just peachy," the woman chuckled. "I'm beginning to feel better already."

How'd that be? Nurse Jacobs thought. *Oh, brother*. She didn't know what to make of this young doctor she'd heard such a great deal about. Just outside the room, he was as worried as a long-tailed cat in a room full of rocking chairs. Now, his bedside manner was downright charming. What caused the quick turnabout wasn't clear, but she simply chalked it up to what the senior nurses referred to as baby doctors on "training wheels" syndrome. Some interns weren't afforded the opportunity to see a lot of different ailments before arriving and immediately found themselves subjected to big city illnesses in an often overcrowded facility. "Sometimes it's too soon, too much and too fast," Head Nurse Robinson surmised when one of the fellows buckled under pressure and washed out of the program in the early stages. "They usually sneak off and turn tail for home if the training wheels start to wobble before they know it."

Delbert looked the patient over thoroughly with his assistant watching his every move. He discovered that her discomfort was caused by ascites, ascitic fluid causing the pain and bulging flanks in the abdomen as opposed to a growth in the abdominal cavity. He explained to Mrs. Collier her need for medication, and because it was less complicated than he'd originally suspected, she was expected to heal within a week. The young nurse followed him outside of the room after grasping his impressive examination technique and heady prognosis.

"You were very good in there, doctor," she politely complimented him. "You probably saved her from the knife. Good for you. Good for her. Nevertheless, I hate to be the bearer of bad news. While we were in with Exam Room Two, another patient has been prepped for you in Number Four. After what I just saw in there with Mrs. Collier, this is a cakewalk for you. A simple external examination ought to do it and then we're off for lunch. Here's her chart. She's experiencing vaginal discharge and discomfort during urination."

Delbert froze. He swallowed hard but didn't want to appear thrown off. "Sure, I've done enough of those to know my way around," he said, envisioning someone as large and equally unattractive as Mrs. Samuella Collier, who was unquestionably older than his mother and several pounds heavier. Delbert wished for the most hideous woman alive to be dreadful and draped on the other side of that door. Unfortunately, the moment his eyes landed on her lying at ease on the examination table with her feet placed apply in the stirrups, a dilemma begun to grow inside of his boxers.

Wearing a surprisingly perky smile and not much else, she happened to be the same woman in the tight pink dress Delbert had fantasized about at the train station. He'd dreamed of her in that exact compromising position, flat on her back with both feet reaching toward the ceiling but this was altogether different. His dream had turned into a nightmare, one that forced him to stand by as it unfolded.

After staring between the patient's thighs for what seemed like forever, Delbert heard a woman's voice. It was Nurse Jacobs beckoning him. "Dr. Gales, is there a problem, something you need me to do?" she asked, for the second time.

"Oh, uh . . . no," he answered, snapping out of an awkward gaze. "No, I'm fine. Sorry. Ms. Alberta Hawkins," he said, reading her name aloud from the chart. "I wasn't sure I had the right notes. I must've confused you with someone else."

"Naw, you got the right one, doctor," she purred shamelessly, while glancing down at the stiff erection in his white uniform slacks. "I ain't ever been so sure about nothing in my whole life."

Cleverly, the patient opened her legs slightly wider. Her ploy didn't go unnoticed by the attentive nurse. She'd seen women with some of the most unthinkable conditions flirt with doctors in mixed company. Likewise, more than a few physicians have sent her away on pointless errands in order to take advantage of the right situation. Delbert appeared to get caught off guard, uncertain how to handle his obvious attraction to the woman regardless of her current symptoms. He hesitated to begin the interview.

Having been through this sort thing before, Nurse Jacobs removed the chart from Delbert's grasp. "Ms. Hawkins, the doctor has had a very trying day. He'll need a moment to compose himself," she said, opening the manila folder.

"He don't have to go composing his self on my account," Ms. Hawkins flirted. "He's a real thrill packaged just like he is now."

"Okay, let's get something straight," the nurse replied, once she'd seen enough. "This is a hospital, not a dance hall. If you can't respect yourself, at least you could save all that cooing until I'm out of the room." That last comment was aimed at Delbert, who until then had become merely a bystander.

"Yeah, she's right," he said, nodding his head in a deliberate and methodical manner. *This is my profession. This is not the time for letting what I really want getting in the way. She's the patient, I'm the doctor, and the nurse ain't missing a beat.* "Let's concentrate on the matter at hand. Ms. Hawkins, how long has this problem existed?" Although Delbert worked hard at training his focus above the draping, what he'd witnessed going on beneath it was getting the best of him.

Smacking her lips in direct opposition to the nurse's interference, the patient answered with her tone subdued and edgy. "The problem started existin' when my no good steady got it in his head to tip out on me a few weeks back. Can you fix it, doctor?"

"I'll do the best I can, ma'am," Delbert answered, feeling sorry for her, but thankful that he wasn't lucky enough to make her acquaintance at the train station and ultimately sharing what her steady had stumbled home and greeted her with. Seeing her as just another patient for the first time, Delbert experienced no additional angst while treating her. He took a seat on the short stool at the end of the examination table. He inspected her thoroughly, collected a specimen and then studied it beneath a microscope on the adjacent desk. Before long, he'd begun humming a mellow tune. Eventually Alberta Hawkins hummed along with him and wiggled her toes to the beat.

"Ooh, that's nice," she said, more relaxed than before. "I always liked that song. Never could remember the name of it though."

"'The Very Thought of You,'" answered Nurse Jacobs as she smiled amiably. "I've always been fond of it too." Somehow decorum was restored in that small white room. Delbert had confronted his demons and with a little help from a crafty assistant, he chartered a route back to respectability, a great place to be for a new doctor trying out his training wheels. And since the specimen he swabbed proved to be a garden variety case of gonorrhea, he was able to treat the attractive woman immediately with a dose of penicillin, although she was all too enthusiastic to straddle the table for an injection. Delbert fought back a laugh when Nurse Jacobs turned her nose up at the sight of the woman's behind readily tooted skyward.

"That's how you ended up with the clap in the first place," she wanted to say, but didn't. "Better luck next time," she told the woman on her way out, after Delbert refused to accept her home number and the standing invitation for late night house calls. Moments later, the nurse checked her watch. She tidied up the room as Delbert made notes in his training journal for his report to Dr. Hiram Knight after each shift.

There was a naiveté about this young man of promise from Texas, she thought. If she didn't know better, she'd have assumed he was afraid of women by the way he initially balked at going near Alberta Hawkins. Good thing for him, she didn't know better.

Delbert was a virgin, despite how hard he worked at concealing it. Coming face to face with one substantiated case of gonorrhea wasn't going to stand in his way either, not by a long shot. Delbert stepped onto the elevator when the same nurse glided between the doors. He'd had the chance to recount the morning's activities in his mind and it wasn't at all as stellar as he imagined it would have been. A quick glance at the nurse conveyed a lot of what she was thinking. Her eyes darted back and forth then drifted toward the floor. "I wasn't that bad, was I?" Delbert asked as they exited the elevator together.

"Excuse me?" she said, knowing exactly what he meant.

"I mean, I did buckle there at the end, but I couldn't have been as lame as that look you saddled me with implied."

"What look? I didn't say a word."

"You didn't have to," he said. "Your expression said it all." Delbert read her name tag and winced. "Nurse Jacobs, Sue, could you do me a favor and keep this between us?"

"I wish I could," she apologized, "only I have to make a report at the end of my shift and hand it in for review. Besides, why should I go out of my way for you when you've just decided to take the time to learn my name?"

Delbert threw his head back and whistled. "This'll be the end of me."

"I wouldn't be so sure about that. When I report how you calmed a patient who was very upset after being sent here and there, made a good diagnosis, and acted professionally when seduced by a naked woman, you'll come out on top. That is, unless you do something to mess all that up this afternoon. See you later, doctor," she said, walking off in the opposite direction from the staff dining hall.

"Sue Jacobs, you're all right with me," he said to himself, standing in the middle of wide hallway. "Yeah, all right with me."

"What's all right with you?" M.K. asked, from the other end of a half-eaten pressed ham sandwich.

"Oh, nothing, just trying to keep up with my first day on the floor is all," Delbert answered. "Hey, was there anymore of that ham?"

"Uhh-huh and plenty of it where this came from. Come on, I'll show you where they keep the good stuff."

Serving trays were set aside in the surgeon's lounge in the event that a difficult case prevented the golden boys of medicine from making it to the cafeteria. Delbert's stomach growled when he saw the buffet. "Man, I know I'm not supposed to be in here. This is fit for a king."

"You're almost right," M.K. corrected him, while grabbing yet another sandwich and a soda to go. "They lay all of this out for the surgical staff. Most of 'em too stuck up to appreciate it though. I know you must be hungry, go ahead and dig in."

"I don't want to get in trouble over this," Delbert objected cautiously.

"Man, what's gotten into you? You belong here, there's good grub, so dig in." When Delbert's hunger won out, he stacked his plate so high that M.K. laughed. "Now, that's more like it."

"You tell him, M.K.," seconded Dr. Hiram Knight, entering the room. "Keeping your strength up is as important as keeping your spirits up." Delbert felt like a sinner listening to a preacher pitching a sermon directly at him. "You did a fine job in there," Knight congratulated M.K. "We might have lost the patient's hand if it hadn't been for your battlefield training. You could learn a lot from him, Delbert, a whole lot." Dr. Knight nibbled on a piece of toasted bread before someone came in to call on him for another case. "Glad to have you back, M.K.," he offered on his way out.

"Thank you, sir, glad to be back." M.K. felt eyes plastered on him, so he stared back at Delbert. "What!" he shouted.

"What? How dare you ask me *what* when I've been up to my elbows in expectant mothers, old battleaxes and wayward women all this time while you're upstairs with the chief performing your first miracle?"

"Any of those wayward women happen to be good looking?" was M.K.'s anxious reply.

"One of them was pretty stacked, enough to get me worked up," Delbert answered nonchalantly

"Ha-ha, the boy is growing up fast. Did you get her private exchange?"

"Yeah, I did, but I didn't have no use for her phone number. She was lying there with the evidence oozing out to prove it," he rattled off quickly. "I'm trying to hear all about you saving a man's hand and you're going on about a patient with a nasty irritation."

M.K. eyed Delbert curiously. "You say she was a looker and stacked to boot. And, you treated her right?" He frowned as Delbert contended that he was right on all counts. "Then somebody needs to sit you down a spell. What am I gonna do with you, Tex? You got all the way to third base and then she opened her legs wider, giving you the signal to slide in for home. Instead you went in standing up. Pitiful."

Delbert replayed the way things went down. He shook his head disappointedly. "I guess I could use some coaching on women."

"Give it some time. You need to walk before you can run. Maybe I ought to drop you by the high school to practice before your next time at bat. You think about it while I head out back for some fresh air and a cigarette. Got another miracle scheduled in an hour. A man got a hammer stuck in his rectum and now he expects us to go up in there and get it out." Delbert clenched his buttock cheeks when calculating the unrivaled pain associated with getting it lodged up there in the first place.

"Damn, M.K., a real hammer?"

"Yep, the end with the nail claw on it."

11

THE MORE THINGS CHANGE

Just outside of the courthouse a large angry crowd swelled. Tensions soared when more than an hour crawled past and the city's deputy mayor hadn't addressed the crowd's concerns after he'd promised to return with full disclosure of passing test results. Opposing parties on both sides grew increasingly more vocal with their comments and unfounded suspicions of the other. Suddenly, two paddy wagons rolled into the town square, parting the rising sea of animosity. As if on cue, the Metro Police Mobile Units idled at the base of the courthouse steps to deter onlookers when the department chief escorted an intimidated city leader out of the front entrance. Despite the fact that he had a platoon of officers in riot gear flanking them on either side to prevent an onset of violence, his eyes darted back and forth as he surveyed the horde.

Henry Taylor had completed the exam over an hour ago and he also had the foresight to utilize the rear exit, avoiding the risk of being recognized by the mob in the event that things got out of hand. He managed to convince three others to do the same but some of them couldn't pass on being showered with thunderous ovations upon emerging through the front doors after completing the lengthy civil service examination. Pretending to be curious but indifferent bystanders, Henry and those friends of his with level heads loitered on the broad sidewalk behind the massive gathering. While watching the situation simmer to a slow boil, each of them wanted cooler heads to prevail, although it seemed highly unlikely.

"All right, that'll be enough of that!" the police chief yelled into the narrow end of a large cardboard megaphone, when several people continually voiced their opinions regarding the city's stand to open the force to blacks. For a man in his mid-fifties with graying hair, Chief Riley appeared to be in decent shape, considering he was as lazy as they came and only appointed to his post after digging up dirt on the last mayor before he was ousted by a front-page sex scandal involving a colored woman. "We all know why we're here and I won't stand for any civil disobedience despite how you might feel over the outcome," the chief threatened, in his finely polished blue uniform. "That means we won't hesitate to haul the lot of you off to jail if your actions demand it." Once the gathering quieted down to his satisfaction, the top cop took one calculated step backward to yield the floor.

"I want to thank you in advance for keeping it down while we get on with the business as hand. Remember that we stand for the city of St. Louis and hope that you accept this class of Metro Police cadets with a measure of respect and dignity. Nothing short of that will be tolerated." After the deputy mayor lowered the boom, a hushed murmur spread throughout the audience. There was no use in getting arrested before hearing the verdict. "Good, we understand one another then," he said, in a tone more resolute than before. "First let me be very candid in telling you that out of sixty-one applicants, our highest number to sit for the exam, we have selected twelve deserving *and qualified* men for the next three-month training class."

"Well, that rules out any niggers getting in!" smarted off a redneck close to the front of the crowd.

The police chief chuckled until he felt his boss's glare burning a hole in him. "Okay, keep it down!" he fired back, with a hint of laughter riding just beneath it. "Deputy Mayor," said the chief, giving a slight nod to get the show moving again.

"As I was saying, I will read off the twelve names. These men will be expected to report for orientation on Wednesday morning at the Police Training Facility, nine o'clock sharp." Jimmy Maxwell's was the first name he read aloud. When no one seemed to object or applaud, the politician continued until there were six names left. He hesitated briefly to brace himself before going on. "The other six cadets will be as follows—James Dodd, Trace Wiggins, Willie B. Bernard, Charles Tennyson, Patton Jones and Henry Taylor." As cheers erupted on one side of the fence, twice as many jeers resounded from the other. Shoving and bickering quickly escalated into inflammatory insults hurled back and forth. Then out of nowhere, someone threw a full soda bottle into the riotous group.

The deputy mayor shuddered. He panicked when angry fists flew wildly. "Do something about this, chief!" he instructed hastily before darting back inside the building to elude danger.

After receiving the go-ahead, police officers stormed the audience to stifle the melée. They wielded night sticks violently, cracking heads without regard. Flashbulbs popped as newspaper cameramen captured the city's ugliest incident in years.

Charles "Smiley" Tennyson, having been near the last one named on the list, gulped hard as he observed the mad brawl. "Is that what we got to look forward to?"

"Nah, not unless you plan on trying your luck with some of that *civil disobedience*," Trace said.

"But Willie B's over there putting his up against those nightsticks. This is bad, real bad. Let's mix in and grab him up."

"Hell, naw, just sit still. Willie B. done made his bed. He'll figure a way out of this jam. Besides, it's way too many white ladies over there to make arrests stick."

Trace couldn't believe his eyes. He removed his bifocals, folded and tucked them away. "Man, the way they breaking heads, I can barely stand to watch."

"You ain't seen the half of it yet," Henry informed him. "It'll get a lot worse before things iron out. Trust me." He tried to turn his eyes away once he recognized several people he'd grown up with being dragged from the bloody sidewalks and hoisted into paddywagons like career criminals. Surprisingly, it was just as difficult watching the same happen to battered and bruised white folk he'd never met. The enormity of what he signed up to do smacked him like the wooden baton he'd soon be asked to carry, when all he set out to do was earn an honest wage and feed his family. Igniting a brutal incident on the shores of the Mississippi was the farthest thing from his mind then.

Now, he could think of nothing else, knowing that the others would not have gone forward without him. Henry felt as if every drop of blood spilled on the city sidewalk was on his hands. What's more, he knew it was only the beginning. "Come on, y'all!" he barked when the men began drifting toward the fight. "I said, hightail it outta here before you get sucked in, hired and fired all in the same day." Begrudgingly, the four men chose the road less traveled, with dubious feeling. It wasn't everyday that colored men got the chance to rumble on the courthouse steps against white men who had openly engaged in hatred and bigotry to their faces. Each one of them went home feeling as though they had missed out on a one in a million chance.

It was late afternoon when Etta finally got Baltimore to return her calls and he was wearing an icepack for a hat when he did. He asked if anything had happened during his novice attempt at drowning sorrows. In addition, he was willing to apologize for misbehaving if it turned out to be the case. Etta laughed. She told him there wasn't anything to be sorry about. On the other hand, she would need him to help square an issue with Penny. Alarmed, Baltimore sat up on his bed and then snatched the melting ice away. Etta had to calm him down before he allowed her to explain that he had done nothing wrong to bring about Penny's situation. Finally relieved, Baltimore listened attentively to all that Etta had to say. He agreed wholeheartedly and then thanked her for including him. Penny's welfare meant a lot and before long Etta's would too, just as much.

When Baltimore found Jinx toiling in some white man's yard in the far end of town, he shook his head disapprovingly. He parked the car next to the curb, not lending much to what the man's neighbors might report to him when he came home from work. It was still a free country, on paper mostly, and he felt free to park his car wherever he got good and ready. "Uh-huh," yelled Baltimore from the driver's seat. He frowned at the patches of grass Jinx had ripped from the lawn. "Etta told me I'd find you around these parts on your knees and such."

"Hey, Baltimo'!" the younger man hollered back. Jinx climbed to his feet and dusted off his brown work pants. He always respected Baltimore and admired him for his brash way of doing things, although it made Jinx nervous as hell the way he carried himself around white people. It was more dangerous than it was crazy, he thought, but admired it nonetheless.

"What you doing up in that man's yard?" Baltimore teased.

Jinx raised his hand to shield his face from the sun. "Don't rightly know yet. Landscapin', I guess."

"Land *scraping* is more like it. That fella's gonna get you for plucking up his grounds. Somebody needs to fetch you away from here before he catches you." Of course Baltimore knew the young man was scratching out a living the best way he could on short notice, but that didn't stop him from poking fun before time came to unload some difficult news. "All right. Don't mind me, Jinx. I'm ribbing is all."

"I ain't stud'n you, Baltimo'. I know you's just around to have a good time with me," Jinx replied, as his smile melted slightly. "Unless they's something else on your mind."

"Well, now that you mention it, there is this one thing I need you to help me with," Baltimore said, looking past him as another thing caught his eye. There was a woman, a white woman, strutting around in the backyard in a two-piece bathing suit. She knew that colored men were watching when she seductively

began applying tanning oil on her arms and legs. Although Baltimore tried to ignore her midday sunbath, there was no way to
shake it off. There was something strangely familiar about her,
but he couldn't place her.

"Okay, shoot. I ain't got much, but whatever it is, I'm willing
to lend a hand," answered Jinx. He was facing Baltimore and
itching to hear what the man traveled across town to ask him.
"Well, what is it?"

"First, let me thank you for helping me put Penny's old papa
in the ground. But see, here's the thing I was getting at. Etta
wants to have a ceremony. You know, for Penny. She's having a
tough time moving on and saying farewell because she didn't
have the chance to before . . ."

"Yeah, yeah, anything for Penny," he answered, sort of perplexed about what was going on behind him. When he couldn't
shake the distinct feeling gnawing at him to turn around and get
a look at what kept drawing Baltimore's attention away, Jinx
peeped over his shoulder. "Ah, naw, naw," he uttered, trying to
keep his voice low. "Uh-uh, Baltimo', I see it and I don't like it.
That look in your eyes and what you's thinking on doing is gonna
get you killed."

Baltimore grinned when he remembered where he'd seen that
lady before. "Calm down, Jinx, it'll be all right after a while."

"You done gone crazy? That's a white lady. She respectable
and she married," he argued. "And . . . and she white!"

"I can see that, Jinx, but ain't neither of 'em got nothing to do
with me," Baltimore said coolly, not taking his eyes of the
woman's pasty skin turning redder by the moment. "She's married, I'll grant you that, but I'm a have to get back with you on
the respectable part." He motioned forward to get closer to the
skimpy swimsuit but Jinx grabbed his arm.

"Come on, let's skin out and take care of that thing you came
to fetch me for."

"Huh?" was Baltimore's faint response.

"Halstead, remember?"

"I can't do nothing for Halstead. He's already dead."

"I know and we got to bury him right, for Penny," Jinx said, hoping to save someone the trouble of throwing dirt over Baltimore. "Baltimo', for Penny?" he insisted quietly.

"All right, Jinx, let's be getting on then. You're a good man. Penny's lucky to have a friend like you."

"I'm a good pal of yours, too," Jinx sighed wearily, while settling into the passenger seat. "If you was to know what I do about that woman's husband, you'd be thanking me for holding you off."

"And if you was to know anything about women in general, you wouldn't be so quick to go patting yourself on the back. Me and her, we got the same idea in mind," he added with a sly wink. "We both share a fondness for intrigue and a broad dislike for her husband, Barker Sinclair." Once the car pulled onto the residential street, Jinx felt like sliding down in the seat to hide his identity. For even thinking about going after Dixie, wife of the meanest white man he'd ever seen, Jinx assumed Baltimore had to be crazy, and stupid.

Two blocks from the hospital, Baltimore noticed several groups milling around on the sidewalks, most of them crying and cursing. He didn't know what to make of it as police cars and ambulances raced past with sirens blaring. "What the hell?" he muttered to himself when discovering that the hospital parking entrance was blocked by a squadron of patrol cars. After a large corn-fed cop waved a baton, telling him to move along, he made a swift U-turn in the middle of the avenue. "Stay here, Jinx," he murmured sternly. "I knew this would happen, just didn't think they'd get into it this fast."

Baltimore marched across the street with long strides. He didn't even blink when the big officer glared at him with cold menacing eyes. Strapped with a .45 caliber charmer in the shoulder holster beneath his suit coat, Baltimore wasn't afraid to gun the man down if he tried to keep him away. Determined to see if Henry was involved in the event that probably had the entire hospital personnel hopping, he pushed his way through the mob of people.

Just inside the emergency room entrance, Baltimore approached the registration desk. "Miss, I know you're busy but I need something," he said to the frumpy duty nurse behind the waist high counter. Then, he noted the check-in area was littered with injured patients moaning, bleeding and carrying on about being innocent and getting clubbed half to death. She glanced up at him, expecting to see another victim of the brutal incident. When her assumption proved incorrect, she frowned and quickly went back to her paperwork.

"Yes, sir, you're right about that. I am very busy and everybody here needs something," she answered. "Now unless you're standing there with an injury that I can't see, please step aside."

Baltimore grimaced and checked his watch. "Okay, okay, I don't have time to fuss. Is Dinah Leonard still on duty?"

"Don't rightly know, but if she is, she's just as busy as me, that I'm sure of," she told him matter-of-factly. "Since you can't seem to take a hint and I'm weary from giving them, why'ont you go on up to the second floor and look for Nurse Leonard there?"

"Thank you, miss," offered Baltimore as he stepped past her.

"And you're welcome, sir," she replied before yelling "Next!" above the noise.

After he'd taken the stairs up to the second floor, the woman he'd met at Ms. Etta's Fast House exited a patient's room while reading a chart. Her uniform was spic and span although her anxiety shone through. "Baltimore, what are you doing here?" Dinah asked, more surprised than excited to see him. "I wasn't supposed to see you until dinner tonight. I'll be needin' some special attention myself by then."

"I'll bet. I was on my way to a meeting when I ran up on a passel of people looking like they been to war and didn't win."

"Yeah, we've been spilling over since that fight broke out at the courthouse," she said, as if it was common knowledge.

"So that's where it went down," Baltimore sighed, with a faraway gaze in his eyes. "When are Negroes gon' learn that white folk don't want us sharing in what they got a lock on?"

"Don't ask me, but it appears we're trying to get it unlocked but fast. I've heard that four or five colored men passed that police test."

"Seems like that lock just got busted clean off," he replied, glancing at his watch again. "Look, Dinah, I need to know where to find M.K . . . uh, Dr. Phipps."

"I could tell you, but you can't get up to see him. Dr. Phipps is knee-deep in broken bones, scrapes and stitches right about now, likely will be for the rest of the day too. Baltimore, I'd love to talk some more but I got to go."

"I understand, Dinah, I understand. I was just wonderin'—" he said, before realizing she had disappeared down the hall. He wandered out of the building reluctantly, without knowing if Henry was badly hurt or worse, dead.

Already on his way to a funeral as it was, Baltimore couldn't see going to another one in the same week. *Henry had better be all right*, he thought to himself as he climbed back inside his convertible. But his attitude was severely distorted when Jinx asked what all of the commotion was about. "Nothing, Jinx," he answered, through clenched teeth. "Some of your friends wanting to be cops got a lot of people's heads broke is all." There was nothing else to be said about that. Baltimore's intense scowl made that crystal clear to Jinx.

1 2

GOODBYE AND GOOD RIDDANCE

On his way to honor a man he couldn't stand, Baltimore pulled his car over on the shoulder of the street a half-mile before taking the dusty unpaved farm road leading to Jinx's property. "Latch the rag top on your side for me," was all he managed to say before subjecting his slick automobile to red clay and pebbles. There was no way he'd let farm living get inside his prized coupe. It was bad enough that he'd have to get it washed and waxed after the dirt settled on his paint job. Penny's safety and well-being meant that much to him and more.

After he guided his car down a long narrow path and over a wooden bridge, Baltimore steered inside a barbed wire fence. Drawing near to Jinx's house, which was a rickety old two bedroom shack sitting atop concrete blocks, he saw an old woman sitting in a brand new rocking chair with two large mutts resting at her feet. Jinx's mother, wearing a long faded duster and a wrinkled bonnet tied under her sagging chin, rolled back and forth with the calm breeze sweeping across the porch. She didn't have words for him as she cradled a large corncob pipe with her right hand and just nodded hello as Baltimore killed the engine. He was a stranger, one she didn't trust. One she saw bringing trouble to her front door and a world of change to her son.

"Afternoon, ma'am," Baltimore greeted the woman, who didn't bother to look his way. She acted as if he didn't even exist, although pretending wouldn't make it so.

"Hey, Muh'dear, we came to finish up back yonder," said Jinx, as if she'd questioned him about being home in the middle of the day.

"Jinxy," she answered softly, before climbing off the rocker and disappearing inside the dingy colored house. Whatever he and that fancy stranger were up to, she didn't want to watch them going about it.

Baltimore lifted his Stetson hat to allow the cool wind to blow through his thick curly hair. "Man, it sho' is getting warm. Etta and them need to hurry up so we can get this over with." No sooner than he said it, a dark-colored four-door sedan came storming up the road.

"That appears to be them now," said Jinx, craning his neck to see over the horizon. "Looks like Reverend Foxmore's car. He wouldn't be coming out here 'less Ms. Etta was bringing him."

"All right then, this is how we'll handle it. I'll stall them, talk to the preacher and slip him a few bills so's he'll say something respectful, while you hurry on back there and smooth out the mound. Make sure it looks nice and kept, like somebody actually gave a damn."

Jinx agreed to do it for Penny and then made himself scarce. "Gimme five minutes, if you can," he requested, jogging briskly in the opposite direction.

When three car doors slammed, Baltimore grunted with a manufactured smile on his face. "Hey, y'all," he hailed, waving to Penny, Etta and a middle-aged man with a limp, dressed in a well-worn black suit.

"Hi ya, Baltimore. I didn't know Jinx's people lived way out here," answered Etta with Penny following closely behind her.

As her head hung low, Baltimore was reminded how young and simple she was, regardless of how much polishing Etta had done.

"Hey, Mistah Baltimore," the young girl said, her eyes still cast toward the ground.

"Come over here. I brought along Reverend Foxmore," Etta said, her voice as shaky as the old house. "He's going to preside over the services. Reverend, meet a dear friend of mine, Baltimore Floyd." When the man of God extended his hand, Baltimore threw his arm around the thick brown-skinned fellow's shoulder instead.

"I want to take a minute and talk to you. See, look here. The man you's about to preside over was the nastiest rabble-rouser there ever was, including the peoples in that bible you carrying, but his daughter is two wings shy of an angel. I care about her and if you know what's good for you, you'd better say something comforting so she can get on with her life." Baltimore pushed a twenty dollar bill into the man's coat pocket to seal the deal. "I figure it all oughtta take about fifteen to twenty minutes altogether. But whatever you do—"

"Sorry, Rev'n. Baltimo' we's got a problem," Jinx interrupted abruptly. He'd kept his voice low so the ladies wouldn't be alarmed at what he had to say next. "The body's gone."

The Reverend stepped back on his good leg and pulled a white handkerchief from his trouser pocket. "What, grave robbers?" he asked, in the same hushed tone.

"Not exactly," Jinx told them. "See, Muh'dear keeps these pooches around and they don't do too much of nothing but eat and flop on the porch to keep her company. Well, they must've thought Halstead was barbeque 'cause they dug him up and . . ."

"Don't say it, son," ordered the minister. "That's blasphemy."

"It's no such thing, Rev," argued Baltimore. "That's a buffet. The devil got his due and the dogs got dinner. Now that's a square deal any which way you count it." Baltimore nearly laughed out loud but held it in as best he could. "Jinx, ain't no skulls or nothing cropped up out of the dirt now is it?"

"Naw, I couldn't find hide nor hair of that old man nowhere."

"Good, 'cause that would mess up the whole proceeding. Were you able to make the spot we put him in fit to be seen?" Baltimore asked, eying the preacher turning greasy.

"Baltimo', I did the best I could and raked the dirt over it nice 'n' even. You can't even tell the dogs done ate him."

Upon hearing that, the preacher tried to hobble away, but Baltimore grabbed him by his sweaty collar. "Where you going? Get back over here, preacher. I believe we's ready for you to earn that twenty now. Make it good and proper or else you'll be sorry."

"Yea, zah, I'll do it justice. You can count on me."

"Good, let's get moving then," Baltimore said, in a manner befitting the occasion. "Ladies, shall we proceed?"

Behind the nervous minister, Etta placed her arm in Baltimore's. Penny followed suit with Jinx. The procession ventured into the back of the house as Jinx directed them to the fake burial site. When the preacher saw the patch of disturbed ground, he headed toward it slowly, watching his step like a man in a mine field. Baltimore noticed his gingerly pace and frowned at him. That shifty country minister had more to fear from the living than he did from the dead, dug up and devoured.

Penny dragged her feet when they approached the makeshift grave. She tugged at Jinx's arm, signaling for him to stop. The bouquet of flowers she'd purchased at a roadside cart trembled in her hands. Halstead was a fleeting memory to everyone in attendance but the girl was just as terrified as when he terrorized her continuously. Baltimore shot a stinging glare at the reverend who had stood too long near the plot without commencing. "Get it started and get it right, preacher!" he whispered angrily.

On cue and frightened, he began with a hardy moan. "Whoaaa, Lawd, we's here to say goodbye to a man You saw fit to bring Your way." Baltimore wasn't the only one thinking how improbable that was, but the preacher had gotten into his patented shtick so he didn't see any reason to go correcting the man. "It's not for us to ask why," he continued, "because we don't have it in us to understand Your ways. This man," he said, looking down at the piece of paper Etta provided, "this man, Halstead King, lived a life we can not judge nor bear ill will to. He's in Your bosom now, Lawd, and we'll miss him. Oh, Heaven and Glory is his new home."

"Stop, preacher!" Penny shouted. "Stop this foolishness right now. Even in death he don't deserve people to lie about all the wrong he done." Tears fell from her eyes effortlessly. She didn't attempt to wipe them from her stained cheeks. "He beat my mama, and he beat me. Hell, he even killed the man whose ground he's laying in. He couldn't do right if he tried and I know good and well he didn't, so let's stop this sham and say what needs being said. Halstead King, you was nothing but a miserable mess of cow crap. The only thing decent you did was make me, and you did that for yourself. You had a slave but now I's free. Too bad you had to go get yourself burned alive first. You ain't never gone get to see me 'come a woman, fall in love with a man or wish you did better by me when I make something of myself. For that, I'm sorry and for that only. I should have shot you when I had the chance but I always hoped you'd change."

Etta left her place and joined Penny to console her when she saw what was coming next. "Why couldn't you be a good man like Baltimore?" she screamed. "Or love me like Jinx's papa cared for him?" Penny dropped to her knees, clawing at the dirt and wailing uncontrollably, while finally letting all her emotions out. Jinx kneeled down and held her close, and he wept as well. Only his tears were meant for the beloved father he'd lost to Halstead's greed and spite. Etta dabbed at her eyes with an embroidered scarf, Baltimore cleared his throat several times to choke back unresolved feelings he'd harbored about his own estranged father, and the preacher looked on thinking that the whole charade was the damnedest thing he ever saw.

One by one, they sauntered away from the plot of land where nothing was buried but their goodbyes. Penny stayed behind to reconcile her own peace. When she was done, she had just what she needed. The ties that bind were tighter than she imagined. The daughter, the slave, the captive, and the woman had to let go in their own way. It might have seemed strange to some, that it was humanly possible to love a man like Halstead with all of his terrible ways, but Penny proved how it could be more than possible for the love of a child to conquer all.

After the funeral, the preacher tore out of the driveway without looking back or passing any parting salutations to speak of. Baltimore didn't blame him for making tracks, considering how he'd forced the poor man to facilitate a farce. Etta knew there was something up but didn't press it. Penny had the opportunity to purge her emotions and put her feelings to rest, and that was worth enduring the ceremony. Now she wouldn't have to be concerned with Penny blurting out something she'd be sorry for later. A forged death certificate from the county examiner's office made it all legal, or close enough to it that no one would be the wiser.

Etta reached inside her handbag and pulled out a small silver-plated case. Baltimore held a lit match to the skinny Chesterfield cigarette and then blew it out. "I wasn't going to bring it up, but have you heard about that big mess went down in the square this morning?" Etta asked, frowning at the thin layer of dust on her black high heels.

Baltimore leaned against the front fender of his car. His eyes dimmed at the thought of what caused the brawl in the center of downtown. "Yeah, I heard. Lots of innocent people got hurt over it too."

After taking an abbreviated drag from the cigarette, Etta lowered her head. "That's why me and Penny was running late. We stopped over at the hospital . . . to see about Henry." Baltimore's eyes filled with alarm. Etta took note and calmed his fears. "Naw, they said Henry wasn't no part of that. Willie B. Bernard was the only one of the boys ignorant enough to mix in. You know he's hot-headed, got that head thumped good too. Say he might lose his job before getting to work a single day on it."

"If you ask me, they's a sack 'a fools for thinking white men are gonna let anything change just because they write it in the daily paper. Putting it down on the front page don't make it so. Too many rednecks around to let it," Baltimore added to prove his point. Suddenly he laid his head to the side and chuckled.

Etta looked at him like he had lost his mind. "You know, I went to the hospital myself before driving out here. I didn't see Henry and figured he was too smart to mess up his chances of passing the test to get any of that scuffle on him and louse it up."

"Well, here's something you might not have heard. It's official," Etta said in a subdued tone. "Henry made the score." When he didn't fly off the handle, she wasn't sure he'd been listening. "Baltimore?"

"Yeah, Etta, I was just thinking how much fun we used to have, us three, you know, you, me and Henry. It's a shame it can't be that way no more. Now, it's you, me and Penny, I guess. And by the looks of it, maybe Jinx too."

Penny had caught her breath and didn't mince words when asking Jinx if he wouldn't mind coming back into town for supper. "I owe you so much, Jinx. Let me do something nice for you, treat you to a big ole steak at Mabel's or something. Anything you want," she said, with her eyes sparkling brightly. "Whaddaya say?"

Jinx blushed due to her forward offer, but he declined. "I'm sorry, Penny, but I done already promised to take Chozelle to the picture show this evening."

"Chozelle? I didn't know you's sweet on her, Jinxy."

"Yeah, we's been going steady near a year now," he answered softly.

"I hope she know what she got 'cause I sho' do," she told him, remembering how Chozelle was cozying up to another man just before they had it out in the store. "If you find out different, you know where I'll be. 'Bye, Jinxy."

Baltimore and Etta witnessed Penny take another broad step toward adulthood and independence. They shared a warm smile over the occasion and felt proud to be a part of it. What Penny inspired in Jinx was something altogether different.

13

HERE WE GO AGAIN

The following evening, Ms. Etta's Fast House was half empty, mostly due to an article written on the front page of the *Comet* newspaper. It warned the Negro citizens to stay off the streets until tempers calmed on both sides of the color lines. Etta knew it was the smart thing to do although it hit her where it hurt, in the cash register. "Looks like it'll be another slow one tonight," she told Penny, as they took the opportunity to inventory her stock of bourbon, whiskey and rum behind the bar.

"Yes, ma'am, I expect it'll be this way until the fellas get good and settled into that police training," Penny replied, after giving it much thought. "City folk sho' can be mean as rattlesnakes when things go changing on them."

"That's the problem. Change has a way of scaring them something awful. Things staying the same, now that frightens the hell out of me."

Penny wasn't sure exactly what that meant so she went right back to counting bottles and tallying the stock, until Henry came strolling through the door behind M.K. and Delbert. Henry's dark colored Stetson hat was tilted down so far that Penny barely saw his eyes. "Ms. Etta," she said softly. "Someone's here to see you." Etta raised her head from the clipboard she'd been writing on, then cast a subtle glance at Penny, suggesting that she find somewhere else to be. "Yes, ma'am," the girl replied before stepping away from the bar area. "I'll wait a while and bring in another case or two."

Without acknowledging Penny's comment, Etta primped her hair with a flat palm and straightened her royal blue evening gown. Despite the low customer turnout, she had a reputation to maintain as one of the classiest dressers in town. Etta blushed right off and tried to hide the surprise her eyes couldn't conceal. "Hey, Henry. I imagined you'd be home preparing for your first day of training tomorrow."

"Jo Etta," he said somberly, with both hands inside the pockets of his brown suit slacks. "I didn't mean to bother your bookkeeping none."

Etta's heart fluttered beneath the fancy undergarments she'd ordered all the way from New York City. "Oh, it's all right," she replied. The way she batted her eyes made Henry uncomfortable.

"Mind if we go in the office a spell?"

"Sure, I'll just get Gussy to come up and tend the bar. Not that there's been much call for it lately."

"That's what I want to talk with you about," Henry said, in an anxious manner. He was married, after all, and publicly flapping his gums with the only other woman he'd had real feelings for.

Once they were both behind closed doors, Henry took off his hat and laid it on her office desk. He paced back and forth slowly with his gaze locked on the hardwood floor beneath him. Etta knew his heart was heavy for a number of reasons. One of which, stemmed from the lack of courage it took for him to tell her that he was getting married. Now, it appeared he was having the same issue again. Only this time it was more important than skipping out on a love affair to run off with someone else. This time, it was a life and death situation. "I was on my way home from getting the police chief to change his mind about sending Willie B. packing," he said eventually. "I told him that this lawyer got all of the white people off by citing it a matter of self-defense, so the same should apply to colored folk. Still can't believe he bought it."

While Etta digested the good news about one of Henry's former teammates, she shrugged. "But that's not why you came by here, is it?"

"You always did know when my shirttail was hanging out."

"Uh-huh, and tucked it in a time or two if I do recall." She was still so much in love with him but the thought of what Henry did to her made her put on a straight face and fly right. "Though now, you got somebody else to do that for you, so what is it you want from me?"

Henry kicked at the floor with the tip of his pointed-toe shoes like there was a pebble he'd decided to roll around under it. "Hell, I may as well come out with it since it's killing me. Etta, look, you got to find a way to talk Baltimo' into leaving town. I've been around those boys in blue and they'd just as likely toss his black ass all the way to China if they knew what he was up to."

"Do you know what he's up to? 'Cause I sure don't," she answered curtly. "He's a grown man and if I do recollect, him and you done some pretty bad things together not so long ago."

After choking back on what he wanted to say, Henry heaved out with a thick measure of anxiety, "Ain't neither him nor you's gone let me forget that, huh? I can forgive him but you ought to know better."

"Me?" she yelled hysterically. "Well, ain't that a kick in the pants? I know you didn't bring your tired, broke ass into my establishment tryna tell me about forgiveness! You ought'n to know better. Henry, that man you all bent on forgetting so fast done saved your miserable life more times than once and I was thankful that he never ran out on you. I was a fool to be wasting my worries over at the hospital thinking some cracker done split your head wide open. Now, I'm sorry one of them didn't. You could use somebody smacking some sense into you."

"I'm aiming to save Baltimo', Etta. That's why I came here," he fussed.

"Shut up!" she spat, slapping his face with her open hand. "You don't deserve to say his name. Get out and don't set foot back in here again, Henry Taylor. You ain't welcome no more."

Henry grabbed his hat and snatched at the door knob. He did what he thought was right, and it probably was the sensible thing to do, but he'd had that slap coming ever since he sneaked up and became someone else's husband on the sly. That notion shot through his mind as he opened the door but it quickly faded when Gussy blocked it with his immense frame. "Jo Etta, you'd want to tell this man to step aside before I have to make him."

"It's okay, Gus," she answered. "He was just leaving." As the weighty bartender backed off, Henry marched past him with lengthy strides.

Penny had also heard the yells that emanated from inside the small office. She knew how Etta felt about Henry in the past, but now she didn't know what to think. To make matters worse, Baltimore was coming in as Henry exited. The two men ran smack into each other at the front entrance.

"Watch out where you's going, slave catcher!" Baltimore grunted viciously.

"You need to let that old stuff go, Baltimore," Henry fired back. "I ain't gone crease, not now, not ever." When he stood his ground, most of the few patrons scattered to safe distances, fearing that a fight was certain to catch fire.

"Ah-ha, you talk big now that you got both of your feet steady on the floor. It was a different story when I pulled you off that hangman's wagon when those Mississippi boys was about to run you up a pole. Or how about the time those Kansas City bluecoats was aiming to hand you over for murder?" As soon as Baltimore unfastened his jacket, Etta lodged herself between the two brooding men. "Clear as I can tell, you don't do nothing but crease."

"That's enough!" Etta shouted.

"I'm sick and tired of living that way too," Henry argued, with saliva mounting in the corners of his mouth. "I'm through going up against the law and I'm through being a shiftless niggah. I done had my fill of that!"

"Beat it, Henry, and don't come back," shouted Etta. "Don't you come back here, never!"

Penny was so scared that her hands trembled over her mouth, especially when Baltimore followed Henry outside onto the sidewalk. "Go on and git, slave catcher!" he howled. "They ain't gone let you wrestle in no white boys, just colored criminals and runaway dogs. They should've had you take the dog catcher test!" Before walking back inside the night spot, he swallowed hard, tasting what had occurred and dreading what was to come. "Damn," he said under his breath, glad he didn't pull his gun and pop Henry like the cocky stranger he'd become. *Damn.*

M.K. and Delbert had both observed the verbal altercation between old friends. When Baltimore re-entered the Fast House, the fellows waved him over to join them. "Here Baltimore, drink this," M.K. offered, shoving Delbert's glass of ice water in his face. "You need to cool off."

"I need something a might stronger than that," Baltimore declared, seeing Delbert and Ollie seated at the same table. "Gussy, get me a bottle of that stuff I had the other night."

"Since when did you start trying your luck at handling liquor?" M. K. queried, not believing his eyes or ears.

"Since the other night, about the same time hell started to freeze," he answered, with sorrow glazing his pupils.

Etta nodded reluctantly to Gussy that it was okay, despite remembering how badly it turned out for Baltimore the last time he settled down with a bottle to contemplate life. "Yes, ma'am, if you say so," Gussy replied, with a mouthful of pessimism. "Here we go again."

Penny hadn't been off the farm any time to speak of and she'd already found herself learning more about human nature than she had in all of her years following behind her papa. It just so happened that Baltimore's hotel bedroom backed up to the Fast House. One night, Penny overheard two people getting after it from an open upstairs window. Since it was dark inside the hotel room he'd rented, she couldn't see a thing, but the sounds of a woman getting everything she needed from a man filled the night air like a heated jam session. Penny listened intently until she fell asleep with her face pressed against a box of bar napkins. The next morning, she saw Dinah sitting on Baltimore's windowsill smoking something that smelled funny, something she'd rolled herself. Penny thought Dinah's wailing and carrying on sounded about as much like pain as it did joy, but seeing as how she'd been back twice afterwards, it appeared joy kept winning out. Subsequently, as Penny caught another view of Baltimore, she was able to see his passions run wild in the other direction. She wasn't willing to bet on it, but if she had to guess she'd say he'd killed men for less than the way Henry hurt him, much less.

"All right then, that's more like it," M.K asserted uneasily, as he made an attempt toward restoring normalcy. "Baltimore, you remember the carnival we broke in down south. I was just telling Ollie and Delbert what a time we had that weekend. Go ahead and tell them, about the Birmingham twins."

"I ain't stud'n no twins scam, M.K. I'm busy trying to make something outta myself."

"Like what exactly? Something other than a shiftless niggah I hope?" he teased, using Henry's rants.

"Yeah, a *rich* shiftless niggah," Baltimore jested, with a raised glass of whiskey.

M.K. drank to that and made a number of other toasts for the sake of tying on a good one, after pulling an eighteen hour shift patching up cuts and wounds. He was willing to drink the night away if it meant getting Baltimore to agree on arranging another fixed beauty contest where the winners owed them personally on the back end. Having to tell the story himself, M.K. didn't leave anything out.

"Three years ago while blowing some money down in Alabama, Baltimore ran across a set of beautiful twenty-year-old twins at the supermarket. He bought a sack of beer and chips then went on back to their apartment. One of them wouldn't give up nothing because the other was watching, so he come and got me to even the odds, but by the time we got there, two other fellas had drank up all the beer and hemmed the girls in for the night. Not to be outdone, Baltimore told the man at a carnival booth that he was sponsoring a prettiest twins contest for women ages nineteen to ninety. The man running the show thought it was a good enough idea, so he worked it up and cleared over three hundred dollars in popcorn and pickle sales while people stood around looking the girls over and voting. Just before the ballots were counted, I snuck around back and dumped them in a trash bin, then I stuffed the boxes to put in the fix. After the carnival closed, me and Baltimore spent all night with the winning contestants, two lovely burlesque dancers who couldn't thank us enough, even though they were still trying to when the sun came up."

After a few more drinks and exaggerations thrown in on the side, Baltimore did come around to seeing M.K.'s point about twinning and winning. Delbert was simply glad to be among men with something on their minds other than bandages and bumps and bruises. He'd seen his share of those to last him a long while. What Delbert wanted was his first female conquest. Twins wouldn't have been a bad start although getting his kicks with two women was more than any man could hope for on his first time out of the gate.

While stumbling back to the residence's quarters after hours of drinking and trading tales about lascivious living, Delbert needled M.K. for his wild stories about loose women, especially a particular pair he'd mentioned earlier. Ollie didn't object because he was looking to get his hands on a pair of identical beauties himself after hearing all about it. "O.K., but this is the last time. Now there I was, waiting for the carnival man to announce the winning contestants. Phyllis, she had the biggest titties of the two, I think, was standing up on that bandstand grinning and waving those melons at me. I had to tighten my belt to keep my pecker in my pants. But when I got her alone that night, I set it free and then went looking for her sister Mildred in the next room, only Baltimore had already ground her down to nothing and sent her off to sleep. Oh, man, we did some wild things then," he reminisced.

"Talk about wild things, I heard Baltimore's got his hooks in that snooty nurse Dinah Leonard that won't let nobody else get close to her," Ollie said, hoping it wasn't true.

"If I know Baltimore, he's put way more than his hooks in her," answered M.K., smiling and nodding as they walked up the hospital lawn. "He's putting a mighty firm piece of meat in her too. Once he gets 'em, he's got 'em."

Ollie grimaced, learning that Baltimore had a reputation for pleasing the ladies as well as attracting them. "I'd better start on the low end on the talent pool and work my way up, least that way I can guarantee keeping my wick wet. I'm so glad those nursing school girls do anything to get on a doctor's lap."

"I managed to hook two of them already," M.K. chuckled as he staggered up the back steps. "It ain't like I've had 'em join in together yet, but I won't give up trying."

"Like those Birmingham twins, M.K.?" Delbert asked, wanting him to tell the story for the third time.

"Hold up, wait a minute." M.K. glanced at Ollie then poked Delbert in the chest with his thick index finger. "Don't tell me you haven't cinched your first big city notch since you've been in town? Come on, Tex, I put you in real good with that healthy ox Belle that night at the Fast House and besides, there's a whole floor of nursing students living over in the east wing dormitories. With all of that possibility in your face, why is your sack still dragging the ground? I mean, you do like girls, don't you?"

"It hadn't occurred to me to ask either," Ollie said, smirking curiously.

Delbert felt like his back was against the wall. He didn't want his contemporaries mistaking him for a sissy so he decided to do a Texas two-step and dance around the truth. "Hell yeah, I like girls," he protested loudly before hushing his own voice. "It's just that I haven't had a lot of experience with fast women."

"Huh, them's the only kind you're gonna get any experience with," said M.K. "Tell you what I'm fixing to do, get me some sleep before they start cracking tomorrow's whip. I'd suggest y'all do likewise. Delbert, I'm expecting you to get some *experienced* pussy before your nuts back up, explode and drown us all. Thank you and good night."

14

HARD DAY'S WORK

Scared to death along with the four other colored men who scored passing grades on the police exam, Henry slipped off his clothing in what appeared to be a supply closet turned make-shift dressing room. He didn't know what he was thinking, trusting white men with his safety as well as his success. The night before, he'd made an appointment to meet with an insurance salesman. In the front room of their home, Henry's wife Roberta cried a puddle on the rented furniture while signing the accidental life policy which made her the sole beneficiary. Although she agreed that it made perfect sense to prepare for the worst, just in case, her tears left a stain on Henry's heart. This police business was serious and so was his marriage. They were tied together, holding him steady, firm against the winds of his past. With Baltimore and Etta standing in direct opposition, he'd need all of the help he could get trailblazing unchartered territory.

His nervous toes danced upon the cold cement floor and added to the chilling aspect of uncertainty. The colored men were asked to undress apart from their white counterparts, who were given full access to the temperature controlled dressing area, individual lockers and running water. Long before the days

of separate but equal, Henry's band of five was relegated to accommodations which amounted to cramped storage space and a
wooden bench. None of them had knowledge of better conditions just across the hall until they were ordered to step into the
examination area in their underwear, for immediate inspection.

As Henry peeped out of the small, non-ventilated room, Trace
and Smiley were close behind. "Stop pushing," Henry complained. "I'm feeling shaky enough as it is."

"Ain't this a bunch of nothing?" smarted Patton Jones, the
smallest of the five by several inches. He scratched at his pea-
sized head and then he smirked. "Y'all been damn near butt-
naked around each other for years and now all of a sudden you
scared for some white boys to see your skivvies. Move outta the
way."

"Where you off to, P.J.?" Smiley asked, with a full set of ashy
knees and elbows.

"To get poked and pulled on by the doctor. They say this
check-up is the beginning of getting into the department."

"He's right, fellas," Henry asserted boldly. "Let's get over
there and show them how real cadets are supposed to look."

Each of them straightened their backs and strutted out in for-
mation, in their multicolored boxer shorts and just as ostentatious
undershirts. Several uniformed policemen gawked, scowled and
laughed at the assortment of loose ends that appeared out of
place and doomed to failure. "Good Lord, it's worse than I
thought. I didn't know the circus was in town," one of the veterans hissed. Others weren't as kind in their assessments of the
new recruits.

Just inside the locker room, they were greeted by a line of pale
farm boys and youthful city slickers also anxiously waiting to get
the process underway. One look at those clean-cut applicants, in
matching white underwear told Henry and his surprised clique
two things right off—they didn't get the memo about generic
drawers and they weren't going to share that posh locker room,
not without a fight.

"Why do they get to huddle up in here and we got to situate in the broom closet?" Willie B. asked, seething beneath the skin. "Henry, you know this ain't right."

"Yeah, I see that, but this ain't the time to make a stand about it. We's got to pick our battles, a little at a time," Henry replied, before being hushed by a superior.

"All right, quiet now!" barked a stout older officer in his street uniform. The policeman's light blue shirt was stretched across his plump belly and his chin sagged like a wet stocking. Years of ordering cadets rounded out his physique. "By the looks of things," he started in, "I don't have to guess that everyone didn't get the word about proper attire for the inspection. However, that's no excuse. Everyone not dressed in white shorts and shirts, drop and gimme twenty pushups." Initially the colored recruits thought he was merely joking but his stern expression begged to differ. "I said drop!" Instantly, those who didn't get the memo assumed the position to answer their first command. While scoffing and laughing, the older cop mumbled to another one, "Now there's no way they'll pass the physical with their hearts racing a mile a minute."

"What the hell is going on here?" yelled the police chief, as he entered the den of prospective policemen. "Somebody better tell me why these men are being hazed and made to dress like some goddam clowns." It was inconceivable to him that men would show up to a paramilitary organization wearing provocative undergarments. When no one spoke up, the stout officer eased out of the side door. "O.K., I was afraid this would get off to a bad start and boy, was I wrong," he barked, with a tone shrouded in sarcasm. "Henry Taylor, is there something you want to tell me?"

Henry's chest was heaving in and out from the brief physical activity but he was more exasperated because of the fools they'd been made of. "No, suh," he answered, staring straight ahead. "We was just getting a jump on the calisthenics, suh."

"I see," said the chief, looking over the assortment of misfits. "Where's Officer Brandish? I thought he was in charge of the uniforms and orientation." The chief surveyed the room and again no one answered. "In no less than ten seconds, I want to see Brandish and the doctor in charge of first-day physicals," he demanded. Within the time it took Henry to blink, men scattered about to locate this Brandish fellow and the physician.

"Here he is, Chief!" hollered the junior officer who came up with Brandish first.

Henry glanced to the side to see the man who was responsible for their initial difficulties. His eyes narrowed angrily when it turned out to be the stout cop who'd embarrassed them in the first place. 'Now I know we's in for it,' Henry quickly surmised, and he couldn't have been more right. Tom Brandish, they soon learned, was out to get them. He'd made up his mind that something had to be done to force each of the colored cadets off the training roster. They would have to take what he dished out in order to graduate and they accepted that from the beginning. Unfortunately, odds weren't heavily in their favor.

"Yes sir, Chief," the fat man answered begrudgingly. "I was getting coffee. I didn't think we were ready yet," he lied, wiping his oily pink skin with a folded handkerchief. "I'd first like to say congratulations to each of you to for making the score on the civil servant examination. That allows you the chance to become a part of the Metro Police Department, but there will be other deciding factors before that happens," Brandish said with a shifty sneer tossed at Henry. Once the chief felt good about things being on track, he stepped out in the hall for a photo opportunity with the local newspapers. "Let me warn you that non-compliance and/or failing to meet upcoming requirements will get you expelled from the training program. And don't let the chief being here make you think I'm not running this operation. It's my duty to put the best officers on the street." Brandish stepped closer to Smiley and whispered, "That means you don't stand a snowman's chance in hell of making it, none of you dumb nigger bastards do." Willie B. was thinking of breaking ranks and decking the pompous bigot, but the chief reentered with the deputy mayor and a host of cameramen. Flashbulbs lit up the room while the brass posed endlessly.

"Good Lord, Chief," the deputy mayor said. "Get a load of their drawers. It's worse than I thought. Do something about that. At least they can all dress alike."

"Yes, sir, I'll get right on that. I've enlisted Clay Barker to lead the training detail. He knows most of the coloreds and is as good a cop as you'll find."

"Chief, is he a man you can trust?" the mayor asked quietly. "The city needs to show the rest of the world that our coloreds get a fair shake in Saint Louis. Make it work and I mean that. It's high time we prove how progressive we are." Again the chief promised to stay on top of it. And for the second time, his boss took him at his word.

"All right, simmer down," said the chief, to a collection of unrelenting photographers. "We don't want any pictures to run below the waist. We're a professional unit and want to appear as such. It's time we left Officer Brandish to his business."

Immediately, the news reporters dashed out like the room was on fire, undoubtedly sprinting to their offices to develop the film. "As I was saying, you will have a hard row to hoe, some more than others," Brandish sniggled, as he read over the names on his list. "This is Doc O'Brien," he announced as an old physician entered wearing a white lab coat and puffing on a foul smelling cigar.

"Morning, gents," he hailed politely. "Let's sort 'em out and get a look at 'em. Whoa, Brandish, you're short one candidate."

"Well, doc, you can forget about James Dodd showing his face. The jiggaboo got homesick for Joplin and beat it back there quick as spit. He was smart to get out while the getting's good."

Despite Brandish's ill-tempered comments, the train to progress started moving and all of the colored men in attendance were glad to be on it. "Spread out, drop your drawers and raise your arms shoulder high," he demanded. After he looked over the recruits, checked their pulses, held their testicles and had them cough, he ordered each of them to stand in line near the wall where a height marker read 5'8". The police regulations demanded officers range between five-feet-eight inches and six-feet-two. All others who passed the exam but didn't measure up could apply for a position within another city department.

When one of the white guys barely made the height, Willie B. squinted his sore black eye at P.J. "This is where you get off, runt," he teased.

"Are you Patton Jones?" the doctor asked P.J.

"Yes, suh," he answered slowly, trying to stretch his short frame up the wall without being detected.

"Well, Mr. Jones, you're also a bit undersized. Son, I'm sorry," he added, drawing a line through P.J.'s name on his chart. "Gotta nix Jones, Patton L.," yelled the doctor loudly, so that the equipment managers could hear him and scratch P.J.'s name off their list.

"Sorry about that, P.J.," said Henry as the slightly dejected man sadly slinked out of line.

"Hell, I'm sorry they didn't blackball me before the doc squeezed my jewels with his ice cold hands. I'll make out all right. There's a position in the motor pool with my name on it. Just give them hell, 'cause you know it's coming." The other men waved so long to him as he trekked back across the hall. P.J. couldn't do anything but laugh when he passed by two officers shorter than him before exiting the building. All he could say was, "It figures," although he didn't overlook it when Brandish laid his fat foot on the scale to help a skinny white kid make the one-hundred-fifty-pound weight requirement.

Over the next three hours, the remaining cadets were shuffled from one room to the next, fingerprinted and measured for workout gear. No one thought it strange when the white men's outfits fit perfectly but the colored men's sizes weren't even close. Everyone knew the score. It was merely an inkling of things to come. Four out of the ten would be subjected to tougher scrutiny than the rest, that's just the way it was. The die had been cast.

The police academy was simply a microcosm of the outside world. There were rules, written and otherwise, to keep black men in their place as best they could. There was no way getting around that. Although Clay Barker was introduced as the training leader, he gave four out of the ten a better hand to play. He was their inside straight, dealt by the chief, which was why he had rushed over to Ms. Etta's with the news about the city's decision to lift the department's exclusive guideline regarding race.

Unfortunately, not even Clay could do a thing about the dressing room conditions during the first couple of days, so at the end of each evening, after studying the procedure book, and jogging miles for conditioning, the training class divided into two groups when retreating to their lounging areas. Since it was unacceptable to wear the soiled academy sweats home, they were expected to change into street clothes before leaving for the day. And, at the end of every evening, Henry's friends were heckled unmercifully and degraded by veteran officers hiding behind their badges while refusing to see the black men as equals. "You coons are smelling up the place" and "Go back to Africa, you filthy animals," were commonly shouted without fear of reprisal, while the other six cadets went home freshly showered and presentable. Smiley quickly tired of stomaching the systematic racism they experienced on a daily basis. He promised to look for a way to get even and it didn't take long to find one.

On an unseasonably warm afternoon for early spring, the training class was on its regular three-mile hike on the city road circling the academy, when someone rolled past on a pickup truck and hurled insults along with a huge bucket of pig excrement at them. Although the foul substance was meant for the black men particularly, it managed to splatter everyone, including Clay, who reeled off a tempest of dirty words, spewing contempt for such a heinous act. He ranted violently until running out of breath.

Steaming mad, Henry rested with his hands on his knees. He watched the truck roar up the road. It was actually getting easier to look past the hatred and see hilarity. For once, all of the men were treated as one and it took a mean-spirited racist to bring it about. Two of the white cadets vomited from the odor. Henry laughed even harder then and so did they, eventually. Before that moment, blatant divisions existed among them as the colored men felt the whip of degradation. Afterward they became closer as a cohesive group, a crap-scented tribe forced to band together as outcasts, as one.

When the funky bunch approached the facility, Smiley discovered a way to cause a major headache. He ran ahead a quarter mile and searched until he located the main water valve to sabotage it. Shutting off the water pipes rendered the training facility helpless. That afternoon, the entire building had to be evacuated because of the stench. Subsequently, every trainee went home smelling the same, like they'd bathed in a hog pen. Henry was still amused when he entered the academy on the following morning, discovering a notice posted by Clay Sinclair and signed by the Chief of Police. It ordered *all* cadets to shower before leaving the premises. Having been forced by Roberta to scrub from head to toe in clothes detergent and then banished to sleep on the basement rollaway bed was a small price to pay for an ounce of equality, a very small price. Staying alive during the next phase of training was certain to cost him a lot more. The five thousand dollars yearly salary wouldn't amount to much then if he was dead.

15

SOUL SALVATION

It was as if the world started spinning out of control and wouldn't let anyone off until tragedy struck.

"Nurse, get another doctor in here now!" ordered the white obstetrician on loan from famed Washington University Hospital. "Hold on, miss, we're going to get the baby out," he assured the frightened teenage patient. "Just breathe slowly."

Nurse Sue Jacobs dashed from the room as instructed. Delbert was sipping coffee from a paper cup when she stumbled upon him. "Come on, Dr. Gales, we need another pair of hands."

"What's going on?" he asked, alarmed by the nurses expression. Typically unflappable, Sue was noticeably shaken.

"Dr. Stanton is here from Wash-U and has signed on for a whopper," she answered. "Come on, he's waiting." Delbert set the cup down at the nurse station and followed Sue. He didn't know what to expect but an experienced white doctor was clamoring for help. He didn't want to imagine what that meant for the patient. "Dr. Stanton, I found Dr. Gales out in the hall," she informed him. "He's an intern. A good one," the nurse added, when the white man questioned her selection with a piercing glare.

"Well, I guess you'll have to do," he said finally, with a look of concern decorating his face. As the young girl in a world of pain lay on the delivery table, with her mother looking on, Delbert slipped into a surgery smock and scrubbed in. "Dr. Gales, what's your familiarity with pre-term births?" the senior physician asked hurriedly.

"Sir, I've seen a few of them in Texas. Assisting mostly." Delbert was looking at the girl. She had medium brown skin and her lips were dry and ashy, with her hair stretching out every which way. He couldn't help thinking how inconceivable it seemed for her to be giving birth when he hadn't been able to talk a grown woman into having sex with him.

"Good, every little bit helps because this baby's breached. It hasn't turned yet and has a mind to back its way into the world." He glanced at Delbert, then at Nurse Jacobs. Her eyes fell toward the floor. When the thirty-five year old soon-to-be grandmother noticed the quiet exchange among the medical staff, she spoke up for the first time.

"Uh, doctors. What's all that mean for my Sadie and her baby?" she asked, her eyes stricken with panic.

"Not to worry, ma'am," Dr. Stanton said in the most affirming manner. "We'll get the child turned, but it'll take some doing. Now, I'm going to need you to step outside with your husband. We'll take care of your daughter," he said, saying nothing about the baby.

Reluctantly the woman clutched her pocketbook, scooted outside of the room and headed down the hall to the waiting area. She nearly turned back when her child began screaming, "Maaaama!" at the top of her lungs but she wiped her eyes and kept on going.

"You wasn't calling for me when Junior Miller was climbing on top of you," the mother said to herself, to lessen the pain of hearing her only daughter coming unglued.

"Just relax, Sadie," Sue said, wiping her forehead and lips with a cool damp towel. She wanted to make the girl comfortable, because a world of heartache was coming down the line.

"Dr. Gales?" the white physician said quietly to get his attention.

"Sir?"

"I have no doubt we can bring the baby here, but do you know the procedure for premature births at twenty-eight weeks?" Delbert nodded slightly, remembering that was barely the third trimester. "Good, what is the protocol?"

Delbert took a deep breath, traveled to the recesses of his mind and came up with the correct answer, a gloomy one. "First, reposition the fetus, secure the delivery and then . . ." he started to say before looking into the young girl's eyes. "I understand Dr. Stanton."

"You shouldn't have a problem following it to the letter? Then let's begin."

For the next two hours, both doctors and Nurse Jacobs worked feverishly. Delbert massaged the girl's stomach, to irritate the fetus into turning on its own, otherwise Dr. Stanton would have been forced to take more drastic measures. As luck would have it, the fetus flipped inside the womb after being bothered continually. The terrified patient smiled eagerly when she saw Delbert's face brighten.

"Is it time?" she asked innocently. "Is it time for my baby to come?"

"Yes, Sadie," Dr. Stanton said, with his hands positioned to receive it. "You've done a fine job. We're almost done. Now give us one . . . good . . . push."

As the girl bore down, the crown of the baby's head emerged. Delbert tried to be happy for her, but he'd learned not to look past the criterion for a healthy life-sustaining birth. In 1947, at twenty-eight weeks, it wasn't possible.

"Push, Sadie," the nurse instructed, "it's almost here." Again the teenager groaned noisily. Soon after a timid little baby boy introduced himself. He screamed and flailed, while his mother looked on with amazement. Nurse Jacobs cleaned the child with a warm sponge and Dr. Stanton passed the honors to Delbert, who was partially disturbed when cutting the umbilical cord. Knowing what lay in store, it almost seemed pointless to do so. As Sadie held her first-born, cooing and touching his fragile body, the medical personnel observing the union waited for the inevitable. Then it happened. The infant slipped into respiratory distress. He began to cough and gasp, then eventually stopped breathing altogether.

"Nurse, take the child to recovery," Dr. Stanton ordered. "Sadie, we're going to do everything we can to get him breathing again. Sit tight." The white physician looked at Delbert. "Dr. Gales, stay here until the nurse returns. I'll meet with you later." Sue cradled the baby and hurried outside of the room before he started crying again, which typically happened one or twice as pre-term infants fought for dear life.

Delbert languished behind, reading his wrist watch as often as he read Sadie's face. She was afraid to ask and he was praying that she stayed that way. There was no perfect time to tell a mother that little chance existed for her baby to survive past a few minutes, because he came into this world before his lungs had been properly developed. There was nothing to be done, as current protocol clearly stated: Do not resuscitate as death was imminent. Finding it difficult to take it standing still, Delbert excused himself and struck out looking for Sadie's baby boy. He caught up to Sue exiting the storage room behind the newborn nursery. "Where is he?" Delbert demanded.

"Dr. Gales, I wrapped him up and put him in the back," she answered, as if he should have known. "That's where we keep them, until . . . you know, they pass on," she explained.

Without another word, Delbert darted past her to break protocol. Sue hated to report him but she had no choice. She struck out in the opposite direction, searching for Dr. Stanton. Instead, she came across her boss and Nursing Director, Geraldine Robinson. When they found Delbert, he was hovering over the child, sweating profusely, administering mouth to mouth with abbreviated breaths and slight one-finger compressions to the baby's

chest, careful not to fracture his ribs. Nurse Robinson had seen
this many times before but it was typically new nurses she had to
pull off dying children.

"Dr. Gales, I'm going to ask you to step away from that baby!"
she declared firmly, as Sue Jacobs looked on. "There isn't anything you can do for him now, Delbert. Sure, he'll get to breathing and then he'll stop again. It's his time to pass on." Initially
Delbert ignored her orders. Nurse Robinson placed her hand on
his shoulder and appealed to his sense of kindness when playing
her trump card. "Dr. Gales, you took a Hippocratic oath to do no
harm. That poor baby is oxygen deprived, son. His brain is mush,
Delbert. Let him go," she pleaded. "It's the right thing to do.
That's the medical protocol we have to abide by, all of us."

Delbert, exhausted and torn, broke down and wept silently as
the boy grew tired of trying to breathe on his own. He took two
quick gasps and drifted away. The seasoned nurse was right, Sue
was right and so was the protocol prohibiting manual resuscita-
tion. Delbert knew it in his heart and had to make peace with it.
And, after Dr. Stanton read him the riot act for abandoning Sadie
shortly after her baby was whisked away, he was reprimanded
again by his mentor and the Chief of Surgery, Hiram Knight.

"Knock off for an hour or so and get your head on straight,"
Dr. Knight ordered. "We'll see more of those here, Dr. Gales, and
the same goes for hospitals across town. That's the way it is and
until God says different, that's the way it's going to be. Shake it
off, doctor, there's lots of work to be done for those who have a
shot at living."

After the long day shift ended, M.K. returned to the residence
quarters and found Delbert lying on his bunk and staring up at
the ceiling. "What's up, Tex?"

"Long day at the office," he replied quietly.

M.K. collapsed on his bed, next to Delbert's, and then kicked
off his shoes. "Whew, I never thought I'd see you whipped. It
must have been a doozie to get you down."

Ollie entered, wearing the same tired expression M.K. had

when he came in. "What's the matter with y'all?" he asked, out of genuine curiosity.

"Ole Delbert got his butt whooped today, as far as I can tell," M.K. answered promptly. "Me, I'm just spent from burning the candle at both ends. After Ruth Anne practically wore me down to a nub last night, I ran into that nursing student who's been following me." When Ollie leered at him, waiting for an answer, he wasn't disappointed. "Like you would have turned your back on the fine brown frame if you was me."

"If I was you, I'd get myself tested for the clap, the heebie-jeebies and smallpox," Ollie joked. "Just be glad none of you ain't me. All day I've been checking up places nobody should be made to look at and examining more rusty peckers than a picky prostitute. Man, I didn't sign up for this. Bill, Claude and Charles are spending more time lounging than the law allows while I'm busy getting propositioned by one sissy after the next. The last one left a message with a nurse for me to call him."

M.K. laughed but Delbert didn't have the energy to join in. "Dont know Ollie, you's a pretty man," M.K. teased playfully. "A honey-boy might get mixed signals while you got both hands tugging at his package."

"The onliest signal I got for sausage smugglers is a stop signal," he argued loudly.

"So, that mean you ain't gone dial him up?"

"Hell, naw, what do think this is? If you wasn't so damned big, I'd head over yonder and bust yo' ass."

"See there, I told you, Ollie, mixed messages. That's what that fella wants you to call him up for. He might even cook you a nice dinner beforehand. You never know."

"Delbert, do something about M.K. before I try my luck upside his head. That's how rumors take flight. Next thing, I'll have a line of 'em trying to feed and frolic me. No, siree, I'm done discussing it. Shoot, I'm liable to up and quit, that's what I'm liable to do."

"Hush up, Ollie, you ain't gonna do nothing but keep your

crack to the wall and your dukes locked and ready. It's all part of the deal, paying the piper."

Suddenly Delbert sat up on his elbows as other interns and residences dragged themselves into the suite hosting eight twin beds. "M.K., you ever feel real bad after a patient's death?" he asked. His colleagues overheard the question and listened closely to see how it played out.

"I knew something was gnawing at you, Delbert. You didn't do something stupid today, did you?"

"Nah, I had a baby die on me earlier," he told them, while reliving the tragic event. "This teenage girl came in ready to deliver but the baby wouldn't turn. I massaged her abdomen until it did. At twenty-eight weeks, that raisin-colored baby boy may have just as well been stillborn. I went against proper procedure and tried to keep him going. It was foolish I know but . . . I couldn't help myself. I've seen babies pass on due to infection, but nothing like this."

Silence loomed ominously in that room until M.K. offered a valuable perspective. "When I was here before, there was a little girl who couldn't have been more than twenty-four weeks in the womb. The mother got killed when a truck smashed into her car at a traffic light. Dr. Knight did what he could to extract the fetus and the baby came out clawing and whining. She wasn't any bigger than a puppy. I ran and hid in the laundry room. I must've cried for two days after she took her last breath. Still think about that baby sometimes, but ain't no use in crying no more. I put that one on God and on Him alone."

Delbert was forced to agree with M.K. because no other answer made sense. "Do you think babies get into heaven?" he asked as an afterthought.

"If they don't, none of us will," M.K. replied, contemplating his own soul's salvation.

"Amen to that," someone seconded from the fringes of the conversation. "Amen." It was difficult to watch an infant pass away. Being a doctor didn't change that for any of them so they left it at that and concentrated on the living.

Early Sunday, Delbert was up and out of the residence hall before the others awoke from their Saturday night carousing. He tried to shake the visions of the dead child from his mind but found it more difficult than he anticipated. At church, sitting in the back pew, Delbert listened attentively to the minister's sermon on forgiveness and felt good about his decision to forgive God. If the Lord held him in the same regard, he was two for two. M.K.'s words rang in his head as the service ended, "Ain't no use in crying no more," and M.K. was right.

With an uplifted spirit, Delbert exited the church and relished the fresh air he'd taken for granted every single day of his life until he saw how priceless it was. "Dr. Gales," someone called out from behind him. "It's me, Sue Jacobs."

Delbert flashed a cheeky grin when finally recognizing her without the long starched apron, marshmallow shoes, unflattering uniform and standard white cap. "Hey, Sue, boy, do you clean up nice," he complimented, taking in her rose-hued sundress, matching shoes and bag.

"You don't look so bad yourself, doctor."

"We're not on the Homer Gee clock, so Delbert will do just fine," he said, actually delighted to see her in less formal surroundings.

"I like that," she replied, with smiling eyes. "Delbert, that's a nice name. It fits you. Oh, yeah, I don't want to pry but I was wondering if I put you in a fix after . . . you know?"

"Not anything I couldn't handle, but you did what the regs called for. I was out of line."

"Maybe so, but I respect you for doing what you felt was right. You have no idea how many times I lacked the courage to do the same myself," Sue admitted. "You're a good man, Delbert Gales, and you're becoming a very promising physician."

"Does that mean you'll go out with me sometime?" he asked, wishing she would comply.

"Nope, I don't cozy up to doctors."

"Do you cozy up with very promising physicians?"

"Uh-uh, them neither."

Delbert couldn't help but laugh. "I heard you were a tough nut to crack."

"Ain't been cracked yet," she said proudly. "My daddy's the pastor here. How would I look if word got back that his only daughter's been getting cracked all over town. Uh-uh, can't have my name sullied nor his." When Delbert thought he understood what she was hinting at, he opened his mouth but nothing came out. "What's with the silent treatment?" Sue inquired, honestly wanting to know. "Not all nurses are willing to raise their skirts for bright-eyed interns, not even for cute ones."

"So you like the looks of things, do you?" Delbert said, fishing for additional compliments.

"Oh, you thought I was talking about you," she chuckled. "Hmmm." As Delbert's smile floundered, Sue propped it up again. "Don't worry, I was. Just showing off my other side which I'm not allowed to do at work. I saw you weep for that baby and it moved me. Showed me you really cared."

"Well now, I can bust a fountain right here if I need to," he jested, showing that he too possessed another side worth noting.

"Huh, that won't be necessary. However you can walk me home if you'd like."

"I'd love to," he answered without lending any thought to local geography. "Wait a minute. That depends on how far you live from here." It didn't matter if Sue's house was on the moon, Delbert was up for making that trip.

16

HEATHENS AND HOUSEWIVES

Spring was in bloom and signs that life had reinvented itself were obvious everywhere. Birds chirped, butterflies soared, couples paraded while holding hands, and ladies with wide-brimmed multi-colored hats spilled out of the churches by the dozens. Penny took it all in gleefully as she and Etta leisurely strolled down the sidewalk, adorned in fashionable pastel dresses, watching busybodies gossiping about various other members of the congregation. As they waded through those milling about, Etta sighed when one of the ladies looked at her and sneered with a heavy dose of contempt. Penny noticed and found it peculiar, but she didn't want to inquire until they had rounded the corner. "Ooh Ms. Etta, I saw that lady back there look down her nose at you. Do you know her?"

"I used to, chile," she answered calmly, with a subdued expression like something from the past was still pinned to it. "Yeah, I was a faithful member of Antioch Baptist, attended every Sunday too. Good preaching and caring families. But then, two things got in the way—righteous sisters and their ugly ways."

"I thought church going folks were different," Penny said, furrowing her brow.

"Different from who?"

"Don't know, just different I guess. I figured maybe they's filled with goodness and some Holy Ghosts or something. I mean, all that singing and bible thumping should add up to a heap of goodness."

Penny's naïve perspective brought an enchanted smile to Etta's face. "That's only on the one hand. On the other, there's people like that old cow who just mooed at me. Those are the ones who can't wait until the church service is over so they can bust down the doors and commence to badmouthing somebody." Etta thought about it before sharing a real life lesson with her young impressionable friend. Before she could stop herself, the truth started seeping out of her mouth like a broken faucet. "Most women don't see things like I do, and I don't mind it much, but I won't be judged by their tight-eyed-squinting, finger-pointing and narrow-minded ideas of how I should run my life. So, I don't go around them to spark the flames and they're smart enough not to set foot around me. That way, we all get along just fine and dandy."

"Seems like all that soul stirring gets people worked up something fierce," Penny concluded, with a toothy grin. "Don't you miss the singing and bible thumping any, Ms. Etta? I mean, since they run you off?"

Etta cut her eyes at Penny, shocked that she'd put two and two together and actually came up with four. "Hush your mouth, girl. Don't get cute," she hissed jokingly. "Truth be told, I miss every smidge of it more than I'd dare let those heffas know."

"Hey, isn't that the doctor from Texas?" Penny asked, spotting Delbert and Sue on the other side of the street. Just that quickly, she'd moved on to something else but Etta was still stuck on having been chased from the church, when she'd never considered it happening that way before. "Yeah, it is him," Penny whispered. "Hey, Delbert," she yelled, across the avenue.

"Penny, don't be hollering out like that," Etta complained, to stifle her. "Especially when you see a man with another woman."

"What's wrong with speaking to him? He's in the Fast House enough and a nice fella at that." Penny frowned sharply, showing her age and lack of maturity. "Shoot, I didn't mean nothing by it. Just speaking was all."

"It's okay, honey, there's some things a lady just doesn't do. Going out of her way to speak to a man with a woman on his arm is one of them. There are others, of course, and we'll cover them eventually." Etta doted on the young woman like a mother introducing worldly boundaries to her daughter.

Penny lowered her head, brooding, as they neared Watkins Emporium. "I know they's lots of things I need to learn and I want to know all of them, too. You're the closest thing I ever had to a mama, Ms. Etta. And, it's just that I'm hoping you don't quit on me like she did."

"You don't have to waste any hope on that, Penny. Nothing can turn me away from you. That's a promise." Etta's eyes began to mist when she saw Penny's tears. She opened her purse and fished around inside it for a handkerchief but couldn't come up with one. "Oomph, we need to step into Watkins before people see us blubbering out here like a couple of dizzy dames."

Inside the dry goods store, Chozelle was listening intently with her ear against the office door, while her father discussed a business proposition with Ollie and M.K. She was startled when Etta eased up on the outer side of the counter.

"Chozelle!" Etta called out.

"Ooh, Ms. Etta, you—you scared me," she stammered. "It ain't polite to go sneaking up on a person like that."

"I've called you three times to see about your selection of kerchiefs but you didn't answer. And, you probably shouldn't be listening in on your daddy's affairs. I'm sure if he wanted you in there, you'd have been invited."

"Well, normally I don't care what goes on in the office, but there happens to be two of those handsome young and single doctors on the other side of that door," she said, as if that made a world of difference. "I'm marrying age and don't plan on sticking here all of my life. I've got dreams to catch, Ms. Etta."

"Dreams, huh? Show me your latest selection and we'll talk about some of them," Etta offered, well aware that Chozelle's mother died of pneumonia several years ago. "And try to mind your mouth with Penny," Etta said, behind a stern expression that insinuated it was more than a mere suggestion. "She's gone through a lot with Halstead dying in the fire and all."

"I didn't know you brung your shadow along today, but O.K., I'll step back. I did hear tell something about Halstead passing on. I didn't think much of him, but it's a terrible thing just the same," said Chozelle, nodding agreeably. She slid a small box down from the second shelf. "Huh, you're all the poor girl's got now. It's like my papa always says, life can turn on a dime. A month ago, Penny didn't even have you."

"And I thought you had Jinx," Etta retorted, as a way to get her nose out of Penny's business, where it didn't belong. "Why are you pausing for other fellas when I hear he's partial to you?"

"Jinxy ain't nothing but a boy, Ms. Etta, a boring boy at that. I needs a man to handle me, a real man with plans, and big ones."

"Not that you asked, but maybe he'd be better at being a man if a certain somebody I know was treating him like he was one. Chozelle, I know Jinx is in love with playing that child's game, but baseball does that to some of them. Trust me, I know."

The younger woman flipped through sheets of linen with Etta, as Penny busied herself sampling a variety of hard candy from gallon-sized storage jars. "I don't want you to think bad of me, but Jinx was fun when the ball team still played together. Now he's a gardener-something or 'nother. What would I look like attached to somebody like that? Without baseball, he's not worth taking into account otherwise. I deserve more, a lot more."

Etta pulled five of the most expensive handkerchiefs from the box to purchase before she gave Chozelle a parcel of priceless advice for free. "Listen closely and then you can throw it away if you can't use what I'm about to tell you. A man's got to know his woman believes in him, whether he's catching his own dreams at the time or not. Having a woman believe in a man makes him wanna try real hard so's he don't let her down, not just in a child's game but also in life. Now, I'm not preaching because I like to live and let live the way people choose to. Throw it away or keep it, don't matter to me. Just a life lesson is all. How much I owe you for these?"

"And this?" Penny squealed, shoving a jug stocked full of peppermints in Chozelle's face.

"Ms. Etta!" Chozelle huffed loudly.

"Chozelle, remember what we said about stepping back?"

"Yes, ma'am," she answered, her lips pursed and pointed at Penny. "I remember, but I don't have to like it."

The office door opened. Mr. Watkins stepped out with M.K. and Ollie bringing up the rear. "Son, it sounds like a grand idea but I'll have to thinks about the proposal some more. Renting a county fair booth on a whim ain't nothing to sneer at," the store owner said, stroking his cheek. "You say I stand to get over real good by being the sponsor of this here contest?"

M.K. nudged Ollie when the older man sunk his teeth into the idea. M.K. grinned harder than he had all day just thinking about it. "Twins proved to be a winning hand, times two. Yes, suh, we got over real good in Birmingham."

Later that evening, Baltimore was wrapping up dinner with Dinah at a fancy restaurant near downtown. Throughout the meal, she could tell something was eating at him because he barely touched the ten-ounce steak on his plate. "It's not like you to waste anything," Dinah said cordially. Her face softened as she gazed at him from across the table at Rudolph's, the most exclusive steak and chop house in St. Louis that allowed colored folk to dine in. "She must really be something."

"She?" Baltimore repeated, as if Dinah was far off base. In fact, she'd hit it right on the head but he wouldn't admit to it. "Now why would you think a woman is behind my loss of appetite? You're the only one in my bed."

"But am I the only one in your head?" she replied quickly, as her jealousy mounted. When Baltimore made a failed attempt at dismissing her question, Dinah pulled out a small gold plated cosmetic compact and checked her teeth. "And don't act like the bed's the only thing that matters. I've been on the other side, baby, the other side saying, he might be her man but I'm on his mind. I know that's just as good as being on a man's lap. The one thing standing between the two is a simple matter of time."

Baltimore smiled, ran an index finger down his thin mustache and then asked the waiter for the check. "Sweetheart, it's not what you think. Really, you's the meat and anything else is gravy."

"That may be," she scoffed, looking at the cold chunk of beef in front of him, virtually untouched. "But lately you ain't been in no mood for steak. So tell me, is she brown or white gravy?" Dinah didn't put it past Baltimore or any other colored man to tip across the race line. She'd done it herself on occasion when the situation paid handsomely and she wasn't deluding herself into thinking that he was beyond doing the same. Baltimore was a hustler, well-versed on what it took to survive, although this go-around he was looking way past surviving. White gravy may as well have been on his lap because it certainly was on his mind while time separated the two.

Dinah didn't protest too much when Baltimore declined to escort her inside the apartment building she lived in off South Delmar. Knowing that a woman could hardly stop a man from making a fool of himself, she didn't bother wasting the effort.

"I've got a few corners to turn, then I'll head on back this way," Baltimore suggested as she stepped onto the curb.

"No, that won't come close to getting it. I ain't no consolation prize," was her cool answer to his lukewarm offer. Baltimore drove away without debating the point, leaving Dinah narrow-eyed and annoyed. She couldn't stand white gravy.

After driving fifteen minutes, Baltimore realized Dinah knew him better than he thought. Sure, it could have been just about anything bothering him during dinner, but she didn't see money troubles being the culprit. So it had to be a female. Since Dinah had an extremely high opinion of herself, she figured there would have been no reason for him to be pondering over another colored woman. But it was like Baltimore told her, this wasn't about his bed. Well, not entirely.

In an area of town called "The Bloody Southern" where the crime rate soared and police steered clear, Baltimore was told he could find the long time pimping, drug-pushing, colored gangster who owed him a debt. Almost two years had passed since they'd done business and the marker was still outstanding. One way or another, Baltimore was dead set on settling it tonight.

The fortress-sized red-bricked house off Piedmont Road matched the address which was handwritten on the napkin in Baltimore's front left pocket. He parked his car in the crescent-shaped driveway and got out. If the gangster was up to his old tricks, Baltimore would be able to tell right off. If not, paying up with his life wasn't out of the question. It didn't make any difference to Baltimore. He'd saved the man's neck before and agreed with the law of the streets, where it was all right to take whatever he possessed, including his life, because it was only borrowed time when you got right down to it.

"I'm here to see the Fat Man," Baltimore told the butler straight out, with his jacket opened, when the man answered the door. "Who may I tell Mr. B. is calling?" asked the ancient butler, visibly indifferent to the visitor's sharp appearance and insistent tone.

"Tell the Fat Man his old pal Baltimore said to get his wide ass out here and be quick about it," he answered the tuxedo-wearing flunky.

The butler flinched then, fearing he'd opened the gate and let the devil in. "I'll-I'll speak with the fat man . . . uh, Mr. B. Please excuse me, sir." Baltimore didn't say another word. Immediately, the man servant made himself scarce and then disappeared behind an expensive hanging tapestry in the front foyer.

"This is how rich folks do it, I guess," Baltimore said to himself while admiring the light-colored marble floors and pricey furnishings. The fat man's taste had improved since they last met.

Standing there too long to suit him, Baltimore wondered what other aspects about the pusher had changed for the better. Suddenly he heard several sets of footsteps headed his way. Baltimore turned, and saw the host flanked by a group of men. He didn't like the addition of bodyguards in the least, because one of them was bound to get cocky and show off for the others.

"Shookie Bush," Baltimore howled, like he was announcing the man's entrance instead of greeting him. "It's sure been a long time." One quick head count told him he'd have to shoot first in order to make it out alive, if it came to that.

Shookie was a resident thug and the self-proclaimed King of "The Ville." His nostrils flared as he stood there in a tent-sized silk house robe. "Baltimo', it has been a month of Sundays since I laid eyes on you, but I figured someday you'd be back to collect on that debt, so let's get it over and done with," he stated flatly. "Then you can get the hell out of my house!"

"I hadn't planned on trouble, Shookie, but if you want to act like these fools can stop me from hurting you, make a move," he grunted, aggravation swelling in his throat. And, just like he suspected, one of the bodyguards went for a long barreled pistol tucked in a waistband. Before he had the chance to slide it out, Baltimore shot him twice in the chest and then marched toward Shookie with both of his charmers poised to close the deal.

The obese criminal rocked back on his heels and threw his meaty paws into the air. There was no reason to act like he wasn't scared to death, so he didn't. "Stop!" Shookie warned the men, who were still breathing. "Don't do nothing stupid! He'll burn me down, right here. I swear it!" His bald head was dripping in sweat now and his heart was pounding inside that barrel chest of his. The brash demeanor he appeared with had abandoned him. "Don't nobody else need to go getting killed, Baltimo'," he pleaded.

"Didn't nobody have to before either, but you come up in my face with men to draw down on me," Baltimore barked. "I oughta shoot you for that alone." Initially the hired guns refused to lower their weapons until Baltimore shoved one gun barrel against the fat man's nose and the other pointed directly at his crotch.

"Put those rods down!" Shookie wailed loudly. "Can't y'all see we're among friends? Friends don't go around capping each other. That wouldn't be friendly, now would it?" The henchmen were confused over how to respond but eventually they did as they were told. "That's more like it. Yeah, that's ideal." Shookie lowered his hands, looking for Baltimore to do likewise. "Mr. Floyd, welcome to my humble palace. I see you done made yourself to home. Just tell me what I can do for you, just name it?"

Although he didn't release his aim on the mountainous gangster, Baltimore felt more relaxed. "Yeah, that does sound ideal. All I need are some answers and we're four corners square."

"Okay, I have lot of answers. Hell, I got answers flying out of my ass. How many of them you want?"

"Two good ones," he said, knowing full well what he needed before knocking at the door. "Who's the police go-between running heroin up from Chicago and where can I find him tonight?"

"Barker Sinclair's the man you want and it being nightfall, he's liable to be at the Red Lantern but I can give you his home address if he ain't." When Baltimore studied Shookie's eyes suspiciously, he bucked them. "What you looking at me like that for? If I'd knowed that's all you wanted, you could've called me over the telephone for it."

"I dont know, Shook, you gave that up kinda easy. If he's the one with the Chi-town connects, why'd you sell him out?"

"'Cause I don't like him and I'm tired of staying up nights waiting on you to show yo' ugly face. In two years, I haven't slept one decent wink during all those nights put together. You got what you came for now you can leave. I'm going to bed," Shookie declared, marching off. "That white man's gone kill you, Baltimo', and I don't even care, 'cause we's even," he yelled from the staircase. "See him to the door somebody and scrape that dead man off of my floor. I'ma sleep for three days."

Baltimore didn't have to get Barker's address from Shookie, he'd already seen the man's house and his wife strutting around in the backyard starving for attention. After a brief stop by the Red Lantern, an exclusively whites-only bar and grill, Baltimore decided to head over and give her some. Barker was wrist-deep in some blonde's cleavage and looked to have a good chance at striking gold when Baltimore peeked in through the restaurant window. Soon after, someone was tapping on Barker's back door.

Dixie Sinclair was sipping from a martini glass in the den when she heard a noise coming from the kitchen. When she went to investigate, Baltimore knocked again. As he stood on the back porch, she recognized him right off through the paned glass. A moment after deciding what to do, she unlocked the door and stepped away slowly. The white woman with shoulder length brunette hair, a slim face and pleasant features never took her eyes from his when he casually strolled in. Dixie pulled down the kitchen window shades so the neighbors couldn't see inside. "How'd you find me?" she asked, as nervous as a sixteen-year-old alone with her first boyfriend. "That day, you came by to speak with our yard boy. How'd you find me?"

"Jinx isn't a boy," he corrected her, "and stumbling over you was an accident," Baltimore added softly, to calm her worries. "I didn't know until I saw you out back that you lived here."

Dixie's eyes sparkled, the slight apprehensions she had all but evaporated. It was hard to dismiss, she liked what she saw, a man unafraid of her husband and his ruthless friends. She could have lied about it but she'd have only been fooling herself. Baltimore was exactly what she needed, a welcome diversion from her un-exciting life. "You coming here tonight, this isn't an accident, is it?" she asked lightly.

"No, no, it isn't. And it won't be an accident tomorrow when you stop on by my place to see me." Baltimore told Dixie where to find him and to call before she came. The married woman listened to him, as she did in the beginning, while agreeing to keep their affair under wraps. In turn Baltimore spent many lustful nights listening to her divulge specifics about her husband's shady business dealings. He could easily envision carving out a huge payday using the information she relinquished during sweaty pillow talk episodes. What he couldn't see coming but should have were the troublesome things destined to get out of hand and spin sideways in a hurry.

17

BARBEQUE AND BEER

Each of the colored cadets promised to ride the training program until the wheels came off. During the week, Henry and the boys sat for one arduous test after another. All of the OIT (Officers In Training) were tired and worn from late night studying and the grueling combat exercises on the following morning. It was a vicious cycle, one that provided men like that overstuffed scoundrel Brandish an open range to sabotage the system. One Thursday, he met with his cronies who couldn't stand seeing the colored trainees compete successfully with the white ones, so they rigged the exam. When Trace Wiggins was asked to hand out the testing folders, he noticed there were two different types pre-assigned. It seemed peculiar that the set with white cadets' names penciled on them were taken from standard department issued booklets, while the others were done on an office typewriter and not professionally at that.

"Uh, Officer Sinclair," he summoned, in the middle of passing them out. "It seems we have a problem with this examination." Clay folded his newspaper in half and laid it on his desk at the head of the classroom.

"Well, let's have a look at those," he suggested, knowingly. At a glance he could see what someone was up to. "You are correct once again cadet Wiggins. First of all, they sent up the wrong tests. These all have pages missing," Clay joked, while tearing several pages from each folder. "I'll have to administer it orally. Please have a seat and get your pencils ready." He winked at Trace, placed the shredded pieces of paper on his desk and then cast a grin toward the window cutout in the door where he knew Brandish would be spying. Sure enough the bigot was present, accounted for, and foiled again. It stung Brandish even more when the oral test scores turned out to be the highest thus far. He should have given up then, but he had one more trick up his sleeve.

Two days later, the men were scheduled for marksmanship trials at the shooting range. Each of them had to qualify by scoring well enough on stationary silhouettes in order to carry a weapon. It didn't take long to discover four revolvers had the sites offset with a filing tool. None of the colored men hit a single target within the first round. Clay couldn't figure out what had gone wrong until he tried to score with one of the guns which had been tampered with. "From now on, we will use only the weapons I select randomly at the beginning of target practice," Clay announced during a lunch break, and loud enough to be overheard by other veteran policemen. "This program will graduate colored officers or the chief will be forced to fire those responsible," he added, to deter any further strategies aimed at sabotaging the colored men.

Brandish and his goons smirked when they heard his rants, dismissing them as idle warnings from a man they still thought of as Barker's kid brother. Clay was on the wrong side of the fence as far as they were concerned, and they wanted to knock him down a peg by damaging his credibility. What they didn't know was the police chief had employed a mole gathering information to ruin theirs. It was time for an historic change in the St. Louis Metropolitan Police Department and the chief wanted it to be on his watch right alongside the deputy mayor. No backwoods paper-pushing cops were going to stand in the way of those men getting their names into history books, no matter what he personally thought of the colored and what they were entitled to.

Later that weekend, West Coast blues singer Aaron "T-Bone" Walker crooned smoothly through an amplified speaker placed in the window facing Henry's backyard. Barbeque and Beer, is what the foursome called their weekly Friday evening cop-n-squat where they'd settle down around a card table to eat, drink and share experiences from the prior week's training detail. P.J., with motor oil underneath his fingernails, stopped by for a rib plate, as Roberta served potato salad and baked beans to the boys out back. Barbeque and Beer provided a casual avenue to blow off steam while they learned to trust and appreciate one another during their internal struggles and the city's growing pains.

With less than two weeks left on their training schedule, everyone was getting antsy. Trace Wiggins had the highest IQ of anyone at the academy in the past ten years, but he was starting to rethink this potentially dangerous vocation involving hand cuffs and nightsticks. His heart was no longer in it but he was determined to see it through to the end.

Smiley Tennyson was so tired of being called boy; he hated that word above all others, including nigger. Around the training facility it was "Hey, boy, what you think you're gonna do when the bad guys start shooting back" or 'Hey, boy, you ain't got no business in that uniform so you might as well go on back to your mammy." So many officers made special trips to the academy to heckle the colored cadets, the chief submitted an edict barring all non-training personnel from entering the campus until further notice.

Willie B. Bernard didn't have a problem handling the political pressures or spending his days playing the game they instituted. His concerns went much deeper. Roll call always seemed to offer a new challenge and surprise. The week before, someone stole his navy police-issued dress shirt, then his wooden baton came up missing, earning him another demerit, and lastly someone went a great distance to get him tossed out by stealing the Smith & Wesson revolver he was responsible for. It wasn't until Clay Barker threatened to expose all of the thefts plaguing the colored cadets to the chief that the shenanigans stopped immediately.

"Funny how Brandish's flunkies cut out busting in our lockers," Willie B. chuckled, from the other side of a half-empty beer can. "I thought they'd drum me out for sure when my revolver came up missing from my hutch. All's I could think of was my pops telling me 'I told you they didn't want no colored policemen, I told you, Willie B,'" he mimicked. "'Now, a colored mortician's got a place in society. A damned good place, yuck-yuck-yuck.'"

"Yeah, that sounds just like old man Bernard," Smiley joked. "'And another thing, Willie B., git yo' ass up to the cemetery and git to diggin'. Yuck-yuck-yuck,'" he added, using the same voice Willie B. had. "Huh, 'least your pops is still talking to you. My old man ain't said two words since I signed up with the department, except for 'What the hell y'all doing in the newspaper in your drawers?'"

Trace sat across from Henry, shaking his head and still as embarrassed as the day they hit the *Post-Dispatch* front page topless and darn near bottomless too. "Could we talk about something else? I've put my past behind me," he said, blowing a stream of cigarette smoke into the warm evening air. Smiley was working on a stack of ribs and almost choked while going after Trace.

"Yeah, but the white paper done went and put your behind on the top of page one."

P.J. sucked barbeque sauce from his greasy fingers. He'd listened to their stories and was actually relieved that he didn't meet the height requirements. He had subsequently took a position in the department's automotive unit, although he experienced hardships as well. "You want to talk about showing your ass. Them white boys in the motor pool ain't no cakewalk. Better than a week ago, I went to get a nip from my coffee thermos and I'll be damned if they didn't put a dead rat in it. I couldn't wait 'til quitting time, because my cousin Lucille stays over at the gov'ment projects on Fifty Third. That evening, I collected a shoebox full of roaches from there, and I'm talking about them great big old flying demons. The next morning I let them loose in the lunch cabinet at the job. Them roaches was the onliest ones who ate lunch that day but I was full off revenge."

Henry laughed the hardest, but what kept him up nights boiling over wasn't funny at all. He sipped on the RC Cola that Roberta suggested he trade in after three cans of brew. "Hey, fellas, I didn't want to say anything at first, but the more I think about it the madder I get all over again." Now that he had everyone's attention, getting to heart of the matter was more difficult than he would have guessed. "We all know how Clay Sinclair is with us every step of the way, but that rotten brother of his ain't nothing but a foul-hearted crook. The first day of ride-a-longs I was partnered up with that lying buzzard Tasman Gillespie. As far as dirty cops go, he's one of the worst. Told me he would make false allegations to have me booted out if I let on to anybody what I saw."

"What did you see?" asked Trace, leaning in.

"We stopped at this apartment building on North Market. Gillespie hollered for me to stay in the car when I went to follow after him. There wasn't a call on the car radio, so's I figured he must've been meeting a chippie or something to past the time. But then Barker's car rolled up and parked in the front. They's in the building for a few minutes until a colored man comes running out screaming and bleeding from his mouth. Barker grabbed him up and then stomped him into the ground. He said, for holding out on him."

No one blinked when Henry paused to catch his breath. "I wanted to jump out of that patrol car and help the man, but that chump Gillespie got his licks in and gave me the evil eye. Hell, I knew what that meant, so's I sat on my hands and looked the other way. Boys, I ain't never been so ashamed in all my life. I've seen Barker a couple of other times too, up to no good each one of them. He was parked up on the hill at Shookie Bush's just yesterday. He come out all causal like with a burlap sack dangling by his side, you know, in a way that looked suspicious, sorta like he was trying to hide it. I always heard of dirty cops and drug pushers throwing in together but I didn't want to believe it. Don't seem to matter who I ride with, Barker Sinclair is always around with me while I'm stuck in the patrol car sitting on my hands. Clear as I can tell, don't nothing happen in "The Ville" unless he's benefiting from it."

"I figured that I was the onliest one seeing the bad side of the blue wall," Smiley said, with disgrace covering his voice as well. "What a fine pickle we got ourselves into. The biggest criminals there is got guns and badges to back them up. Ain't nobody gone do nothing to sway them, especially not some colored cadets they'd just as soon shoot and claim a robber did it. Most of the veterans carry a second gun they use for that kinda thing, when they don't want the mess to get on them. I got enough trouble trying to keep my body off a slab at the Bernard Mortuary. Dead men tell no tales. And believe me, I'm shutting the hell up."

Willie B. bit into his bottom lip and exhaled slowly. Out of nowhere, a single tear crawled from his eye. "After all we's going through and been put through, I think Helen's tipping out on me. She's likely to be getting it on with one of them doctors at Homer Gee. Policeman ain't good enough for her, I guess."

Henry put his can down and frowned at his friend's accusation. "Ah, man, scratch that. Helen is true as the day is long. She's probably just putting in more hours so she can move up and get in deep over there. Don't let this police business mess up nothing between you and that good woman."

"Yeah, Henry's right," Trace asserted. "This is just a job, they come and go, but a woman like yours is forever. After putting up with your janky ways for the better part of five years, she ain't fit for nobody else."

"I'm glad y'all see it that way, because I'ma kill the sonabitch who's jooking Helen when I find out. I ain't looking to share that good woman I got," he chuckled in a sinister manner. "And if I catch her spreading her legs away from home, I'ma kill her too." Willie's mean streaks and fearlessness were legendary. He'd once stared down the muzzle of a loaded gun and didn't blink when the man pulled the trigger. If Willie B.'s wife was sleeping around, there would be hell to pay, all the way around.

18

ALL'S FAIR IN LOVE AND HOUSE CALLS

On Saturday afternoon the county fair was in full swing. Children had their fill of popcorn, hot dogs and cotton candy. The rodeo was a major attraction, as were the amusement rides, but the event which had M.K. and Ollie foaming at the mouth was the contest they had convinced Mr. Watkins to sponsor, the Prettiest Twins competition.

To the store owner's delight, herds of on-lookers showed up to view the contestants. While having their undivided attention, he made the best of it. Scores of white and colored customers feasted on bags of peanuts, corndogs and waffle cakes. He was making money hand over fist while Chozelle flirted with every adult male who looked half decent and looked at her twice. She consistently shooed Jinx away when he hung around the booth too long for her liking. "Go on and check out the rodeo or something, Jinxy," she scolded him, not waiting for an answer. "I can't keep the cash drawer straight with you lurking about. Go on now, git. I'll see you later." With his feelings hurt in the process, Jinx wandered away. Loving Chozelle was bittersweet at times. She was a doll when the mood hit her and a dragon when she developed a taste for something other than him.

Baltimore held a secret meeting with Ollie and M.K. on the side, while Dinah, Penny and Etta applauded the twins' talent portion of the competition. A pair of white teenagers, who dazzled the crowd with a baton twirling exhibition, appeared to be leading the pack early on by three o'clock. But a stunning colored duo, in their early twenties, tap danced their way into the voters' hearts. Baltimore teased M.K. about the remote chance of an elderly set of sisters, who recited the Gettysburg Address in perfect tandem, making off with the trophy, and the men's dreams of bagging the tap dancers while doing it. It wasn't until Ollie exposed several stacks of blank ballots he had run off at the printer that Baltimore conceded the fix was properly administered. He congratulated them on their deceitfulness and aptitude. M. K. had previously promised a matching set of tiaras and fifty dollars prize money in return for the dancers' agreeing to show their appreciation over drinks and devilment afterwards. The only thing standing in his way was working the tail end of a split shift with another resident, and then it was all over but the moaning.

Penny, dressed in new blue jeans, a white cotton pullover and loafers, excused herself from the festivities when she saw Jinx being banished from his steady's company. "Hey, Jinxy. Where're you off to?" she asked, with traces of powdered sugar from the waffle cakes she'd eaten on both cheeks. "All the fun is going on right here," she mentioned suggestively, "unless you want to be around some smelly ole animals over at the rodeo." Jinx smiled as he took the corner of a rag from his back pocket, dabbed it on his tongue and then wiped the white powder from Penny's face.

"You always did have a thing for waffle cakes," he said, smiling even brighter now.

"You wanna know what else I always had a thing for?" she asked shamelessly.

"What's that, Penny King?" he replied, pretending that he didn't have an inkling what she was referring to.

"Well, if'n you don't know, maybe I should keep it to myself," she teased. When Jinx hunched his shoulders as if he was willing to let it go at that, Penny popped him on the head with a bag of cotton candy. "Ooh, silly boys. I can't stand y'all sometimes, I swear." Jinx let her fume for a minute before kissing her on the forehead.

"I know, Penny King, I know," he confessed. "I's just funning with you. And truth be told, if I didn't have Chozelle, you'd make a fine steady, I'd bet. You've grown into a right nice young lady. Everybody says what good Ms. Etta's doing for you." Penny blushed and tossed her big brown eyes up at Jinx. She wanted to kiss him back and not on the forehead either, but she feared making a fool of herself because she didn't know how.

"Well, if Chozelle don't know what she's got, she stands a chance of losing it," she said, with a playful shoulder wag to emphasize her point. "Seems that a lady ought to know a good catch when she has one. I sho' do."

"Come on and walk with me, Penny. 'Spite of all these people around, I feel kinda lonesome. Don't seem possible really."

"Yes it do, Jinxy," she countered. "I get that same feeling sometimes, like I'm the only one who knows I'm alive." Penny placed her hand in his as they strolled down the carnival aisles, sharing cotton candy and feeling alone, together.

When they discovered a tent where a man was asking twenty-five cents for three baseball throws to win stuffed animals, Jinx's smile stretched out like a limousine. "Mistah, I'll take a dollar worth of tries," he said, with four quarters in his palm. Penny stepped aside and watched as his entire countenance altered. "Without one of these in my hand, Penny, I feel like a fish out of water. A fish drowning on dry land," he confided. "Mistah, get ready to snatch down and give this woman what ever she wants 'cause I'm about to dive in the water and breathe." One, two, three, he fired the baseballs, knocking down all of the wooden milk bottles as easy as breathing. In less than a minute, the tent minder was scowling at Jinx and snatching down two of the biggest stuffed animals he had on display. Penny was partial to both the lion and unicorn. She brimmed with excitement when Jinx told her she deserved a lot more than those and in due time, she'd have her choice of men as well as carnival prizes.

The crowd observing the twin competition had doubled in size when Penny made her way back to the platform to show off her gifts to Etta, Baltimore and that stuck-up date of his who everyone thought was so beautiful. Penny tugged on Jinx's arm when he stalled a few feet away from the Watkins's booth. "What's the matter?" she asked before seeing her answer written up and down Dinah's face. Etta was shaking her head while watching Dinah go off on Chozelle, making a spectacle of it.

"If I told you once, I told you a thousand times, little girl," Dinah spat. "Keep your greedy eyes off my man and I'll try to keep my fist off of your face." Baltimore tried to ease the tension by ushering her away but she dug in her heels. "Uh-uh, I'm not gonna let her think she's getting away with this. The brat probably wouldn't know what to do with one man at a time, much as she's chasing 'em by the dozens." After Dinah had run her mouth a little more, Baltimore tipped his hat to nosy bystanders and wrestled her to the far corner of the fair to settle her down. Unfortunately, it was too late to spare Jinx's feelings and to make matters abundantly worse Etta spoke out of turn. She had no idea Jinx was standing on the other side of Penny's overgrown unicorn.

"Dinah had to learn sooner or later," she said to Penny, in retrospect. "You can't take that man out in public and not expect women to be fighting over him. That's just the way it is, chile. Chozelle done went from curious to crazy."

"Sorry, Jinxy," Penny whispered softly. "Miss Dinah didn't know about you and Chozelle." She was extremely saddened by the turn of events. Jinx saw it on her face and now he finally recognized how love had blinded him.

"That's okay, Penny, people tried to tell me about how things was but I had too many rocks in my head to listen. Chozelle's willful and wayward. I don't have what it takes to alter that. Guess that's a joke on me. I'm a head on home. Thanks for showing me a good time, while it lasted. See you around." Having his heart stomped on twice in one afternoon was too much. Finally it was so clear, the way Chozelle led him around by the nose and toyed with his emotions as she saw fit. Jinx had seen it for what it was at last, and it hurt twice as much for others to have recognized it beforehand. Chozelle was just incapable of loving anyone as much as she loved herself.

Penny saw Henry before Etta did as he made his way up the main aisle with Roberta and their small boy. She nudged Etta to get her looking that way. "Everybody's at the fair, I reckon."

"Yeah, everybody and his mama," Etta hissed, after she saw him too, "though you'd hardly know him with his clothes on."

"Ooh, Ms. Etta," Penny giggled.

"What? Oh, I don't mean that," she argued. "I'm talking about those darned newspaper photos."

Penny looked at her cockeyed. "That ain't the way I heard it," she said playfully. "Mistah Baltimore told me y'all used to be crawling on each other like a tub of crabs."

"Shut yo' mouth," she chuckled. "That's ancient history and I'm a have a talk with Mistah Baltimore, you wait and see."

"Uh-uh, Ms. Etta," Penny pleaded. "If you say I told, he might not tell me nothing more about your old belly rubbing days with Mistah Henry."

"Penny, I'm a get you!" Etta hollered as her protégée dashed away dragging both of her animals behind. "You're wrong for that, Penny!"

In so many ways Etta wanted to forget how much she loved Henry, less than a year ago. The wound was healing rapidly but it had a strange manner of reopening whenever she saw him with his new family. Since it was easier to look the other way, she did then too, although suddenly the county fair didn't hold nearly as much allure as it had moments before. Besides, it was high time to be getting back to the Fast House, Etta had decided conveniently. That's where she belonged.

At nine o'clock that evening M.K. whistled as he handed off his closing report to the nurse he requested to assist him weeks ago, because of her knowledge and skills. Nurse Helen Bernard enjoyed working along side the popular doctor as well. He wasn't like a lot of the physicians she encountered. Sure, he was a skirt hound like most of them, but he often made her feel more like a person instead of merely a part of the medical machine known as Homer G. Phillips. M.K. shared pertinent information about the patients and explained why he did certain things to treat their infirmities. Helen admired him for taking the time to include her. All of the extra hours she logged were paying off. She was being considered for advancement in the nursing ranks.

"Nurse Bernard, here are the remaining charts for the night," M.K. sang gleefully. "One of the attending doctors will be here by the time I'm showered and ready to hit the town. I've got a hot date, two of them," he boasted. "Maybe they'll let me take turns."

"Goodbye Dr. Phipps," the slim, dark brown-skinned nurse replied cordially. "You'd better watch yourself, though. Been having a rash of disease lately, the nighttime variety," she submitted for clarity sake.

"I ain't worrying, these are clean churchgoing girls. Twins."

"Not that it's any of my business, but churchgoing girls got to keep busy doing something when they ain't in church."

M.K. thought about it for a split second then frowned at the nurse. "You're right, it ain't your business. Good night, Nurse Bernard."

"Good night, Dr. Phipps," she answered, after he'd disappeared down the hall.

"Paging Dr. Phipps," a voice called out from the hospital intercom. "Dr. Phipps, please contact the emergency room nurse, right away."

Nurse Bernard chuckled when she heard M.K. yelling at the top of his lungs. *That's good for him. It's probably a stab wound that needs stitching but at least it'll help him keep his pants on.*

Neither of them had any idea that two men arrived after a nasty knife fight, both requiring complicated surgeries. Because M. K. was still listed as emergency room duty doctor when they were signed in, he was responsible to assist in their operations. Cursing profusely throughout, he stabilized their conditions and passed them on to his replacement. After showering and dressing on the fly, M.K. caught a cab to the Remington Hotel and sprinted up the side steps to suite number four-seventy-three, the room he had gone in on with Ollie.

Huffing and out of breath, he knocked on the door. "Come on, Ollie, open up," he said under his breath. "I need this, don't let me down." M.K. grew increasingly excited when he saw the doorknob being twisted from the other side. "Oh, yeah, that's it. Come on, man."

"Hi, ya, M.K.," Ollie mouthed in a tired tone, with a bed sheet tied around his waist. "What took you so long?"

"Damned that, where's Dora and Cora?" he asked, craning his neck to look inside the dimly lit room.

"We waited a couple of hours for you. Drinking, slow dancing and such," Ollie informed him, with sleep in his eyes. "They're still back there in the bed."

"Oh, yeah, that's good!" he howled, before being shushed.

"M.K., you're gonna have to keep it down. After all that tap dancing and then all that stuff we did together, they're plum tuckered out."

In disbelief that his luck was that bad, M.K. wanted to cry real tears. "Ollie, you telling me you had them both?"

"When you didn't show, I stepped in. I had Dora first and then Cora, I think that's how it went." Ollie appeared just as exhausted as the girls.

"Nahhh, you weren't with both of those beautiful girls at the exact same time?" M.K. whined, fearing he missed out on that kind of action.

"Hell, I had to, Cora got tired of watching. Man, I never knew such a petite little thing could be so greedy."

"Shoot me now, Ollie," he wailed. "Please hit me over the head with something heavy and put me out of my misery." Ollie stood there grinning, while M.K. kicked himself for being out-foxed by circumstance. He was just about to turn and walk away when he heard something in the back bedroom. M.K. pushed Ollie aside and then wandered a few paces past him. "What was that?"

"Sounds like the shower running to me," Ollie answered, with a raised brow. "It could be the beginning of round two."

"Ooh-wee, paging Dr. Phipps!" M.K. moaned hungrily. "I'll be right there. Do wait up. Hey, Ollie, send out for some sandwiches and soda pop. It's gonna be a long night. The doctor is in, and he's making house calls. Which of 'em did you say was the greedy one?"

19

A TWISTER'S COMING

Baltimore learned that Dinah worked the late shift at the hospital on Wednesdays, and he also knew it was Barker Sinclair's poker night, both providing him the perfect opportunity to work the crooked cop's wife into his busy schedule. Going on three weeks, he'd met her at his apartment and each time she grew more attached to his charming ways and sexual prowess. Baltimore was a tiger in the bedroom and Dixie had a bad case of jungle fever, a very bad case.

Over the past two days, Baltimore was haunted by the eerie feeling that someone was following him. As long as he didn't have to pump hot lead in Barker before he'd made some good money, he could deal with casting a long shadow even if it landed on someone else. When Baltimore stepped out of his apartment building, that someone emerged from his shadow and into the street light. An early model Dusenberg limousine rested along the curb with the motor running. Baltimore pretended to ignore it until the chauffeur leaned on the horn as he glided past. Before he opened his mouth to voice objections to being tooted at, the same square-shouldered brute from the Jewish mobster's mansion climbed out onto the city sidewalk and thumped a lit cigarette into the gutter.

"What?" Baltimore barked rudely. He contemplated going after the hired muscle but wasn't much in the mood for getting his clothes dirty. Besides, it would have been more trouble than it was worth to make a point, so Baltimore decided not to make a fuss.

"You're that Floyd guy, right?" the large thug asked. Considering how the two of them came extremely close to blows once before, Baltimore almost knocked him on his square behind for insinuating that all colored men looked alike.

"Maybe next time I'll leave you with something to help you remember me better," Baltimore answered instead.

"No disrespect, the light ain't so good," he lied. While Baltimore studied his expression for signs of insincerity, the back passenger side window of the expensive automobile lowered and a stubby white hand poked out to summon him over.

"I was starting to think you'd forgotten our agreement, Mr. Floyd," Schmitty Rosenberg grumbled, once Baltimore was seated inside. "It's been quite some time since you barged into my home claiming to organize a hefty fortune for me."

"For us," Baltimore said curtly. He appraised the rich man's fancy tuxedo and top hat resting on the seat before remembering how bothered he was by the surprised visit. "And I don't appreciate you coming around here laying for me. I told you what was going to happen and none of that's changed. I put my time in and it's about to pay off. By this time Friday, I'll deliver as promised." The brooding white man wanted to know Baltimore's strategy specifically, but that was not going to happen, since he'd just put the finishing pieces together courtesy of pillow talk with Dixie Sinclair. It didn't matter that she was sharing intricate details of her husband's business dealings. That woman would have gabbed all night long if Baltimore hadn't convinced her to get on home before Barker was finished with what he'd been up to.

"So far, Mr. Floyd, you've been all bark and no bite," Rosenberg complained. "I rather looked forward to having a ravenous wolf in my midst so don't disappoint me. By the way, I have secured that sizable item that you requested. It's parked at the landing near the waterfront, next to the drydock warehouse. You know the place?" When Baltimore nodded that he did, Mr. Rosenberg pulled out two black satin gloves to wrestle on his thick hands. "Good, then you have two days, or I'll send someone by to get your attention, and Mr. Floyd, you don't want that."

"Let me tell you what you don't want, Mr. Rosenberg, that's for me to get my dander up due to white folk hanging around my place. You'll get what's coming to you, I'll see to that."

"You, as well, will get what's coming to you," the mobster replied calmly. "*I* will see to that. Now, if you'll excuse me, I have tickets to the opera and I won't be late."

Baltimore found himself standing on the sidewalk, watching the European antique slip off into the night. If he hadn't already put in a call to a couple of associates he could count on, the situation might have gotten dicey. As luck would have it, two very capable operators were headed toward St. Louis on the northbound redeye, two men Baltimore trusted with his life.

The following morning, Baltimore was up at the crack of dawn. He pounded the decorative ceramic tile inside of Union Station until the schedule marquee changed. A company man dressed in a black and white uniform came around and changed the sign reading "On Time" to "Arrived" for the train from Kansas City. *Right on schedule,* Baltimore thought, as he marched out onto the platform to greet his partners in crime.

With a host of others, he stood patiently while passengers stepped down off the Midwest Express. Baltimore smiled big and wide when reliving the gambling room caper he pulled with a group of fellas he'd put together almost a year ago. The situation intensified when a hot-headed fool deviated from his plan and got himself shot after getting cocky. Subsequently, he was recognized by an off-duty Kansas City cop moonlighting as a security guard. Baltimore's smile evaporated when the thought of something like that happening again crossed his mind. He'd gotten away by the skin of his teeth and wasn't planning on going back to jail, not for anybody.

Pudge Gillis exited the train first. Seeing him dressed in a tailored suit caused Baltimore to swell up with laughter because Pudge, shorter than average height, had always worn his clothes a size too big like he expected to grow into them. The natty pale blue suit was a good look, he was a grown man wearing expensive clothes that actually fit him. Baltimore extended his hand to the nut-colored man with almond-shaped hazel eyes and gushed with joy. "Pudge, you're sharp as a tack and a sight for sore eyes."

"Hi ya, Baltimore. You don't look so bad yourself," said Pudge, carrying a small suitcase.

"Where's Dank?" Baltimore asked when the other man didn't appear immediately.

"Oh, he'll be off directly," Pudge answered, speaking of his traveling companion. "We dealt gin rummy most of the way, so he's probably on board try'na scrub off that whooping I put on him."

"Yeah, I'm still licking my wounds," admitted a tall, deep ebony-hued man with an athletic build. "Move outta the way, Pudge, so's I can shake my friend's hand."

"Dank Battle," Baltimore howled as the ex-boxer shook with him. "You look like a million dollars with a ham sandwich on the side."

Dank beamed at the compliment, then he ran his thumbs down the lapels of a brown colored wool-blend five button suit. "Yeah, but I lost my last three dollars to Pudge on the way up."

"Come on, fellas, I'm sure y'all could stand some grub and black coffee to pep you up," Baltimore assumed.

Pudge patted his full belly and sucked on his front teeth. "Naw, we caught a meal on that iron sled we just hopped off of. But I could use a bed big enough to swim in. It took some considerable effort to shake Dank's folding money from those giant mitts of his."

"Don't fret, I've worked all of that out," Baltimore assured them. "Let's head to the car and catch up before getting down to brass tacks. Boys, it sure is good to see y'all. I know Kansas City won't be the same while you're gone."

Dank chuckled, in step behind Pudge. "Huh, Kay Cee ain't been the same since you left," he offered with a wink. True, Baltimore had spent some time in their city and stole a few hearts while putting his hands on some very important men's money. He fled town leaving behind a lot of scorching memories and lovesick women. Unfortunately, he could never return without risking a murder rap for gunning down a pair of colored police-men in order to rescue Henry from their clutches. Both Dank and Pudge had difficulty believing it when Baltimore informed them how his ex-best friend was now very close to becoming a lawman himself. They viewed it as a ridiculous career move. After all, Henry had skirted the other side of the law too many times to go changing his ways, even for a woman as demanding as Roberta.

When the threesome reached the parking lot, Pudge admired a fancy cream-colored convertible. Being a lover of fine automo-biles, he was tempted to steal it until Baltimore explained that it was his car. Dank suggested Baltimore hide his keys when his back was turned, but Pudge reminded them he was an expert at boosting anything with wheels, that's why he was invited in on the heist. Dank was the brawn, quick on his feet and faster with his hands. Baltimore proved to be the valuable brains behind the outfit. Together, the trio was efficient and effective. They didn't need Henry for this one, not unless the house of cards collapsed on top of Baltimore's business venture.

The motel where he stashed the new arrivals was an out-of-the-way "Colored-Only" lodge off Aldine Avenue, a quiet stretch of road bordering "The Ville." Since Baltimore had procured a room with double beds and stocked the pantry with enough food to hold them over, there was nothing left to do but clue them in to the entire set up. "Let me lay it out for you, so you can sleep on it until I come back later this evening," Baltimore said, with the utmost sincerity. "Here's the long and short of it. There's a white cop running smack and supplying the local dealers."

"Aiche?" said Pudge, with a surprised expression. "You brung us up here to steal heroin? I don't mind a lot of things, but I ain't one to get too close to the pump."

"Me neither, but there's this man, a Jewish mobster, who's willing to pay a lot of money to get his paws on a major shipment. We're taking it not so's we can get involved in pushing that poison," answered Baltimore. "Our deal is sweeter than candy, so listen up and watch those cavities. All the smack pumping through these parts come from Mississippi or Chicago. Those Miss'sip boys got way too much fire power to take down, but it just so happens I got an inside track to the load rolling in from Chi-town. It's simple. We pull a snatch and grab, nice and easy-like, and y'all catch the next train with twenty grand each to play rummy with on the way home."

"Twenty thousand? Dollars?" Dank yelled eagerly. "Man, them's the kinda cavities I like. Hell, my teeth starting to hurt already. When can we get at that candy?"

"Hold your horses, Dank. I need everybody to be clear on a few things. First, I'll need Pudge to swipe a car this afternoon. Nothing too flashy, just sound enough to make it to Springfield, Illinois, 'cause that's where the drivers like to take a dinner break. We'll ditch the stolen car there and pick up another one on the way back. There's less of a chance to get pulled over with one on the hot list when you cross over state lines. Next thing, these white boys are crooked cops, so if it gets ugly, shoot to kill. We don't need state troopers spoiling our getaway. Now here's how it'll play out from there." Baltimore went on to share only the details he deemed necessary. Tell a man too much and he'll have too much to remember was his philosophy and he stuck to it.

At six o'clock sharp, Baltimore returned to motel to get the ball rolling. He left his car in the parking lot and rode away with the fellas in the Chevrolet Pudge had boosted from a nearby supermarket. They drove it to the three-ton cargo truck Schmitty Rosenberg provided by the Mississippi River landing, and then jumped on Route Fifty-Five North, headed toward Springfield. After the sun disappeared over the horizon Baltimore pulled into a service station and filled the gasoline tank to the brim. When they reached the outskirts of the small town, Pudge swapped stolen cars and waited near the roadside diner where the robbery was set to take place. He passed the newly acquired vehicle off to Baltimore, joined Dank in the truck and then waited. Baltimore pulled over on the shoulder of the highway and kept an eye out for a St. Louis squad car traveling south. He couldn't afford getting too close to the jack point and risk the chance of Barker recognizing him beforehand.

A little after an hour of watching cars whiz by, a police car roared past with two white men inside. Baltimore went to start up the Buick Pudge had pinched when they hit Springfield, but it wouldn't turn over. "Come on, you raggedy death trap!" he cursed. "Come on and crank for your ole buddy Baltimore." He continued rubbing the ignition wires together to kick it over, while peering up at the road. Just as the police car drifted out of sight, the second-hand car fired up. "Yeah, baby, yeah!" he cheered. "Let's go get that candy." The vehicle sputtered and spun its tires until eventually lurching onto the road.

Baltimore gunned the motor and gave chase. He appeared across the highway from the roadside diner just as Barker Sinclair sat down to a cup of coffee. His partner and Henry's ride-a-long superior, Tasman Gillespie, took his seat at the booth near the front window so he could watch the patrol car. As Barker headed for the restroom to relieve himself, Gillespie flirted with the busty waitress like he always did on the way back to the city. Baltimore waved a yellow handkerchief out of his passenger side window to alert his crew it was time to move.

Gillespie didn't give it too much thought when a large cargo truck rolled off the highway into the tiny lot, although it momentarily blocked his vision of the police car. He glanced at the muscle-bound colored man who'd climbed out of it, seemingly to test the tire pressure on the driver's side. Gillespie had no idea that some-one else was working feverishly at hotwiring his ride home. It wasn't until the truck had ventured back onto the thoroughfare that he hopped up from table, screaming his head off. As if it had disappeared into thin air, the patrol car and their shipment van-ished into the night.

Barker flew out of the restroom, zipping up his pants and ready to strangle his partner for letting a trunk full of uncut heroin out of his sight. Within minutes, he was on the phone to St. Louis telling an interested party what had happened. Officer Brandish agreed to set up a net along the highway with designs on captur-ing the men driving Gillespie's department-issued vehicle when they re-entered the city limits. Barker realized the car had to be headed south because Chicago was one hundred and ninety-eight miles away. The thieves would need a big city to fence that large amount of drugs and St. Louis was the closest.

Brandish's men could have searched the highway for days and found nothing. Dank had lowered a ramp a few miles up the road from the diner and Pudge drove the missing patrol car into the cargo compartment and locked it down tight. Once it was se-cured, Baltimore followed them into town, past the weary eyes of officers taking dirty money for their dirty deeds.

By morning, Brandish had relayed the bad news that Gille-spie's police car never resurfaced. Barker's blood boiled when it occurred to him someone in his inner circle was responsible for him losing a two-hundred-thousand-dollar load of smack. Some-one was going to die over the betrayal. There were no two ways about it. Retribution was imminent and lightning was destined to strike, just as Etta predicted.

20

BENT WISHES AND BAR STOOLS

It happened Thursday while Baltimore slept. Barker Sinclair, Tasman Gillespie and that fat mule Officer Tom Brandish met to decide two things, how to get their stolen shipment of heroin back and how overt their attack would be when going about it. After an early morning meeting, each of the men reported to duty so as not to draw any attention. Besides, going into work provided the perfect cover they needed to shake a lot of trees and pass it off as aggressive community policing.

On the last day of the trainee ride-alongs, Barker started out on a wild tear. He visited several of his smack dealers in colored neighborhoods before heading toward the other side of town to rattle a number of upscale cages. Henry sat back quietly, counting the hours until the shift was over. He was eagerly anticipating the cadets' graduation scheduled for the following afternoon. If he could somehow remain calm and keep his thoughts to himself, he would become one of the first Negro police officers in the city's history. While spending countless hours watching Barker and Gillespie terrorize the neighborhood he grew up in, he felt the clock wasn't ticking nearly fast enough. He didn't feel relaxed until they crossed the railroad tracks. Even though Henry couldn't decipher exactly what had the two rogue officers in a very bad mood, he knew it wouldn't likely change as long as they hadn't come up with a solution to their problem.

During their third stop on the list of Barker's white dealers, he and Gillespie left Henry in the car to drop in on a pool hall owner who'd made the mistake of complaining about losing money due to a skittish supply of drugs. His grievance was met with hostility and a rash of violent threats. "I don't give a damn what you have to do, Marty," Barker grunted, inside the man's office. "We're all in a pinch and it'll be at least a week before I can get my hands on some more unless . . ." he began to explain before catching himself. Business in the streets was already unsettling, and steadily declining. Telling his pushers how he'd gotten ripped off would cost him credibility in a hustle built on reputation and the ability to deliver. "Anyway, you see to it that your stash carries you through the weekend."

Marty was shaking, partly because Barker had him by eight inches and thirty pounds. The squirrelly pipsqueak was a long-time junkie as well. He didn't have it in mind to share what little heroin he did have with his customers. "But I can't cut it no more," the scared pool hawk debated, against his better judgment. "I've stripped it down once as it is. If I sift it again, it won't go right and my neck will be on the line."

"Listen, you slimy little toad!" Barker yelled. "I know for a fact you've stepped on my deliveries twice when your pool tournaments lasted two days, so don't go screwing with me now. Just do what I tell you and we'll all come out on top when the smoke blows over." What Barker assumed was correct. Marty had secretly created a slush fund to facilitate serving his own habit. He mixed in as many additives as he could get away with as it was. Stripping the chemical content further was sure to render it unfit for human consumption, but going against psychotic cops meant a certain death sentence. Marty reluctantly agreed and did what he was told.

More than a few minutes had passed while Gillespie and his drug boss puttered inside the pool hall harassing Marty. Henry's frustration took a toll on him. Against departmental policy, he got out of the squad car to stretch his legs. He pondered over the things he'd observed while trying to piece them together. It was unnerving to watch his mentors' nasty dispositions spiral out of control since the day began with Gillespie filing a false report to the shift commander about having the police car he'd signed out stolen from his front driveway. None of it made sense at the time so Henry pushed it to the back of his cluttered thoughts and said to hell with it, when suddenly he heard a man bellow loudly as glass shattered behind him. Henry ducked his head and cautiously turned toward the noise, expecting to see some poor soul come crashing through the pool hall window. Instead, the action was coming from somewhere farther down the sidewalk. A white man dressed in a soiled warehouseman's jumpsuit sprinted from the jewelry store with a cloth sack hanging from his hand. "Stop him!" the immigrant jeweler wailed in Henry's direction. "Police! Police!" he shouted frantically.

Every bit of moisture vanished from Henry's mouth when he realized the man was begging him to foil the robbery. He was for all intents and purposes on duty to uphold the law. Without waiting for Gillespie to join in the chase, Henry took off after the thief on foot. He mentally replayed all of the drills from the academy regarding the correct methods in apprehending criminals. As Henry grew nearer to the man who was running short on enthusiasm and gasping for breath, Gillespie and Barker exited through Marty's front entrance just in time to catch a glimpse of the pursuit in progress.

"Where the hell is he going?" Barker questioned, casually viewing Henry close fast on the suspect. "Dammit, let's go see what he's gotten himself into." They sprinted for their vehicles parked at the far curb and barreled down the street after them.

"Stop, police!" Henry growled bitterly but the thief kept on running. "Stop or I'll shoot," he managed, short of breath himself. Henry nearly tripped over the man when he actually gave in and threw his hands up. "All right now, don't move. Don't you move an inch!" The man peeked behind him, fearing that the copper just might make good on the threat to fire at him. When he saw a colored man with his gun drawn, the robber chuckled and then started down a narrow passageway. Annoyed when it appeared he might have to scurry after the man again, Henry took out his night stick. He flung it at the crook's legs like he'd practiced a million times. His eyes widened when it worked to perfection, causing the jewel thief to stumble. As he lay sprawled out on the cement groveling painfully, Henry had the last laugh. "Ah-huh, I bet it ain't so funny now. I got you, sucker. Yeah, I got you."

When the veteran cops located them, Henry was walking his captive out of the alley with abrasions on his face and a nice set of handcuffs to replace the diamond bracelets he'd made off with. *Just wait until the boys hear about my first arrest,* Henry thought, *just wait. I'll finish at the top of the class behind this.* No sooner than he'd patted himself on the back, Barker tore into him with venom dripping from his twisted mouth.

"Have you lost your goddamned mind, boy?" he shouted at Henry, followed by fast violently strides. "What do you think you're doing?"

"What?" Henry answered, as proud of himself as a man could be. "I know I'm not full-fledged 'til tomorrow, but I figured I'd get a head start when I seen this man trying to make off with this bag of loot. It took some doing but I caught him, got him good too. Took this knife off him myself," Henry gloated, showing off the long blade he confiscated single-handedly.

"Naw, what I mean is what do you think you're doing putting your hands on a white man like that?" Barker reprimanded. "Hand him over to me and don't you ever go after anybody that ain't as black as you. Damned spook's as dumb as dirt, I swear. What are they teaching y'all at the academy these days?"

The man Henry risked his life to apprehend lifted his head

and spat in his captor's face. "Ain't no nigger hauling me off to jail," he reveled smugly. "I'd die first."

"Next time you'll get your wish," Henry whispered under his breath as Barker marched the man he'd arrested back to his unmarked car.

"Talk to your boy," Barker told Gillespie, just as he drove away with the criminal locked down in the back seat.

"Don't you say nothin' to me," Henry warned, as they followed closely behind Barker's car to the station house. It was difficult to watch another man taking the credit for his hard work.

"Are you threatening to get something off your chest, Cadet Taylor?" Gillespie snapped back.

"Ain't no threats, Gillespie, just a heads up," he answered plainly. "You go on ahead and push me. I'm ready to push back."

"It ain't too late to blackball your coon ass, you know."

"With what I know about you and Detective Sinclair, I reckon we'll all get what's owed us. Think on that before you go running your mouth over me." Henry had been pushed to his limit whether he knew it then or not. Baltimore's words rang in his head until he shook them out. "They ain't gone let you wrestle in no white boys, just colored criminals and runaway dogs. They should've had you take the dog catcher test!" Henry had seen Baltimore beat a man to death with his bare hands during a heated conversation gone wrong, now he was wishing someone had knocked some sense into him. What Barker had put on him hurt a lot worse than a busted lip and left much deeper bruising. By the end of the day, Henry was forced to second guess his decision to join the force and reexamine himself as a man.

As the sun faded into the landscape, Delbert loitered outside of the superintendent's office. He had been having dinner with M.K. and Ollie, laughing it up about the scheme they pulled with the carnival contest and how much fun it was congratulating the winners when Hiram Knight stormed into the dining hall demanding M.K.'s presence immediately. The party ended abruptly as Dr. Knight sneered down his nose and then breathed fire from it.

Almost an hour had passed and still M.K. hadn't returned to the residence dorms for a game of poker with the fellows, so Delbert went looking for him. "Nurse Bernard, have you seen Dr. Phipps? He took off with Dr. Knight and no one's seen hide nor hair of him since."

Willie B.'s wife Helen glanced up from her evening report and smile amicably. "Sorry, Dr. Gales, but I haven't seen him since he signed out for dinner. You might want to check the third floor, either the tub room or the soiled linens closet. That's where he usually takes that second-year nursing student he's sweet on. If he don't watch his step, he's liable to help her get booted but good." Helen drew a line through several items on her report, before continuing. "Poor girl can't see for dreaming. She's missed curfew so many times, Knight's probably been getting an earful from Nursing Director Robinson and is passing it on down the line."

Delbert had his suspicions that M.K. was keeping time with one of the young ladies from the nursing program, but that confirmed it. He thanked Helen and then wandered up to the third floor and searched the hiding places she mentioned. When his friend hadn't turned up in either of them, Delbert felt compelled to hang around until M.K. finished taking a tongue lashing from the chief.

"M.K., this is not what I expected out of you, son," Dr. Knight scolded him, with his hand on his star resident's shoulder. "Well, it is what it is, I guess. Crying over spilt milk won't help the situation, but I know one thing that will. There's nothing left to do now but buying the cow," he concluded, much to M.K.'s chagrin.

"No, please don't put that on me, Dr. Knight. I can't marry that girl, I'm-I'm already hitched, sir," he lied.

Hiram frowned while picking up the telephone. "We'll let's just see about that. Operator, get me Washington D.C., the home of Mr. and Mrs. Walter D. Phipps. Yes, ma'am, I'll hold." He sat his bony behind down on the corner of his desk, glaring at M.K.

"Please don't call my folks with this, Dr. Knight, I'm begging you. Please."

"Don't you try to make me out a pigeon, boy. Come clean and take it like the man who's been up that nurse's skirt on the regular."

Dr. Knight waited to be connected. M.K. paced worriedly. "O.K., O.K., I'm not married, but I don't want to be either. Can't we do anything about this before it goes too far?"

"Sorry, ma'am, wrong number," the wise old surgeon said into the phone receiver before placing it back on the cradle. "First off, you lied to me and I can't stand a liar. Second, the girl says she's carrying your child, so it's already gone too far. What the hell did you think was gonna happen after sliding that rusty thang of yours between her legs every chance you got? The only people who act in such a reckless way are no less than fools . . . or parents. You have effectively worked your way into both categories."

"Yes, sir," was all that M.K. could say on the matter. Dr. Knight ordered him to propose to the young lady after shopping for a wedding ring. He was given a two-hour break to facilitate his responsibilities, quick, fast, and in a hurry. Once sharing the dreadful news with Delbert, neither of them felt like shooting the bull over poker. M.K. asked that Delbert not mention a word about his plight until he'd had the chance to follow Knight's strict directions. He had changed out of his uniform into street clothes and disappeared before Delbert blinked twice. Feeling terrible about the young couple's dilemma, he called up Sue Jacobs at her parent's house and asked if she was available for a late movie. Unfortunately for him and M.K., she agreed to meet him downtown.

With both hands stuffed in his pockets, an old acquaintance of M.K.'s followed closely behind him while he pounded the pavement in search of solitude. He was convinced he had shaken it once and for all after his enlistment in the Army medical corps ended but there it was again circling him like a bothersome fly. The urge was so great that it caused M.K.'s head to spin. Although a few stiff drinks wouldn't make it stop, he had to slow the merry-go-round which had become his life. Ms. Etta's was open, so he slinked inside to get a handle on his misery.

21

DIRTY DANCING

For a weeknight, the joint was hopping, but then again end-of-the month paychecks were rolling in by the dozens. Etta enjoyed Baltimore cutting up like he did in the old days, when money came easy and Henry was alongside him to help spend it. Despite only recently meeting Pudge and Dank, she could tell they enjoyed being around Baltimore as much as she did. He knew how to be downright engaging when he wanted to. The fact that M. K. dropped in to party with him made it that much easier to watch.

"Penny, look at them," Etta said, wiping down shot glasses behind the bar. "They put me in the mind of a pack of boy children showing off while mama's away."

"Sho' do, Ms. Etta. I can't remember Mr. Baltimore laughing and carrying on since before all of the colored police business kicked up. It's a grand sight to see him like that." Penny had learned a lot about life and how grownups sometimes experienced highs and lows from seeing them down on their luck and searching for answers in the bottom of whiskey bottles. Seeing Baltimore and his buddys pal around seemingly without a care in the world reaffirmed that adult life wasn't all bad, all the time, either. It occurred to her the best parts of it were spent with good friends over a hearty laugh. That was really living.

The ladies relished what appeared to be an impenetrable bond until Blinky the shoeshine boy hustled in through the front door. "Mi-Ms. Etta, I-I-I needs to-to-talk-to-Mistah-Ba-Baltimore. It's private," he said, with pleading eyes.

Etta folded her arms and squinted her peepers at him in a suspicious manner. "Blinky, didn't I tell you to stay away from here until the weekend? You have school work and I don't want to get into it with your pa again."

"Yeah-yeah I know," he said rapidly. "Bu-but this-here diff'rent. I-I-I gots a me-message for him." Blinky held a folded note up for Etta to see, thinking that just might change her stance on his making a few pennies. Wisely, the boy conveniently forget to mention that a white lady parked at the corner store paid him a whole dollar to hand deliver the note.

"Go 'head on, then," Etta conceded. "I guess it must be important, but soon after you get on home and 'tend to your lessons."

Gushing with unbridled excitement, the boy smiled thank you and then scampered off to deliver the message. Once he found Baltimore, Blinky yanked on his suit coat sleeve. "Th-this lady t-told-me to carry this over to-to you." Baltimore leaned back in his chair to listen as the boy whispered something he didn't think should have been overheard by the others. Baltimore flashed an impish grin, handed Blinky a silver dollar and sent him away. That was the fastest two bucks he ever made and still had time to get home and finish his school work.

Baltimore looked over the note before tucking it away inside his breast pocket. *Meet me at your place. I want to see you immediately. Please hurry. D. Sinclair.* After finishing his bottle of cream soda, Baltimore apologized for having to dash out. "Fellas, I'm going to call it an early night. Got a little something needs my attention," he told them, insinuating that little something was a woman.

"She must be in a powerful need at that," Dank jested, "to be ordering out for it?"

"Yeah, don't forget to send up a note if you find yourself getting outdone," Pudge offered, from the other side of a stiff jigger of gin. "Heck, send up a patch of smoke signals if you can't find no paper." All of the men laughed out loud. M.K. was having such a great time, he'd forgotten about his woman troubles, hunting for engagement rings and being due back to the hospital for the remainder of his shift. After another couple of drinks, he'd forget himself altogether.

Baltimore had excused himself and said goodbye to Penny and Etta before hitting the door to answer a peculiar note sent by another man's persistent two-timing wife. Dank and Pudge carried on about the beautiful women they missed attending to back in Kansas City while M.K. pretended his old habit hadn't begun to itch. When he saw Gussy coming in from the back alley, he got up from the table with more than half a mind to scratch it. "Hey, Gus', I need to bend your ear a minute," he said, darting his eyes at the same door the hefty bartender had just walked through. "Let's talk out there." Right away, Gussy recognized the glint in M.K.'s eyes.

"A lil' chat's gonna cost you."

"I got enough to whisper at you," M.K. answered, slipping two dollars in the man's thick paws.

"Hey, fool, not in here. Come on out yonder and see what the speaker's got to say."

M.K. followed him into the rear of the busy nightspot. Gussy stepped outside and raised a tin trashcan lip to get at an ordinary brown paper sack. Inside of it was a hypodermic needle, a bent spoon and other drug paraphernalia. He looked at M.K. and shrugged. "You one of them doctors, ain't you? Never figured you for a hype-head," the bartender said crassly. The offhanded comment didn't go unnoticed. M.K.'s hands trembled as Gussy prepared a measure of smack to cook on the spoon.

"Uh-huh, it takes one to know one," M.K. responded in the same rude tone he'd been insulted with. "It's been a while since me and this bitch danced but I'm feeling kinda lonesome."

"Oh, she's wicked," Gussy replied, behind a devious grin.

"After y'all get reacquainted, take your time coming back in. Ms. Etta finds out about this, she'll have my ass in a sling."

M.K. made a fist and tied the rubber hose, constricting his favorite vein. His eyes rolled back in his head when the heroin raced through it. "Ahhh, there she is. Oomph. Whewww. Baby, I'm back." M.K. leaned against the wall, fading into another world where drug fiends traveled to the other side, the dangerously dark side.

Gussy sneered at him, languishing there both helpless and hapless. "Look at what you done got yourself into. That's a mean . . . mean bitch. Ride her good now. Don't let her buck you." There was no room to pity M.K. because she had Gussy strung along too.

Penny teased the bartender when he returned after a long stint away from his post. "Gussy, Ms. Etta had me come look for you. She say, if your breaks get any longer we's got to find us another somebody to bother when things is slow."

"Good, the missing link done found his way back," Etta heckled him from her office door. "Gus, mind the bar so Penny can run upstairs for some extra ashtrays and matchbooks."

"Yes, ma'am," he answered assuredly. "I ain't going nowhere."

"Hurr'up, Penny, it's liable to spill over tonight. Folk's will be huffing and a puffing."

Penny pointed her finger at Gussy, insisting he stay put. He threw his hands up like a father playing along to appease his child. "You've been up to something," she said peculiarly. "I don't know what, yet. But you' been acting funny lately."

"Well, that makes us a fine pair because you *look* funny all the time," he teased right back.

"Forget you, Gussy, I ain't stud'n you right now, no how," she jested. "You just wait. After I fetch those boxes, I'm a have at you some more."

The burly teddy bear suddenly felt sick to his stomach but didn't want Penny to notice his discomfort. "Go on now. I'll be right here hankering to fight with you, too."

Penny shook her fist jokingly on the way up the side stairs. She continued smiling when she opened the storeroom door with her master key. Curiosity called her near the window, where she'd watched Baltimore make love to several women. Penny didn't feel like a snoop, well not exactly. She viewed it as an education in womanhood to learn how lovemaking was supposed to pan out, what sounds to make when doing it and approximately how long it was supposed to last. School was still in because Baltimore acted differently with each of the ladies he treated to that love den of his. He took his time with Dinah and let her stay the night, Penny remembered, but he always seemed to be in a terrible rush when the white woman slipped by for adult entertainment.

Penny placed her hand over her mouth and giggled when she spied on Baltimore with Dixie Sinclair, who was opening the window and pulling down on the shade to hide her indiscretions. "Huh, you'd better get what you want before he do, white lady," Penny murmured, "'cause he'll be sending you back to wherever you come from if he finishes moaning first. That's a fact." She leaned closer to the window to see what else there was to spy but someone turned the lights out inside the room, impeding her from seeing anything worth looking in on. Anyway, Penny was on the clock and raring to get back at clowning around with Gussy.

Back on the bottom floor she sat both small boxes on the bar. Her sparring partner wasn't anywhere to be seen, but she had a good idea where to find him. It occurred to Penny she'd better poke her head in the office to tell Etta about her mission to locate the absent bartender and subsequently give him a friendly piece of her mind. "Gussy, you somewhere's about?" Penny yelled out of the back door. She looked in both directions, without seeing a soul. No one answered. Then, there was movement in the trash heap stacked along the wall beside her. Startled, Penny lurched backward. "Ahhh! Who's there?" she screamed, in response to an unrecognizable gargling sound. Sensing that someone or something was hurt, she wrapped both hands around a broom handle which she'd used to sweep out the passageway many times. Cautiously, she nudged at the heap against the wall. "Gussy, that bet' not be you playing a mean trick on me, or else I'm a tell Ms. Etta."

"Help me," a strained voice pleaded. "Please help me." A closer look revealed M.K. huddled over in immense agony.

"Oh, shoot," she winced. "Mistah M.K., what's happened to you? Don't move. I'll get Ms. Etta. She'll know what to do." Penny flew into the night club and pounded on the office door. "Ms. Etta, open up!" No one answered back so the girl used her key to gain entry. What her eyes found was disturbing. After one glance at Gussy lying face down on the floor with foam bubbling from his mouth, Penny assumed the men's ailments were somehow connected. "Not you too, Gussy," she whined.

"Shut that door, Penny," Etta ordered solemnly, her eyes trained on the massive lump of flesh. "We done called the ambulance but ain't no use now and I couldn't find that M.K. friend of Baltimore's nowhere to help out. Ain't never a doctor around when you need one."

Softly, Penny explained why that happened to be the case. "That's what I came to tell you. Mistah M.K. is crumpled up in the alley saying he needs a whole mess of help. Ms. Etta, he looks near about as bad as . . ." Penny couldn't bring herself say the fallen bartender's name.

"Come, chile. Show me where to find him," she said firmly.

With Penny leading the way, Etta grabbed Dank and Pudge from their table to assist. Sirens in the distance became alarmingly closer as Etta worked at reviving the young physician.

"Looks to me like he's been poisoned," Penny guessed. "It must be eating at him from the inside."

Dank pushed M.K.'s sleeves up to his elbows. He discovered a fresh needle mark on one of them and a trail of dried blood as well. "Yeah, it's poison all right, the evilest kind at that."

"Maybe you ought to send the girl back in to tell those meat wagon fellas where to find us," Pudge suggested.

"No, no medics," M.K. grunted painfully. "Find Delbert . . .

Dr. Gales or Helen . . . Nurse Bernard at the hospital. Oooh . . . get them. Please."

"I know 'em," said Etta, "That's the boyish looking Texas doctor and Willie B.'s wife. She works over at Homer Gee. Penny, mind the bar and if Baltimore comes around, tell him what happened."

"Ain't no need for that," Penny replied. "There he is right over yonder."

Baltimore appeared behind them wearing an opened dress shirt, slacks and a mean unrelenting grimace. He'd put the gun away when stumbling onto a collection of his friends instead of a would-be attacker molesting Penny. "I heard you scream," he said, staring at her like she was a blood relative. "Who's that stretched out?" he asked before investigation for himself.

"That friend of yours," answered Penny. "Mistah M.K., he's sick as a dog."

Without hesitation, Baltimore rushed to his side. "What's happened to him?" he asked feverishly, while checking his torso for stab wounds or worse. When discovering what Dank had moments earlier, Baltimore's heart sank. "Dammit, M.K., you said you'd let loose of that fix on smack. Said you licked it."

"It started . . . hmmm . . . fighting back," he said, before a swarm of laborious convulsions took hold of him.

"This is just what I need," Etta fussed. "Hell, I got two hypes on my hands. Carry him on upstairs and the ambulance can take Gussy back with them, I guess, since he don't want to go." Etta was afraid that more trouble would show itself that night. Her intuition didn't let her down.

"M.K. can't show up to the hospital like this," Baltimore agreed. "They'll sack him sure as shooting."

"We were just about to send for Delbert and Willie B.'s wife Helen. M.K. said to," she added, before Baltimore began to question her motives. "I can't have my customers seeing him strung out like this, so you'd better bring him up the back stairs and put him in one of the cozy'n rooms."

M.K. hollered out when the men began moving him. Dank had no choice but to shut him up so he popped him in the jaw with a right cross to sedate him during transport. "I didn't mean nothing by it, Baltimore," he explained, just to be on the safe side.

"I know you didn't, Dank. Carry him up to bed. I'll head out and wrangle Delbert and Helen. Try to keep M.K. calm so he don't hurt himself."

Penny refused to linger behind when Baltimore started toward his car. She said there wasn't a thing she could do at the Fast House but worry and she was never any good at that. Not taking no for an answer, Penny jumped in the car and suggested he had better get going.

Baltimore checked with Ollie and the guys playing poker but no one had seen Delbert for hours. Penny had better luck finding Helen. She was seconds from signing out and didn't want to believe a budding surgeon like Dr. M.K. Phipps had succumbed to dangerous street drugs. Even though Baltimore explained how M.K. had been on the straight and narrow for quite a while, the nurse didn't feel any better about his choices in life. She was skeptical that anything could be done if it wasn't already too late. There had been a rash of overdose victims arriving at the hospital that evening and the same was happening at white hospitals across town, Helen informed them, adding that not many of those patients made it.

There was a twin bed in the upstairs room at Ms. Etta's where M.K. struggled for dear life, two wooden folding chairs, a small dresser and a wash basin. Helen sent Baltimore down to the kitchen for a loaf of bread and black coffee as soon as she laid eyes on him. "He'll be needing some food on his stomach. I'll be needing the coffee to keep me awake and alert."

Predicting they were in for a long night, Baltimore stopped into Etta's office to place a call. He reached the registration desk, managed to get patched up to speak with Ollie, but still no Delbert. After Dank had completely blown his buzz, he and Pudge lit out for the motel, sulking. Once they were off, Baltimore watched the coffee pot percolate in the back of the kitchen area of the club. As if it was choreographed by an elderly band leader, time marched on slowly.

22

CRAWFISHES

With the grim reaper tucked in his pocket, Willie B. Bernard busted in the front door hollering for his wife, wearing contempt on his face because she'd sneaked off with Baltimore and Penny while he waited outside of the hospital for her. Willie B. said he felt like a fool having a wife running around with another man. Etta tried to explain but he had his mind set on wreaking havoc. Seeing that he wouldn't listen, she ran to the kitchen area to get Baltimore. Several of Etta's customers shrieked when three shots rang out upstairs. *Bang! Bang! bang!*

Penny flew down the staircase, frightened, saddened and shaking her head the entire way. "It's that undertaker's son. He's shooting up the room with Mistah M.K. and that nurse lady."

Baltimore rushed past her with a full head of steam. He sprinted up the stairs so fast his feet barely touched any of them. Willie B.'s black revolver was still smoking as Baltimore entered the room with his pistol drawn. Offering no resistance, the shooter wore a vacant expression that spoke volumes. "They had it coming," he told Baltimore. "I figured she was giving it to one of them doctors. You can't blame me for doing what a husband's got the right to. I told Henry 'n 'em what'd happen if it came to this. I told 'em."

Out of his periphery, Baltimore saw M.K. move his fingers after taking one slug to the chest. He snatched Willie B.'s gun from his hand and sent him downstairs. "Wait on the police, they'll want to talk to you, but this man is still alive. I'm taking him over to Homer G. Phillips myself. Get in my way and you'll join your wife directly." The man was understandably shaken but was more than coherent enough to know what that meant so he stepped aside agreeably.

Baltimore hoisted M.K. in his arms and staggered with him out to his convertible. "Come on, M.K.!" he cried, when his friend lost consciousness. "Hang in, just a tick longer." He maneuvered his roadster through the emergency room loading dock and leaned on the horn until two white-jacketed orderlies raced out with a gurney.

"We'll take it from here," one of them shouted at Baltimore.

"The hell you will," he objected. "He's a pal of mine. I'm coming with him."

"If you really care for him, you'll let us get him inside with the doctors."

As soon as they entered the emergency room area, the attending nurse called out to the men wheeling the gurney passed. "What you got there?"

"A gun shot wound, male, around twenty-seven."

"I'll call for the surgeon on duty. Hold on a minute." The nurse ran her finger across the schedule and read the name of the attending emergency room doctor for the evening. "Paging Dr. Phipps," she announced over the public address system. "Paging Dr. M.K. Phipps to the ER dock."

Dr. Hiram Knight sucked on the moist end of an expensive cigar as he marched up to the check-in nurse. "Don't tell me M.K. isn't back on duty yet?"

In an effort to comfort the man who'd just been wheeled in, the nurse stood from her desk and circled it. When she saw the patient's face and his clothes soaked with blood, she lowered her head. "Sorry, Dr. Knight, but Dr. Phipps won't be reporting this evening."

The chief surgeon followed her eyes to the victim's face. He rushed to check his vitals, but there was no pulse, no signs of life whatsoever. M.K.'s eyes were opened, still and gazing up at nothing at all. Painstakingly, Dr. Knight pulled the sheet over his protégé's head. He took a deep breath and choked back on the thought of sending that young man to his death. "My God," he sighed. "Please have mercy on us all."

Baltimore remained at the hospital for hours after M.K. was pronounced dead on arrival and taken to the morgue in the basement. A shockwave spread throughout Homer G. Phillips. Nurses gathered to comfort one another and console the young lady who had a baby to carry without a man to help raise it. Baltimore ran down what happened to Delbert and the surgery director. However, he conveniently left out the incriminating details of M.K.'s drug overdose, merely stating that the doctor was too sick to be moved and implied he'd experienced a severe bout of food poisoning. Baltimore went on to explain that when the nurse's jealous husband heard that she'd sped away for Ms. Etta's, he was enraged and immediately assumed the worst. Helen was leaning over M.K. trying to hold him still when Willie B. broke the door down. Imagining how it must have appeared, Baltimore couldn't fault him one bit. He'd have done the same if snared by a similar set of circumstances.

Exhausted and visibly disturbed, Baltimore wandered out to his car. Dinah emerged from a city cab, wearing something she'd thrown on and a stunned expression. The phone call she had received from Delbert sent her rambling out of her apartment dazed and dismayed. "Honey, I'm sorry," she said, clinging to Baltimore's shirt, stained beyond repair. "Baltimore, it's terrible, I know, but Delbert told me there was nothing you could do. He's a doctor and he was friends with M.K. too."

"You shouldn't have come out this late alone, Dinah," was his somber response. "It'll be dangerous around here for a while. Get in, I'm taking you home."

"Okay, honey, okay," she cried. "Whatever you say." Dinah never did care for the way Willie B. treated Helen, always accusing her of tipping out on him. The nurses used to laugh about it on their dinner breaks because they knew how loyal she was. Helen thought her husband's jealous insecurity was adorable and a stark indication of his love. "He loves me so much it makes him sick sometimes," she'd say. "He don't mean nothing by it, just can't help hisself." Dinah reflected on that while Baltimore collapsed on her bed and drifted off to sleep.

"Yeah, Helen, you were right," she heard herself say quietly. "That man loved you too much for your own good. Don't fret. You're with the angels now. Go on and rest. Put in a word for me if you can." Dinah propped a pillow against Baltimore and nestled beside him. She wondered what he meant about expecting danger to abound. Why would he get such a ridiculous notion like that?

Friday morning came too fast for Dinah to arise and greet it. She was asleep when it arrived, but her man had up and gone.

"Get yourselves together," Baltimore grunted into the phone receiver once he'd driven back to his apartment building. "I'm a be there in 'bout an hour. We got to turn some corners and I mean fast."

Pudge yawned wearily. "Sure, whatever's clever. Are we about to settle up with that Jew gangster?"

"Yeah, and I ain't in the mood to be crawfished neither. We'll need a work van to cinch it. Pick one up and I'll tell you all about it when I get there."

Baltimore sat on the edge of his bed, cleaning both of his pistols and loading them to the gills. He had a bad feeling about sticking around town, so he plotted a prompt escape while he showered and changed clothes. The colored radio station blasted the story about M.K.'s homicide, reporting that the shooter was one of the police trainees due to graduate later that day. The announcer also went on to say that Willie B. had been arrested for murder and awaited his fate in the county lockup. It was difficult for Baltimore to feel sorry for him, so he didn't bother faking it.

By the time Dank had gotten dressed and his hands on something to eat, Pudge was returning to the motel with a newly acquired green panel van. The words *Piedmont Yard Services* were stenciled on the side of it in white lettering. "What are we supposed to do with that?" Dank inquired, poking his head out of the motel room door.

"Don't rightly know, but Baltimore says we need it and that's good enough for me," Pudge answered. "That appears to be him pulling up now. You can ask him yourself when he gets out."

"Naw, he still looks mighty upset about last night and that doctor friend of his getting all shot up. I'll hold off 'til he comes out with it on his own."

Baltimore didn't waste any time filling them in on the next order of business. His plan was simple and to the point. The men expected it to be fairly simple to follow but were caught by surprise when he handed them boarding tickets for the evening train back to Kansas City. "Don't nobody but Etta know y'alls' with me and I aim to keep it that a way," he told them. "So I can't carry you over to Union Station once we settle up and split. You'll have a stack of bills to roll with so catch a cab afterwards, catch a meal, and if you have time stop by a cat house on your way out, catch yourselves some mattress bass." Dank really liked the sound of that and Pudge wasn't too far behind him. Both of them had been hankering for female companionship.

"Good, I'm glad we all see eye to eye," Baltimore said, a mere hint of a smile on his mouth. "But first, here is the address and directions to the place I need y'all to sit on a while. Get there right at a quarter to ten and not a second before. Park on the street for fifteen minutes and then meet me back here. If somebody tries to tail you, shake them first." Once again, Baltimore didn't divulge what their part was in the scheme, only what their duties involved. It always worked out better that way and there was no reason to go fixing something that wasn't broken.

Much like the time before, Baltimore's car was searched when he approached the wealthy mobster's estate. He'd called ahead and told Schmitty Rosenberg that the heroin he'd swiped from Barker Sinclair was on its way. Baltimore also warned that under no uncertain terms should he try to back out of their deal. The mobster laughed but Baltimore failed to see the humor in it. In a matter of minutes, Rosenberg would as well.

"Hand me the bag and come on in," demanded the big goon when Baltimore walked through the spacious entranceway.

"I'm not turning this over until I'm square with Schmitty," Baltimore declared, stone-faced and steady.

"Stay put then. I'll tell *Mr. Rosenberg* you're here." The hired thug gave Baltimore a thorough once over.

"What you stalling for? Run and tell him, unless there's something you need to get off your chest first?" Baltimore exchanged his icy stare with one of his own until the thug blinked first. "And tell *Schmitty* I ain't got all day." Although it only took a few minutes before he got the O.K. to meet with the boss in his enormous den, it felt like eternity and then some.

"Mr. Floyd, wonders never cease," was Rosenberg's peculiar salutation. He was sipping on a glass of orange juice and reading the latest edition of the *Post-Dispatch* newspaper as if he didn't have more pressing issues to facilitate. "Do you have my entire parcel in that satchel?" he asked, neglecting to look up at Baltimore.

"It's all here but it's not yours until you've paid me my entire hundred gees."

"It seems that I have a dilemma," Rosenberg said casually, flipping past the front page to an article that interested him. "Some changes have occurred, since we last spoke. While I'm appreciative of your cunning nature and well-thought-out execution, I am undecided on what to do about it. I could compensate you for your efforts, say fifty thousand dollars perhaps?"

"Fifty? Why should I accept fifty thousand when we have a deal for twice that?" Baltimore said, in a manner of a flat refusal rather than a question. "You wouldn't be try'n a crawfish and back out on our agreement, now would you?"

"Well, I could do a number of things I suppose, but I am willing to do either of these—put fifty grand in your hands or cut them off and feed them to my dogs, boy."

After hearing two gunmen enter the room and position themselves behind him, Baltimore sighed heavily. "There's always option three. See, there're some extras you haven't calculated from my standpoint. I'm not willing to let some fat pit-faced pusher jerk me around. And before you go underestimating me again, call your mama."

Rosenberg looked up from his morning paper then. He knocked the glass of juice off the desk with the back of his hand. His eyes narrowed. "My mother? If you think about touching her . . . that woman's a saint."

"If you don't pony up every dime of the money owed me, she'll be in the hereafter with lots more of them saints." Baltimore wasn't sure if Jews believed in heaven or hell but it sounded like a credible threat so he went with it. "Think I'm bluffing, dial her up."

The telephone trembled in Rosenberg's hand as his placed the call. "Hello, mother, good morning. Is everything there all right?"

Baltimore glanced at his watch. It was four minutes to ten. "Ask her if the green yard service van is parked out by the curb. Two of my partners are keeping an eye on her for you." He watched Rosenberg's jowls contract when his beloved mother confirmed that two colored men were parked on the street outside of her house.

With all the power Schmitty Rosenberg had amassed, he didn't have a chance at saving his own mama's life. He plopped down in his leather wing-back chair defeated. He demanded Baltimore be fully compensated as agreed. When his head henchman objected, he slammed his meaty fist on the desk. "I said, pay the man!" For the second time, Baltimore proved more cunning than the mobster predicted, and it made Rosenberg furious. Despite being guaranteed one hundred percent profit by selling Barker's drugs back to him for two hundred thousand dollars, he hated being manipulated most of all.

After Baltimore played his trump card, a briefcase filled with stacks of large bills rested on the passenger seat atop a large ring of M.K.'s blood. He'd never been more happy and sorry at the same time. That's what he told Etta while stuffing nearly eighty grand in the safe hidden in the floor beneath her office desk. "Don't be looking at me that way, Jo Etta, ain't nobody gonna come to get after this money," he assured her. "I didn't steal it. Just traded it for something I did steal."

"I didn't say nothing," she replied, well aware that Baltimore's countenance didn't convey one inkling of remorse. After safely putting the money aside, Baltimore didn't care who might have come looking for him.

"Maybe you don't say nothing with your mouth but with that look that's burning a hole through me, you're saying more than enough."

"When are you leaving?" she asked, after her apprehension waned. "You know how you do, make your mark and then move on. I thought you'd blow out today until you showed up with all that money. More money than is supposed to be lumped together at the same time."

Baltimore didn't respond to Etta's comment about the vast fortune he recently amassed. "Don't worry, I'll say goodbye before I get in the wind. I was thinking on taking Penny with me."

"Penny? Uh-uh, she can't go gallivanting all over tarnation with you. She ain't even full grown yet."

"And I ain't stud'n on bedding her neither. Penny is a lamb and always will be, as far as I'm concerned, Etta. Look, I just want to show her some of the things she'll never get to see staying here in St. Louis. There's a lot of beauty out there, a lot to behold." He hadn't once taken into account what Etta might like to behold and neither did she, until then.

"Well, why shouldn't the same go for me? I mean, I like beautiful things too. Besides, Gussy done went and keeled over, so I don't have a decent bartender and I'd just as soon not have to go out and hunt one up." When Baltimore offered Etta a loving smile, her expression dripped with intensity and anticipation.

"Well, I'll be, I'm flabbergasted. 'Couldn't guess you'd be willing to tramp around with me and leave the Fast House behind."

"Pret' near as I can tell, there's over fifty thousand or more you just shoved in that hole. Now, I could be wrong, but that ain't nowhere close to trampin'. Don't hold me to it but I wouldn't might mind a change or two coming my way."

Baltimore saw something in her he hadn't before. There was a fire behind her eyes, a blaze he'd witnessed coming from other women, one that cried out to be quenched by striking out toward new, bold and unknown territory. Etta was afraid to miss out on something she'd never had, a wide-opened trail and close friends to help her experience it.

"We'll have to sit down and discuss it then," Baltimore agreed. "Right now, I've got two fellas itching to go fishing. M.K.'s body needs to be sent home to his folks and that girl carrying his baby is going to need some money when it gets here." Baltimore didn't come right out and say he'd be the one paying to have his friend's remains flown back to the east coast or he'd make a substantial donation to help support the child, but Etta knew his heart was made of gold. "Tell Penny I'll be around later. Don't worry, everything will be fine," he said persuasively. "Trust me." Etta was pleasantly although nervously optimistic, and she had reason to be. Baltimore was still lightning in the jar. Unfortunately, the lid had already been removed.

23

WHAT'S GOT INTO YOU?

What should have been one of the happiest days of Henry's life turned on him like a woman whose love had grown cold. He awoke to breakfast in bed, a wonderfully prepared plate of pan-seared fish and grits. After his wife Roberta served the delicious platter, she climbed in the bed with him and then served up a good old-fashioned stack of hot loving to top it off. Henry didn't want to run the risk of throwing a wet blanket on the moment, but a troubling thought nagged at him while he relaxed beneath the sheets, running his fingers along the curvy contours of Roberta's ample hips.

"Ah, now that's the kind of stroll through the garden a man won't soon forget," Henry cooed, as his wife rested her head on his thick dampened chest. "'Berta, I can't remember you taking hold of things like this before. Not that I'm complaining mind you but it is mighty peculiar. What's got into you?"

Roberta pulled the cotton bed sheet over her shoulder then she slid her leg out from underneath it. "Ooh, I just caught a chill. You got me running like a furnace on the blink, hot and cold all at once," she said before answering his question. "Whew! I've been watching you, pacing about and bottled up over the past three months. It's been rough on me too. The more thought I lent to it, the harder it got with me not knowing if you'd get tired of those ornery white boys making it tougher than it has to be. I didn't want you to get hurt or throw in the towel either, so I kept it to myself. This morning I felt the time came to open up and let loose."

"Uh-huh, you've been keeping it to yourself all right," Henry teased, since discussing his fears didn't particularly appeal to him. "You need to know I never meant to bring you in on my sorrows. I reckon it has been hard on you too. Good thing that graduation ceremony fires up in a couple of hours. Me and the fellas deserve all the respect they'll be forced to give us then. The chief says there ain't no officer's badge any bigger or more important than the next and I believe him. You know, some of those boys carrying that tin got hearts full of hate. The department is rotten down to the core."

Roberta raised her head. She glanced up at her man's face and blushed. "That's why we need more men like you to straighten it out."

"I ain't ever been one for straightening. Done spent too much time knocking wrinkles in, mostly."

"That was the old Henry," she told him, as she nestled her cheek against his warm skin. "You're new and improved like the man on the radio says about the showroom Cadillac. I love your new bells and whistles."

Henry beamed proudly, fighting off an awkward grin. "Come on now, Roberta, keep talking like that and I'll be asking you to blow on that ole whistle for me."

"Huh, you must have me mistaken for some other woman. I don't wrap my lips around that kinda screecher."

"Don't go frowning on it until you tried it," Henry suggested lewdly.

"Have you . . . tried it?" she smarted back.

"Heylll, naw, who do you think I am?"

"My point exactly," Roberta argued convincingly. "There're some things I don't have to sample to know the taste won't suit."

"All right, 'Berta, all right," Henry said, giving up on what he thought was a good idea. "I'd better be getting around to putting on my dress blues and heading over to the courthouse." Just then, the telephone rang. "Hold up, dear, lemme get that, it's probably one of the fellas checking to see if I'm up and running."

Sitting up on the iron framed bed with a sheet covering her breasts, Roberta sneered at the thought of succumbing to Henry's sexual desires, then she smacked her lips and chuckled. *That'll be the day, when colored women stoop to serving a man's filthy whims like white girls do. Huh, ain't no telling where Henry's thing has been or who it's been in for that matter.* When she'd given it a second thought, Etta came to mind. She was really steaming then. "Henry!" she yelled, expecting to pick a fight about his ex-lover and what she'd likely done to his whistle when they were together. The ghostly expression he wore, standing naked in the doorway, caused her to shake loose from going against him. "What is it, Henry? Who was that on the line?" she asked, with short and snappy breaths.

"Trace, Trace Wiggins," he answered quietly, as if a myriad of other things zigzagged through his mind simultaneously. "He said they got Willie B. Bernard locked up for murder."

"Murder?" she repeated, in as much disbelief as her husband. "Who? When?"

Henry's mouth was bone dry when he told her. "He killed Helen and some doctor friend of Baltimore's last night . . . at Etta's place." His knees were shaking because he'd initially assumed it was Baltimore at the wrong end of Willie B.'s gun barrel. Feeling somewhat relieved that it wasn't, he breathed heavily. "I didn't know the dead doctor, but I'm awful sorry for Helen though."

"Poor girl," Roberta groaned sorrowfully. "Helen didn't do anything but love that fool with all her heart. However it happened, I'd bet Baltimore had something to do with it, and don't let me get started on Jo Etta Adams."

"Don't," Henry huffed, in an insolent manner that caused Roberta to shrink back. "There's been innocent blood spilt any which way you look at it. This ain't the time to go pointing fingers and calling names."

"I just thought—"

"I'm running late," Henry interrupted. "Gotta go." Henry didn't share the information Trace had about the number of dead-on-arrival heroin victims turning up at the hospital during the night. Henry easily connected the dots back to Barker Sinclair and Tasman Gillespie's illegal enterprise. Immediately, he regretted the decision to let Barker ride off with his prisoner, keeping quiet about it, and his lack of fortitude when witnessing police brutality. He'd grown accustomed to being a second-class citizen but refused to be a second-class police officer who wouldn't take a stand any longer. Henry promised himself the next time he was faced with stepping up to the plate, he wouldn't be sitting on his hands again.

En route to the long awaited ceremony, Henry parked the car in front of Watkins Emporium. When he told Roberta he'd be right back, she merely grunted that she heard him, but offered no reply. The way he'd handled her when Etta's name came up still had her seething. Henry had to work his way back into Roberta's good graces before she was ready to say two decent words to him. A great deal more was required if he ever intended on taking another stroll through her garden, a great deal more.

"Well, looka yonder," the store owner hailed, proudly. Mr. Watkins's face rounded out into a grandiose smile when he laid eyes on Henry's impressive uniform, dark blue from shoulder to shoe, a double-pocketed shirt, brass and leather belted accessories and a perfectly shaped black and navy colored cap to compliment it. "I declare, this is a big day for our people and the city of St. Louis," he said, admiring the uniform as much as he did the man wearing it.

"Thank you, sir," Henry said softly, not used to being ogled and appreciated by grown men, unless he was decked out in his baseball gear and knocking the hide off fast pitches. Henry was uncomfortable with this type of adoration, although he wasn't turning it down. *If only everyone felt the same as Mr. Watkins*, he thought, as a familiar face sauntered through the door with her shadow bringing up the rear.

"Hi ya, Etta, hey, Penny," the older man greeted them from the opposite side of the checkout counter. "I was just telling Henry here how dashing he looked in his parade duds."

"Afternoon, Mr. Watkins," Etta offered. She neglected to comment on Henry or his slave-catching clothes, as Baltimore called them. "I've got white detectives breathing down my neck about a double murder and that colored newspaper has been snooping high and low, too, so I give less than a damn about brass buttons or the trained baboons wearing them." Mr. Watkins winced in embarrassment at Henry, unable to pretend Etta hadn't blasted him with a personal attack, which he assumed was the result of a jilted woman scorned.

"She always was a ball of fire," he whispered to Henry, while handing him change for the cigars he'd stopped in to purchase. "But then you'd know that better than most, I guess." Henry dumped the coins into his trouser pocket and winked at Mr. Watkins.

"Yeah, always was," he agreed, as he turned to leave. "Miss," Henry said to Penny in passing. Her eyes glimmered at the big man in the striking suit and she smiled at him the way the store owner had when he arrived. She watched Henry strut all the way out onto the sidewalk, but her smile vanished when Etta eased in to block her view.

"Come on, chile, you need some new scarves and hose," she hissed disappointedly. "Wait 'til I get you home, we're gonna have a long talk about the way things is."

"Ms. Etta, all's I did was wave at Mistah Henry," she protested. "Is there a rule says I can't be nice just because y'all can't get along?"

"Hell, yes," Etta informed her, "and that's what I'm aiming to tell you all about soon as we get along."

"Is it gonna hurt?"

"I'm gonna do all I can to see that it does," she answered, with a frown on her mouth and laughter dancing in her eyes. "Women-folks and friends got to stick together against any form of foe, even if they got absolutely no other reason to other than because one of them says it ought to be so."

"Seems kinda silly to me," Penny said after pondering on it a while.

"Seemed silly to me too until I saw you swooning over Henry's broad shoulders wrapped in that getup. Then it made perfect sense that I needed you to be as spiteful as I'm willing to. That's what you call a true friend."

Penny mulled over the issue some more before making her stand. "I don't like that rule, not even a little bit."

"And nobody asked you," Etta reprimanded her. "If I wanted your say, I'd have asked you for it."

"Whew, it's a mite tougher being a friend than I thought. They's too many rules for one."

"Now you're getting the picture. On second thought, setting you straight might not hurt so much after all."

Penny furrowed her brow awkwardly. "Tell that to my aching head."

At the steps of City Hall, the very place where the colored cadets were initially selected, Roberta was staring upside Henry's head the way she had since he glided out of the emporium on Cloud Nine. She imagined his smile was due to something Etta said instead of what Mr. Watkins put in his mind about her.

Seeing as how his wife didn't have words for him, Henry didn't speak up to tell her any different. "That ought to hold her," he told Smiley Tennyson as the host of wives cordially introduced themselves near the front of the proceedings.

"That's something I haven't seen," Smiley responded, looking over his right shoulder, "white and colored women shaking hands and grinning at each other. Too bad Willie B.'s wife Helen couldn't be one of them. Clay Barker said the prosecutor is aiming to send him up for life without parole if he can't guarantee a hanging. Etta's telling detectives a misunderstanding is what caused it. You think Baltimore put her up to saying that so's to save Willie B. from the hangman's noose?"

"Naw, Baltimo' never did cotton much to Willie B. and Etta

wouldn't say it was so unless that's the way it was. This city is going to come apart at the threads."

"At the seams too," Smiley answered, with his gaze locked on the trail of cars parking at the curb. Henry's eye found it disheartening as well. On one side of the street, a contingent of sixty or so colored men gathered. The other side served as the rendezvous point for twenty off-duty officers who were actually selected to sit in attendance, in full regalia, as a sign of support. They openly defied orders when they appeared in faded jeans and other casual clothing, in silent protest against the induction of colored officers. The chief was so embarrassed he pulled a stunt to rival theirs.

"To commemorate this special occasion," he said, after the band played a few numbers, "I would like to announce the unanimous choice for Best Cadet of the Metropolitan Police Department's Spring Class of 1947. On second thought, I'll let their training leader present this highly coveted award."

The chief moved aside when Clay ascended the podium steps. He scanned the meager audience while humming on the inside with enthusiasm. "It is with the utmost respect that I salute this officer with the most sought after training award we have. This class has voted you, Henry Taylor, the unanimous winner for Best Cadet and would like you to receive this plaque on their behalf. Come on up, Henry, you deserve it." To the wildly thunderous applause from the congregation of colored supporters, he stood from his chair, arched his back and went up to accept his award with his peers cheering him on.

Roberta cast a lengthy glance toward the row of off-duty protestors. Because the ceremony went off without a hitch, she found herself wondering what their alignment meant, down the road, if anything other than making time to shake people up by staring. Roberta didn't have long to wait before the good-ole-boy network validated her darkest suspicions.

24

HIGH HEELS AND BIG DEALS

Friday night at the Fast House, Etta marveled at how many customers and curious patrons appeared to take in the excitement which spilled over after Willie B. shot up the place. It became the story of the day once word had traveled through the black community. A would-be police officer supposedly catching his wife with a colored doctor and blasting them both was too much of an event to disregard.

Penny and Etta hustled drinks from opening time to the wee hours of the morning. Madame Clarisse helped out behind the bar for kicks, although Etta insisted she take fifty dollars for being a friend in a time of need. Clarisse didn't mind the close proximity to Baltimore throughout the night and would have gladly done it for nothing. Unfortunately for her, when the Fast House shut down, he slipped out the back door with someone else while her back was turned. Penny giggled under her breath as the hairstylist ranted about her need to be made love to by a handsome man like Baltimore. "There's nothing like having a fine man rubbing up against my skin," she said, from the other end of a lit cigarette. "Hell, the way I feel right now, I'd even take an ugly man with smooth hands, a strong back and a big ole-"

"Uh-uh," Etta interrupted. "Don't you dare dive into all that in front of Penny. Let's get this place locked up and maybe you can make a call or two and see who's in the mood and still available."

Clarisse blew a dense stream of smoke into the air as she leaned back against the bar. "If I can get one on the line, I can put him in the mood. You can take that to the bank and cash it."

Etta laughed as she puffed on a Chesterfield herself. "You know, all this talk about menfolk got me missing something I ain't had in a while," she said in retrospect.

"What's that, Ms. Etta?" asked Penny, with wide wondering eyes.

"Huh? Oh, uh, headache powder," she lied quickly. "Never you mind that. I was thinking out loud when I should have kept it to myself."

"Maybe that's the problem," Penny said, cutting her eyes at Etta like a sly fox. "Maybe you've been keeping it to yourself for too long."

"Penny?" Etta said, caught off guard by her innuendo. "What do you know about grown folk's affairs?"

"What don't I know?" she answered, twirling a damp dishrag like a child's toy. "There ain't a night goes by that I don't see some fella try'na get it or some woman try'na to give it away. Even seen one or two of them cathouse girls offering to make a profit selling it. Seems to me that pleasing is what makes the world go around. If it ain't, I sho' don't know what beats it out." She tossed the same foxy leer at Etta and Clarisse she'd pitched at them moments before. "Headache powder, that's a new one. Heard it called everything but that. I'm awful hungry, y'all. Who wants to settle down to a red eye hot plate at the Smokey Joe's Café? I'm buying."

"Etta, don't look now, but you've got a woman on your hands," Clarissa said, marveling at Penny's sudden maturity. "Better still, a woman who's treating us to breakfast."

"I'll say," was all that Etta could say, without drilling her protégée on exactly what else she might have learned under her very nose. Etta was even more astonished than Clarisse. It took everything she had to keep her mouth shut, afraid of getting more than she'd bargained for.

Penny had already shared a lot of what she picked up from hustling tables, but she was not prepared or willing to make known the number of steamy sex scenes she observed through Baltimore's rented room window. Penny figured on keeping that to herself. It was also clear she had matured in many ways since taking up with Etta, including learning a valuable lesson: to keep quiet when something was better left unsaid. Running off at the mouth could have brought pain to so many.

The following afternoon, in Baltimore's room, Dinah was casually dressed in an oatmeal-hued pleated shirt and argyle sweater, while she lounged on the small loveseat with her arms crossed. She'd listened to Baltimore's plans to leave town by sundown while he neglected to tell her where he was headed and for how long. "That's not gonna cut it this time," she objected, staring at his back as he placed folded clothes into a new set of expensive suitcases. "I know you've been up to something so don't stand there and lie to my face." When accused of being untruthful, Baltimore turned toward Dinah in a slow deliberate manner that caused her to cower away from him.

"You know I ain't got no cause to lie to you or no other woman and I ain't gave you any cause to put that label on me," he panted. "I done told you all you need to know, for now. If that won't do, there's the door."

She didn't know what to think then. Baltimore had been honest, she was mindful of that before challenging him further. "So tell me then, why are you in such a rush to storm away from me? If I didn't know better I'd think you was giving me the sack."

"It'd be more like me to give you the latch," he joked. "But we've had good times, Dinah. Good times are all I can offer going forward. You could come with me, you know."

"And do what, Baltimore?" she asked, while standing up from the loveseat. "Come with you and be your whore? I didn't hear nothing about you loving me coming out your mouth, now or ever. I have a home here, a job that keeps money in my pocket and all of my friends to keep me company. That's a good life. Unless you're stud'n on trumping what I already got, we might as well fold them right here and walk away from the table." Confidant he wouldn't call her bluff, Dinah rolled her eyes at him to appear more geared up to let him go than she actually was.

Before he answered her, someone knocked at the door. Baltimore furrowed his brow and raised his hand to shush Dinah. Not expecting any visitors, he grabbed the revolver from atop the bureau. "Yeah, who is it?" he asked, with an insistent tone.

"Open up and I'll show you," a woman's voice answered.

Baltimore recognized it immediately. Dressed in a pair of casual trousers, he glanced at Dinah to note her reaction, then he reached for a suitable shirt to make himself presentable. "Hold on a minute, I'm throwing something on," he answered through the door.

"You shouldn't bother on my account," the woman responded in a sensuous tone. "I like you best in nothing at all."

Listening to the woman carrying on outside the door, Dinah was ready to blow a gasket. There was no skirting around this one. It couldn't help but get ugly. She was chomping at the bit to see who Baltimore had been splitting her time with. "What you waiting on?" she whispered, while watching Baltimore stall. "Unlatch it!" she demanded, louder than before.

After a deep sigh, he opened the door. Before uttering a single word, Dixie Sinclair sauntered in showing off her sleeveless red and crème sundress. Wasting no time getting at the reason she showed up out of the blue, she purred and tossed both arms around Baltimore's neck. Uncomfortable as could be, he peered down at Dixie while she pressed her face against the opening in his unbuttoned long sleeve shirt. "Whoa now, Dix, I've got company," he said, trying to pry himself away from her exuberant clutches.

"Ohhh!" Dixie squealed. Backing away from Baltimore as if he were a leper, she shot a barrage of fiery looks in Dinah's direction. "Sorry, I had no idea you were entertaining. But now that I'm here, she can run along." Dixie's elitist outlook gave her the inclination that Baltimore would arbitrarily choose her to stay, assuming he favored white meat if he could get it.

"Don't go getting any ideas deary," Dinah asserted broodingly. "I don't like getting pushed around unless I ask for it and you're hardly my type."

"Baltimore, if you wouldn't mind seeing her out," the white lady suggested with a dismissive stare flung at her colored competition. "Three's a crowd and Barker's in a fit of rage about a missing police car or something having to do with it. In either case I don't have all day." Baltimore was in no hurry to force the issue of someone having to be sent home so he held his cards close to the vest and his mouth buttoned tight.

"So this is Mrs. Barker Sinclair?" Dinah said coolly, as she looked the intruder over carefully. "I thought you'd be old, mean, and fat. Boy, did I get a false report." Of course Dinah was merely going off what Barker had said about his wife when he was with her.

"Excuse me, have we met?" Dixie asked.

"No, but I've had a long running . . . understanding with Barker." The corners of Dinah's lips curled into a sheepish grin. It was all she could do not to laugh at the white lady's stupid expression.

"You and Barker, really?" Dixie said defensively, insinuating that was too ridiculous for words.

Finally Baltimore came across an invitation into their conversation that suited him. "Well, ain't this cozy? Barker's woman and his whore brought together by chance."

"I'll say, Baltimore. It's just peachy," Dinah contended. "Him and you's in the same fix." Her astute observation flattened Baltimore's smugly self-righteous smirk. "Come to think of it, y'all belong together. I'll take my hat and handbag and leave you two alone. Yes, it has begun to feel a bit crowded for my taste as well. And Baltimore, this could not happen to a more deserving person. I have no doubt you'll get everything you got coming to you." Dinah collected her personal items and strolled out of the door.

"Dinah, hold up!" Baltimore hollered down the hall. "I wasn't thinking on asking you to leave. Dinah!"

"You can go straight to hell!" she hollered back.

When Baltimore stepped inside the room, his dander kicked up something terrible. So put off by the order of events, he could barely stand the sight of Dixie, especially after she had run off the lady he had intended on staying with. "Are you happy now? Huh?" he shouted. "I sho' hope so 'cause there's no sense in both of us trapped in a rut."

"Settle down, lover. The very thought of you with that woman gives me the shakes."

"How you think that niggah-hating husband of yours might hold up imagining the tricks you do with me?"

"If I didn't know better, a woman might get the wrong idea and get her feelings hurt. That colored girl's gone now. You don't have to pretend any longer that you'd rather I go."

Baltimore drew in a measured breath and frowned wearily. "Pretend? Is that what you think, I was pretending? Oomph, if that ain't the damnedest thing I done heard all day," he barked curtly. "You had no business coming here, Dixie, and that's just for starters."

"Wait a minute!" she said, her voice rising. "I'd hate to be unreasonable, but unless all of that good loving of yours knocked one of my screws loose, you needed my help to rob Barker's heroin shipment." When Baltimore's eyes exhibited his surprise, Dixie made it plain she had paid her dues and wasn't in any disposition to be shortchanged. "Oh, boy, don't tell me you thought I was in this for the pillow talk alone. I wasn't expecting to split the take down the middle, but I certainly didn't look for the old heave-ho on the back end." While she had Baltimore wrapped up in his loss for words, Dixie sashayed up to him and nuzzled his hairy chest again. "Now don't you go getting all quiet on me," she cooed softly. "What do you say we settle after getting down to the nuts and bolts of our arrangement? Hope you don't mind,

I'd planned on rewarding myself first." She ran her palm down his pants, easing her thin fingers inside of his zipper.

Baltimore was taken aback by the woman who had a lot to gain, but he hadn't counted on cutting her in. Additionally, it was especially annoying when discovering he hadn't masterminded the takedown of Baker's shady enterprise alone and that caused him to react in a hurtful way. "If business is what you came here for then you shouldn't have chased off my company. Dinah was all pleasure and then some. You can get a second opinion from Barker."

Dixie's face tightened. She couldn't believe her ears. "You really weren't playing around? That girl, you do want her more than me?" She gasped, pulling her hand from inside his boxer drawers. "You-you ungrateful animal!" she ranted, clawing at his face. "I'm nobody's fool. I'll show you who you're messing with."

"Cut it out, Dixie, it's over," Baltimore argued, diligently blocking her frenzied blows. "Stop it, now!"

She tore at his clothing, ripping the pricey shirt he'd moments before slipped on. "I'll get you, you black bastard!"

"You need to quit . . . this . . . foolishness before somebody gets hurt," he said, growing tired of defending himself. He snarled and grabbed Dixie by the arms, then dragged her toward the door. Fueled by spite, she wasn't willing to go quietly. Baltimore needed her to leave and in a hurry before his prediction became an unfortunate reality. Digging in her heels, Dixie tussled mightily. She struggled to remain inside of the room.

Her husband's Ford, which she'd parked in the alley, was being hitched to the tow truck, after Etta reported it blocking her back door. The white truck driver heard what he figured to be a couple working out the kinks in their relationship, but he couldn't tell which room it was coming from, nor did he care, for he assumed both the man and woman were colored.

Refusing to be thrown out like yesterday's trash, Dixie snatched herself away from Baltimore's grasp and sprinted toward the other side of the room. When he caught up to her, he locked his wrists around her waist. She gritted her teeth and held firm to the window frame just as the truck driver peered up. "Goddammit!" she yelped loudly. "Let me go! Let me go!"

The white man was familiar with the neighborhood. He knew the adjacent building to be colored only. After seeing Baltimore tear Dixie's fingers from the window, he became a lot more interested. He rambled to the end of the alley howling "Police!" to the high heavens.

Baltimore didn't believe in men putting their hands on women. However, for the first time in his life, he wished he did, as sweat poured from his face with trails of blood marking Dixie's claws. Her blouse tore as they wrestled violently. "Hell, girl, you's trying my patience, now. Don't make me get rough."

"You can't treat me like this," she ranted wildly, slapping at his face to work herself free. "Let me go!"

"Uh-uh," Baltimore grunted. "It ain't no use. You might as well give up." He was adamant. There was nothing left to argue when he heard the hammer of a pistol cock mere inches from his head. The hairs on the back of his neck stood on end.

"You heard her, nigger," spat the police officer, with the rancid smell of stale chewing tobacco on his breath. That was the last thing Baltimore remembered before feeling a sharp pain shooting through the back of his head and the cold hard floor slamming against his face.

25

BETTER OFF DEAD

Baltimore's life had been strung together from a long list of fast times and jagged edges. Etta fully understood how a man was made from the things he'd done or had done to him. The minute she heard about a colored man having been beaten and dragged away in chains from the Ambrose Arms apartments, her heart sank. "Penny, call over to Madame Clarisse's," she ordered, praying that her intuition had lied to her.

"What do you want me to say when I get her on the line?" she inquired innocently.

"Ask her if the man who the police beat . . . if the one they took was Baltimore." Etta stared into space with a blanket of uneasiness shrouding her face. It was difficult to think of anything else until she knew for sure.

Penny's mouth popped opened when she played Etta's words back in her head. "But, Ms. Etta," Penny said worriedly.

"Call her, chile," Etta demanded in a subtle manner. "Go 'head and get the pilot on." Penny nodded slowly as she reached for the telephone sitting on the office desk. Etta would have made the call herself but her hands wouldn't stop trembling.

"Yes, ma'am, get me Bedford one-seventy-three, please. Yes, ma'am, the beauty parlor," she affirmed for the phone operator. Penny pressed her lips together when Clarisse answered on the other end. "Uh, Madame Clarisse, this is Penny . . . Huh, that's why Miss Etta had me to call you . . . Naw, ma'am . . . we's just relaxing mostly . . . Naw, ma'am. Uh-uh . . . Yes, ma'am, I'll tell her. 'Bye." The way Penny's gaze drifted downward after hanging up caused Etta to place a hand over her mouth, afraid she might release the scream she held in the pit of her stomach.

"Well, Penny, what exactly did she say?"

"Said she'd be right over."

It startled Etta when Clarisse barged into the building. "Girl, don't be busting in here like that," she said, placing her left hand over her chest. "You're liable to fool around and stop my heart."

"Sorry, Etta but I have to hurry," she apologized, in abbreviated breaths. "The whole parlor is buzzing more than usual today." In the five minutes Clarisse spent situating her customers with other stylists and then traveling from her salon seven blocks away, Penny had almost put two and two together from the snippets of information she'd overheard in the storeroom between the soda pop and ice house delivery men. For Baltimore's sake, she crossed her fingers on both hands and hoped she'd heard wrong.

Clarisse paced around the table where Etta and Penny had planted themselves by the office. Her face was plagued with hesitancy as she watched the two of them staring back at her. "What?" she asked, as if they hadn't been dying to get the news.

"Don't play that game, Clarisse. I know you didn't fly down the street like a Kansas cyclone to stand there holding it in," Etta hooted, although she wasn't nearly prepared to deal with potential life-altering information head on. "You may as well take a load off and get to it."

"Okay, but it won't be easy. I assumed y'all already heard from the grapevine, seeing as how things was between you and Baltimore," she said, more in Etta's general direction.

"Was, what you mean by was?" Etta inquired suspiciously. "You sound like somebody done died . . ." she spat before catching herself. There was an old wives' tale that warned of speaking things into being, so Etta closed her mouth abruptly.

"Madame Clarisse, I know how Miss Etta feels about Baltimore and I'd 'preciate it if you just jump right into what you know about the police beating."

After the woman lowered her head momentarily, to summon the appropriate words, her eyes floated up to rest on Etta and then on Penny. "From what I hear, everybody in town is talking about Baltimore and the policeman's wife." She was surprised to see that Penny appeared unmoved in a time when colored men typically went out of their way to avoid being in the same room with white women.

"Yeah, like I was saying, a man was sent to move a car from an alley not too far from here. The white man operating the wrecker truck heard a woman yelling that somebody had mugged her and was still at it, so the fella went for help. He found two cops down at the corner and told them what he heard. It wasn't until the truck driver mentioned the woman was white that they paid him any mind." Etta was afraid to make a sound while Clarisse divulged the rest. "The story goes all over the place from there depending on who you want to believe. Some say Baltimore dragged her up to his place, slapped her around some and was smack dab in the middle of forcing himself on her when those white boys broke the door in." Etta pleaded with her eyes for information she dared not ask with words. "No, they didn't kill him," was Clarisse's response to her friend's unspoken concerns. "But they leaned on him so bad, he probably wished they had."

For Clarisse to go spouting off something like that, she couldn't have possibly ever known a man like Baltimore, Etta thought. With her lips tightly pursed, Etta released a bittersweet chuckle on the inside of her mouth. That chuckle eventually erupted into full blown unbridled laughter. Penny was confused until she caught on to what Etta found amusing, then she joined in and shared in the merriment.

"Is both of y'all drunk?" Clarisse queried, with painstaking honesty.

"You tell her, Penny," Etta laughed, "It feels too good to waste."

"Tell me what?" Clarisse prodded.

"See, the worst thing that could happen to Baltimore is being mistaken for something he ain't, like a man who forces things on women or even like being dead. As long as he ain't dead, he can take care of the other." Penny glanced at Etta to see how the explanation measured up to expectations. "Good, Penny, I couldn't have said it better myself. Whew! Thank God he's still alive." Etta sighed evenly. "Is anybody saying where they got him now?"

Clarisse wasn't quite sure of anything anymore. Penny had shown more rational intuition than a woman twice her age and Etta was behaving like a giggling idiot, as far as she was concerned. She presumed that the news would have demolished the ladies' love for Baltimore beyond repair, even if the story were only partially correct. Having invited a white woman up to his room alone should have sufficiently accomplished that. "Uh, I suppose I could do some checking about Baltimore," Clarisse offered, still oddly puzzled by their unyielding devotion to a man neither of them shared a bed with. "Give me a half hour at the parlor," she added, feeling suddenly more confident herself. "You can bet somebody there knows something about where they got him."

Penny wanted to share how she'd seen Baltimore with a white woman on several occasions through his window, but she wasn't sure if that would do more harm than good, for him and her, so she tucked it away in the same place it originated, in her heart. "Thank you, Madame Clarisse," she said finally. "We's going up to see about him as soon as you nose around and get word to us." The hairstylist couldn't do a thing but admire her adoration of Baltimore and agree to do some mighty powerful nosing around, all in the name of fidelity.

Clarisse passed Delbert on his way in through the door. She smiled politely as he held it open for her. Just as he approached the table where Etta and Penny chatted, Etta explained they'd be closed for business until further notice. "That's fine with me, Miss Etta. Hi ya, Penny," Delbert said, hunching his shoulders. "I worked all night and didn't have the chance to thank Baltimore personally and on behalf of the medical staff for putting up the money to send M.K.'s body home to his folks. It ain't every day a colored man's remains ride on a sky taxi."

Penny's forehead wrinkled when she didn't understand a single thing he just said. "What's a sky taxi, Dr. Delbert? And why do they let dead men ride in it?"

"That's just what they call an airplane, Penny. Some states have laws about non-breathing colored cargo. Missouri is one of them, but Baltimore fixed it with a white fella at the air strip. I'd bet the only color he saw was green when a wad of bills was flashed in his face."

"Yeah, that sounds like Baltimore alright," Etta reasoned.

"So is he around or should I leave word with y'all?" Delbert asked, after he didn't get an actual answer to his question the first time. "What he did, meant a lot to a whole bunch of folks, myself included. M.K. was an ace as friends go."

"Delbert, maybe I should pour you a settling drink to sip on," Etta said, sorrowfully. "There's something I need you to do." She explained what the skinny on the street was and how nothing shy of a miracle aided Baltimore in surviving his arrest. To secure his safety behind bars, serious decisions had to be made and a plan of action instituted. Most importantly, time was of the essence. "So you understand why I couldn't possibly make this happen by myself?" she asked him afterwards.

Penny cleared her throat. "Uh-huh, *we* can't do it without your help, Dr. Delbert."

"Well, that's a serious proposition," he said apprehensively. The look on his face showed how scared he was to involve himself in it. "I'm just a country doctor trying to find my own way."

Etta's eyes softened as signs of distress revealed themselves but Penny's expression hardened. "Look here, doc, they's some things a man is forced to do because it's right," she said, holding his gaze with hers. "Baltimore is that kind of man. I'd like to think you is, too." Before Delbert had the opportunity to mull over Penny's challenging declaration, someone kicked the front door open. The loud crash sent chills through Delbert and Penny. Etta squinted spitefully when she saw him, the one who'd put his foot against her door and had shaken her down more times than she cared to remember.

"Jo Etta Adams," Barker announced soberly, trouncing in with two uniformed officers she hadn't seen before. "I'm not interrupting anything, am I? Because I sure would hate that."

"Detective Sinclair, it's always interesting to see you," Etta replied. "As you can see, we're not open for business now so you should come back later on and have a few on me." She wasn't in the least bit intimidated. Predators like Barker sensed fear in others, and too much was on the line to snivel in the shadow of a desperate cop.

"Ms. Etta. That is what they call you, huh? I like that, the way it evokes respect. Respect is a good thing too, it separates the haves from the have-nots. You, Ms. Etta, are definitely one of the haves." Neither Penny nor Delbert had experienced the war of wits common between night club owners and white officers who wanted to share in their good fortune and hard work. Etta had seen and stood up against tougher white men than Barker, smarter ones too. She knew how to stay pat without overplaying her hand. That's the only kind of respect Barker understood, unrelenting nerve.

"Listen, detective, why don't you tell me what you want and I'll see about accommodating you? What, are you here for a police protection fund donation?" That's the term Barker used for his extortion racket.

"No, I'm afraid I'll need a lot more than a donation," he answered, circling the table where she and the others sat. "This time, I came for something that belongs to me." Barker studied her face for any tell-tale signs of incrimination. "See, somebody stole from me and I want it back. All of it." Etta glanced down at the table, thinking about what he said and the words he used as clues without giving up more than he was willing to. "A hired gun came in town asking about a man, a slick pool hustler, who liked to run with Henry Taylor and a pretty matron who we both know is you. I didn't bring any heat to your door after his trail ended here the first night he flashed the gold caps on his teeth. That's respect," he added as an exclamation point. "Now, that slick hustler has seen fit to put his hands in my business."

Etta knew then, without question, Barker's visit had nothing to do with extorting money from her to feed his own illegal enterprises; his Gestapo tactics had everything to do with Baltimore. She also suspected that the bundle of cash Baltimore placed in her floor safe was tied to it somehow. What she didn't get right away was Barker's wife sneaking around with colored men when he clearly detested them so vehemently. Suddenly, it became clearer. The white woman wanted to hurt Barker for something he'd done, she wanted him to suffer in a manner that suited her. Baltimore and Dixie weren't merely heating up the sheets for kicks, they were also business partners, only she had her hands in his pockets before letting him in on it. Mrs. Sinclair manufactured a devious ploy to stick it to her husband but good. Baltimore was her well-played pawn.

"Well, as you can see, Baltimore ain't here," Etta answered smugly. "And we both know why that is. When I see him, I'll be sure and let him know exactly how you feel about things."

Barker closed his mouth to hold in the anger erupting inside. Then, he let out a bitter laugh. "If you know what's good for you, you'll see that I get what's rightfully mine. It'd be a damned shame for someone else to lose what they've worked so hard for." Without any clever farewells, Barker gestured for his men to move on and then he followed after them.

Delbert got a good look at what Etta, and Baltimore for that matter, were facing. After he saw her snap back, unwavering, to a powerful white man there was only one thing he could do, back her play to the end. He smiled at Penny while deciding to get his hands dirty. "If we're gonna do this, it needs to happen now," he asserted. "Call and see if that hairdresser has found out where he's locked up and meet me at the hospital in thirty minutes. If this is the way they want to play, I'm stacking the lineup and bringing in some home run hitters."

26

SORROW'S STONE

Night was fast approaching when the taxi dropped Etta and Penny in front of Homer G. Phillips. Before they entered the hospital, a long black Lincoln Continental wheeled around the corner like a bat out of hell. Tires screeched as it skidded to an abrupt stop just a few feet away from them. "Hey, y'all, glad you made it. Get in," Delbert summoned hurriedly from the passenger side door. "We'll talk things over on the way." The women gladly obliged. Etta was eager to get started. Penny marveled at the expensive car as it glided along the city streets like an ice cube on a marble floor. Even in times of peril these people sure know how to make the best of it, she thought, while looking down on the back of the driver's head. "Ladies, this is Dr. Hiram Knight. Dr. Knight, meet Penny and Miss Etta. These are two of M.K.'s friends and family of Baltimore's, the man who tried to save him."

Once the introductions were concluded, Delbert filled them in on the strategy they hemmed up in the short time they had to work with and it sounded great to Etta. Although Penny couldn't understand why all of this had to take place in order to see Baltimore, she went along with it from top to bottom. In the fifteen minutes they traveled toward the county jail, her conscience gnawed at her. Penny couldn't help but wonder if the jam Baltimore landed in could have been avoided had she confided what she saw to Etta beforehand. Attempted aggravated rape of a white woman was a hanging offense in the state of Missouri. A colored man getting accused of it had it even worse. Baltimore faced the penalty of death and she blamed herself. Tears streamed down her cheeks when they pulled into the jailhouse parking lot.

"You stop that crying now," Dr. Knight demanded. "Ain't no need for tears, young lady. We're going into the battlefield. It's no place for the faint of heart."

"Yes, suh," she replied. "I'm a do my best to push 'em back."

"See that you do. These kinds of people prey on the weakness of colored folk, always have." Penny sniffled and wiped at her face with a lace handkerchief as the shortest grown man she'd ever laid eyes on marched across the street with choppy determined strides.

As they approached the mammoth building, made of dark-red brick, Delbert continually surveyed their surroundings. He checked over his shoulder so frequently it made Etta jumpy. She had seen her share of jails because of past affiliations, and actually viewed one from the inside of a cell. Running with shady associates carried a heavy price tag. Possession of stolen goods carried a jail term. Despite the poor decisions she made in years past, she wouldn't trade any of them for a king's ransom. Etta reasoned that serious mistakes were priceless lessons in life, building character and wisdom one foolish blunder at a time. Hopefully, Baltimore's fortress of foolishness wouldn't get walled in by the Department of Corrections like thousands of other colored men's had. One thought traipsed through Etta's mind as they entered what loomed ominously like a wasteland for repentant souls. Baltimore was in a small fraternity of inmates locked away in perpetuity; he was an innocent man facing a guilty lie.

Just inside the metal doors of the St. Louis County Jail, an unnerving chill climbed up Delbert's spine and hung on with a death grip. He followed closely behind Dr. Knight, who didn't seem bothered in the least, while Etta prodded Penny along. She lagged behind, taking it all in like a baby duckling in strange water. There were uniformed desk officers pushing papers and others pushing around men is handcuffs. Numbers of colored women and an assortment of white ones too, all reciting their personal hard luck stories in efforts to get their husbands back, saddened Delbert. Flies on the off-white painted concrete walls had heard them all, some more than others. But one thing they had yet to see was a single teary-eyed sister leaving with what she'd come for, her man's freedom.

Several of the desk officers glanced up to take note of two colored men wearing white doctor getups strolling through the maze of misery. Since they had enough on their plates as it was, none of them broke a sweat inquiring whose business they'd come to intercede on. The officers who'd heard about the colored rapist they had sneaked in the back dock had a pretty good idea. His appearance was far too appalling and disfigured to send through the normal intake channels. All the desk jockeys needed was an assailant beaten to a pulp to stir the grieving gabbers they already had to deal with into a frightened frenzy.

"Y'all should go over there and have a seat," Dr. Knight strongly suggested to the ladies, as their entourage neared the sergeant's desk situated at the rear of the first floor. The grumpy doctor didn't have to say it twice. Etta pulled Penny by the hand in the other direction. It was game time, a boys-only game where the rules changed by the minute.

"Maybe you ought to go and have a sit down with them," said the middle-aged white man sitting behind the tall duty desk. He sucked on the wet end of a cheap cigar the way Dr. Knight was accustomed to doing, but neither of those men had anything else in common.

"Wouldn't it make more sense for you to find out who we are and why we're standing here?" the older doctor said rhetorically. Delbert glanced around feverishly, to see if any of the officers overheard his mentor's blatant disregard to their white commander.

"I don't need to ask a damned thing," the thick-headed sergeant replied belligerently. He peered down at them crossly to display his displeasure. "From where I sit, I see one-and-a-half nigger doctors wasting my time. One sawed-off wise ass and the other who's about to crap his clean white pants."

"Perhaps I'd better get to it then. I'm Dr. Hiram Knight and I have in my company an associate, Dr. Gales. We know for a fact that a man, a colored man, was arrested and brought here, through the back. Furthermore, he has not received medical attention after being worked over by the men who detained him."

The cop smashed the limp cigar in his right hand and slammed his meaty left paw against his desktop. "A nigger named Night, that's one for the books," he teased. "Listen to me, boy. I don't care what you think you know. We don't have that Floyd fella here and if we did, I wouldn't give a rat's ass about helping him."

"How did you know I was referring to Baltimore Floyd if they didn't bring him here?" asked Knight. "I never said who we were here to see after."

When the sergeant's top lip quivered, he was exposed as a liar. "Looks like we have a problem, officer," said a white man approaching the duty desk. The cop raised his eyes eventually only to rest them on two other men, by the looks of it, two wealthy men.

"Naw, sirs, we're just about to end it right here and now. Ain't no problems at all," said the sergeant.

"I beg to differ," argued the younger of the white fellows, who was in his mid-forties, dark-haired and handsome. His spiffy tailored suit said what he didn't have to, money was on his side. Unfortunately for the sergeant, the law was on his side too. "I'm Albert Hummel, legal counsel for this Floyd fella you claimed not to have in your possession."

"I should have known, a slick mouthpiece to muddy up the waters," the cop fired back sternly, as if not impressed.

"And I'm the stick in the mud," answered the older of the white men. "I'm Dr. Fredrick Stanton, from Washington University. If you're not quaking in your boots yet, this might speed

things up a pinch. See, it's worthless human waste like you that
gives decent white men a bad name. That probably doesn't mean
much to a lazy self-righteous dunce but it does to me and I can
guaran-damn-tee you it won't sit right with the mayor. And if he's
too busy to take my call, sergeant, the governor will be happy to.
We make it a point to golf together at least once a month." The
doctor, who had introduced Delbert to the premature birth protocol when delivering the teenaged girl's baby, was just as matter-
of-fact when rendering the gruff officer's attitude ill-effective.

When the cop picked up the telephone, Delbert grinned on
the inside from head to toe. His team was in the game and slapping the ball over the fence. After having been asked politely, he
signed his name quickly, nodded to Etta and then smiled affectionately at Penny. Although he had no earthly idea what to expect
on the other side of the long corridor leading to the containment
cells, he was certain to emerge from the point of no return. "Thanks
for showing up when you did, Dr. Stanton," said Delbert. "Are
you and the governor really that chummy?"

"Of course not," he answered slyly. "I'm a die-hard Democrat.
But the governor doesn't know that."

Delbert felt good about asking the famous doctor to accom-
pany them. He didn't have to get mixed up in a colored man's
struggle of survival, and he didn't have to lie about being pals
with the head of state, but Delbert was so glad he did on both
counts. The three-hundred-pound jailer, who opened the huge
steel door leading to the immense rows of cells, looked as if he'd
never experienced a good day or a meal he didn't like. With a
military crew cut, rotted teeth, and a four inch scar carved into his
right cheek, he seemed quite comfortable frowning at the strangers
he was ordered to assist.

"Two things 'fore we get on the block," the jailer announced.
"Walk the middle path and don't wander too close to the cells.
Most of these boys are animals, so don't get careless." None of
the doctors blinked, having administered life-saving medical procedures to gunshot and stab victims, some of which they didn't
feel needed it. Physicians had the propensity to be a surly bunch

when the need arose. The lawyer, who hadn't been that close to hardened criminals, did as instructed, walking farthest from the line of small cells sectioned off by concrete dividers. He hadn't been subjected to traumatic episodes of blood and guts either, nor had he designs on starting then.

When that steel door slammed shut behind them, Delbert's mouth went dry. The stench of soiled clothing, dried sweat and urine almost caused him to gag. The lawyer did, three times. He pulled a handkerchief from the breast pocket of his suit coat and pressed it against his nose. "Fellas, let's get in and get out. Jailer, take us to him and be quick about it," he demanded, trying to sound as if he weren't about to lose his lunch.

Near the end of the cell block on the first floor, the jailer stopped and turned to face the door. His hesitation caused Dr. Stanton to force the issue. "Get to it, man!" he yelled, after looking inside the tiny den.

Dr. Knight grabbed the bars with both hands, trying to pry them apart. "Open it!" he demanded, his voice trembling with rage. It was hard to imagine that the man with his head cracked opened, thrown across the iron bunk in his blood-stained clothing was still among the living. "If that man's dead, he won't be the last one."

Delbert was shocked at Dr. Knight's threats. He had no qualms believing harm would come to that sour-mouthed dinosaur if Baltimore had been left to rot, mainly because no one bothered to search Knight's leather doctor bag. Packed among the scalpels was a Derringer pistol, locked and loaded. What he was willing to do with it hadn't been discussed previously; with any luck he wouldn't have to decide.

As the heavy gate swung open, each of the men felt the same fear but none of them voiced it. The lawyer ducked inside the cell with the others, wincing regretfully. Delbert held his breath and his place while more seasoned personnel headed the examination. He'd seen dead people before, lots of them with their faces bruised and swollen, lacerations slashed here and there, split lips, and broken ribs. But none of them appeared half as doomed as Baltimore did when they rolled him over gingerly on his back. Surprisingly, he howled loudly when they moved him. That ole crew-cut jailer seemed the most relieved upon hearing it.

"See, he-he's all right," the big man stammered frightfully. "He's alive. He's all right."

Dr. Knight carefully pulled on Baltimore's severely torn and saturated shirt. "He's alive but he's not all right, not nearly all right," he argued, shooting the jailer a hateful glare. "He's got at least two bruised ribs and possibly some internal hemorrhaging."

"This patient is in desperate need of medical care," added Dr. Stanton. "And this poorly lit cell won't suffice. Get me the man who runs this place, now!"

"But, I can't leave with . . ." he started to debate until Knight stared him down again. "I'll be right back but I got to lock the gate. County regulations," he explained.

Albert Hummel, the lawyer, agreed to go with him. The others stayed behind, enclosed with the prisoner. While they were off searching for the administrator, Delbert kneeled down by the bedside and noticed that the eyelid that wasn't swollen shut began to flutter. "Baltimore," he whispered. "Hey, Baltimore, it's me, Delbert. You know, Tex. We've come to help you. You're hurt something awful."

"No shit, doc," Baltimore answered. He uttered a slight chuckle until the pain caused him to groan in agony. "They wasn't gonna kill me," he said assuredly. "Crackers wanted to d'stroy my spirit first. Said I was resisting arrest. You can't trust 'em."

"Those crackers almost took care of both simultaneously," Dr. Stanton mused. "But we won't let them finish the job, son."

Baltimore heard something in the man's voice that didn't register. He forced his head up, saw the white doctor's face and then he eased out another hurtful laugh. "I . . . must . . . be in heaven," he sputtered and gasped. "Get me hid . . . 'fore they learn about the mix-up and put me out."

The lawyer returned with the jailor. When he found laughter spilling out of the cell, he didn't understand. "I got the head cluck to bite but they don't have the wherewithal to operate on Mr. Floyd. They're sending an ambulance right away." He noticed how the mood had changed since he'd been gone. "What, I miss something?"

"Yeah, this man's in hell and he just don't know it yet." answered Dr. Knight. "Wait until I get him on the operating table. He'll be sure of it then."

Barely able to breathe without spitting blood, Baltimore tried to sit up and make off with the one shoe he was wearing when they locked him in. "Yea, though I walk through the valley . . . of the shadow of death . . . I fear no evil," he mouthed quietly before collapsing on the bunk.

"Get that door open," ordered Dr. Stanton. He was armed with a worrisome scowl. "We need to get him operated on before he's really knocking at heaven's door, or at least standing at the gate."

The jailhouse clinic, normally used to treat common mishaps and minor injuries, served as a makeshift operating room. Surgery to repair a small puncture in Baltimore's lung and sutures in several necessary places took over an hour but they closed him up without discovering any serious internal complications.

Baltimore was put together better than most, Hiram Knight joked afterwards as he and the white doctor shared a smoke in the clinic. Delbert thanked them, filled Dr. Stanton in on what Baltimore was accused of and the way it really went down before the cops came crashing in. Stanton didn't comment on whether he believed Delbert's story. "There was a man in trouble," he said respectfully. "My friend Hiram called me up saying how the fella was worth seeing about and that was good enough for me. Besides, I don't trust crackers either."

The entire processing area stopped on a beat when Baltimore's hot-shot lawyer and personal medical team re-entered from the great unknown behind the steel door. Word had circulated during their eighty-seven-minute absence, during which Etta kept track of each and every tick on the wall clock. The white people in attendance were more curious than compassionate, but each of the colored spectators displayed genuine concern. For them, it was a lot like rooting for the home team even after they had been suspected of cheating. Regardless, it was far better to win against an opponent. The very moment Delbert flashed a noble nod toward the back of the room where Etta and Penny stood in anticipation of a sign, several of the colored women and men applauded excitedly. From the white police officers, Delbert was pelted with snide remarks and dirty looks.

Albert Hummel had practiced law for more than twenty years, but he had yet to experience how life played out in the black community and generally viewed it from the other side of the color line. For that moment in time, amidst the cheers and jeers, he was one of them, and he liked it. "Whoa, boy, this case is bigger than I thought," he said as they exited through the front doors.

"It'll get bigger still," Dr. Stanton cautioned openly. "Lace up your boot straps and get ready to meet the devil's angels head on. Oh, and Albert, it wouldn't hurt to get the wife and kids out of town." Suddenly the inspired attorney's good vibrations and feelings of inclusion waned. Life on the other side wasn't nearly as appealing after all, not even close. In actuality, it was scary as hell.

27

SOMEBODY'S LYING!

The Law Office of Albert Hummel occupied part of the fifth floor of the Regalia Building in the heart of downtown. His busy practice thrived on hefty retainers, settling the estates of St. Louis's elite and the business of protecting wealthy white men whose unfortunate habits had gotten them crossways with the district attorney's office. Albert was expensive but well worth it. When clients followed his instructions, they were much better off than those who initiated an alternate strategy, and subsequently discovered the error of their ways, in prison. Because Baltimore's case was high profile, receiving daily front page ink in both of the city's newspapers, Albert had his work cut out for him.

The established *Post-Dispatch* newspaper smeared the story with a different spin, each time warning white women of black men's predilections including the irresistible desire to bed them. The *Comet*, a leading source of news and gossip among the colored contingent, had more unanswered questions than various suggestions to explain what occurred in the private room of Baltimore Floyd. *Comet* readers had read about this sort of thing before, a white woman exposed for running with the "wrong kind" and later screaming rape when her recklessness came to the light.

The *Comet* readers imagined that a white woman who didn't get exactly what she went there for was unthinkable, while the white population found that notion to be horrendous and inconceivable. Albert knew he would be hard pressed to find one white juror to believe otherwise, at least in public where he'd need them to. Since blacks were prohibited from serving as jurors in cases involving whites, the deck was stacked against him and his newest client, now known as "the notorious Baltimore Floyd."

The attractive red-headed receptionist asked the ladies sitting in the law office reception area to meet in the conference room. Etta and Penny eyed one another apprehensively because of this impending discussion. They had been shaken up, talking between themselves while doing their level-headed best to ignore a multitude of inquisitive white clients looking down their noses at them. Etta, decked out in a pink satin dress, which was cut just above the knees, and a fetching bow-tie shaped hat, pulled on Penny's hand when she'd battled second thoughts of giving her deposition.

"Ms. Etta, I ain't too keen on having all these white folk gawking like they want to hurt us."

"Don't worry about them, Penny. These people haven't seen such a pretty girl dressed like she just stepped out of a magazine is all," Etta replied pleasantly. "I told you that green outfit was a winner." Penny lowered her head to appraise her fashionable mint-colored skirt and jacket ensemble. When her eyes rose up to meet Etta's reassuring smile, she agreed to go forward.

"Yes, ma'am. You probably right. These folks ain't never seen the likes of us. Let's go see what that lawyer man wants. Baltimore's counting on his friends and I'd hate to break down on him." She remembered how he didn't hesitate to step between her and Halstead's wrath that day in front of Watkins Emporium. Now that she had the opportunity to return the favor, Penny was determined to step up and stay on course on his behalf.

The room was spacious, with two walls a lot longer than the

others. Penny figured it must have been designed that way in order to get the rectangular-shaped mahogany wood conference table to fit inside it. Placed on the adjacent credenza against the short wall closest to the door was a crystal serving set. Penny admired it but she was even more infatuated with the idea of enjoying a cool drink of water from it. A tiny freckled-faced woman, wearing a plain amber-colored dress with her dark hair wrapped up in a tight bun, noticed the young lady flirting with it.

"Oh, you can have some, sweetie," the stenographer offered kindly, as if she had prepared it herself.

"Thanks, ma'am, this is a nice place y'all got here," Penny complimented, in exchange for the woman's generosity.

"Why, yes, this is very nice come to think of it," she answered.

"You did come here to help Mistah Albert with Baltimore's case, didn't you?" Penny asked, concerned as to which team the lady with the tiny machine was pulling for.

"It's okay, Penny, she's with us," Etta explained. Privately, concerns about who could be trusted had crossed her mind too, especially after no one had seen or heard from Dinah since the very moment she left Baltimore's room. Rumors swirled that she was Barker's chocolate plaything and wasn't interested in telling what she knew, if anything. Other chitchat resonated as well, implying either Barker or Baltimore had Dinah disposed of because she knew too much. Stories circulated throughout the entire city. No one was certain which tale to believe, so every kook with an opinion had a shot at being right. The pot had begun to simmer and everyone was anxious to sit and watch it boil.

"I'm sorry to have kept you ladies waiting," Albert apologized. "Miss Adams, Miss King." Penny batted her eyes after being called by that name for the first time ever. It had a nice ring to it, rolling off the nice looking white man's tongue. When Etta asked if everyone could go on a first name basis, Penny rolled her eyes and looked the other way as she pouted. "Good, we're all friends here," Albert agreed. "Let's move on then." He began by informing them he'd contacted Baltimore to ensure his well being.

"I've seen Mr. Floyd again and I assure you that he's coming along just fine, although he is still extremely tender and stiff in more places than I'd care to detail in the presence of ladies."

"Good. When can we go down to see him for ourselves?" Etta asked, raring to go.

"Well, that's a problem," he informed her reluctantly, choosing his words so as not to offend. "Mr. Floyd does not wish for either of you to visit him. I know that might sound heartless, but try to see things from his vantage point. He obviously cares a great deal for the both of you and can not bear to have you feeling sorry for him. You must know he's a very proud man."

Angered by Baltimore's refusal, Etta let her feelings get the best of her. "Why doesn't he want us to see him? Humph, best hope he don't let that fat pride of his end up tied to a rope." Penny glared at her for voicing such a thing after preaching how they should watch what they said while in the company of white people.

"Ms. Etta, you shouldn't have," she challenged. "I know you's missing him something awful, but Mistah Baltimore be a proud man like he says, too proud to let you see him down like he is now, in that pen, like some chained dog, Ms. Etta. Please don't fuss over it and take that away from him." Penny wanted to apologize for confronting her elder in mixed company but she meant every word. Tears spilled from her eyes when the stenographer began sniffling at the end of the table. Although the white woman was as removed from this case as any other, Penny's deeply felt sentiment moved her deeply.

"Oh, no, please don't cry," Albert pleaded. "This is a tough case and I can't get what I need if . . . geez, Cindy, not you, too." When he heard his employee boohooing, he leaned back in his chair and sighed. "Okay, it's contagious. I really need you all to try and calm down. This could be a long process and Mr. Floyd needs you all to be strong. Cindy, I need you to be a better example."

"Sorry, Mr. Hummel," she whimpered, wiping at her tear-stained cheeks with a thin folded sheet of tissue. "That has to be the bravest thing I've heard in years."

Albert left the room briefly to let them do whatever it took to clear their heads. When he returned, the trio managed to pull it together. "Outstanding," he said in grand business-like fashion. "That's better. Oh, and before I forget. There is the matter of the fee for my firm's services. Mr. Floyd told me you had access to his funds." He was waiting for Etta to respond, but Penny came out of her handbag with a yellow ribbon tied around a thick bundle of bills.

"How much you think it'll take to spring him?" she asked plainly. When Albert didn't speak up right away, she hunched her shoulders. "I got more if this won't do it."

Etta shared the dumbfounded expressions plaguing the others. Each of them looked at Penny, amazed she had such a great deal of money and didn't seem to mind parting with it. "Don't worry, I can spare it," Penny offered matter-of-factly. "My papa left me some, what you call a inhur'tance." Etta couldn't wait to discover what additional information Penny neglected to divulge regarding her inheritance, but that would have to sit and stew a while.

"Penny, you can put that away, Baltimore left some money with me. He can spare it too," Etta asserted. Albert was licking his chops after previously predicting he'd get pieces of money as they scraped it up, but he didn't plan on receiving the full amount he normally billed for a case going to trial. "I'll make a draw on the funds he had me to keep by tomorrow, Albert. Why don't you get back to telling us what to do today?"

Etta thought two-thousand dollars sounded kind of high-priced when he filled her in on the amount he charged, until she realized all the money in the world wouldn't be too much to ask if it meant Baltimore's acquittal. The eighty grand in her floor vault wouldn't be worth a dime either, if the man who deposited the money couldn't rightfully reclaim it. "You'll get your money, trust in that," she concluded on that particular subject and didn't want to hear another word about it.

"Good enough," Albert said lightly, as he watched Penny place her money back into her purse. "The next item on the agenda is a serious concern. I have detectives searching high and low for Mr. Floyd's female companion, Dinah Leonard. She hasn't been to her job in days now. I'm afraid she skipped town. It's probably for the better, although she's supposed be in possession of valuable information. Would either of you have prior knowledge about what happened the day of Mr. Floyd's arrest or of Miss Leonard's sudden disappearance?"

The look on Etta's face was puzzling. She contemplated all of the scenarios she'd heard on the streets but the lawyer was strictly seeking facts. Eventually, she shook her head regrettably indicating she had nothing to offer. There was something peculiar about the way Penny shielded her eyes by staring down at the glossy finish on the conference table.

"Penny, is there something you want to tell us?" Albert prodded carefully.

"If you know something to help Baltimore, now's the time to tell it," Etta added, with bated breath.

So much had happened that the girl who'd gotten caught up in a woman's predicament didn't know where to start. "Don't rightly know where to begin," she muttered, having been taught that family business was supposed to remain in the family.

"Don't worry about what you've learned bending anybody in the wrong way," said Etta. She had an uneasy feeling Penny wasn't holding back for Baltimore's sake alone. "Just tell it and Albert will decide if its useful."

"Yes, ma'am," Penny answered. Her voice was so weak that Cindy had to lean in to hear them. "He didn't suspect I was spying on him but I did, a lot." Albert wanted to ask if the *he* she was referring to was his client but he decided to let her go without interruption. Cindy's stenograph tape would help him later if he had any questions when preparing for court. "He had some women over to that place of his that backs up into the storeroom at the Fast House. I wasn't snooping at first but I got an eyeful of what he did to those lady friends of his and how they liked it so much.

I ain't have no idea all that grabbing and groaning they did was the same as what happened to my old sow to get them piglets Halstead sold off last summer. It was kinda fun to watch him carry on with Miss Dinah. She was just as wild and twice as loud. They had a hot time together—just pumping, sweating, laughing and whatnot. Then one night, Miss Etta had me go upstairs and fetch a box of paper napkins. I was happy to get into that store-room like always and maybe get lucky enough to watch him with a lady he really liked. I could tell easy when he did because he'd let her quit moaning first before he went to rolling off. Some times he would take a woman to that room of his, get to cutting up and soon as you know it, he'd go and fall off to sleep faster than a brand new puppy with a belly full of milk."

"Penny, this is very important. What did you see that night, when Etta asked you to get the paper napkins?" Albert asked, to get her back on track.

"Well, that's the first night I saw her up there with him, fooling around and blowing cigarette smoke out the window after they . . . you know," she answered, thinking there was nothing left to say until she peered up to discover three sets of begging eyes asking for more. "That ought to help some. Huh, Mistah Albert? My friend Baltimore didn't have to take nothing from her. I seen her giving him all she had and then some. She was stuck on him. I heard her hollering how she couldn't get enough."

"Okay. You did fine, Penny." Albert took a deep breath and drew her gaze to his and then he held it for the big question. "I just need to know one thing. Who? Who was the lady Mr. Floyd wouldn't have any need to take . . . from her?" Cindy stopped typing so she could hear the name clearly. Etta didn't have to guess. The way Penny deliberately omitted Baltimore's name from the story until adamantly defending him explained why she'd kept secrets. Penny knew the level of trouble a colored man faced if it was discovered by the wrong somebody he was having a naughty tryst across the great divide.

In the moment of truth, the lawyer swallowed hard and re-moved his spectacles. "Who was the woman, Penny?"

"That white lady all the fuss is over," she said, making an ugly face like those words left a bitter taste in her mouth. "In the paper, they say her name is Dixie Sinclair. She's the wife of that mean policeman called Barker."

Albert was so relieved. He'd been holding the anticipation in so long his head almost exploded onto the table. "Penny, you've done a very good thing," he said wearily. "Mr. Floyd's going to be quite proud of you."

"He's not gonna be cross with me for spying on him none?"

"I can't see how he could," Albert predicted, from an extremely poor vantage point. He didn't realize it then but his job had just gotten a whole lot harder.

28

YOU HAD TO ASK

In the lower level of the county lockup, Baltimore rested while recuperating from his arrest and surgery as best he could. The male nurse assigned to the medical care ward played checkers with an injured inmate in what scarcely could have been considered a clinic. It didn't amount to much more than a twenty-by-twenty-foot room with cots and a table with cotton balls and rolls of bandages aligned on it. Patients with serious ailments were generally carted off to various hospitals, depending on their race, under armed guard.

Baltimore was somewhat of an enigma because of his impromptu surgery and the bi-racial staff which performed it. His celebrity status grew once rumblings of his near death beating circulated among the other six hundred inmates. Several colored convicts sent him treats from their personal commissary accounts. Although Baltimore wasn't a fan of sweets, he respected their kindness and generosity knowing how prisoners coveted their snacks as prized possessions. The shoe box beneath his bed stored the assortment of chips and mini-cakes. Baltimore shared them with a mentally challenged patient named Husky Maywood, who had recently eaten a hand full of mothballs thinking they were candy mints. After having his stomach pumped, Husky was on suicide watch, because they couldn't classify his behavior otherwise without shipping him off to an insane asylum. That was a fate worse then death for a slightly retarded man serving six months for stealing smokehouse steaks to feed his mongrel dog.

Baltimore had taken a liking to Husky, too slow for his age and too big for his small IQ. His dark complexion was dusky and dry. His hair was matted on his round head and looked as if it never once had a comb pulled through it. It was hard and bristly but the man's heart was soft as butter, something Baltimore believed was set aside for women, children and fools. Husky barely qualified by the skin of his severely bucked teeth.

"Tell me another one Baltimo'," Husky begged after he'd heard his new acquaintance spin the third parable of the day. "I like the way you tell them bible stories." As he bit on a chocolate cupcake one tiny morsel at a time, like a last meal, his eyes impatiently anticipated another tale.

"All right, Husky, I'll tell you one that I heard as a lil' chip on my papa's knee. Well, it seems some time ago that this king they called Herod ruled over the land. Everyone was getting along just fine until some pretty smart fellas called wise men showed up at his castle looking for the place where the King of the Jews, a baby, was to be born."

"Why was they looking for the baby?" Husky asked naively, with crumbs wedged in the corners of his mouth.

"The ruler wanted to kill him 'cause he was afraid the boy would take his kingdom and put him out in the cold. Nah, old Herod wasn't about to let that happen, so he went out and got some fancy thinkers to figure out where he could get the boy." Baltimore grinned when he saw Husky's starry eyes shining brightly as he nibbled cake continually. "Yeah, he tried to work the wise men in his favor but they had a dream, warning them that the old king was up to no good."

"I'll say he wuddin, old rascal," Husky agreed, with a frown exhibiting his distaste for the story's antagonist. "So did he get at that po' baby?"

"Uh-uh, but he did something terribly, terribly bad instead. When he couldn't find the baby boy, with his mama and papa, the king got mad. He then did a thing so rotten I don't even want to tell you about it."

"Please, Baltimo', I gots to know now," he whined. "Come on, pleeease?"

"Okay, but you asked for it," Baltimore reminded him, just as he used to when reading bedtime stories to his younger sister. She would pull on his arm, pleading in the same way Husky did. And so he finished the tale like he always had. "Seeing as how King Herod couldn't locate the boy after a while passed, he sent a whole batch of his killers to the place where the wise men had gone to meet up with him."

"Did the batch of scoundrels catch up with that lil' lamb?" he asked, wishing they hadn't.

"Not to speak of, but that's where the story takes a dive. Since they didn't come up with him after searching pole to pole, they got orders to kill all of the boys in town and nearby towns too, all younger than the age of two, guessing that's how old the child had to be then. He couldn't seem to get at the boy he wanted, so's he killed every other one hoping that'd do the trick." When Baltimore noticed it had grown quiet in the clinic, he raised his head off the pillow and glanced over at Husky. The big fellow was holding himself and rocking back and forth in a disturbing manner. The tears, which watered his face, made Baltimore sorry for picking that particular bible tale.

"You was right, Baltimo', I didn't wanna know about all them dead chil'rens," he wept, while slinking under the covers and pulling them up to his neck like a frightened child after hearing a ghoulish yarn. "That wuddin' fair, not a bit," he groaned.

"Life is like that, Husky," Baltimore said, reflecting on the many crimes he'd committed in the past and escapes pulled off by a hair. "Yeah, it just don't make a damned lick of sense," he added, when it occurred to him how he had been falsely accused and imprisoned.

"I don't wanna hear nuthin' else about it. Nuthin'," the blubbering man complained.

"Husky, listen to me, it's a sad tale, but I think it might make you feel a lot better knowing that the lil' lamb that got away was none other than baby Jesus."

"Oh, Lawd have mercy for that," he whimpered, with hints of happiness in his eyes. "His papa spared him, and took the udders in his place?"

"That's right, Husky, that's right. And that baby boy grew up. He's been returning the favor on us every since," Baltimore explained. "It's a hard pill to swallow, I know, and I aim to ask the Lord if all that was necessary if I ever make it to heaven."

Husky shuddered softly beneath the sheets until a question came to him he wouldn't let pass without asking. "Baltimo', whut if you don't make it up there to see Him?"

"Then you can ask Him for me, Husky. I'd like that," Baltimore answered as kindly as he could, imagining that's how it was likely to play out.

"It's good to see that you're a spiritual man," Albert Hummel remarked as he approached Baltimore's cot. "It doesn't mean much in the courtroom unless you can get a believer on the witness stand."

"Hi ya, lawyer man," Baltimore greeted him amicably. "I ain't been much on believing lately, especially when paddling upstream don't seem to be getting any easier. My pappy is a fire and brimstone preacher, but he can't stand the sight of me. Huh, it'd strike his fancy to know I ended up like this. He always said I was living in a fool's paradise. Up 'til now, I'd have sworn he was wrong."

Albert pulled a metal folding chair to the bedside and shook his client's hand. "You're getting along much better than the last time I saw you. And after what I'm going to lay on you, you'll feel even better yet." The lawyer opened his brown leather satchel and reached inside. "Every now and then a miracle falls from the sky. Here's one for the books if I do say so myself." Albert grinned and cleared his throat. He handed the deposition toward Baltimore before a renegade thought occurred to him. "I'm sorry, Mr. Floyd, I didn't think to ask. Can you read?"

"How are you gone fix your mouth to insult me while reaching your hands in my pocket? Sure, I can read and write. On a good day, I can decipher Latin," Baltimore quipped. He snatched the papers from his attorney and sneered at him as long as he could before laughing so hard he nearly ripped his stitches. "Don't go getting bent out of shape, Albert. I's just funning with you. Us colored boys keep a sense of humor handy. It pays to, nowadays."

"Well, I'm glad you didn't take offense," Albert remarked, with an extreme sigh of relief.

"Oh, you don't get off that easy. I'm offended plenty but you don't know no better so I won't hold your ignorance against you. Let's take a look at this and see if it was worth leaving your cushy office to show me."

Not quite sure how to respond, Albert cleared his throat again and leaned in, lowering the pitch of his voice for the sake of confidentiality. "As you can see, this is a bomb we can drop on the prosecution's case. It proves that you and Dixie Sinclair had been involved in a consensual affair. The fact that she was in your room only strengthens this deposition." The trace of a smile he'd worn quickly faded when Baltimore's hand clinched into a fist. "What's wrong? Is there a problem?"

"Yeah, I've got a big one," Baltimore responded, in a manner puzzling to his legal advisor. "I didn't have no idea Penny was looking in my window or I'd have been more secretive."

"Well, it's a good thing you were not as discreet as you thought. It's like I said, some times a miracle falls when you least expect it."

"You're gonna have to cancel that miracle, Mr. Hummel," Baltimore demanded, using a formal tone. "I can't let that child climb up into the witness chair, in front of all those people and testify. They'll hit her with all the hate they've been saving up for me. She's too good to be ruined on account of my mischief.

I'd just as soon hang first. Anyway, Dinah Leonard's the one you want. She can vouch that I didn't have to take nothing off the white lady." Baltimore was still bothered that Dixie had neglected to fess up to their torrid affair.

"Mr. Floyd, I've met Penny and I agree, she's a doll, but you may very well be faced with the most extreme penalty if we lose this case. Now, hear me out before you make up your mind. The D.A. is going full speed on this. At nine o'clock this morning he dropped the charges against that colored police cadet who shot his wife and that young doctor at Etta Adams's night club so he can concentrate on railroading you."

Baltimore was astonished. His stomach churned as he replayed the deadly scene in his mind. "I was there, man. I seen Willie B. Bernard do it in cold blood. You're telling me they just opened up the gate and let him go free?"

"The travesties don't stop there. So far we haven't been able to find Ms. Leonard, and the district attorney is petitioning for the trial to start in ten days."

Baltimore's eyes displayed with inconsolable surprise. "Why'd they get in such a hurry? It's not like I'm going nowhere."

"They're afraid if it doesn't get under way soon, there'll be retaliation from the locals. My office is swarmed with death threats from the Ku Klux Klan for representing you. What Penny saw could save your life, Mr. Floyd. I'm not certain that anything else will. Can you give it some thought before turning it down?" Albert's question stayed unanswered so long he couldn't be sure Baltimore heard it. "Mr. Floyd?"

"I heard you just fine. But, I got to draw a line in the sand," he replied eventually. "I know you're risking a lot helping me and I'm grateful. It might be a heap better for everybody if I throw the case and let them string me up." Baltimore didn't mean it, but he reasoned Penny's life was more valuable than his own.

"Unless miracles come in pairs, that line in the sand of yours could very well put you in the death house. Being a man of principle is one thing, but this is loony!" Albert bellowed louder than he meant to.

"Now I know I'm in the right place," a man's deep voice sounded from the door of the small room. Henry, dressed in his daily uniform, strolled in. "Baltimo' Floyd swearing off somebody's help because he's too pig-headed to accept a hand up. If that don't beat all."

Baltimore felt a sudden chill roll over him when he heard Henry's voice. He propped another pillow behind his back and peered toward the gentle oaf in the next cot. "Husky, remind me to tell you the one about the prodigal son. It's got these two brothers in it, who parted ways over money, fast times and overripe envy. It's a doozie." Husky nodded slowly, closed his sad eyes and then drifted off to sleep.

"I can see you need some time to work out matters," Albert said, as he stood from his chair. Baltimore returned the deposition and he stuffed it back in his fancy satchel. "I'll stop by in a few days. We'll keep looking for that missing witness." He glared suspiciously at Henry in his brand spanking new uniform, wondering why his client was taking meetings with the local police. It didn't add up, so he made a mental note to inquire about it with Etta later.

Curiosity had spun its shameless web on Henry. He had to stop in and see for himself. A man unjustly accused was as rare as a two-headed snake. Henry was positive of Baltimore's innocence because he'd been a close friend, through thick and thin, and never once knew him to force his desires on any woman. He didn't have it in him, to be that kind of man, under any circumstances. Of all the fights, shoot outs, and tough spots Baltimore landed in, it was inconceivable for Henry to think of him as anything less than unflappable. "They finally caught you dead to rights?" Henry said lightly, not ready to believe his eyes.

"Yeah, they caught me with my pants on backwards all right but they got it all wrong."

"At least they got to you while you was still in them or else they'd have killed you on the spot." Henry tried to make sense of Baltimore's actions but his history of unpredictability made that impossible. "You just had to go and give it to Barker's wife of all people? I've seen him put in some pretty rough work and he ain't no slouch."

"I've seen his wife put out and neither is she. Couldn't deny that even if I had a mind to. Hell, I done heard white boys singing about being way down south in Dixie since I was a pup, I saw my chance to see what all the fuss was about and I took it," he joked. "And I have to say, screwing with Dixie was worth it."

"Don't play yourself stupid, Baltimo,' or the last laugh will snap your neck," Henry warned. "You done stirred up a mess of hornets by shaking that big ole thang of yours at the queen bee's nest."

"Man, you don't know the half of it. Come busting up in here like you're bringing me the news. It was me, fighting and scuffling against two farm boys who tried to split my scalp. Dixie Sinclair played me like a flute in more ways than one. I thought she was a pushover, but I had her pegged all wrong. She picked me out from the start and flipped on her man the first chance she got. I'm the one who took his boatload of smack and she's the one who lead me to it."

"I ain't ever known you to be a liar, Baltimo,' but that can't be close to the truth. Why would that lady help you con Barker and then hand over that much money to some . . ."

Baltimore sat up on his bed. "Go on and say what you think of me—some niggah! Yeah, because she's a white girl you think she's above rummaging in the sack with me and cutting a hole in Barker's pockets while she was at it? It was never that hard for a woman to put one over on you. Tell me something, did the Metro Police make you buy those slave catching clothes?" Baltimore asked, with a terribly disheartening stare. "You's mighty high hat for a gullible field hand, buck." Henry stared at Baltimore in disbelief before he could reply.

"That's kinda funny coming from a man who's got to ask if he can take a piss," Henry replied bluntly.

"I don't need you to tell me what the hell I can and can't do. I've made it this far by my damned self, no thanks to you. Ain't there some stray dogs roaming the streets that need picking up?"

"You still too full of yourself to see what's standing in front of you," Henry said, sneering at Baltimore's current status. "They got your stubborn ass locked up, ready for tar and feathers, and you got the nerve to look down your nose at me. Maybe that ditch those boys knocked in your head leaked out some of the starch that's put you in this hole in the first place."

Baltimore's face darkened with resentment, in a way that startled his visitor. "What you doing here then, Henry Taylor? Since it's plain to see you's with them from scoot to skip. Matter of fact, why'ont you shove off before I bust a stitch putting my foot square up the back of that monkey suit. Go on and get out, slave catcher. This is one niggah you's too late to snatch!" Henry choked on the words knotting up the back of his throat. Instead of retaliating with damaging rips at Baltimore's ego, he frowned pitifully and walked away.

"That's right, get on back across the water before your rowboat pop a cork. You ain't the man I used to know and you ain't my friend no more. You done forgot, Henry Taylor!" he yelled hysterically as his unwelcome visitor exited the cell block. "Shame on you, Henry Taylor, you done forgot!" Baltimore felt the tear in his heart being pulled further apart. Too mad to give it any reasonable deliberation, Baltimore cursed up a mighty storm and then vowed to get even with Henry in hell unless he had the chance to settle up sooner. Henry hadn't forgotten how they were once two of a kind, he just didn't want to remember.

29

CASKETS AND CHARADES

For three days, a quiet trance held the staff of Homer G. Philips Hospital hostage. In the business of saving lives, dealing with death was inevitable, but the recent murders of M.K. and Helen loomed heavily over the doctors and nurses who knew them best. Dr. Hiram Knight took it easy on the residents and made it a point to speak to each nurse he passed in the halls. Geraldine Robinson, the nursing director, asked to take a leave of absence after she first received the bad news. It was a difficult matter having to sedate the hospital's tough-as-iron matriarch. She'd been the strong shoulder to lean on for so many people over the years. Seeing her toppled from the grief of two senseless killings left an indelible stain.

Delbert wrote his father for the first time since arriving to St. Louis. Although the words didn't come easy, he relayed his thanks for the sacrifices made. He shared how his matriculation and ability to keep pace with his contemporaries were both fairing well. While writing the next passage, Delbert broke down and cried when he attempted to explain what happened to one of the residents who had taken him under his wing. Becoming a skilled surgeon, playing God with patient's lives, and handling the pressures of life were all interrelated, he'd discovered. If any of the three faltered, the others came crashing down as a result. One saving grace, which Delbert held close to his heart, was the love that blossomed with the skilled nurse he couldn't stop thinking about, Sue Jacobs, the pastor's daughter.

Aware of Delbert's struggles and his suffering over his lost friend, Sue worked at consoling him with kind words and warm embraces as the funeral service for Helen drew near. M.K.'s remains were flown out of town the day before and Delbert was on hand at the air strip to say his goodbyes. Moving past it seemed impossible until a peculiar occurrence changed that.

In the rear seat of Pastor Jacobs's long black Buick, Sue held Delbert's hand tightly, as if she had no intentions of ever letting go. Her father observed them from the rearview mirror on the way to the cemetery. He wasn't keen on his daughter playing nursemaid to any man, other than him, but he didn't utter a single word. Burials, births, and blushing brides were about letting go, so it was clear to him that he needed to loosen the reins holding Sue close to home. She was a grown woman, despite how much he despised viewing her that way. Besides, if they traveled the blessed aisle, the pastor wouldn't be losing a daughter, he'd be gaining a doctor, and that wasn't a bad deal any which way he cut it.

At two o'clock, the Buick eased inside the cemetery gates and passed the funeral procession which stretched out for two city blocks. It seemed that every friend and acquaintance Helen had made in her lifetime turned up at her service as well as countless others who felt sorry for the likable nurse they'd read about in the *Comet*. The event had culminated as a veritable who's who see-and-be-seen. Local celebrities arrived in droves. Singers, wealthy entrepreneurs and hospital employees were given the VIP seats up front. Etta and Penny were among those shown to the middle rows. Henry, Roberta, Smiley, and the other colored policemen were offered sitting accommodations farther back. Because Sue's father was the presiding minister, his car was allowed to roll past the long line of vehicles ahead of him.

The broad-built gray-haired man with even dusky skin exited the automobile thirty yards from the burial pavilion and lead the way. Sue clung tightly to Delbert's arm as he made his way toward the casket, marveling at how many people appeared to pay their last respects. Adorned in dark suits and classically tailored mourning attire, a horde of colored women and men migrated closer to the plot of land where a previously virtual unknown was to be laid to rest.

The sun-drenched skyline was overshadowed by the disastrous occasion. Murmurings persisted as the mourners and meddlers discussed the gloomy details which lead each of them to that place. Rumblings of Willie B.'s release from jail had just begun to surface. He was beside himself for ruining three lives, M.K.'s, his loving wife's and his own. The Metropolitan Police Department retracted his training credits, closing the door for a position within the force. Adding to that, Willie B.'s biggest regret was knowing his wife's body had been prepared at the family mortuary. Helen was stored there for three days while he was incarcerated and his father was faced with the daunting task of embalming his own daughter-in-law.

Willie B. roamed the streets since his release because there was no place for him to hide his shame. In every bar he entered, someone was reading about the crazed mortician's son who shot up Ms. Etta's Fast House in a jealous rage, ending the lives of two respected members of the community. During his search to find solace and a medium to exorcise his guilt, Willie B. sat on a stack of worn tires behind an old service station on the edge of town. After drowning his sorrows with a bottle of cheap liquor, he'd set out again, fueled this time by an undeniable yearning for closure.

Pastor Jacobs opened the funeral program and exhaled a heartfelt sigh. He had the privilege of facilitating over Helen's christening. He watched her develop into an upstanding young lady and later he presided over her wedding to the man who ultimately ended her life. It wasn't a long stretch imagining his daughter Sue lying still and void inside of the expensive hand-carved coffin ready to be lowered into the ground behind him. He kept that in mind when reciting his opening address.

"Welcome, one and all to the final send-off for our beloved daughter, sister, and friend Helen Medford Bernard. She was a wonderful child, who blossomed into a beautiful, kind woman and nonetheless was taken from our midst far too soon." Someone in the back wailed loudly, as if on cue, so it went virtually unnoticed by the minister.

When several women screamed simultaneously, in mass hysterics, he peered up from his notes. "Oh, my God!" the pastor exclaimed. The crowd gasped when a man came traipsing through it, weaving about in a policeman's parade uniform and white gloves. Like an epidemic, women began to faint one after the other while a number of men ducked for cover. So inebriated he could hardly stand, Willie B. pointed a loaded revolver toward the minister as he marched closer to the podium.

"I ain't gonna say this but once!" he shouted. "Don't try and stop me."

"Son, this isn't the way," an elderly man reprimanded from the sidelines.

"Shut the hell up, Daddy," the gunman barked, his quick temper not yet running its course. "I've listened to your mouth long enough and I'm tired of hearing it. If you don't want to see tomorrow, then just keep on flapping your trap." "All right then, I'm glad to see y'all come out to say so long to my Helen. She's the apple of my eye and . . ." Willie B. was becoming overwhelmed. "And I want to see her one last time, then I'll be on my way." He motioned with the gun barrel for his old man to unlock the coffin lid. As ordered, his father whipped out a key and inserted it into a small metal clasp, but he refused to do his son's bidding past that point. "Still stubborn as a mule, I see. Get on out the way!" he shouted. The mortician stepped away from the mound, fearing what would happen when his irrational son saw his wife's corpse.

Willie B. waved the gun at the audience erratically. "Stay back! This is my wife! Mine! I got the right to say goodbye proper." With the pistol secured in his left hand, he heaved the lid open. The lid rocked back as the weight shifted on the leather belts used to secure and lower the casket. A ghastly roar resounded from the crowd. "Shut up!" hollered Willie B. in response. "I can't hear myself think with all that damned noise going on back yonder." Angry and out of sorts, he pivoted on the soles of his new shoes to face the remnants of his wife. He stuck his hand inside of his coat pocket and came out with a poorly folded sheet of stationary paper. Tears began fleeing from his tired eyes.

"I wrote you a poem, baby," he cried, sniffling intermittently. "I know how you was always after me to put something down. See, I done it." He held the paper near the dead woman's face to confirm it to her while the audience gawked in total disbelief. "It goes like this, Helen. 'You was the world to me. I lost you and I lost my way. I don't want to live without you another day.'" It seemed as if he was going to continue reading, but he decided to plant a tender kiss on her rouge colored lips instead.

Willie B.'s father closed his eyes when his son turned the gun on himself and squeezed the trigger. The deafening blast reverberated as the crowd was shocked into silence. Willie's body jerked forward, falling on top of Helen. The leather straps beneath the casket gave way, sending both husband and wife plunging into the newly dug hole.

30

SECONDHAND HEARTACHE

"You're saying he jumped *in* the box?" Clarisse asked for the fifth time after Etta painted the horrifying picture for her on the following day. Clarisse's face scrunched into a prune-like contortion just thinking about it. She swayed in the beauty salon chair from side to side as Etta fiddled about in her purse. "You know I've heard people say they wanted to follow loved ones to the grave, but I ain't ever heard of nobody actually pulling it off."

"It was more like he threw himself in it, but what a sight, girl," Etta recalled, as she passed Clarisse an opened pack of smokes. "Then, it was just like that newspaper said, folks started screaming and knocking each over trying to get out of the way. It was a holy mess. I feel so sorry for that poor woman. Nobody deserves to be laid to rest like that. Plain pitiful."

"They always said that undertaker's son wasn't right in the head. Ain't no doubt about that now."

Etta took a long drag from her cigarette and frowned with a far-away reflective gaze in her eyes. "Naw, naw, it ain't."

The newspaper recounted the event from beginning to end for those who didn't attend the funeral. It was the *Comet's* first edition in three days that didn't have Baltimore's arrest and impending trial as the headline. Albert Hummel felt like a heel when he called Etta to share Baltimore's refusal to let Penny testify on his behalf. Against his client's wishes, Albert deliberated pushing her into it regardless, but Etta laid down the law. She enlightened him as to how close Baltimore felt to the girl and that he wasn't to become the first man to use Penny after she'd broken free of her father's tyrannical prison.

Furthermore, the detectives Albert employed to snoop around came back scratching their heads. No one they interviewed was willing to provide information that remotely benefited Baltimore. The neighbors on the same floor, who did open their doors, had mixed emotions regarding why the white woman was in the room but weren't willing to offer testimony under oath. Back to square one, Etta forked over the attorney's two-thousand dollar fee and came up empty as a bottomless washtub. It wasn't until Penny reappeared in front of the shop, with two grown men, after making a run for boxed lunches that she saw a glimpse of light at the end of a very dim tunnel.

"Who is that Penny's got with her?" Clarisse asked cautiously, as she stared at them through the glass door. She was particularly interested in the tall dark one. He had a brick-layer's physique which was more to her liking than the shorter man's less impressive frame. However, she did loops over his light colored eyes once she saw them up close.

Etta sat up on her perch and then squinted in their direction. "Is that . . . it sure is, those boys from Kay Cee." Etta eased down off her seat and met the fellows as they approached, in step with Penny. "Pudge, Dank, what in the blue blazes are y'all doing back here from Kansas City?"

"Hey, Etta, ma'am," Pudge said, greeting both ladies simultaneously. "We didn't get back 'cause we never left. Baltimore convinced us to take it easy before rushing off for home. We've been taking in the sights, so to speak," he added, with a sneaky wink so Penny wouldn't catch on to their conversation.

"I hope you didn't get nothing on you," she teased. "Fellas, meet Madame Clarisse. This is her shop, so mind your manners."

Dank tipped his brown derby-styled hat and smiled cordially. Clarisse caught it and threw him back an even bigger one for his troubles. "Madame? I sho' like the sound of that."

"Boys, it's so nice to make your acquaintance. Bright eyes, muscles, it's too bad I missed you the last time around," Clarisse flirted shamelessly. "We's right fond of showing off the sights we got around here."

Dank quickly glanced in Etta's direction. She just shrugged her shoulders with a look on her face that said go at your own risk. "Don't mind if I do see what's what. Come to think of it, I thought you might be with the neighborhood tourism society. We got to discuss some things with Etta, then I'm available to see what new attractions might be opening up," Dank said with a sly grin.

Penny smacked her lips loudly, interrupting their flirting and reminding them that business waited in the wings. "Ms. Etta, how long you gonna let them carry on that way? Madame Clarisse likes the man and his eyes are wide open for her too, even I can see that. Now, let's talk about how they can help Mistah Baltimore. That is why they's standing here after all," she huffed, growing increasingly annoyed. "Well?"

"Yes, ma'am," Pudge said respectfully, to boost the young woman's ego.

All of a sudden, Dank was in a hurry to get that Baltimore business over and done with too. With any luck, he could help straighten out his pal's affairs and do a lot of good for his own situation in the meantime. Pudge had known Baltimore long before introducing him to Dank, so their roots ran much deeper. He was anxious to get the ball rolling.

"Me and Dank was ready to sail on down the railroad line when these four white boys took the bench next to us at Union Station," Pudge eagerly explained. "They looked to be real rough around the edges, you know, like farm hands. They were whispering but I heard every word just fine. Said they was gonna set fire to the jailhouse to get at the 'nigger rapist' the cops got locked up for putting it to a white woman against her will. Hell, since that didn't have nothing to do with me, I kept to my own. Then another fella showed up. A law man, they called Tin-man or Tazz-man or some such strange name like that. Anyway, they pointed to this story in the colored newspaper. When they hustled off, leaving the daily rag where they'd huddled, I wanted to know whose goose they was about to cook. And damned if it wasn't Baltimore's name right there on the front page."

Etta knew outside instigators meant trouble in the worst way. They were known to storm in, bring the Negro community worlds of hurt and then they'd disappear into the night without being held accountable for the havoc caused. "We'd better act fast, then," Etta asserted firmly. Her demeanor was solid as steel when she apprised them of what Penny had observed through the apartment window. Clarisse chewed on what she'd heard, then rolled her eyes and pursed her lips in opposition. Etta took note but forged ahead, despite her inclination to defend what Baltimore had done. The details involving Dinah's untimely disappearance were sketchy, she told them, adding that it didn't look good for Baltimore unless someone found the woman alive and willing to stand up for the truth, if not for him. Next, Etta informed everyone of what she'd gathered about Baltimore's relationship with Dixie, and his flat-out unwavering stance against including Penny formally. Albert's detectives couldn't get anywhere with their canvass for potential witnesses either, so they were left with a big pile of nothing, more than enough to go around.

Pudge slapped his soft hands together as he was struck with an idea. "Etta, did you say that lawyer fella sent white detectives over to grill colored tenants about a colored man getting in the sack with a white woman?" And just like that, it occurred to Etta that not all of the stones had been sufficiently overturned.

Dank stared at his newly purchased wristwatch then at Clarisse. "It won't take long getting them to spill it to us," he boasted assuredly. "We can get kinda persuasive if need be. Ain't that right, Pudge?"

"Uh-huh, downright charming," he replied, with a raised brow.

For ten dollars, the local mail carrier spit out the names and door numbers of every tenant on Baltimore's floor when the K.C. Detective Agency sent their only gumshoes out later that afternoon. Pudge distracted the unfortunate and unsuspecting soul who had found himself staring down a forty-four caliber cannon when Dank cornered him in the side stairwell to have a meeting of the minds. Another ten spot changed hands after the mailman dropped nuggets of information about the residents, including secrets they'd rather be kept hidden from public scrutiny.

Three of the tenants on the list Pudge had scribbled down in a small tablet warranted discussion before ascending to the third floor. They didn't want to run the risk of calling on someone who'd put the city cops on them and stall their investigation. The first person they approached was Rosa Lee Teacart, a forty-year-old woman receiving monthly checks from Topeka, Kansas under the name of Marla Speeks. The fellows didn't have to guess that she was on the lam; the mailman threw that one in free of charge because she wouldn't let him rest his hooves at her place without leaving something she could spend on the dresser. Knowing that she was a woman with money on her mind, more than most, gave Pudge a few angles to shake her down. He convinced Dank to hold off on any strong-arm tactics unless it was absolutely necessary, because they'd hate to rough up the wrong person who could corroborate Baltimore's claims.

The number on the center of Rosa Lee Teacart's door was made of cheap black tape. The corners had turned up, making them hard to read in the dimly lit hallway. "That does say three-fourteen, don't it?" Dank asked, as he reached forward to smooth out the numbers with his long fingers.

"Looks to be the one," answered Pudge, mostly guessing. "Baltimore wasn't putting on the Ritz. I was almost mad at him for sticking us in that dive motel, but he stayed low budget too." He glanced down the corridor in both directions before getting

Dank to knock. "The coast is clear. Go ahead and beat on it some." Before Dank wrapped against the wood, they heard someone approaching from the other side. "Save it, she's opening up," Pudge whispered.

Dank backed off and assumed an authoritative position directly behind his smaller counterpart in the event whoever opened the door tried to dismiss his partner's non-threatening stature. Pudge wouldn't have admitted it but the world seemed a good deal more manageable with a former prize-fighter backing his play.

"Uh . . ." was all the woman got out before laying eyes on gloom and doom blocking her path. Her mouth flew wide open a millisecond before losing her breath. The woman was exactly what they expected, a chameleon who altered her appearance as often as she changed her wigs. The dress she'd undoubted wrestled with in order to get it zipped was a dark shade purple and made from shiny synthetic material that clung to her generous hips and breasts like cellophane. She wasn't exactly a large woman but two more hot-buttered biscuits would have easily qualified her. Dank surveyed her body with his piercing eyes, wondering why their mail-carrying informant refused her demands to cough up a couple of bucks. Her silky cinnamon-brown skin, cute button nose, thick legs and full lips had the money in his pocket fighting to get out.

When she noticed how the big fellow was sizing her up for durability, she began inching backwards slowly, flicking glances at the doorknob. Pudge stuck his foot inside her apartment so she couldn't shut them out. "Don't fret, Rosa Lee, we just need to talk to you about the man them white police dragged off," he told her, in a straightforward voice. "We can do this inside, nice and quiet-like, or standing here for busybodies to listen in, if you want people to know your business, *Marla Speaks*." The way he used her alternate name made the woman shudder. "If we wanted to harm you, you'd have never seen it coming until it was too late to matter," he explained, to ease her into the gear he wanted to drive in.

"O.K.," she said, with reluctance and a dead-eyed glare at Dank.

"Don't worry about me," he said, reading her thoughts. "If it comes to that, you'll get more out of it than I will. And, I pay in advance." There wasn't any reason to deny she'd made extra money when times called for acts of ingenuity in order to get by, so she let his lewd comment pass without addressing it. Besides, rent was due and her pocketbook was light.

"Come on in, then," she muttered. "It's not like I have a choice from where I stand. And since we's all chummy, I'd rather go by Marla. It's been a long time since I heard somebody call my name." She invited them in and then pulled the door closed afterwards. Her small domicile was an exact copy of all the others in the hall, but she'd done a lot of work making it her own. Decently framed country landscapes hung against dingy walls on the sides. One of them wasn't half bad, actually. An eggshell-colored sofa sat in the middle of the front half of the room while a metal framed bed occupied most of the back side. The kitchenette area was small, but the elegant hand-painted flower vases placed here and there gave the apartment a smile they didn't expect to find. Everything in the room was a reflection of who she was, a woman on the run with an unquenchable desire to enjoy the second-hand slice of life she'd carved out for herself.

"Now that y'all in, get to asking so's you can get out," she huffed, with both arms folded rebelliously.

Pudge understood women like her, sick of running and tired of everything else, so he took it easy on her. "Marla, tell us what you know about the colored fella and who he was in the habit of bringing up to his room."

She nodded sympathetically before voicing her regret. "I liked Baltimore," she said as another thought traipsed through her head. "He didn't care too much for me, in the way I wanted. Wasn't his cup of tea I figured, even though he was always nice enough to say hello when we passed on the stairs. Most men try to look up my dress when they's heading down, but not him." She was disappointed that Baltimore hadn't tried to cop a free peep show and didn't appear all that ashamed about it. "That day, I had a trick in here with me." Marla's eyes floated up to rest on Dank then, noting his reaction. After his lips curled into a slight smile, her gaze drifted toward the floor again. "He was in a hurry to get home so we had to rush things. Baltimore had that pretty little chippie of his over. The walls here are paper thin so it's easy to make out what folks say in the next room. He told her he was blowing town but offered to include her in the deal too. They was about to fight about why he had to go and then there was this knock at his door."

"Was that the same day he got pinched with the white girl?" Pudge asked, nearly apologizing for making her envision Baltimore with yet another woman. Again she nodded, sadly indicating it was. "Why'ont you tell us what you remember?" Pudge pressed, eager to get to the truth.

"I was getting to that," Marla panted, not wanting to be rushed. "Well, then a white lady showed up, telling him to run the colored one off. That didn't go over like the white lady wanted, so she hung around. I missed some of what happened after that because my customer went to getting a little excited, you know, right about then." Marla walked toward the kitchenette and poured herself a glass of water. "The colored girl must've left 'cause I didn't hear her no more. Baltimore was alone with the white one in there. They were arguing over money, it sounded to me. He tried to throw her out! Then all hell broke loose. She was knocking about and hollering but not the way you'd think. It was like she got madder over being told to leave than she was about whatever money stood between them. It's strange though, how that white woman didn't say two words in Baltimore's stead when the police crashed in on their disagreement. They the ones hollering rape, not her, then again she wasn't saying no different."

Pudge took copious notes as he followed Marla's story line by line. "Anything else?" he asked, sensing she was reluctantly holding something back.

"Nah, that's all of it," she concluded, as if a heavy burden had been lifted from her shoulders. "I wish I could do more."

After being silent long enough, Dank cleared his throat. "You wouldn't mind telling your story to the judge at the trial, would you?"

"Mistah, that's too far to fall," she answered. "I know Baltimore's in a jam, but they want me back in Mississippi for killing my no-good husband over an affair I had with his brother. If I get looked at too hard by the police, they liable to ship me off to pay the debt I owe. This ain't Park Avenue, but I get a little money from my ex brother-in-law who was around a lot. It ain't much but it helps me out some." Her story was one of many colored women during that time. She craved to be something other than what she'd been. Born to sharecropping parents and married by age sixteen left lots of room to spread her wings. Adopting the name of her best friend back home, hustling tricks and slaving at the nearest five-and-dime store wasn't what she had in mind, but it was better than prison. Anything was better than that, even wearing another woman's name and never going home again.

Next on the men's list was a man called Pete Larson. He was rumored to sell underground skin magazines to sex degenerates who liked young boys. Larson wouldn't get the good cop routine awarded to Marla Speeks. He ranked at the very bottom of the criminal gene pool and was treated as such. Pete answered the door like a dangerous thug but the visitors saw something else deep inside of him at first glance, a scared little man acting tough to ward off bigger predators. He had to be convinced by Dank's rock-hard fists that he wasn't as tight-lipped and obstinate as he initially thought. A couple of stiff blows on the jaw had him singing like Lena Horne. Pete Larson agreed to offer the same tune in court if he had to, as long as Dank stayed away from his apartment.

Pudge waited another hour before Abigail Langtree decided to find her way home. She was an old prickly woman, fencing stolen department store goods out of a building two blocks away. The old woman said, "I don't care what y'all have on me, it ain't going to get me to doing nothing to help that triflin' niggah after dipping and doodling with that white gal. Anyways, he got what he deserved for bringing that white heffa in a colored-only lodging house where she didn't have no business. Those cops should've beat on his black ass like an army mule!" Abigail Langtree was still barking vehemently at Pudge, when Dank exited Marla's door fastening his belt. He'd felt sorry for her, enough to leave two months' rent on the dresser. He dropped twenty-four dollars in advance. It was one thing for a man to say he was sorry and another to prove it.

"Well, you heard that old biddy," Pudge vented. "She wouldn't give a flying flip and it don't matter what we held against her."

"Yeah, I got that. We have that dirty picture peddler, Larson, sewed up. Sad thing about Marla though."

Pudge glanced over at Marla's door, "Yeah, she's had it harder than some," he said in a weary voice.

"Nah, I meant it's sad to know Baltimore passed on that. She rides like a Cadillac and spins like a top. I done put a few bucks down on the cow and I'm coming back for the milk. Whew! I need a cigarette."

Annoyed that Dank made the best of a bad situation and he couldn't, Pudge retaliated. "What you need is to wash the smell of that lady's tail off your face, twice."

3 1

NICKELS AND NIGHT CRAWLERS

Three days had passed since Pudge and Dank's investigative maneuvers. Pete Larson conveniently got the notion to leave town, trying to avoid working with Baltimore's defense team. Courtrooms made him antsy and he was already as jumpy as a pregnant toad due to the underground operation he ran. There was money in child pornography, and a lot of it. He'd decided to hoof it with all of the inventory stored in his luggage. When Dank snatched him up by the collar and dragged him back up to his apartment, Pete fell on his knees and begged for his life. Dank took his collection of photos instead then warned him that begging wouldn't save him if he tried to skip out again. Pete sat in the middle of his floor and cried like a baby when Dank left with his working inventory underneath his arms. He'd have been even more heartbroken after testifying because that suitcase and every photo in it were torched as soon as Pudge learned of their existence. Afterwards he spat on the ashes. Robbers, bandits and the like, those who made their money by taking from other men, were typically more tolerant than others who exploited people for profit. However, very few were willing to do business with kiddie flesh peddlers. If they didn't need Pete Larson's song and dance to help sway the jury, he'd have been dead and done away with already.

Henry kept his mouth shut while spending his first full week as a police officer. Tasman Gillespie was up to his old tricks, running drugs with Barker, shaking down nightclub owners and slapping around pushers when the mood struck them. Henry had no idea where Barker came up with an additional supply of heroin so fast. Since Baltimore admitted hijacking the cargo from under his nose and fencing it, Henry could only deduce that Barker was forced to purchase his own drugs back at a hefty markup or lose his business altogether. Unfortunately, being forced to do anything he'd rather not made him extremely coarse. Having to pay Schmitty Rosenberg top price to stay in the game made him mad. Henry observed silently, made mental notes about the addresses of drug houses, drop locations and the place Barker stashed the goods.

As soon as Baltimore's trial ended, Henry was going to ask for a transfer and a new partner. It was one thing to know what was going on but too much to stomach when seeing it up close. He drove home one day thinking how difficult it was being on the right side of the law when lawmen were doing most of the wrong. Henry had a lot of animosity building inside of him. He was beginning to tire and fray at the edges, something he hated to admit, even to himself.

With one week remaining before Baltimore learned his fate, Henry had constructed a hedge around his life and family. Rarely did he leave the house after returning from work and he didn't allow Roberta on the porch after nightfall. Henry felt the world around him was shrinking into a dangerously poisonous pill dancing on the tip of his tongue and he couldn't stand the taste of it. Fear seeped into his heart, fear that he'd likely one day take too deep a breath and swallow that pill. Roberta had begun to watch him carefully. She'd heard of white policemen who didn't take to the pressures of protecting the public successfully. Most were re-moved from the department because of long-term drunkenness, while others ended it all by splattering their brains on bathroom walls. Roberta prayed all the time, hoping that Henry would come back to her after he left for work. Her son Denny, all of five years old now, prayed as well. Unsure what brought on her pan-icked expressions and silent babblings, the boy prayed his mother wouldn't need to pray as often going forward.

Two days later, Henry sat on his bed with his head in his hands. Roberta called his name. He heard her clearly enough but didn't respond right away. The next time she summoned him from the bedroom doorway, he was caught off guard. Startled, Henry pulled a pistol from underneath a pillow and aimed it at her. "Wait, Henry!" she cried. "It's me, honey, Roberta."

Acknowledging his wife finally, Henry blinked his eyes rapidly as if coming out of a trance. "Huh, oh . . . oh," he stuttered, now staring into the face of a woman terrified of what her husband had become, a rabbit among wolves. He was afraid, of what ex-actly she didn't know, but the man she married was overcome by something he was hiding.

"Uh . . . I'm sorry, Henry," she uttered stoically once he'd low-ered the gun to his side. "I hollered for you but there wasn't an answer so I came to see what kept you."

"I'm the one who needs to apologize. Things gots me so agi-tated I almost shot my own wife. Forgive me?" he asked, with pleading eyes.

"Sure, baby, I know you didn't mean to hurt me. It's just that I came to tell you there's a white man at the door," Roberta said, as an afterthought.

"A white man?" Henry grumbled, with the weapon poised in his thick fingers.

"Yeah, it's your friend from the academy," she answered, as if he only had one of them. "The fella who helped the colored men get a fair shake."

"Clay," he replied, almost chuckling. Due to his embattled

soul, Henry had all but forgotten how much he had respected Clay Sinclair. His presence was welcome come hell or high water, but an unannounced visit after dark put him on the ropes.

With a loaded thirty-eight revolver stuffed in the waistband underneath his shirt, Henry peered out of the screen door before opening it. "You alone, Clay?" he asked, wisely looking for signs of a set-up.

"Yeah, Henry, and I didn't expect to show up here anymore than you did." Clay affirmed slowly.

"Come on in, then," Henry offered. "I'm glad to see you. Sorry Roberta had you standing out there like a stranger, but things being what they is—"

"Save it, I understand," Clay answered quickly. He followed Henry into the small living room area, quickly noticing the impressive furniture filling the room. "Nice digs, Henry. Maybe you've found a way to make a little extra on the day shift," Clay said, questioning if he'd taken money for keeping quiet about Barker and Gillespie's drug distribution ring.

"Naw, all of this stuff is being paid off the old-fashioned way, slow, a few nickels at a time."

"Glad to hear it," the night caller responded, genuinely relieved. "I didn't risk my job and pension just so's you could hop the fence for some extra . . . nickels."

Henry eased back into a relaxed stance then. "You didn't go wrong with me," he answered, although he was growing quite interested as to why Clay was paying him a visit. "I'm liable to be paying on these front room fixings when you start drawing on your pension, but that ain't why you're here."

"No, it's not, and if Barker knew about this, he'd have my head. Truth be told, it's the soft spot I have in my heart for people getting dealt from the bottom of the deck. Guess I never could stand seeing any man being shafted, regardless of what his skin looks like." He noticed Henry's wrinkled brow. There was a tough question in his head trying to tunnel out.

"Uh-huh," was Henry's way of asking for more information without actually having to admit being lost in the conversation.

"Well, it's like this," Clay began, after Henry nibbled on the bait, "I know my brother pretty well and I also know his wife. Now, Dixie ain't all bad, but she ain't no saint neither. For one, she's high strung and kinda greedy when you get right down to it."

Henry was totally turned around then. Again he stalled, waiting for something he could sink his teeth into. "You don't say," was his way of getting another taste.

"What I'm really trying to say is, that sister'n-law of mine is very likely to have been with Baltimore and for more reasons than you can shake a stick at. She sold him out, though, to save face. I'm sure of that. He should have seen it coming. A man like him should have known that a white woman and a colored man don't ever see eye to eye, once they got white men with guns staring down on them. I know you and him has always been close until you hooked up with us." When Henry's mouth opened, Clay laughed. "If you think this town can hold in a secret, you'd be sadly mistaken. I heard about y'alls' falling out, it had to happen, you're on two different sides now. I also heard some other things. The prosecutor is going after Baltimore hard, soon as he can. That district attorney wants a conviction and a fast hanging so he can run for mayor in the next election. If your buddy loses, D.A. Winston wins in a landslide, guaranteed." Clay had a lot more to say, but didn't. He wanted to see how Henry would react to the free meal he'd served up on a silver platter.

"O.K., that's an awful lot to chew on, Clay. But, I don't know what you intend on me doing about any of it."

"Let's just put it like this, if it was my best friend facing a rigged jury and a known hanging judge, I'd sure as hell come up with something." As Clay shook hands with Henry on the way out, he turned toward Henry and whispered. "Don't look now but the same car has been idling up the street for some time now. Watch yourself, Henry."

"Yeah, I'm grateful to you, Clay. Thanks again." Henry's chest heaved a heavy sigh after such an unusual encounter. He stepped out onto the porch as his friend drove away. The minute Henry remembered being told about the car idling suspiciously nearby, he turned in that direction, entertaining the idea of an investigation.

Roberta stood on the other side of the screen door. "Are you going to be all right?" she asked, having overheard every word.

"You tell me," he said, as an attractive woman strolled up the walkway with a stylist black leather handbag dangling from her wrist.

Etta didn't have time to second guess her difficult decision to swallow every ounce of pride she had and go to Henry for help. She felt twice as small as a flea, standing there on the cement path leading to Henry's home, with his woman and family inside. It took all that she could muster to raise her head and face Henry and Roberta's stunned expressions. "Evening," she said finally, forcing the word out like a ten pound newborn baby. "I wouldn't have come here if it wasn't the absolute last place..." Etta started to say. When her head fell forward it appeared she'd sufficiently overstayed her welcome already. Something way down in her core stopped her from aborting her mission. She wouldn't leave unless being told by Henry to go. But surprising all of them was Roberta's voice telling Etta it was okay to stay.

After marching up four steps to reach the door, Etta's legs were burning like she'd hiked Mt. Everest. Henry hadn't said two words to her and he wondered if it was smart to offer any at all. She smelled pretty, he thought to himself, but Etta went through great lengths to dress down. Her skirt was uncharacteristically long and pleated. The sweater she had pulled over her cotton blouse was buttoned above her breasts. Etta didn't intend on competing for Henry's affections and she didn't want Roberta to think that she was.

Etta eased off her lacy black evening gloves and then crossed over an unfamiliar threshold and into a married ex-lover's home. She surveyed the furniture in the same way Clay had earlier and in the manner Baltimore did before him. "Nice taste your... Roberta has. This is a lovely place." Etta was disappointed in herself. She'd planned on paying homage to Henry's wife, but couldn't manage to execute it the way she'd practiced while sitting in the car waiting on the white cop to complete his business first. "Whew, believe me, Henry, I don't like being here any more than you do."

"I believe you," he answered in earnest, as he struggled feverishly to avoid eye contact. "It's better you go on ahead and get off your chest what it is that's got you standing there staring a hole in my floor."

"Perhaps you're right," she agreed wholeheartedly. "I know you been down to the jail to see about Baltimore," Etta said nervously, her voice soft and unsteady.

"Soon as I stepped in, he went off on me like I was the one who put him away all broken up and bandaged. He didn't give me the respect you'd give a dog. Even fixed his mouth to call me a dog catcher and worse," he confided scornfully.

Having had her share of bouts with Henry as of late, Etta gulped her remorse. "I'm sure you saw how Baltimore ain't at his best, so I'm asking you not to be sore at him. He's fighting back the only way a man in his position knows how. He's biting everything close to him. Especially those he loves and don't want to see getting hurt because of something he done."

After hearing her speak about Baltimore, it was his turn to be honest. "Jo Etta, despite what kind of fool he thinks I am for wanting something better for myself than what I had traveling around on a lark, I ain't sore at him. I feel sorry for him."

"Don't do that," she objected passionately, as Penny had at the attorney's office when she made the same error in judgment. "He can't use no pity, not from any of us who know him better than to think he could ever be guilty of what they said. Your mind appears to be made. Maybe if I'd had more practice putting my thoughts together, I'd be able to change it. But—"

"Now don't you go doing that," he reprimanded her sharply. "Baltimo' was like a brother. Him and me were two of a kind . . . once. There was a time I would have followed him to the ends of the earth and back again, and all he had to do was ask. The scrapes we staggered up against and walked away clean from would have been the end of most men, white or colored," he reminisced fondly. "It seems that you and him are picking up where you and me left off. Don't try to deny it," Henry warned when Etta opened her mouth to refute his claims about falling for Baltimore. "You wasn't ever any good at it."

"I'm sorry."

"For that I should get sore, but I won't," he mused. "I got what I needed in Roberta. Maybe you can be to Baltimo' what he's been missing but didn't know it. You and him, is all that's left of my past, like clothes that don't fit no more, but you still hate to give them up because they used to make you feel so good about having them."

"I never heard it put that way, Henry. I reckon me and Baltimore quit being your size about the same time you realized you had a lot more growing to do." Etta was glad to see that Henry had matured beyond her expectations. He was a strong man, and a good one, just not the man she recognized from her memory. That fellow was dead and buried.

After listening in, Roberta had no reason to believe Etta wanted him back. The Henry Taylor who once lived to hold her against his heart was gone. And, in the blink of an eye, so was Etta.

Henry pulled a chair out on the front porch and took a seat. He was staring up at the stars trying to shake Etta and the space she'd previously occupied in his mind when Roberta brought out two cold bottles of beer. Henry reached out for them with a warm thankful smile. "Don't go getting too happy," she said, handing only one of the beers over to him. "This one's for me."

"Since when do you take in the devil's elixir?" he teased, using the term she had on several occasions.

"'Guess I deserve to twist the cap off at least one vice, seeing as how you're getting picked at from both sides and in the middle." She scooted her chair next to Henry's and then tipped her bottle back as she drank some beer. "Oomph, it still tastes like Tennessee slop jar water. I'd hoped it changed since my days of knocking back a few at the teacher's college."

"What you know about that?" Henry asked, delighting in her carefree attitude.

"I know about a lot of things that are better not to share with my husband," Roberta answered him. "But, what I've come to know most of all after your company passed through is that I hate agreeing with both of them. I don't have a choice when you think about it. If it wasn't for Baltimore having saved your life all those times I've heard about, I wouldn't have you. Neither would our son."

"Would it matter to you whether it was Baltimo' who put me in harm's way before plucking me out, all of those times you've heard about?"

Roberta bent her elbow, took a long swig then smacked her lips like a liberal drinker who knew exactly how to enjoy a cold one. "It's not up for me to say, Henry. The two cents I gave is all you're getting from me. That decision now belongs to you, and you alone. I'll be inside if you want to break out that whistle. I'm starting to think that a girl could do a lot worse than learning to blow one, if it's her husband's."

As the screen door slapped against the wooden frame, Henry realized what Roberta was offering. He planned to coach her on the finer points but she didn't require much instruction in the least. That's when a funny notion struck him. Either his wife was one heck of a fast learner at whistle blowing or she'd had plenty of practice with husband number one. Whatever the case may have been, Henry was glad to be with a wife who loved him, wanted to make a good home, and cared enough to bend over backwards to please him. He did have Baltimore to thank for a number of things, but he'd worry about settling his conscience in the morning. At the time, he was busy persuading Roberta to bend over forwards too.

32

You Don't Say?

The day before the big trial, no one seemed to know what happened to Dinah or whether she was important at that point. Penny, riddled with grief, worked hard at clearing her mind. She owed Baltimore so much as she remembered how kind he had been with her. She feared his death would somehow bring about hers as well. Etta suggested she occupy herself by shopping to ease the tension knotted between her shoulders. Since it was easier to window browse than ponder on far more serious issues, she agreed to casually browse and pick up a few things along the way.

After treating herself to a set of satin panties, one for every day of the week from the Woolworth's department store, Penny caught a taxi to Hanson's Shoes. There, she purchased three pairs from their most expensive selection. The white salesman stared at her for a long time before accepting her money. A young colored lady shelling out thirty-five dollars a pair without batting an eye had him more than a hint suspicious. The man was flat out green with envy. Before she knew it, Penny had stuck out her tongue at him, goading him to risk his best sale of the day with a bigoted remark. Wisely, he placed good old fashioned common sense in the path of racist ideas and saved his commission. His behavior, and her own for that matter, rubbed Penny the wrong way. She was a new consumer but quickly learning how it felt to spend her money with people who would rather lose a sale than to treat colored customers with the same respect afforded white ones. That's when she hopped in another cab and told him to carry her back to her neighborhood, "The Ville."

The moment Penny stepped inside Watkins Emporium she noticed how it was buzzing with people who looked like her, colored folk. Immediately, she felt better about herself and Baltimore's situation. Surely someone would find Dinah and she most certainly would say something to clear him. If coloreds couldn't count on one another, she thought, where were they supposed to turn? Something had to give. It simply had to.

"Hey, Penny, it's frenzied today," Chozelle yelled when she passed by with an arm full of fabric. "People are buying up the place, getting sporty for the trial, I guess. I ain't seen nothing like this since the war ended."

"Me neither," Penny mouthed silently, taking in all the excitement. "Chozelle, hold up a minute."

"Move it, honey, I'm running as it is. Papa's in his office checking on something for Jinxy. A telegram or some such foolishness, I think. That leaves me to handle this dizzying crowd. By the looks of it you've been getting a little dizzy yourself. You know them white stores don't care about colored money."

"Oh, these, I gave it to that last sales fella pretty good. Wagged my licker in his face and dared him to leap."

"How much did that sort of satisfaction cost you?" Chozelle asked, suggesting she'd overpaid for the honor.

"A hun'ed and change, but it was worth every dime watching his head swell up like a melon," Penny answered, with a satisfied smile. "Did you say Jinxy was in here?"

"Sure did," Chozelle confirmed with a carefree wave. "Check up front." Obviously she'd gotten over their lopsided relationship and had subsequently moved on to the next three or four men to fill her social calendar. Penny was grateful nonetheless.

She merely wanted one tall skinny suitor who wanted her just as much, that was her idea of having it all, despite her lack of understanding regarding exactly what to do with it.

Jinx was bent over the counter, dressed in worn blue work pants and a dirty long-sleeved shirt of nearly the same hue. Penny sat her bags on the floor and then tugged at the red rag hanging from his back pocket. Jinx turned around to get a look at who was bothering him. When he saw Penny's flashy clothes and made-up face, he gushed with surprise.

"I should have known that only you'd be willing to get this close to a dirty yard man in your fancy duds. I declare, Penny King, you's one of a kind and prettier than a picture."

"Why, thank you, Jinxy, but I ain't willing to let but one man get me dirty regardless," she replied, as grown-up as she knew how. Just about then Mr. Watkins came out of his office hoisting a yellow telegram high in the air.

"I told you we had it," he hailed gleefully. "It came last week. Must've been misfiled under 'B' for baseball instead of 'D' for Dearborn. Sorry about that."

"What do I owe you, suh?" asked Jinx, behind a puzzled expression. He couldn't understand why a telegram addressed to him would be regarding baseball.

"Ah, don't mention it, Jinx. Those folks in Canada paid for it on the sending end."

Penny handed the store owner a silver dollar. Mr. Watkins refused it initially, saying it was too much money, but she refused to take it back. Jinx thanked her as they headed off toward the exit. "You is something else. I don't rightly know what yet, but you's really something."

"When you figure out what that something is, you need to let me in on it," she said, just this side of scandalous. "Well, open it up. Somebody done saw fit to get your attention from a far away place for a reason." Penny wasn't sure where this Canada was, but it didn't sound like it was any place near Missouri. Jinx ripped the seal off the telegram and unfolded it. He read it once, squinted his eyes into narrow slits then he read it again, this time more deliberately.

Penny took that piece of yellow paper from his trembling hands when he appeared too disturbed to speak. "'Dear Sam Dearborn, Jr.,'" she read aloud. "'It is with esteemed pleasure that the Montreal Royals Professional Baseball Organization offers to you an audition with our ball club. Stop. Please appear on or before June 17th, for an examination and workout with us. Stop.'"

Before she'd finished reading the message, Penny wore the same befuddled expression Jinx had. "Jinxy, this is big news. Why ain't you jumping for joy? Baltimore says you's good enough to play with Jackie Robinson and those white ball clubs. He said you had the right stuff." Penny peered down at the telegram again in an odd fashion. "I thought you said this note came from some Canada folk. It says here they's sending for you to play with the Mon-tree-all Royals."

Chuckling like a man who heard a bad joke, Jinx explained that Montreal was a town in Canada, as best he knew, and that it was a great honor indeed to be invited to try out. It was his dream come true, but it was also a hollow victory. "I'm not sho' I can head way up there all by myself, Penny. I'm a country boy, but that Canada is a whole 'nother country from this one. I was thinking on sticking it out here and seeing how you and me get along, steady-like, well, until Baltimore got pinched."

"Sam Dearborn, Jr., you'd best to forget about me and Baltimore. It's your big chance to be somebody famous and do what you love most. What you should be thinking about is how you gonna make it to join up with them Royals in four days. That's a lot of thinking you need to do. First, get on home and tell your mama. She's liable to bust wide open with pride. Congratulations, Jinxy! Ain't that what they say when something good happens to you?"

"Whoa, Penny, we can't tell anybody about this just yet. I need to settle down first. Promise?"

"Sho', Jinxy," she agreed, although she couldn't see why he'd want to keep a lid on it. "Mum's the word. I won't spill it to no-body."

"Thanks, Penny, I'll catch up to you later. You sho' is some-thing. There's a lot I needs to figure out right away."

"Way to go, Jinxy," she yelled, as he trotted off toward his old jalopy.

Chozelle stuck her nose out of the door sharply. "What you fussing over Jinxy about? Why all the fanfare?"

"Ah, it's nothing really, he's just happy to be looking at another job to get more of his clothes dirty," Penny answered slyly. "Man, he sho' can run."

"Too bad ain't no real money in running or that boy would be rich. Oh, well." Chozelle ducked back inside when her snooping didn't amount to anything substantial.

"That's what you think," Penny said to herself. "That fella can run, throw, hit and catch with the best of them. There's more than riches in that. They's also dreams come true to boot. Con-gratulations, Jinxy," she sang like a phrase to a lover's song. "Go on, boy, show 'em what you's made of. They'll sign you up as soon as they see you. I know I would."

Penny kept her word when returning to the Fast House for work later that evening. She was finding things to smile about for the first time since Baltimore had gotten arrested. Etta didn't un-derstand it at first but soon enough, she recognized the rhythm in Penny's steps. She didn't have to ask who was to thank for her improved outlook. Etta could see nothing but Jinx's reflection in Penny's eyes. In her own was Baltimore's wide-mouthed grin. She shared in Penny's happiness like a mother would after her daughter crossed over into adulthood, ready to find her way. Penny was breaking free, but Etta wasn't ready to let her go or give up her visions of Baltimore, laughing and loving life as it was in-tended, at full speed. She hated to imagine him being any other way although that didn't make it so.

*   *   *

Thirteen days in lockup as a guest of the county granted Baltimore more than enough lonely days to sort out his life and the times he'd rather forget but couldn't, because they made him feel alive. He'd spent a few nights behind bars before, mostly for misbehaving in small backwater towns, zigging when he should have zagged. Of all the ladies who surrendered to his pleasing ways, those still renting space in his head were the hot-natured, hot-tempered, head-strong lionesses who shined while loving him hard and long. Dinah Leonard was a lot like them, he insisted, when warring with a natural inclination to hold a grudge. It was difficult to harbor ill will after he replayed the scene which turned her against him. Dixie Sinclair was simply a by-product of his reluctance to settle down and stake a claim. If it hadn't been her, Baltimore would have pressed his luck and driven Dinah away with someone else eventually.

During those thirteen days, he reminisced privately about the father who disowned him for living a wild lascivious life and the mother he prayed for often. Baltimore couldn't understand why a beautiful and vibrant woman chose to stay in a toxic marriage, which yielded four outside children. Then, as suddenly as the question surfaced, it faded from his mind. Mulling over the pain men brazenly brought upon women, especially his own past transgressions, came at too high a price. He'd rather not be reminded just how much of his father's son he'd become. That alone was his biggest regret.

Everything happens for a reason, Delbert advised Baltimore after overhearing him thinking out loud. He'd arrived the day before the trial, removed twelve stitches from Baltimore's abdomen and several others used to patch head wounds suffered during the arrest. Although Baltimore had experienced a lion's share of devilment and hard luck, it never occurred to him that some things happened purely by chance because they were supposed to. He'd previously subscribed to the cause-and-effect school of thought but his untimely incarceration easily proved Delbert's theory.

"Thanks, Doc," Baltimore said, with newly uplifted spirits.

"Everything does happen for a reason. It makes perfect sense. I should have thought of that myself. Sometimes one bad hand follows another, that's just the way it goes." As he tried on both sets of clothing Delbert collected from the apartment building at his behest, the pressures associated with rethinking the bad decisions he'd made in the last month dissipated. "All I could do was play the game. There was no way to know the next card would be the suicide jack of spade. I did what I could with what I had. I owe you, Doc. I owe you."

Delbert stared at Baltimore oddly, as if he'd begun to lose his grip on reality. Taking into account what lay directly ahead, he fully understood if the man needed to back away from the pressures of imminent danger. He'd have taken a mental holiday long before then, if it were his head on the chopping block with the entire town waiting on the axe to fall. "Now that I got your attention, chew on this," said Delbert. "Etta told me to pass a few things your way."

Baltimore took a seat in his small cell and crossed his legs as if he were at a cocktail lounge tossing back drinks with an old friend. He listened attentively as Delbert reenacted Willie B.'s erratic conduct at Helen's funeral. He did such an astounding job performing the scene that Baltimore had him reproduce it three more times. Etta was right, Baltimore also found it absurdly hilarious, once he'd gotten over the shock.

While catching his breath, Delbert relayed certain additional messages and brought him up to speed on Dank and Pudge's efforts at investigating his case. Baltimore was glad to hear his friends had hung around when most men would have cut and run. He didn't know how to feel when learning about Penny falling deeper for Jinx. On second thought, he liked the idea of those two building a wonderful but simple life together. Delbert hurriedly explained how their union wouldn't be simple at all if Jinx decided to strike out of town and accept the audition with the Brooklyn Dodgers' farm team in Montreal.

Baltimore grinned proudly like a brand new daddy then. "Jinx tell you this?" he asked, wanting to be certain of the information.

"Naw, I came by it second-hand, but you can set your pocket watch by it. The news is supposed to be real hush-hush but can't nobody keep a secret in this town," Delbert told him, with the utmost confidence.

"Hell, don't I know it," Baltimore asserted, most assuredly.

Delbert neglected to tell him how he had promised to keep it under his hat when getting the scoop from Ollie, who'd been told by Chozelle, after she read an arrangement signed by her father and Jinx from the locked desk drawer. Mr. Watkins agreed to travel out to see about Jinx's mother once a week and keep her pantry filled with necessities. Penny left him one thousand dollars on deposit. She assured him there would be more when the situation called for it.

"Folks need to mind their own business," Delbert huffed ferociously. "That's what I always say."

Baltimore tossed him a crooked smile. "*Always?*"

33

BUCKING THE ODDS

In less than two hours, the second biggest trial gripping the city of St. Louis would be bearing down on them. The first landmark proceeding culminated in the Dred Scott Decision, that disallowed slaves their freedom after previously living in free states. While Dred Scott initially won his liberation in the St. Louis Circuit Court in 1850, he later lost it to his master's widow by a Supreme Court reversal seven years later; ruling that Scott's time spent in a free society didn't override the fact that he was born a slave and didn't have the right to challenge it.

Baltimore's case was different in many ways. He was born into freedom experiencing life throughout the United States and he didn't have seven years to burn while litigators decided his fate. However, their cases shared notably similar characteristics. Baltimore's liberty hung on the testimony of a white woman who was out to get him, most of the white population in the town wanted him dead for brazen disrespect to the establishment and the selected jury was not comprised of his peers. Putting it bluntly, like Dred Scott, Baltimore was also in big trouble and betting against the house.

When the cell door opened, Baltimore stood from his bunk,

straightened his flashy silk necktie and eased on the tailored jacket. It was the ritziest suit he owned. Fashionably designed with wide lapels, the light-brown fabric decorated with soft hounds-tooth checks, the suit was a show stopper. He was immediately reminded of that as he exited his current dwelling in the colored wing, escorted by two guards down the long catwalk. The men on his cellblock stared, hooted, and hollered as he strolled toward the transporting area on the first floor. "Give 'em hell, Baltimo'," one convict asserted solemnly. Others howled and applauded loudly as he glided past them.

The charges he faced weren't the driving force behind their overwhelming support. Baltimore embodied the kind of man they'd like to be, fearless, confident and polished. He had received so many love letters from local women praying for his release, the jailhouse postal office began returning the sweetly scented packages to the senders. Those they allowed him to keep amounted to three full boxes beneath his bunk. There was a secret inmate lottery to be held on the day of Baltimore's verdict reading. Lust-filled letters detailing hundreds of young lady's explicit carnal desires were worth more than gold on the inside. Those with photographs included, priceless.

Baltimore anticipated being found guilty and then transferred to the state penitentiary's Lifer's Row or their famed Death House by nightfall. With that in mind, he stopped at the massive iron door and tipped his hat to the boys, believing he'd never see them again. Despite their motives, they cheered him heartily then. Some of them held high hopes for Baltimore's release. Others couldn't wait to get the lottery underway. Together, they all cheered.

The State of Missouri vs. Obadiah "Baltimore" Floyd was scheduled to run for one full day because the police were said to have caught him in the act. It was an open and shut case, the kind that D.A.s built political careers on the backs of. At ten o'clock sharp, D.A. Dudley Winston, a brash forty-four-year-old Republican, entered the courtroom ready to lay his foundation. The county's biggest courtroom was packed to the gills, evenly divided down the middle with white citizens jammed shoulder to shoulder on the left and the colored citizens stacked deep on the right. And, much like Helen's funeral guest list, the colored section was laced with famous notables seated near the front—although for this spectacle, Etta, Penny and the dearest of Baltimore's friends were awarded ringside seats. Delbert, with no wiggle room to spare, leaned over to Dr. Stanton. "I hear this judge is the no-nonsense kind. You think Baltimore can get a fair shake?"

"He's a good man, tough as nails though," the white doctor answered. "And he's a hunting buddy of mine."

Remembering how the doctor had bluffed the racist sergeant at the county lockup, Delbert wasn't sold this go-around. "I mean, do you know him well enough to trust him?"

"You bet we can, Delbert. He's a Democrat too."

Three minutes past the hour, the defendant's chair was still vacant. Judge Atticus Sumner banged his gavel to hush the courtroom. With poorly groomed white hair, he appeared several years older then he actually was. He'd presided over cases for two decades and wasn't about to let this divisive mob turn unruly under his charge. "The trial beginning today is very serious and so is the sanctity of my courtroom," the judge announced sternly, his eyes bulging from their sockets. "I will not tolerate insolence or over-exuberance in any way. Keep your comments to yourselves and I'll let you keep your seats." Judge Sumner pointed his finger at both sides of the aisles, then he motioned to the thick-framed bailiff guarding the prisoner's entrance.

After taking his cue, the bailiff unlocked the door and opened it. Albert Hummel walked into the room carrying a brown leather lawyer's briefcase. Baltimore entered three paces behind him with his head held high. He strutted in like a millionaire playboy, controlled and confident. Thick coal-black wavy hair covered the wounds previously inflicted upon his head. His classy attire masked what they had done to his body. The even smile he aimed at the front row concealed his apprehension of facing twelve angry white men sitting in the jury box. The atmosphere was overwrought with disharmony. Almost half of the viewers to his left scowled and sneered while Baltimore's friendly faction eagerly welcomed him among their fold.

Etta couldn't stop thinking how tired and thin he appeared. Baltimore was well-rested but tired of living with a great degree of uncertainty. There was no way to conceal that from himself. Penny was altogether giddy because he was seated close enough to reach out and touch, but she dared not attempt it. Being near Baltimore, despite what he was involved in or with, that was its own reward.

After shuffling papers in front of him, the D.A. rose from his chair and tucked his snazzy burnt-orange silk tie inside of his expensive tweed jacket which he then fastened. Dudley Winston had the distinction of being overly handsome and cocky to a fault. His thick mousy-brown hair was worn slicked back and tapered. The athletic build he was once so proud of had softened considerably. He was refined, from a powerful family with old money, but that didn't stifle his aspirations or impede his bulldoggish assault on the defendant's character. "We all know why we're here, so I won't waste your valuable time with slick lawyering because it isn't necessary. There stands a man accused of a heinous crime against humanity. Mr. Floyd lured a married woman up to his apartment under false pretenses and subsequently tried to force the act of fornication on her, against her will. In this beloved state of Missouri, we called that attempted rape." He glanced at the defendant to see if it shook him up. Staring back at him was a man who didn't seem fazed by the harsh depiction of the crime. Baltimore was cool as ice.

"Dixie Sinclair is not present because we feel it is too arduous a task for her to relive an assault on her person any more than she should have to. Her testimony will be provided later this afternoon. Moreover, don't let the victim's absence in any way keep you from listening carefully to the testimonies and finding that man, known as Obadiah 'Baltimore' Floyd guilty, guilty, guilty!"

The judge squelched the murmurs circulating from the audience with two expeditious raps of his trusty gavel. And as easy as that, quiet was restored.

D.A. Winston found his seat as Albert Hummel greeted the jury box with both hands stuffed in his pockets. He stared at them, panning over their faces one by one. It was an old lawyer's trick which forced jurors to search deep within themselves, knowing the defense attorney would be doing so at every turn. "Gentlemen, yes, this is an extremely serious case. And yes, you will be asked by me to free my client once I've proven what the police walked in on was not a man taking advantage of a woman, but was nothing more than a lover's quarrel that got out of hand." Venomous shouts rang throughout the courtroom. Albert's opening statement had successfully tagged him as Public Enemy Number One, steering the focus away from his client as planned.

"Order in the court! I said order!" the seasoned judge bellowed insistently. "If I hear anymore outbursts like that from my *civilized* constituents, I will clear out every white man and woman that does not have a direct role in this case. And I mean it." The colored spectators thought that sounded like a grand idea, one that probably occurred to them from the outset.

"As I was saying," Albert continued, "I will prove beyond a shadow of a doubt that the district attorney's office should not have wasted your valuable time getting mixed up in a private, and completely consensual backdoor romance." Albert cleverly evoked the worst sentiment from the heated horde while standing between them and the jury. They didn't have a clue he was pitting the angry masses against them. It was a magician's ruse to keep them looking at one hand while he hatched the trick with his other one. Before sitting down, Albert's agenda was so well implemented that D.A. Winston, who was absolutely positive he couldn't lose, overlooked it.

"Whadda you trying to do, start a riot?" he whispered to Albert, in passing. "Your honor, I'd like to call my first witness at this time. Mr. Bud Riddle, please step forward."

The tow truck driver emerged from the fourth row wearing a

snug-fitting outdated suit. He was of average height, with thinning reddish-brown hair. He had a soft chin, with a thin beak nose and poor posture. He was also cleaned up, freshly shaven and anxious to tell his story, the one he'd rehearsed a hundred times in his bathroom mirror. As far as he could tell, what he did saved that white woman's virtue.

After having been sworn in, he took a seat in the witness box. D.A. Winston approached him eagerly. "Mr. Riddle, please tell us what you recall happening that brought your attention to the opened window on the third floor of the Ambrose Arms apartments on the day in question."

The witness gazed toward the same side of the room he'd vacated moments before. "Well, it's like this here. I went to hooking the drudging winch up to an abandoned car left in the alley behind Ms. Etta's Fast House, that's a colored night club, when I heard a man and a woman getting into it. You know, like an argument. Didn't think much of it 'cause it wasn't none of my business what went on in that colored-only apartment house."

The prosecutor shook his head as if he agreed with the man's description of things thus far. "Yes, Mr. Riddle, then what happened?"

"Well, I heard a lady screaming."

"What did the lady you heard screaming say?"

"'Goddammit, let me go. Let me go,'" he answered nonchalantly. Again, there was a slight murmuring until one disconcerting gaze from the judge hushed their voices.

"You stated that a lady screamed to be let go. Did you see her being accosted?"

"Objection, your honor!" Albert shouted. "He's leading the witness."

"Sustained," Judge Sumner answered. "Rephrase the question."

"Yes, after she screamed, did you see her? And if so, what was she doing?"

"Yeah, sir, I seen her. She was grabbing at the window frame. I thought she was about to be pushed through it, but she wasn't. A man had his arms wrapped around her waist, trying to get her away from it."

"Is that man here in the courtroom today?" asked the prosecutor.

"Yes, sir, he's that colored fella sitting over yonder." He steadied his index finger at Baltimore like a child pointing out a schoolyard bully.

"Thank you, Mr. Riddle," the D.A. said as he returned to his table.

The defense attorney sauntered toward Bud Riddle slowly, as if trying to set a counterattack. That worried the witness and he began to fiddle uncomfortably. "Mr. Riddle, we've heard you testify that you heard a man and a woman in the colored only apartment building getting into it. And since you were hooking up—what was it called, to the car?"

"A drudging winch," Riddle answered proudly.

"That's right, how could I forget that? I'm guessing it's a quiet piece of machinery?"

"Naw, sir, it kinda makes a loud clacking noise," he answered, much to the D.A.'s dismay.

"O.K., you were operating loud machinery, during which time you heard what sounded like people arguing? Try to think back now, because this is very important. Before you hooked up the loud machinery, did you hear what they were getting into it about?" Albert wisely stood directly in front of the witness to block his view of the D.A., who might have been inclined to coach him by using slight hand signals.

Mr. Riddle lowered his head and thought about it. "You know what, I did hear something. When I first climbed off my truck, I heard a woman say, 'Blankity-blank, you black bastard.' That's another reason I assumed they were both colored." Albert was almost sorry he started this line of questioning until the truck driver remembered a helpful piece of information. "Then a man's voice yelled back at her, 'Quit fooling around or somebody's gonna get hurt.' Yeah, that's what he said. I'd forgotten about that, but I'm sure that's what he said."

"No more questions, thank you, sir." Albert had softened Riddle's solid testimony to even things out. As Mr. Riddle walked by the prosecutor's table, he was given the evil eye and a big fat thanks-for-nothing frown.

"Mr. Winston, your next witness," the judge said, to keep it moving.

"Officer Timothy Rankin, please come forward," D.A. Winston announced like he'd done with his first unsatisfactory witness. The uniformed leather-faced cop rambled to the witness box, carrying the pride of the white race on his back. He was determined to sink the defendant, even if he had to stretch the truth in order to do it.

"You were called to the Ambrose Arms apartment house. What did you find when arriving at Room Number Two-Twelve?"

"I was the first one in the door after hearing a loud ruckus way down the hall. When I made it in, I saw the defendant straddled on top of the white woman," he mumbled, as if it pained him to recount what he saw.

"Did she say anything to make you think she was in trouble?" asked the prosecutor, expecting the defense to make the same objection to that leading question like he'd done before. When Albert didn't object, Officer Tim Rankin delivered the most damaging statement thus far.

"Yeah, she did. She told that boy to let her go and that he couldn't treat her like that."

"And Mr. Floyd, the defendant, did he respond to her protests at being held down?" Again no objection came from Baltimore's lawyer. Albert decided to offer the cop some extra rope so he'd feel secure. Later, he'd use it to tie the prosecution's witness in knots.

The officer squinted his eyes at Baltimore and locked his jaw before answering. "He said, 'No, it ain't no use in fighting. You might as well give me what I want.'"

"No further questions." The D.A. pranced to his seat smugly, after getting in a solid left hook.

Albert smiled at the cop, who embellished his story much like he'd anticipated. To stir the gritty policeman, Albert leaned toward Baltimore as if he was asking him pertinent information to refute the cop's claims. Officer Rankin froze up like a small stiff-backed child when he predicted a dose of trickery was headed his way.

"Mr. Rankin," Albert addressed him, purposely neglecting to use the officer's title so he'd be viewed by the jury as a civilian and more likely to have seen things with a particular slant. "Please tell us the very first thing Mr. Riddle, the tow truck driver, said when he ran toward you at the end of the alley?" The brooding officer peered up at the ceiling, working diligently at remembering that part of the incident. He'd shared his role in the actual arrest and subsequent beating after Baltimore was handcuffed so frequently he'd committed it to heart. Albert's question was a lot tougher. "Well, Mr. Rankin, the same question is still on the table. What did the truck driver say when he came to you?"

"Uh . . . He said something about a man and a white woman tussling. 'Come on and help this woman' or something like that." Rankin shrugged his beefy shoulders "what-ever" style and dismissed the question's importance.

"Based on your testimony, Mr. Rankin, the truck driver did not say anything about a white woman being molested by a colored man, is that right?"

"No, he didn't say that exactly, but when he pointed to that address, which we know to be colored and it registered to me that a white woman was involved, I knew what must have been going on."

"That's what I like, an honest man. *Officer* Rankin, you assumed what must have been going on when a white man comes to you, he's running, and then tells you a white woman is tussling with a man in a building known to be occupied by colored tenants. Officer Rankin, if a bank is being robbed and you happen to see me driving away, please don't shoot before learning whether I was in on it or not," Albert scoffed.

"Objection!" yelled D.A. Winston. "Is there a question coming out of all this posturing?"

"Yes, there is," answered Albert. "Officer Rankin, you testified just a minute ago that the defendant was on top of the woman saying—" He paused and pointed to the court reporter for clarification.

"'He said, 'No, it ain't no use in fighting. You might as well give me what I want,'" the female transcriber read from the papered reel.

"That's right, were those the defendant's exact words or yours, Mr. Rankin?"

"I'm sure I heard him say that," the cop answered confidently. "Yeah, I'm sure of it."

"Mr. Rankin, I have your partner waiting outside. If I bring him in, and I plan to, will he tell us your words or the defendant's when asked face to face? Think before you speak, Mr. Rankin, perjury carries a jail term too. I'll ask you again, did he say "You might as well give me what I want" or 'You might as well *give up?*'"

"Yeah—yeah, that's what he said," the officer recanted. "It was a lot like that. 'You might as well give up.'"

"Was it those words or something like that?" baited Albert.

"It was exactly those words," answered the middle-aged policeman. He was willing to agree to anything to get off that hot seat.

"One further line of questioning, Mr. Rankin. When you said to the defendant, 'You heard her, nigger,' did Mr. Floyd release the woman voluntarily? And I'll remind you that your partner will not have heard your answer when I drag him in."

The hinges had been removed from his previously iron-clad story. "Yes, sir, the defendant got up right away and let us put the chains on him without making a fuss." Rankin didn't have to guess what was coming next.

"Then, sir, during a peaceful arrest, why did you and your partner work over Mr. Floyd with your nightsticks, fists and shoe heels?" Albert counted silently to ten while the jury members' eyes filled with resentment, one by one. "You're done, Mr. Rankin," Albert sighed wearily. When he sat next to Baltimore, his client was impressed.

"You sharp as a tack, counselor."

"Truth is a mighty fine tool in the hands of the right man, Baltimore, a mighty fine tool."

"Nice, who told you that?" Baltimore inquired.

"Albert Hummel—Senior. My father was a big-shot lawyer back east."

34

BOLD IS SO BEAUTIFUL

Baltimore confided to his lawyer that he felt the trial was going better than he'd presumed. Albert wisely advised that he not get too excited just yet. The district attorney asked to defer questioning of the last witness until later in the day. Albert saw this wrinkle as a chance to break the case wide open. He petitioned the judge to permit the addition of a surprise witness that his private detectives had suddenly located. Of course it was a bit of a stretch, but D.A. Winston couldn't prove that a certain woman hadn't been put up in a cushy white hotel and treated like a queen, so he was forced to roll with it. The D.A. returned to his seat reluctantly when Albert's surprise graced the courtroom with her presence.

Baltimore was among the multitude left dumbfounded and deceived when Dinah Leonard strutted in, dressed to the nines in a designer outfit, a flashy crimson skirt and jacket. Her hat and shoes were black, ornamented with miniature red silk bows, to set off the stunning ensemble. She sashayed down the aisle like a movie star taking a stroll along a glitzy Hollywood red carpet instead of into a musty municipal mélée. It took some convincing to get Dinah on board for Baltimore's sake while Albert's detective's had her hidden all along. He couldn't chance letting any-one discover where his bombshell was safely tucked away. She was too valuable. Now that she was poised and polished, he hoped she didn't remember how deeply it hurt when she learned about Dixie.

"Hello, Ms. Leonard. I know you're a very busy woman, so I won't detain you too long," Albert said, with the utmost admiration. He openly flirted with her to suggest that attraction, in spite of race, was difficult to dismiss. "Ms. Leonard, were you inside or near the defendant Baltimore Floyd's apartment room on the day in question?"

Dinah wiggled her hips while adjusting her position in the hard wooden chair. It didn't go unnoticed by the white men sworn to consider all of the evidence before deciding Baltimore's guilt or innocence. Once she'd aimed more hip and thigh at the jury box, she tilted her head and wide-brimmed hat to the side. "You know I was there," she answered curtly, while avoiding eye contact with Baltimore. Albert backed away to get a clear picture of what was about to transpire.

"I'm sorry, Ms. Leonard, is that a yes or no?"

"Yes," she huffed, "I was in Baltimore's room that day." The D.A. had been making notes and jotting potential questions when he determined that observing the surprise witnesses demeanor might prove more prudent.

"Good, now that we've established that, please tell us what if anything you saw before leaving the room."

"I didn't see nothing," she replied, her lips spitefully pursed.

"I'm not so sure of that, ma'am," Albert contended, as he approached the judge's bench. "Your honor, permission to treat Ms. Leonard as a hostile witness?" He was given the go-ahead to mix it up with the sultry sandbagger. "Ms. Leonard, isn't it true that you and the defendant were alone until Dixie Sinclair, the alleged victim in this case, came knocking at the door *voluntarily*?"

"Yeah, that happened," was her cold response.

"Isn't it also true that you saw the two of them arguing like good friends on the bad end of a misunderstanding?"

"No, sir, I didn't see nothing like that," she spat defiantly, with her expression souring. Baltimore didn't know what to expect next. It was poetic justice he reasoned. The prettiest lady in the entire room was holding out because she had assumed incorrectly that he had once done the same to her. It appeared that Baltimore's legal counsel also agreed because he let her off the hook so easily.

Just when it seemed the momentum had begun to shift, the district attorney had the bright idea to wow the audience with a bout of grand standing. As far as he could tell, Albert left several interesting questions on the table. Since he neglected to ask the obvious, D.A. Winston did. "Ms. Leonard, I also thank you for coming here this morning."

"You're welcome," Dinah replied pleasantly.

Her change in demeanor caused everyone on the right side of that auditorium to wince collectively. Her body language suggested she'd rather be on the prosecution's team, and that's what Albert counted on when prepping her. He'd seen the D.A. rush into court unprepared before but lucky for him, the defendant confessed when his first year public defender put him on the stand. He may as well have shoved the poor sap in the electric chair himself. Albert Hummel, Jr. had the element of surprise on his side, aligned with that fine tool in the right man's hands, truth.

"Ms. Leonard, I'll be brief. There are a couple of things bothering me. See, I'm contending that Mr. Floyd lured the victim to his room and then attempted to assault her sexually after becoming violent. And for the record, you did not recall seeing any animosity between them?"

"Yes, sir, that's what I said. When I lit out of there, that white lady wasn't fighting with him none, at least not with her hands."

Rumblings traipsed through both sections of the courtroom then. The only person who saw it coming was Albert. He had carefully laid a half-baked trap for his opponent and the D.A.'s over-inflated ego caused him to get snagged in Albert's crafty snare. District Attorney Winston flew off the handle. He'd been upstaged, not once but twice. In a desperate attempt to cork the hole in a sinking ship, he committed sin after sin against the barrister's code. First, he asked a question he didn't know the answer to, and then followed it by taking a wild swing with a dull blade.

With embarrassment fueling his wrath, the D.A. opened the lid to Pandora's Box. "Ms. Leonard, please enlighten us as to why you left the defendant's apartment when Dixie Sinclair arrived, if the defendant didn't throw you aside with designs on raping her?" He was sure Baltimore had asked Dinah to leave the room, or the defense would have strengthened their position by getting her to say otherwise.

"That ain't the way it went down," Dinah answered meekly.

"That sure sounds like what happened to me. The defendant saw an opportunity to be with another man's wife, a white woman, and he threw you out, didn't he?"

Dinah pulled a handkerchief from her dainty purse and dabbed at her eyes in grand dramatic fashion. "Baltimore didn't put me out!" she fired back at him, as if struggling to hold in an entire tribe of tears. "Dixie Sinclair did! She ran me off so she could have her way with him!"

The courtroom erupted. Newsmen darted through the doors to phone in the latest break in the case. Judge Sumner did his best to shout above the noise but failed miserably. "Order! Order!" When no one seemed to give a whirl, he slammed the gavel until pain shot through his hand. "Bailiff, clear the courtroom! Get everyone out of here. Maybe they'll be more respectful after lunch."

As Dinah stepped down from the stand, she ever-so-slightly peeked beneath her wide brimmed hat then relayed with her eyes what she couldn't say with her mouth. Baltimore had received his formal acknowledgment of forgiveness wrapped in a stunning red package.

Albert hustled him out the side door during the moment of

mayhem for his protection. He was grinning from ear to ear as Baltimore looked him over curiously. "You had Dinah do all that?"

"Yeah, it was my daddy's idea. He can't stand the prosecutor any more than I can. Said D.A. Winston reminds him of a fellow he hated for years, Winston's old man. How's that for a second generation ass whippin'?"

"First class all the way," Baltimore chuckled, appropriately amazed. "Remind me to stay on your good side, Junior, where it's safe."

During the lunch hour, Baltimore nibbled at a chicken-salad sandwich delivered from the nearby Market Street deli. Because he didn't care for mayonnaise, he ate the crust around the edges while Albert studied evidence from the morning round. He liked what he saw. "We're not out of the woods yet. They'll put Dixie Sinclair on the stand and you'd better believe she'll come in with some waterworks to beat the band," he predicted soundly. "I'll do the best I can to rattle her, but it'll boil down to your word against hers." Baltimore appreciated the way Albert handled the jury and made a fool of the prosecutor, so he paid close attention to everything his lawyer said. "You'll have to tell your side of the story after the Sinclair woman sobs through hers. Winston will come at you with all he's got. He'll rant and rave, try to put words in your mouth and insinuate foul things about you. No matter how much or how long he yells, you need to remain calm, like we practiced. If you don't let him catch you slipping, there's a good shot you'll walk out of here a free man."

Barker Sinclair stormed into the D.A.'s office with a vengeance. He charged up to Dudley Winston and grabbed him by his fancy lapels. "You son-of-a-bitch," he growled. "You had Floyd's ass handed to you on a platter and you're still getting your ass kicked in there. Maybe I ought to get the police officer's association to pull our support and back another candidate for mayor."

Winston placed his sweaty hands on top of Barker's and pressed hard against them until he let go. "You've got some nerve barging in here like I haven't spent the last two weeks trying to clean up after your wife's mess. She had to go and make a damned fool of the both of you with a connected colored man. Perhaps you didn't see Dr. Stanton sitting in his back pocket. He's coming off as a goddamned hero to those people out there and I'm shoveling shit to stay even." The district attorney openly exhibited his displeasure for being attacked with unwarranted malice. "Don't you ever come marching in here again like your house is in order. If that coon-chasing wife of yours would have managed to stay off her back in Floyd's bedroom, we wouldn't have to take this lying down now." When Barker stormed out of the office, D.A. Winston was stretched out on the floor with a sharp pain shooting through his rattled teeth.

Outside on the courthouse steps, Barker's Ku Klux Klan buddies squabbled over pulling a fast one to stall the proceedings. They determined that the sissy D.A. was doing a terrible job of wrangling the coon's attorney. "The brotherhood came to see a spook-buck get his," one of them asserted solemnly, "not let him slip out of the hangman's noose." A white lady shouldn't be subjected to public ridicule at the hands of a nigger-loving Jew lawyer. Albert's family was Presbyterian, but that was of little consequence to them. It was easier for the hate-mongers to despise him if they thought his roots traveled back to the Middle East. One of the rednecks proposed snatching Albert from his bed as soon as they kidnapped Baltimore for an old-fashioned necktie party.

When Barker relinquished complete control, he was informed they'd already orchestrated the defendant's demise and a strategy to spare his wife from being gawked at by all of those filthy jiggaboos in the gallery. Barker was then told that the afternoon portion of the trial would be cancelled immediately due to an unforeseen incident. And, sure enough, a law clerk came out and announced the postponement. Five of the twelve jurors suffered intense stomach pains and vomiting after eating contaminated lunches, delivered from the Market Street deli. Barker knew then that it was possible to get at Baltimore, and all he'd need was a little help from his friends.

After an hour passed, the judge's clerk was sent to get Baltimore's lawyer. Albert Hummel gathered his briefs and headed toward the judge's chambers. Several things traveled through his mind as he followed the young attendant's footsteps. His biggest concern was receiving a heated reprimand for sneaking in Dinah Leonard as a surprise witness under their noses. When Albert saw D.A. Winston standing at the window holding a bloody handkerchief over his swollen lip, he knew something else was wrong, very wrong.

Judge Sumner unzipped his robe, slipped it off his narrow shoulders and then hung it on a wooden coat rack in the corner of the office. "Thanks for coming straight over, Albert. It seems we have a problem," said the old arbitrator. "Dudley here has heard the news so we'll let you in on it. Sit down, the both of you, and Dudley, don't get any of that blood on my chair. Why'd you let the husband into your office in the first place?" Albert, seated beside the district attorney, turned slowly to closely examine the result of the embittered detective's rage.

"Barker Sinclair did that?" he asked, wearing a shocked expression.

When D.A. Winston lowered his head shamefully, the judge pointed his finger at him. "Don't think this lets you off the hook. We're postponing the trial, for one day, time for the jurors to get over whatever has them hugging toilet stools in the men's room." Again, the defense attorney was a step behind and waiting on answers. "Oh, don't look at me like that, Albert. If I didn't know for a fact that you also had lunch delivered from the same sandwich shop, I'd hold you in contempt of court for jury tampering."

"Who, me? I never . . ."

"Shut up," Judge Sumner barked abruptly. "I know you weren't behind this, but it still doesn't sit right with me." He leaned back in his chair and growled some more before spouting directions. "Dudley, I'd get your so-called *victim* prepped if I were you. And Albert, you need to get that slick thug of yours out of sight before somebody gets up the gumption to do what Dudley might not be capable of."

The moment Albert realized what that meant for his defendant, he grabbed his things and shot down the hallway in the direction of the small prisoner holding room. When he pushed past the guard and opened the door, Baltimore had his head down on the table. Albert stopped in his tracks, thinking the judge's prophecy had come to pass. "Baltimore, tell me you didn't finish that sandwich?"

"Nah, I tossed it in the can," he answered, peering up curiously. "Too much white spread on it for my taste." Baltimore's lawyer didn't have to inform him that was the very reason he was presently chained to the floor. Conversely, he did discuss what he'd learned about the trial postponement and at least five violently ill jurors. Albert had rather not alarm his client but there was no getting around it, Baltimore had to be told.

"There is no easy way to say this," he whispered across the rectangular shaped table. "That food poisoning incident wasn't likely an accident. It's obvious they think we're winning this case, Baltimore. Your life is in jeopardy."

"Considering how that's the first time you used my common name, you really believe it is."

"Yes, I do, unfortunately. If you're a praying man, I'd devote some time in that regard," the attorney recommended.

"Shoot. That ain't gonna work," answered Baltimore as he rose from the chair. "It's been so long since I said something to Him, the Man probably won't even recognize my voice."

Albert got up and walked over to Baltimore then placed his hand on his client's shoulder. "But then again, He just might."

35

GOT A HOLD ON ME

That afternoon, Henry sat at the restaurant counter with his mouth wrapped around a half order of ribs and coleslaw. The diner was humming over the news that the big trial had been shut down because of bad chicken served to the jurors at lunchtime. Henry's first response was one of relief. He didn't have the chicken. Soon after he dismissed it as bad luck for the jurors, he smiled in Baltimore's honor. In a desperate fight for his freedom, the man was still drawing aces. Some men were lucky that way, he thought, too fortunate for their own good. That's when something tugged at him to look up from the plate of bones he'd picked clean.

A burly white man, whom he had not laid eyes on before, was placing an old duffle bag in the trunk of the patrol car he shared with Gillespie. Henry was halfway out the door before his partner came into view. Like two casual friends meeting on the street, the two men shook hands and parted ways. Another stranger drove up in a beat-up Plymouth that Gillespie's acquaintance climbed in. Henry reasoned it was an old friend saying hello, until he mulled over the cold stare he got for asking.

"Hey, what was that about?" Henry inquired as they pulled away from the curb.

"Nothing that concerns you," Gillespie replied. "Just some fellas I used to know visiting for a few days." Henry carefully debated needling him about the man's bag in the trunk but he didn't want to get into a hassle over an unfamiliar white man he didn't plan on seeing again. Their frigid discussion blew over as quickly as it began, Henry thought. His partner could have let the afternoon slide by without racial politics creeping in but it simply wasn't to be.

Gillespie rolled a toothpick into the corner of his mouth, flicking at it with the tip of his tongue. His mind was speeding a mile a minute by the way he worked that thin sliver of wood in and out of his mouth. His mind must have slammed into a wall and disintegrated because he said the dumbest thing possible. "Hey, Henry, you think they're gonna hang that friend of yours by the end of the month? I mean, ain't no sense in the state feeding him, if all's they're gonna do is snap his neck on the gallows." Henry's blood boiled, not in the way he was accustomed to. This time, it was slowly percolating. He peered out of the passenger side window with the best intentions of focusing on something else but Gillespie wouldn't let up. "Come on now, and tell me when you think they'll do it? Henry, I got twenty dollars that says he don't make it to the end of the week."

Henry immediately became suspicious and knew he had to divert Gillespie's attention so he could examine what was in the trunk. "Oh, I don't know when the sentencing is, but they ain't likely to pin this one on him. Sho', they'll try but it won't stick worth a damn," Henry asserted, with the same dry tone that baited him.

The moist toothpick dangled from Gillespie's bottom lip now. The die had been cast and he was put out with Henry for being so uppity. "You can put some money where your fat mouth is. I got twenty bucks says that friend of yours is the one who won't be worth a damn come tomorrow. There're some mean folks around here that don't like what he did to Barker's wife and they hate the way other white folks are kissing his butt afterwards."

"I don't have nothing to do with none of that," said Henry. "I'm on the right side of the law. Which side you reckon you fall on?"

"I *am* the law," Gillespie gloated. "If you don't have some dough to put on the barrelhead, then you should learn to keep your mouth shut when a grown man starts talking."

Suddenly Henry yelled for his partner to pull off the city street so he could make a restroom pit stop. "What the hell has got into you?" Gillespie questioned. Once before, when evading Kansas City police detectives, Henry got away clean by faking a severe stomach virus. Since it worked to perfection then, he didn't see any reason to forego pulling the same routine.

"Ah, man, I think I got the piles," hollered Henry, pretending to writhe uncomfortably. "Pull over to that service station on the corner and let me out around to the side. If you don't hurry, I'm a go right here in this car and soil the seats."

"Oh no, hold on, Henry! In this heat, that'll stink something awful."

Laughing to himself, Henry wrinkled his face and howled as if his insides were coming unglued. "Oooh, you got to hurry up then. I think it's about to gush out!" Gillespie guided the patrol car into the service station and slammed on its brakes. "Sorry about this, have a soda pop on me. It might be a while." Henry tossed a quarter on the front seat then pushed the door open. He sprinted toward the rear of the building with one hand on his stomach and the other pressed against the back of his pants. "Yowwwwl!" he shouted for good measure, as he disappeared out of sight. Leaning on the wall near the restroom door, he crossed his fingers, wanting Gillespie to leave the car exactly where it was. The trunk was not in the line of vision for the station clerk. If Gillespie went inside, his visibility would be cut off too. Henry was willing to wait as long as it took to flush him out. He didn't have to be a genius to suspect the stranger and the faded green bag in the trunk had a lot to do with Gillespie's overconfidence. He needed to get a peek inside. He needed to.

After the longest minute of Henry's life, he heard a car door close. He inched along the dingy white wall. Gillespie was nowhere to be seen. Henry decided it was time to move, regardless of the outcome. If the crooked cop caught him rummaging through the duffel bag, he'd come up with some lame excuse. A mental midget could fool Gillespie.

Squatting down to keep out of sight, Henry duckwalked to the rear of the car and felt the trunk latch. He reached inside then yanked out the canvas sack. As soon as he opened it he saw an embroidered patch sewn to a white cotton garment and it rattled him. The black cross circled by red stitching was undeniably Ku Klux Klan insignia. Henry's heart raced when he shoved the bag back in and pulled the trunk lid down. A few seconds passed before he heard footsteps coming his way. In that fraction of time, Henry cooked up a scheme to get off the hook.

"What you doing back here?" asked Gillespie. "I thought you were sickly."

"I am, help me up." Henry leaned on him, forcing all of his weight onto his suspicious partner.

"Damn, you're heavy. Open the door and slide in," said Gillespie, completely buying into Henry's ruse. "I'll take you to the station house and let the sergeant get a look at you."

"Uh-uh, ain't no time for that. Take me by the hospital first."

"Henry, I know you don't feel good but I've got too much to do today to be get stuck at the nig—uh, the colored hospital waiting on you to come around."

"Then don't hang on," Henry whined. "Just get me there, then you can tell the desk sergeant where I am. I'll take it up with him later."

"O.K., just relax," Gillespie ordered, in a panicked high pitched tone. "Don't crap in this car. They just washed it." Henry smiled beneath his phony grimace and fake stomach pains. He had to find out what Gillespie was planning to do with that hood and robe.

Gillespie didn't lift a finger to help as Henry faked convulsions and extremely painful dry heaves. As Henry stumbled inside the emergency room door, the patrol car blew out of the ambulance delivery dock. He watched it zoom in the opposite direction of the station house. Henry could always count on his partner to do what suited him and nothing more. At least he was consistent.

When Henry saw the coast was clear, he started out of the same door he'd used to ditch Gillespie, then thought better of it. So many potentially perilous scenarios raced through his head, he couldn't think what to do first. "O.K., Henry," he said, pacing in circles. "What would Baltimo' do if it was me in trouble? Think. Think. One thing, he wouldn't be here thinking, he'd be out there doing it."

The emergency room duty nurse sneered at the colored officer peculiarly. For starters he was the only one she'd ever seen and for two, he was blubbering to himself like an escaped mental patient. "Excuse me, sir, but can I help you with something?"

"What?" Henry answered, oblivious that he wasn't alone or that he'd been stared at by several people waiting in the reception area.

"I said can I help you, because you've made it clear that you do need some," she replied, slightly more tickled than annoyed at his strange behavior.

Henry gave his immediate surroundings a thorough once-over. Several pairs of eyes glared at him. He glanced down at his uniform, forgetting just that quickly he still had it on. "Uh-uh, listen here. I'm with the Metro Police," he muttered hurriedly.

"Humph, I can see that," she scoffed playfully.

"Well, yeah, and I'm on a special case. I need to know where the head man is. He'll know where to locate the doctor who's been working on the colored fella standing trial for being with that white girl."

Cautiously, the nurse stood up, while continuing to sneer at Henry. "Come here, officer." Henry approached her desk, uncertain whether she'd call for him to be thrown out on his ear, uniformed cop or not. "Let me tell you something," she whispered.

"Since you're here to help Baltimore Floyd beat this bad wrap, I'll help you. That man has done a lot of good to some friends of mine around here. I don't know what business he had with that woman, but he's been an angel to Dr. M.K. Phipps's family and that nursing student carrying his unborn child, an angel, I tell you. Now, Dr. Hiram Knight, he's the hospital superintendent but he ain't available. Go see a good buddy of Baltimore's, Dr. Delbert Gales. He's the one been going down to the jailhouse seeing about him. You can find Dr. Gales in the south wing. I'll call ahead and let 'em know you're coming."

Henry remained motionless for a brief moment, digesting all that she'd told him. The hardest part was listening to a perfect stranger going on about Baltimore like he'd hung the moon. Henry felt silly for being jealous because it wasn't that long ago he thought the same thing.

"Thank you, Ms.?" he said, reading the name tag on her uniform.

"Friends call me Belle and believe me, it's the least I could do."

"All right, Belle, I'm beholden to you. Oh, how will they know it's me when I make it to the south wing?"

"Unless there's two colored police wandering around over there, they'll figure it out," she said.

Henry smiled politely as he went in the direction she pointed him. He wasn't intending on wasting any precious time by visiting with Baltimore's personal physician. Dr. Gales may not have known a single thing going on behind the scenes but it was a good place to start, just in case. Besides, Henry didn't believe he had any allies in the matter and he wasn't in any hurry to face Etta.

After one nurse passed him off to the next, Henry was in the presence of a young man who appeared too young to be a doctor of any kind. Delbert had been pulled out of an examination room to speak candidly with a colored officer everyone seemed to be fairly impressed with so he obliged. Once the two men had a viable degree of privacy, Henry realized he was inept and down-right clueless as to the first order of investigation.

Delbert looked up at the towering peace keeper, puzzled at his presence when nothing came out of his mouth. "What exactly do you want with me?" he asked eventually.

"Uh . . . you're the Dr. Gales who's been working on Balti-more Floyd?"

"Yeah, I've treated him, but he's doing fine now," Delbert said, growing leery.

"I know this might sound kinda screwy, but I think some white boys are putting together a scheme to lynch him before the trial is over." Henry quickly explained what he had seen and heard.

Delbert agreed it was better to err on the side of caution, then he suggested Henry inform the police. That's when reality struck. A lone colored cop couldn't take unfounded accusations to the establishment, especially when they wanted to see Baltimore burn. "I know what you can do. Call Baltimore's lawyer, tell him what you told me and then contact Etta Adams, the club owner. She knows where to get a line on two of Baltimore's closest friends. They'll stand up for him." Henry was getting sick and tired of people telling him who Baltimore's associates were.

He should have known better than anyone where to get help and it hurt him down to his soul that he didn't. It was apparent after visiting with Dr. Gales that Baltimore had nestled in a place in those people's hearts and he was on the outside looking in. Unless Henry wanted to be pegged at every step, he had to get out of that slave catcher suit and into civilian clothes. But, there was one stop he had to make beforehand where the uniform would come in handy.

The taxi driver who drove Henry up to the lavish mansion atop an elevated parcel of land had another fare waiting on him about a mile up the road. He didn't dare pull off for fear of having a colored lawman mad at him. Car services were often used by the department when beat-walking cops needed extra wheels.

He was likely to see Henry a lot and he'd rather they be on good terms. "Don't you run off," Henry warned with a nasty expression. "I won't be long and if you're not here when I get back, you won't have to worry about another pick up, ever." Frozen by the threatening words of a pistol-packing Negro, the white driver killed the motor. "That's more like it. Be back in a tick."

Henry marched up to the house, thinking how much bigger it looked up close, a lot bigger than it had when he sat in the patrol car with Gillespie. Now it was his turn to call on the fat man, instead of playing security guard on Barker's dirty money pickups. Henry banged on the door harder when he felt ridiculous for having to wait longer than the white detective. As the colored butler opened up, Henry pushed past him yelling the home owner's name. "Shookie! Shookie Bush, get yo' big ass out here!" he wailed. "It's the goddamned law." Henry was prepared to use his gun when hearing what sounded like a herd of elephants stampeding across the marble floors.

"Who told you to be stupid enough to run up in my house like you paying the mortgage?" Shookie ranted. "I usually have niggahs come through the back." The tan and white striped suit was immaculately tailored for a man of his girth. The frown he shoved in Henry's face was cheap and off the rack. Shookie had plenty of those and saw to it that Henry got plenty of them before he left. "And another thang, Baltimo' ain't at your back no more, so I'd tread lightly if I was you."

"Funny you mentioned him right off, Shookie, 'cause he's why I'm here."

"Humph, riding around with those white boys must've warped your brain. Me and Baltimo' settled up and done parted ways once and for all. Wasn't long ago, I heard the same about y'all." Shookie puffed from a long cigar and flicked the ashes in a crystal jar held by his manservant.

"Don't pay that no mind, Shook," argued Henry, as he began to show signs of a thin skin. There was yet a third person telling him about Baltimore's business. "There's something more important I need from you. I understand that don't nothing go down in the neighborhood without you either knowing about it or being in on it."

"And, why should I offer crumbs off my table to you? That is what you after, ain't it, a piece of Barker Sinclair's pie?"

"Naw, I came to pitch for Baltimo'," Henry admitted.

"Ah, I see. You don't know when to stop running behind that fool. He's a done deal. They's gonna lynch him all right. I hate to see that happen to any colored man but the Klan done sent up some out of town talent to bump him off." Shookie was in better spirits just talking about a threat on Baltimore's life. He offered Henry a seat in his extravagant sitting area, also decorated in white. After they spent five minutes reacquainting, Henry threw his best ball at the oversized gangster to hit. With any luck, Shookie would take a wild swat at it.

"Let me tell you why you should do everything in your power to keep Baltimo' outta harm's way, Shookie."

"Yeah, you's a bigger fool than you look. Everybody knows I can't stand Baltimo's ass. Goodbye and good luck. Hell, I let him haunt me for two years before I paid my dues and got him outta my head."

Henry saw his pitch rip past Shookie's face. It was so fast the fat man didn't even see it coming. "Well, now we're talking. How'd you feel about living in his head for a while?" Shookie tooted on the stogie, while holding out for the count. "Now, think about it for a minute. If you help pull him out the lion's mouth, he owes you. Wouldn't you want him to know what it's like having to look over his shoulder and every time somebody rings his bell unexpected, he gets the shakes hoping it ain't you coming to collect on the marker?"

"Ooh, shit!" howled Shookie. "Yeah, man, I like the sound of that. That's the best proposition I heard all year. Just make sure Baltimo' knows it was me who helped spring him. If he ain't buzzard bait by the weekend, I'll own his narrow yellow behind."

Henry decided having a drink wasn't such a bad idea after all. He wouldn't be the first or last officer to take a nip while in uniform and on the clock. The shot of bourbon loosened the wheels just enough to ease the tension. It was hard concentrating on the information Shookie provided without kicking himself for being so far removed. And if it were divine intervention, subsequent to the fat man making good on his word, Henry was reminded of a debt he'd promise never to forget. Baltimore owned the marker on his life as well.

36

BEFORE DAYBREAK

Roberta hung damp clothes on the line in the backyard. When Henry came through the basement door, she was surprised to see him two hours earlier than he usually signed off his shift. "Hey, honey," she greeted apprehensively. "I hadn't too long made it in from the school myself. Dinner's not ready yet, but you can find some cold cuts in the icebox if you can't wait."

"That's all right, 'Berta," Henry answered, fastening the last button on a dark colored short-sleeved shirt. "I'm a have to grab a bite on the run." Roberta hadn't paid close attention to him up until then. There was a hitch in his voice, one she hadn't heard before and it scared her.

"Henry, you didn't lose your job, did you?" she asked, noting his relaxed attire during working hours.

"Naw, don't worry about that. I took sick time today."

"Sick?" said Roberta, scanning her husband for visible ailments. "Honey, what's bothering you?"

"My conscience," Henry replied quietly. "It's got me down, way down."

"Smells like bourbon played a hand in it," she huffed smartly, before returning to her laundry. "I guess now is when you'll tell me what you're doing home in the middle of the afternoon."

"They's gone try to kill him, Roberta, Baltimo'," Henry informed her. "Some Klansmen done rolled in, from out of town I suspect, to help Barker Sinclair and Tasman Gillespie grab him up." He watched a petrified expression wash over her face and thanked his stars she didn't try to stop him. "I'm rounding up some old partners to gum up the works, if we can. Please don't fret. I love you and I love Denny. And as God is my witness, I'm coming back to spend the rest of my life with y'all." Roberta's lips trembled. There were so many things she wanted to say but couldn't come up with a single word. Instead, she nodded lightly and then threw her arms around his waist. Roberta's heart skipped a beat when he walked through the fence and into the place cowards dare not go, along the road paved with good intentions.

The same cab driver acting as Henry's personal chauffeur for the time being was told to take him to his vehicle at the police precinct. He laid a sizable tip in the man's palm, then climbed into his car and double-timed it to the Fast House. At four-thirty on the nose, Henry wrapped on the door while reading the posted sign which read: *Closed until further notice.* Prepared to beat on it again, he inched back when someone opened it slightly from the inside. "It's me, Henry," he announced, when seeing a pair of eyes peeking through the thin crease between the door and frame.

"Come on in, we've been nesting on pins and needles," answered Dank.

Henry was wearing a worrisome grin but was delighted to see the man who'd gone up against Kansas City's finest with Baltimore to protect him. "Hi ya, Dank. It's good to see you. I heard you and Pudge came up to shake some limbs."

"It's better to shake them than dangle from them, I always say," Dank jested. He hadn't been fully informed of how they decided to get close to Baltimore, let alone do anything to assist in his escape. Henry's half-baked plan was almost feasible, if

Delbert got Albert Hummel to bite like he anticipated. He wouldn't have long to ponder before learning the outcome.

Dank barred the door, then lead Henry to a little room near the back. It was off the kitchen and served as a catering hutch for preparing finger foods and the like. Henry didn't let on that he knew every inch of that building, including the safe he helped install beneath the office desk. Until meeting and falling for Roberta, he'd owned a third of the business. Selling it back to Etta put money in his pocket but drove a wedge between them.

"Henry Taylor!" yelled Pudge as he entered the room. "I heard you caught on at the department. They ain't made you captain yet?"

"Hey, Pudge," he responded, shaking hands with the wheel man from his getaway. Looking at him ambivalently, Etta forced a smile. "Jo Etta," Henry said, as if paying respect to the woman's home. "Miss Penny," he hailed, to complete the salutations. "All right then. I don't know what Dr. Gales told y'all, but I've been thinking on something. Did he happen to get my message to Baltimo's lawyer?"

Etta explained that she'd received a call from Albert after he'd petitioned for a temporary transfer. Judge Sumner agreed that death threats supposedly emanating from inside the jail system warranted that Baltimore's request be granted. Albert also discussed why notifying his client of the dangers associated with being transported was the prudent thing to do. Albert and Etta shared several ideas to further discredit Dixie Sinclair on the stand, if it came to that. Unfortunately, none of them seemed viable after having been sufficiently fleshed out, so Henry and the boys put a game plan together with duct tape and wire, just enough ingenuity to keep their faith running.

Baltimore paid close attention when he received a call from his lawyer after the seven o'clock hour that evening. Albert had been right about everything so far and he didn't want to stall progress by changing seats at the table. Baltimore was handed a convict's shiv, a knife made by scraping the rounded sides of a spoon down to a sharp point, when the news of his relocation circulated around his cell block. If the state troopers were in on some diabolical plot to hand him over to a local hate group, he was prepared to take out a few of them before going down. That much he'd promised to Albert before hanging up the phone.

Albert's next call was a direct ring to D.A. Winston's home, advising him of the numerous harassments received, leading to the judge's immediate ruling and concern for the defendant's safety. The district attorney slammed the telephone down at breakneck speed, then he contacted Barker at the Red Lantern tavern to fill him in on the judge's orders. It was difficult to believe Baltimore's attorney and his buddy, the judge, could have both been so stupid. Overjoyed, Barker shared the enormous mistake made in their favor with his cronies. They cancelled the late night wake-up call scheduled for Baltimore in his cell. Having him out in the open presented them a much more exciting opportunity. Three state employees were no match for an incensed detective, a truckload of drunken Klansmen, and a blood thirsty henchman with a license to kill.

It was half past midnight at the county jail. None of the prisoners on the colored wing slept as the steel door leading to the quiet cell block slammed shut. Baltimore stirred on his bunk when he heard it. Hushed whispers were passed along until they reached him. "They're coming, two of them," the murmurers advised, giving him a hand in deciding his own fate. Baltimore approached the cell bars, sliding the home-made knife on the inside of his county-issued ankle boot and remained poised. When their steps grew louder, he remembered his lawyer's recommendation that being moved was far better than being found dead in his cell with no witnesses to come forward. Baltimore sized up both state-employed police officials in brown and khaki colored uniforms. Neither of them was as large as him but they made up for it with menacing revolvers strapped on their hips. Disturbed thoughts of destruction and damnation did loops in his head as the jailer recited instructions before turning him over.

"All right now, this is the notoriously famous Baltimore Floyd.

He's what you might call a celebrity around here. He's been a good boy, though. You won't have no troubles out of him. I'll open it up, cuff him and walk him out. At that time, we'll sign him over to you." Baltimore felt like a slave at auction when listening to the jailer, who spoke as if he was transporting livestock instead of a human being. An urge to strike out rose inside of him, beckoning to be unleashed. Then, the jailer made another extremely dubious move. While frisking his prisoner, he felt the knife, paused to glance up at Baltimore then went on as if nothing concerned him. "Like I's saying, as a man walks, so shall he be lead," the jailer stated, in a way that suggested it was of vital importance. "Their shoes," he mouthed, standing in front of Baltimore to cuff him; which was another deviation from procedure. All prisoners were cuffed from behind unless shackled by leg irons collectively. The jailer brought no leg irons. "All right, that's nice and tight fellas," he announced sternly. "Why don't y'all head out and we'll follow?"

Baltimore exited the cell, surrounded by guards and gloomy faces offering muted goodbyes. Eventually, he noted the trooper's shoes, one brown pair and the other black but neither was standard issue. While contemplating what to do about it, Baltimore asked the other inmates to look after Husky and keep his belly full of sweetcakes. They chuckled over his requests but agreed wholeheartedly to abide by them. "So long, boys," Baltimore said in passing. "See you on the front page." Even though he couldn't predict what awaited him on the outside of that massive door, leading to the rear end of the building, he was sure it would make headline news.

"Goodbye, Mr. Floyd and good luck," said the jailer, as both of the other men forged signatures on the release document. He'd given his word to Judge Sumner to look after the high-profile inmate while in the county's custody and he kept that promise. The jailer's protection ended when the sliding gate closed.

Baltimore offered his thanks, and kept an eye on the men now in control of his well being. A third man, too chubby to meet the rigid requirement of the state police, settled in behind the steering wheel of the transportation vehicle. Baltimore thought he looked familiar but then so did a lot of white men in the state of Missouri. The driver was Officer Brandish, the wickedly obtrusive Metro officer from the academy, who ushered him into the backseat. Brandish would be the first to die.

Through the main avenues of St. Louis, they traveled at a moderate speed due west. In the meanwhile, Baltimore sat quietly with his hands between his knees, where the knife was easily accessible. An eerie feeling kept him company in the minutes which passed before any of the men uttered a word. The sounds of tires rumbling over uneven road, metal shocks creaking and the annoying scent of cheap aftershave blending with perspiration kept him fully vigilant. Baltimore's desire to stay alive kept his eager fingers mere inches away from the blade.

"This is the turn," the driver announced northwest of Kings Highway, the outer reaches of city living. He flashed the headlights when maneuvering the vehicle onto a narrow, dusty rural route. Immediately, a severely battered pale blue pickup truck scooted in behind them. "That ought to be the boys," Brandish chuckled. "We're really cooking with grease now." Baltimore's chest filled with anxiety as the car swerved down the darkened unpaved surface. "Sit still, nigger, we'll be there before you know it."

The men posing as troopers were the same two Henry had seen earlier in the day passing a Klan outfit to Gillespie. Barker invited members of the area redneck chapter to join in on the fun, vowing not only to get even with Baltimore for hijacking his drugs but also for screwing with his wife. Barker was dead set on getting downright evil.

The truck followed for more than a mile. Another set of headlights swung in line behind it. Brandish laughed in a sinister manner while glancing in the rearview mirror. "Ha-ha, looks like Gillespie finally decided to get his ass in gear. I see a patrol car closing in." Baltimore struggled to catch a glimpse out of the back window.

"I thought I told you to sit still," the man to his left grumbled, before landing a mean right uppercut to his chin. Baltimore's head jerked against the backseat. He didn't see it coming.

"Okay, man," Baltimore exclaimed woozily. "All right, I ain't moving. I'm still. I'm still." Hazy and disoriented, he shook his head to snap out of it. He regained focus when the driver fussed about a missing pickup.

"Hell, they must've fell in a ditch but there's enough of them to rock it out just fine," Brandish assumed. He couldn't have guessed the truck had been flipped over purposefully by the police patrol car tailing them. "Hold on, here they come. No, that's Gillespie. He knows he should have stopped to help them out. Probably didn't want to miss out on any of the fun."

"That's mighty white of him," Baltimore cracked. Sensing another jaw-snapping blow was headed his way, he dodged it. The man who'd thrown the punch doubled up with another one. Baltimore swayed back and forth banging shoulders with his captives. Brandish skidded along the road yelling for the commotion to cease.

"Don't kill him yet! Wait 'til Barker's had a poke at him. We're coming up on the farmhouse now."

The headlights shone on a two story wood-framed house just down the road. Two cars were parked in front, behind was a big red barn which reminded Baltimore of a Norman Rockwall painting he was fond of.

"What the hell!" Brandish questioned, pulling alongside a police vehicle. "If Gillespie's already here, who's that behind us?"

"You ain't never gone find out!" shouted Baltimore as he jammed the knife into the base of Brandish's skull. Blood squirted from the gash in his neck like a busted water main. The car surged forward as each of the men in the backseat screamed shamelessly. One of the captors worked feverishly to get the door opened but couldn't. The car roared off the road, crashing headlong into a large oak tree. The radiator hissed and spewed steam into the light of a crescent moon. There was no initial movement inside the ravaged automobile.

The barn door flew open. Barker emerged hastily, wearing a white sheet. Gillespie and two other men accompanied him with their racist uniformed ensembles intact. As they moved toward the wrecked vehicle, the city cruiser which had bumped off the pickup screeched to a halt just yards from the farm house. Simultaneously, both passengers wrestled Baltimore out from the car wrapped around the tree. Barker was awed by the absurdity of the event.

"Brandish!" he yelled. "Where's Brandish?"

"This jig killed him," the stiff slugger said apologetically. "Had a knife hid in his boot, I guess."

"You guess? Didn't anybody think to search him and who in the hell is that?" Barker shouted angrily, when four men in Klan paraphernalia stepped out of the police car idled in the road. "How many boys did y'all bring up here from Joplin?"

"They must be local Klan," answered the other man guarding Baltimore. "They sure ain't with us."

"Hey, there. We got him," Barker hollered in the stranger's direction. "It was supposed to be a private affair but I won't be selfish. There's enough for everybody to take a slice or two." Barker was confused when they approached with guns drawn. "Loosen up, guys. Let's boil this monkey then peel the skin off like— like—" He froze, gathering that none of the four gunmen had their weapons trained on the colored prisoner, but rather at his men.

Baltimore's head throbbed violently until he recognized the way one of the hooded men wielded the shot gun. "Blast them, Dank!" Baltimore hollered, wisely hitting the deck before shots rang out toward him. Dank followed orders, reloaded and then popped off two more rounds. He splattered one of the night riders, then mowed down another. The men in Dank's posse fired at will. Their targets hustled inside the barn for cover. Baltimore heard Smiley Tennyson's goofy laugh as he sprinted past in hot pursuit. The barn door closed after Barker and two others scurried frantically. The men who took Baltimore from the county jail bolted toward the open pasture. Pudge ripped off his hood and gave chase. Considering all that transpired up to that point, Baltimore was equally surprised by the fourth rescuer's identity.

Henry dived underneath the police car when multiple shots sounded from inside the barn. He rolled in the dirt, cursing and spitting.

"Henry?" Baltimore bellowed. "Where'd they get you?"

"I ain't hit. I stubbed my damned toe getting outta the way," answered Henry, while Baltimore climbed to his knees laughing and pointing. Barker eased out from behind the barn with a pistol steadied at his head. "Watch out, Baltimo'!" cried Henry. Then, from out of nowhere, something went thud as it ricocheted off the policeman's chest. Barker coughed and gagged during his slow descent to the ground. He clutched at his chest with both hands. Baltimore stood over him, eyeing the baseball lying in the dirt near his feet.

"What happened to him?" asked Henry, with bright unsuspecting eyes.

"Ain't but one man in this county who can hurl a perfect pitch hard enough to stop a man's heart," answered Baltimore.

"Jinx?"

"Yeah, he ought to be standing on the other side of that car y'all rolled up in."

As Barker took his dying breath, Henry turned to see someone strolling in from the shadows of darkness like an apparition. It was Jinx, as Baltimore predicted. Earlier, he heard Barker and his cronies discussing where they were taking Baltimore, so he set out early and hid.

"Hi ya, Jinx," Baltimore said, waving to him casually as if passing him on a street corner.

"It's good to see you, Baltimore," he replied warmly.

"It's also good to see you've been practicing. That ball sailed in with some steam on it. Uh-huh, you'll do fine up there in Canada."

"I guess it's true, you can't keep a secret in St. Louis," he replied, while studying the damage his right arm caused. "Ain't nobody gonna miss him, not even that wife of his."

"I won't forget him, though." Baltimore said, as he walked toward Henry with his hands cuffed.

"Naw, and I didn't forget you either," Henry confessed, removing his hood and robe. "I couldn't forget any of it. But, what I can't figure out is why a grown man wants to wear this hot ass dress in this Missouri heat."

"You wouldn't have a key to these bracelets in your purse, now would you?" Baltimore joked.

"Naw, I keep it in my brassiere," Henry answered, with a smile full of teeth. He handed Baltimore a small key to remove the shackles. "'Should have seen your face when we hopped out from that car. I thought you's gonna piss your pants."

"I thought I did," Baltimore admitted, shaking the cuffs from his wrist. "Let's get to it and give the ones in the barn what they was saving for me."

"No, suh, you stay put out here," Henry objected. "Dank's got them penned in. Besides, they's hiding in the haystack and it'd be a shame to get you killed after all the scheming it took finding where they's bringing you."

Smiley returned from the pasture huffing mad and out of breath. "Man, I hate this country bullshit. Let's push on back to the city." He'd ruined a pair of good shoes by stepping in a pile of moist cow manure.

"What happened to the boys you chased off?" Henry inquired apprehensively.

"I can't say for sho'. All I do know is they's two of the fastest white boys I've seen, who wasn't streaking down the first base line." That's when a rifle blast echoed in the distance. All of a sudden, Baltimore collapsed on the ground in agony. Blood trickled from his side like water from a cracked flower vase.

"Dank, Pudge, forget about them!" shouted Henry. "Jinx, get out of here! Smiley, help me get Baltimore in the back of the car."

"We can't take him to Homer Gee," Smiley contended sadly. "That's the first place they'll come looking when he turns up missing."

"Well, he's gonna die if we don't get him somewhere quick so's they can stop the bleeding."

"Take me to Etta's Fast House," Baltimore groaned before losing consciousness.

"I'll go and get help from the hospital," Jinx said loudly, then he sprinted to his car.

Under constant attack from the shooters staked out in the pasture, they carried Baltimore's limp frame to the car and flew down the same road they used coming in. Pudge mashed the gas pedal against the floor board. Baltimore grimaced painfully, while Henry applied pressure with one of the folded cloth hoods sewn by Penny and Etta. Without it, Baltimore didn't stand a chance of seeing another sunrise.

37

AFTER THE DAWN

Pudge listened to Henry yelping from the back seat, begging him to go faster. He pushed forward, recklessly side swiping parked cars during dangerous turns. While they traveled along Newstead Avenue, a green sedan raced beside them. The driver gunned the motor to keep pace. Dank stuck his shotgun out of the front passenger window until he realized the person roaring down the avenue wasn't a team of white men out to pursue them. It was Dixie Sinclair. "It's a lady, y'all!" Dank yelled, shocked to see her handling the big four-door so effectively. "It's a white lady!"

Pudge drew closer to Etta's Fast House but Dixie wouldn't let up. Her car raced forward inch for inch. Smiley arose from the backseat. He recognized Dixie's face. "Ah, hell, it's Barker's wife. She's saying to follow, but it smells like a trap."

"That's the one who got this whole mess going from scratch?" asked Dank, cocking his shotgun. "I'm a blow the front end off her car."

"Nah, she's okay," Baltimore grunted. "She needs something I got."

"Baltimore says to stay with her," Henry shouted, praying that a dying man knew who to trust. If proven wrong, he wouldn't get a second chance to make the same mistake. No sooner than Dixie slowed her pace and made a right at the next corner, they saw three police cars parked next to the curb in front of the Fast House. Uniformed officers had been told to keep an eye peeled for bundles of heroin while searching for an escaped fugitive from justice. Six cops, sent by Tasman Gillespie, were encouraged to gash the place beyond repair. By the distraught looks on the colored men's faces as they passed by, the cops were highly conscientious about their duties, swinging axes at tables and chairs, knocking holes in the bar, smashing bottles and ripping everything in reach from windows to the walls with sledgehammers. Watching them mangle Etta's dream and livelihood was difficult to take, but Baltimore's injury forced them to press on. Pudge tailed Dixie for three more blocks. She swung wildly into the alley behind Watkins Emporium. Remembering what Smiley said about it being a double cross Pudge gave Dank the go-ahead to blast anything that appeared suspicious.

Parked in the rear of the dry goods store next to Dixie's Chevrolet was Etta's Chrysler Imperial. Pudge leapt out while Dank circled around. Before they reached the door leading to a storeroom, Delbert stormed outside to meet them.

"Get Baltimore in here and hurry. Jinx called ahead so we sent Mrs. Sinclair out to find y'all," he explained hurriedly. "Glad she ran across you fellas first. There's a death squad tearing through "The Ville" out to get you."

"Yeah, we saw. They's well into getting Etta's club," lamented Pudge, with the image of it being gutted down to the pipes still in his mind.

Henry panted as he and Smiley carried Baltimore inside the back door. "You'd better ditch that squad car, Pudge," he wisely advised. "It could lead them right to us. Smiley, why don't you run along with him and see that he finds his way back?" Smiley took one long breath, glanced at Baltimore again then trekked out of the door with Pudge. Henry had seen Dank operate in a hail of bullets when they raided a high stakes gambling establishment a year ago in Kansas City. Pudge was a great getaway driver although his nerve as a shooter was still suspect. Smiley could get it done if someone needed to be killed. Likewise, Dank lacked compunction when it came to doing the deed. Henry was smart to hold him back as a safeguard in the event they were discovered.

Once they secured Baltimore on top of the sturdy cutting table, Chozelle tipped in with them. She'd planned to run off with him before observing firsthand what painful uncertainties an association with a man like that could bring her way. Baltimore hadn't asked for her companionship, but she assumed he wouldn't turn it aside if she offered it in the right way. Now, Chozelle was sorry for considering it. She felt like a fool with a secret, too silly to share. "Dear God, is he dead?" she cried nervously before vomiting in the sink.

"Nah, he ain't, just fell off is all," answered Henry. "The doc's gonna fix him. Ain't that right, doc?" Delbert prepared anesthetics and alcohol. He glared at Henry, in defense of his personal commitment. His was equally as thick as theirs.

Penny filed inside the crowded room like always, in Etta's shadow. Dixie slinked in at the back, purposely not getting too close. When Dank laid eyes on her his teeth clanked together. "I'll be damned if it ain't that witch again. Haven't you seen enough of colored folk? Cause I know I'm tired of looking at you."

"Leave her be, Dank," growled Etta. "She told us everything and she's mighty sorry about the way things played out. Without her help, we couldn't have known where to send or none of y'all."

"Come on, now, it's her fault Baltimore's laying there on that table," argued Dank. Just thinking about the trouble she'd caused had gotten him mad at her all over again.

"When those lawmen galloped in on her and Baltimore's spat, Dixie wasn't grappling by herself on that bedroom floor," Etta debated intensely. "Was she?"

"You didn't have nothing to do with it and they's down the street splintering the club apart," answered Dank.

"They're not trying to hurt me," she said knowingly. "Somebody's got them looking for something is all. What they've been sent after ain't there, though." Etta had seen trouble coming a mile away. She'd packed her bags, emptied out the safe and hid all of the things she'd planned on taking when she left town. Penny was an utter mess. She shivered continually while Baltimore laid still. Etta had to pry her from that very spot when Delbert began fishing at the bullet from his side. "Come on, chile, this ain't the kind of thing you need to see," was Etta's honest assessment. "Come on, Dixie, you neither." The three of them departed into the dimly lit emporium and ducked behind the counter, out of sight from passersby.

"Hold him down!" ordered Delbert. "He's got to lay still or the bullet might start to move around in him." Dreadful screams came from that back room during the hour that lapsed before Delbert located and then extracted the bullet. His clothes and surgery gown were soaked throughout with sweat and blood. When Pudge returned with Smiley, Baltimore appeared half past dead. His skin was washed out, a peculiar shade of ash white.

Delbert peeled off his mask and gown to greet them. "What took y'all so long?" he whispered wearily, worn to the bone.

"He didn't make it?" asked Smiley. "All of this was for nothing." He slammed his fist down on the table near Baltimore's head.

"Watch it, boy," Baltimore whined. "You still got bad aim."

"He's gonna make it!" Smiley shouted triumphantly.

"Not if you don't keep your big mouth shut," Dank threatened harshly. "We all got to clean up and skin out of here."

Henry wiped his face with a blood stained towel. "You did a great job, doc. How far you reckon we can move him?"

"Move him? Man, he just underwent surgery. He'll need time to heal and rest. Moving him at all could kill him."

"If those Metro cops find us here, he'll die here for certain," said Dixie, with Etta co-signing her assertion. "He can't be here when the sun rises and the way I see it, that'll be about thirty minutes from now. I filed for divorce, so I've got no reason for sticking around." Dank didn't have the heart to tell Dixie that her petition to the courts wasn't necessary. Barker couldn't contest it from the grave. Etta thanked her, paid what Baltimore said she deserved and then wished her well. Dank wished her the hell away from him.

Delbert washed up and suggested Baltimore see a doctor with a real examination room, informing them that his procedure was merely patchwork to hold him together. Etta shushed his modest rants, slipped him two thousand dollars and handed him the keys to her sporty two-door Chrysler Imperial. "Just a little pre-wedding folding money for you and that pastor's daughter," she told Delbert on the sly. "That's one pretty nurse you found yourself."

"Nobody knew about me and Sue's engagement," said Delbert, before catching on finally. "Oh, right. This is St. Louis."

"You's kinda slow for a smart doctor, but that don't stop us from counting you as a friend."

"Thanks, Miss Etta. I'll remember y'all, always," Delbert promised, shaking hands and gathering various surgical instruments. "One question, though, how is it you're gonna leave after giving away your car?"

"That old thing? For what I got in mind, I'll need more space than that." She informed him how to stop the right window from sticking when the temperature rose, then she waved so long. Pudge helped Baltimore into the back of his roadster and covered his spotted bandages with a blanket, then offered to hang back a few days to see about Etta's safety. Penny hugged Etta tightly, handed her a note, then she settled into the front seat of the convertible with Jinx and drove away.

Seven miles into their journey, Jinx passed by the bus stop on the way to Union Station. Chozelle sat patiently with a small suitcase at her feet and a pre-paid train ticket to Detroit in her purse. Penny glanced at Jinx when she saw her. He'd noticed too but didn't blink. "You ain't got no love left for her?" Penny asked.

"If I did, Chozelle would've known I was driving to Detroit and catching a train to Montreal from there. I got who I need with me." That was good enough for Penny and music to her ears. If it hadn't been for the roadblock heading out of town, their trip would have gotten off to a beautiful beginning.

"Oh, no, what should we do, Jinxy?" Penny asked, watching the police inspecting one car after the next.

"I think I'll break line and turn around. Maybe I'll come back and try again later on."

"Uh-uh," Baltimore objected. "You break and they're liable to come after you. How many cars before they get to us?"

"Uh, six or so," Jinx answered, counting those ahead of him. "Yeah, six."

"Good. Don't get scared and don't say no more than you have to. Make up something simple if need be, but something believable. Y'all can pull it off, I know you can. Whatever you do, don't look back here."

They heard rustling in the rear seat but remained calm like Baltimore demanded. As the convertible approached the blockade, Tasman Gillespie and Clay Sinclair confronted them. "Hey, I know you, boy," said Gillespie, tired and rattled from the night before. "You're that nigger going to try out with them Canadian cold fish eaters."

"Nah, suh, I don't know nothing about eating on cold fish," said Jinx, keeping his eyes focused straight ahead.

"I bet you will before long. Who's this you got with you? She seems kinda young to be taken across state lines. That might pose a problem for those who uphold the Mann Act, prohibiting the interstate transporting of girls for prostitution and/or malicious activity. You got malicious activity on your mind, boy?"

"I only got baseball on my mind, suh," Jinx replied. "Don't know what that other thing is you called out." Clay positioned himself on the other side of the car. Gillespie hadn't told him his brother was dead and his sister-in-law missing. As far as he knew, Baltimore was as good as dead too, that's why seeing Jinx driving

Baltimore's fine automobile all the way to Canada didn't surprise him.

"Hey, Jinx, who's this young lady?" Clay inquired, with his eyes on the back floor board.

"H—h—her?" he stammered.

"I'm Jinxy's li'l sister, Penny. Our ma say we can go any god-damned where we damn well please, long as we send her some money when we get there."

"You'd better keep a muzzle on this sister of yours, boy," Gillespie ranted, stunned by the girl's fiery tongue. Clay saw what looked like a pile of white bandages hanging from underneath the rear foldout seat. He was willing to let it pass but then Gillespie caught a glimpse of it. "What the hell is that? Bloody bandages? Clay, go ahead and let up the trunk."

As Clay circled to the back, he steadied his weapon. He lifted the trunk cover and cautiously recoiled. When he only found luggage, Clay shook his head. "Ain't nothing here but travel bags and such," he reported evenly. "Let 'em go. It's gonna be a long day."

"Naw, not yet," Gillespie snarled. He yanked on Baltimore's bandage. "They're gonna tell me what this blood soaked cotton is doing back here?"

Penny craned her neck and gawked at Gillespie as if he were an ignorant dolt. "Oh that's just one of my monthly woman-hole-pluggers, what was meant for the trash heap back yonder. If you don't watch out, that thing will get to stankin'." Gillespie shrieked and wiped his hand against his uniform as he released his grasp as quickly as he could. Clay laughed while Gillespie cursed like a drunken sailor.

"Y'all get on outta here before I throw up!" he yelled, looking at his hands as if expecting them to melt after fondling what he thought was a colored girl's feminine hygiene products.

Jinx was glad to follow his orders to get going but he couldn't understand what happened to Baltimore. A few miles down the road, he drove the car onto the shoulder of the road. Immediately, there was a thumping sound. Baltimore had wedged himself beneath the folding rear seat, which was also used as a secondary storage unit. He had the foresight to crumple himself inside it but couldn't muster the strength to let himself out. It ached unmercifully when he spoke up to congratulate Penny for her crafty improvisations. He suggested a future in motion pictures if she had an inclination. "You're a natural born persuader, Penny King. A natural." When she turned to thank him, he'd fallen off to sleep, bundled under the blanket.

"Hear that, Jinxy? I's a natural," she repeated, wearing a huge screen siren's smile.

Penny wore that natural smile for three hours until coming to a speck on the map, with a decent amount of colored folk and a midwife, who knew how to properly dress wounds and change bandages. After they'd had a bite to eat and shoved on, Baltimore grew increasingly stronger. They arrived in Detroit by midnight, rented two adjoining rooms in a fancy downtown hotel with a stunning view of Toronto, Canada not five miles away.

On the following day, Delbert read an account of Baltimore's daring escape in the *Comet*. The *Post-Dispatch* merely posted an arrest photo stating the notorious Baltimore Floyd was killed while fleeing capture south of the city. D.A. Dudley Winston wanted the story to disappear the way Baltimore had, even if he had to tell another lie to hasten it on.

Delbert drove to a nice spot along the Mississippi River in his new car to ask Sue's hand in marriage, nice and proper. Her father had given his blessings and Delbert spent all afternoon shopping for the ring. It was a beautiful white diamond cluster, a real eye-catcher. Of course, Sue said yes, again.

Henry struck a deal with the D.A. and served up Tasman Gillespie on a silver platter for racketeering, drug distribution and breaking Baltimore out of jail with the intent to murder him. Henry's name was skipped to the top of the detectives' list, as a shoo-in. When he rolled by Etta's Fast House, broken and boarded, in his patrol car with his new partner Smiley Tennyson, Henry wanted to pretend it wasn't once the hottest joint in St. Louis for colored patrons to rub elbows with their heroes, drink like kings and dance like their shoes were on fire. Unfortunately, there was no use in pretending.

His wife Roberta took on a new attitude immediately. She was walking their son to Woolworth's like she'd always done, when something happened. As two white women sauntered toward her on the sidewalk, they busied themselves with conversation while neglecting to make concessions for the colored woman with her child. Roberta was tired of being invisible. Considering what her family had experienced during the previous three months, it was high time she be seen and respected. Clutching Denny's hand, she stood firm, forcing the women to walk around them. The women sneered and Denny did likewise. Not only did it feel liberating but the little boy smiled for the first time since learning of his biological father's death in the war. That alone made it all worthwhile.

Etta arrived in Detroit in a chauffeur-driven limousine with Baltimore's money and a wooden storage chest she'd paid Pudge and Dank a hundred dollars apiece to dig up from Penny's front yard, before they caught an afternoon train to Kansas City. Etta was glad to see everyone had made it there safely, although it was killing her to know what cost two hundred dollars to excavate. Penny eagerly anticipated the opening too. It had to be something important because Halstead beat her for watching him lower it in the hole she was forced to plow. Jinx cried real tears when it turned out to be his family's missing fortune. He cried again when he was offered a contract to play major league baseball. After all, it was more than just a game, to him, it was sort of like breathing. And boy, how he loved to breathe.

While sitting in a fancy downtown café, Baltimore read over the telegram from Albert Hummel's office. He learned that there weren't any outstanding warrants filed for his arrest in the state of Missouri. However, it was made known that he wasn't welcome back there either. With a bag full of money, his freedom, Penny's upcoming wedding with Jinx, and Etta getting dangerously anxious and ornery, Baltimore had the waiter pour four glasses of champagne. "I want to propose a toast," he announced. "Let's raise our glasses to getting by and good friends," he cheered, before sharing the thought running circles in his mind. "Y'all, I've been doing some thinking on going into business for myself, with a few partners of course. You think they got any Fast Houses around Canada?"

"Probably so," said Etta. "But not the kind we had back home. I'd bet they could use a proper fire pole in the middle of the floor to stir things up a mite."

Penny grinned brightly at the thought of it. "Yeah, I reckon they could at that."

MS. ETTA'S FAST HOUSE

VICTOR McGLOTHIN

ABOUT THIS GUIDE

The questions and discussion topics that follow are
intended to enhance your group's reading of
this book.

DISCUSSION QUESTIONS

1. Discuss how meeting Baltimore led to a defining moment in Penny's life.

2. Do you feel that Halstead got what was coming to him, as Jinx asserted?

3. Discuss Delbert's plight as an overachiever who set out to please his father while finding his own way.

4. Dr. M.K. Phipps' character had several layers. What importance did his role play in the story?

5. After Ms. Etta took Penny in, the young lady's life changed dramatically. Name some of the occurrences that forged a strong relationship between them.

6. Ms. Etta endured internal struggles regarding falling in love with Baltimore and letting Henry go. Which do you think was more difficult? Why?

7. Henry wanted to move past the fast times he experienced while running the streets with Baltimore. Should Henry have kept out of his old pal's affairs, considering he had a new family depending on him?

8. Did Baltimore's troubles result from Dixie's decision to remain quiet at his arrest or was it a simple case of reaping what he'd sown with her?

9. Jinx admired Baltimore a great deal despite his affinity for Dixie. Did you expect him to risk his life and baseball career over their friendship? Why or why not?

10. When Baltimore killed the pool hustler who had been paid to hunt him down, he convinced himself that murder was inevitable. Did you agree with his assessment?

11. Baltimore proved to be generous on many occasions. Is that why so many people stood up for him in his time of need?

12. Clay Sinclair was an honest and good man. Discuss how his sense of fairness impacted the colored characters.

13. How did the underhanded tactics of some white police officers galvanize the Negro recruits?

14. Dr. Hiram Knight carried a lot of weight inside the hospital walls because it was necessary for the training of young surgeons. Discuss how he took the same fearless approach when coming to Baltimore's aid.

15. Discuss Penny's peculiar attraction for watching Baltimore make love to other women.

16. Why do you think Dixie helped Baltimore in the end? Why did Dinah?

17. Baltimore sent for Dank and Pudge when he realized he needed two good men to hijack Barker's heroin shipment. After hearing that Baltimore was headed for a hanging, they returned to put their lives on the line for him. Did you find their loyalties refreshing or senseless?

18. Where you surprised at how M.K.'s death affected so many people? Discuss why you think everyone took it so hard.

19. Henry had to grow into the man he ultimately became. How did his struggles with Barker Sinclair and Officer Gillespie contribute to it?

20. After Ms. Etta's fast house was ransacked by the police, she pulled up stakes to follow her adopted family. Do you think she ever got over Henry marrying Roberta? Did it really matter in the end? Why or why not?